Thistlefoot

Thistlefoot

GennaRose Nethercott

ANCHOR BOOKS
A Division of Penguin Random House LLC
New York

AN ANCHOR BOOKS ORIGINAL 2022

Copyright © 2022 by GennaRose Nethercott

All rights reserved. Published in the United States by Anchor Books,
a division of Penguin Random House LLC, New York, and distributed
in Canada by Penguin Random House Canada Limited, Toronto.

Anchor Books and colophon are registered
trademarks of Penguin Random House LLC.

Cataloging-in-Publication Data is available at the Library of Congress.

Anchor Books Hardcover ISBN: 978-0-593-46883-8
eBook ISBN: 978-0-593-31417-3

Book design by Christopher M. Zucker

anchorbooks.com

Printed in the United States of America
10   9   8   7   6   5   4   3

For my father, Michael Nethercott
For my mother, Helen Schepartz
For my brother, Rustin Nethercott

And for all our ancestors who waltzed,
baked bread, loved, fought, and survived the impossible
so that we could at last, here in this gentle sliver of time, meet

Thistlefoot

PROLOGUE

BEHOLD: *KALI TRAGUS*, THE Russian thistle. A bushy lump of a plant, green flowers vanishing into green leaves. Its stem, striped red and violet as a bruised wrist. The leaves are lined with spikes, sharp like stitching needles. You are advised to wear gloves when handling it, if you must handle it at all. Should the thorns prick you, pretend you don't feel it. It doesn't do any good to gripe in times like these. There are worse wounds to be had than a thistle prick. Much, much worse.

The Russian thistle swells to life in the most arid climates. It thrives on disturbed land—flourishes in those places where a strange violence occurred. Among burned crops. Thirsty fields. Once-thriving farmlands ravaged by blight. Despite it all, the Russian thistle survives. Multiplies. It can grow between six and thirty-six inches tall. When it dies, it breaks off at the base and journeys across the earth, dropping seeds as it travels. The thistle moves like a living beast, rolling and waltzing in the summer wind, licking up dust, shimmying against the unhinged expanse of the land.

There's a story people tell about a man back in Russia who was executed by the state. His head was severed. When the head thumped to the ground, it turned into a fat fox and ran out through the crowd of onlookers, out of the city limits, out into the forest where it lives to this day. The Russian thistle, it's not so different—rent from the root and running, running.

But then, you knew this plant already. Even if you've never been to the old country, nor dragged your fingertips along photographs of the steppe, nor paged through yellowed tomes of Slavic folktales, you know it. You've seen it in old films, somersaulting down desolate stretches of highway. Coyote plant, wind-howler, the starting pistol of every good standoff. When you see the *Kali tragus*, you can almost *taste* lonesomeness, bitter somewhere in the back of your throat, or smell it in the air like a perfume. It represents all words left unsaid, stories untold, the memories that have been kicked up by storms and carried off across the untamed prairie. So many meanings, many names. *Kali tragus*, the Russian thistle, windwitch—the tumbleweed.

Did you think the tumbleweed was from here? Montana, perhaps? Nebraska? No. It is a foreigner, too, like so many of us. In 1873, Russian immigrants arrived in South Dakota, selling off and planting flaxseed they had carried with them from their home villages. The seed, unbeknownst to them, had been contaminated with thistle. Before long, the invasive species spread across the western United States, quickly becoming one of the most common weeds of the West's drier regions. The seeds traveled by threshing crews, wriggling out into wheat fields and orchards. They hopped trains, hiding in boxcars. They voyaged in wagons and bootheels, in the bellies of rodents and the talons of birds. They traveled in great windblown wheels, churning up dust. They fed mule deer and sheep, elk and prairie dogs, quails and small mammals scrabbling in the soil. During the Dust Bowl, when grazing was scarce, cattle farmers filled their herds' bellies with thistle.

Soon the tumbleweed had become one of the Wild West's

most iconic characters. A grand joke, no? This paragon of Americana—secretly an immigrant, after all. The Russian thistle disguised itself well. Put on a costume built of country songs and sharpshooters and pale rivers of smoke.

They say that if you wear a mask long enough, you become what you pretend to be. Perhaps the Russian thistle is more story now than anything else. Perhaps the tales we tell about it have replaced what it once was. No more women clucking in Yiddish over thistle caught in their skirts. No more European winters graying the weeds to ash. No more shtetl gates to tangle into. Instead, a slow, long whistle under an open sky. Who can claim to know the weed's true home anymore? Even the seeds themselves have forgotten.

. . . and yet.

Back in the old country, fires bloom like fields of red poppies. Kyiv, Chernihiv, Odesa. Shops and homes looted. Villages pillaged. Jews hanged in their own kitchens from the rafters, brown bread still rising in the oven. Who can tell if the room is warm from the baking, or from the torch thrown through the open window? Outside a burning synagogue, a spark catches a stray thistle plant aflame—a gouge of gold light cutting open the dusk. The thistle is swallowed by heat. A fireball howling within a crumbling city.

At this same moment all across America, tumbleweeds burst into fire. They blaze tangerine orange, a nation of lanterns swaying in the breeze. And still, they roll, thousands of Moses' burning bushes spinning across the prairie. Even an ocean away, something of them remembers. Even though they cannot see their old cities burn, the thistle burns with them. Even in a new land, their molecules reach backward, through time, through their own name, through a thousand stories, and erupt into beacons of sorrow. Beacons of light.

CHAPTER ONE

"WELCOME, MY ULTIMATE BABES, you thieves and lovers, to the greatest spectacle this side of the Mississippi!"

Isaac Yaga curtsied before the crowd, his black thrift-store suit splitting slightly in the knees. He had obsidian hair that levitated in soft waves around his head, as if experimenting with gravity. His face was pale and narrow, punctuated by a leaning, crow-like nose and pupils sharp as polished lead. If he had eaten well in the past month, you wouldn't know it, his skeleton floating inside the old suit with room to spare.

Standing atop a sagging milk crate, he widened his arms to the crowd below. An invitation. Applause and a few rough hollers overtook the audience as Isaac straightened up, sweeping a charcoal curl from his forehead, where it had drooped. On a square of cardboard at his feet, a svelte black cat lounged, licking a paw. The cat ignored the clamor with poise. The show continued.

Thirty or so spectators had gathered in the street around them. It was the same horde of French Quarter tourists Isaac always lured in—drunken businessmen who spent their meager annual vacations chugging passion fruit hurricanes out of disposable goblets and wreathing themselves in plastic beads, their mistresses peacocking on their arms. Isaac winced at their endless guffawing as they stumbled through Bourbon Street's gutter milk after dusk. He despised the way they treated the city like a playground, rather than a breathing, thrumming home where real people lived. Where real people died.

But it wasn't as if Isaac was much better. Wasn't he, too, only flickering through? Here a few months, then gone—the same as ever.

"First off, welcome to the great city of New Orleans. If you like my little show today, I'd greatly appreciate any small tokens you might care to offer me, a wretched showman. I know you came here dreaming of the lowliest ways to spend your hard-earned wages—and I assure you, friends, no money is dirtier than cash spent on street barkers." Isaac winked at the audience. The cat blinked.

Isaac always had a way of wooing a crowd. His voice was clipped and dexterous like a trained acrobat, his tightrope-tongue rarely interrupted. When he spoke, people listened. Were you to encounter him up close, near enough to catch the amber flecks in his tobacco-brown eyes, you'd be surprised to find Isaac's sight peering not outward at you, at the world, but rather, reversed, down an inward tunnel. Yet, the performer Isaac was bold as a cannonball. A master manipulator, able to tug small, invisible strings in the air and make an audience's attention leap up like a marionette. If such a thing as possession exists, one could surely make a case that Isaac Yaga was prone to it, overtaken by some stage demon, an actors' poltergeist, a thousand players' ghosts overflowing from him and bounding out into the onlookers' laps.

"Now, if y'all can take out these little devils"—he waved his phone in the air—"and please turn them up as loud as possible. All the way up. That's it. If your phone rings during the show, you have to buy me a drink, and we're all in favor of that sort of thing."

He didn't truly care about disruptions. But the banter put the crowd at ease, and he needed them to trust him. In reality, a phone chiming amid the cacophony of Royal Street was a single droplet of noise in a great ocean. The Quarter was swollen with sound: clarinet wails boiling over like kettles too long on the stove, hollering soap sellers looming in shop fronts with candy-like samples slivered on mirrored trays, kids tap-dancing with bottle caps glued to the soles of their sneakers, and farther off, beyond the levee, the haunted calliope of the Steamboat Natchez, whose carnival song could be heard even a mile away, two miles, ten, onward . . .

It was nothing like performing in the cold silence of the Yaga family puppet theater where Isaac was raised. There, the slightest cough would reverberate like thunder through miles of green velvet curtains. He had always felt that quiet as a presence, rather than an absence. A molten hush, like liquid mercury swaying in thick silver waves. When he was a child, there had been times when the silence felt suffocating, like being held underwater. Other times, it felt like a friend. In any case, it had been a long while since he had stood on that dark stage, or felt the suspension of a held breath just before the curtains rose. Busking for drunk sightseers, on the other hand, was one disturbance after another. You got used to it.

"You, sir, with the yellow tie. Yes, you. Come on up here. That's it— What's your name?"

"Brian," replied the man. Three men beside him—friends or colleagues—chuckled and clapped him on the back.

"Tell me three things about yourself, Brian. Can be anything: favorite food, shoe size, what you do for work, the last time you had your heart irrevocably shattered. Any three facts about you, Brian."

"Uh, favorite food . . ." The man in the yellow tie struggled, blank-faced.

"These are just examples, Brian. Anything. Anything at all. What are you doing here in New Orleans?"

"I'm here from Cincinnati, for the orthodontics conference down at the convention center. I design parts for X-ray machines. I don't know, what else do you need?"

But already, Isaac had begun clicking into place—thousands of tiny clockwork gears in his body aligning with all the little gears in the man across from him. In the milliseconds between words, Isaac memorized the precise way Brian's muscles tugged his mouth to move—and readied his own mouth to mimic it. He studied the shapes of the eyebrows, one arching slightly higher than the other, which triggered a ligament connecting to the apple of the man's right cheek, easing it upward to match. He took in the precise degree at which the man's knee bent while leaning on the right hip, the notes in his vocal range as he spoke, the way he divided his sentence for breath or emphasis. And lastly, always last, Isaac looked directly into the man's eyes. Isaac was a mirror, and the man named Brian's reflection tumbled in, heartbeat by heartbeat, cell by cell.

"Brian, old boy, are you ready to meet your match?"

Then, Isaac transformed. There was no Isaac anymore. Only Brian, standing face-to-face with himself.

Showtime.

Fools without an actor's keen eye might have mistaken this display for pure magic. A bodily alchemy, exchanging one form for another. And surely there *was* some enchantment to it, though if prodded, Isaac would insist on his skill and skill alone. A cartography. Each body, he'd say, is a map, rivered with tendons and capillaries, peaked with mountains of muscle, bone, cartilage, fields of skin. Isaac had spent years training himself to read this map and duplicate it with a surgeon's precision. By studying a person closely enough and isolating the muscles in his own narrow body, Isaac could reproduce the gentlest tic of each limb, the slope of an eyelid, the elbow's birdlike angle. Simple, scalpel-sharp imitation.

Brian squinted and took a startled step back. What he saw wasn't possible. *Couldn't* be possible. It was as if he had caught his own reflection in a shopwindow—somehow, the young man across from him had *become* him. Brian's colleagues began to notice the change, too. One let out a single booming chortle like an angered horse. Another tossed his head back and forth between Brian and the Isaac who was now Brian as if trying to shake water out of his ears. Hopping down from the milk crate, Isaac hoisted Brian's arm into the air like a victory flag, parading in a circle through the audience so every member of the crowd could observe the transformation. Each footstep of the two men, in tandem. Every little twitch and gesture, perfectly aligned. By now, Brian had become the secondary version of himself, a shadow, while Isaac was undoubtedly the more genuine Brian of the pair. As if joining the charade, the little cat marched alongside. Two Brians, one feline, and a mass of tourists all thrumming with the electricity of what appeared to be a terrible, demonic miracle taking place in the center of Royal Street.

And what came next? Chaos. Releasing Brian from his theatrical duty, Isaac wove through the crowd. He zeroed in on face after face, body after body, chameleoning between identities. A crooked-spined old man. A set of young twins, increasing their rank to triplets. A handsome couple on their honeymoon. An entire Norwegian bachelor party. A librarian with a broken leg. The mass went dizzy keeping up, Isaac spinning through a carousel of faces and postures and personal tics until at last, he stopped death-still and let the many identities shed from his bones like old snakeskins. The audience shattered into applause. Wallets flung their leather wings wide, cash fluttering toward Isaac in emerald flocks.

Before the crowd's frenzy calmed, Isaac slipped away, the little black cat still bobbing at his feet. He had almost rounded the corner onto Dauphine when someone grabbed him by the shoulder and shoved him hard. Isaac's face collided with brick. One hand was gripping him by the hair, another smashed into his back, squeezing him chest-first against a wall. *Muggers.* It wasn't uncommon to be held up while walking alone—though rare in the daylight. Isaac couldn't see the person pinning him, but he could feel hot, ragged breath on the back of his neck. *Drunk?*

"Got him, boys!" the owner of the hands called out. Two sets of footsteps followed, running. "You think you can steal from us, you little shit?"

Okay, maybe not muggers. Isaac twisted his head against the wall just enough to glimpse two men running toward him. White guys in button-downs and khakis, slicked-back hair, expensive watches. Conference fashion. They were Brian's colleagues, the ones who'd ogled dumbly as Isaac had mimicked their friend. Isaac strained against the first man's hold. He tasted blood where his teeth ground into the inside of his bottom lip.

"The little fish is wriggling!" Isaac's captor laughed. "Look, fellas, I caught a scrawny one. Think I should throw it back? Won't be much good to fry up." His hold tightened. Who knew orthodontists had so much nauseating machismo?

It would be only a few moments before the man flipped Isaac face forward to search his pockets. Isaac closed his eyes. He inhaled. Forced the small muscles of his face to squeeze and move, let his posture slump, his spine compacting in the man's grasp. Another yank of Isaac's coat, and he was jostled around to face the three men.

Isaac's eyes were wide and moony, filling with tears. "Please don't hurt me. Here, do you want money? I have money!" His voice had leavened two octaves higher, and his hands trembled like a little boy's. He gestured with his chin toward his pants pocket. His face looked impossibly young, no more than twelve or thirteen. Even his height had changed, barely reaching the men's shoulders.

One of the pursuers stumbled, drunken confusion clouding his expression. "Cramer, that's not him."

"Course it's him," said Cramer, his hold on Isaac still firm.

"I don't think that's him, man."

The third colleague weighed in. "This is what he does, he's a con artist, he impersonates people."

"Please," whimpered Isaac, "I don't know who you people are. I want my mom."

"Are we *sure*, though? 'Cause if it's not him . . ."

The black cat hissed at the assailants, scratching at the nearest man's shin.

"Come on, you moron," Cramer sighed, kicking the animal away. "That's his frickin' cat, it's *him*."

But in the debate, Cramer's grip had loosened just slightly. That was all Isaac needed. His full posture snapped back, the age returning to his face. He ripped free of the man's hold, scooped the black cat up in one hand, and bolted down Dauphine, rounding onto Ursulines. The men bounded after. It might be three to one, but Isaac knew the map of the city by heart, and his pursuers were clumsy with drink. Half a block behind, he could hear the slap of dress shoes striking pavement as the men pounded after him. He whizzed past Burgundy Street. If he could make it to the busy intersection ahead, he could lose them, vanish into another crowd. He grabbed a signpost, using it as an axle to swing his body around another sharp corner. As he did, he nearly collided with two girls on bicycles, who shrieked, swerving to avoid him. Just ahead, a red trolley chugged lazily down the street. *Come on, almost . . .* Isaac sped up. Just as the trolley reached the intersection of Ursulines and North Rampart, Isaac dove in front of it, landing neatly across the road. The men skidded against one another, trapped on the other side. Between them, the red trolley car chugged sweetly past. He'd lost them. Their shouts faded into the Natchez's song.

"Not bad, eh, Hubcap?"

The little cat rolled onto her back, belly up. Isaac took the gesture as an agreeing nod. He tongued his bruised lip.

Isaac was crouched on the back stoop of his shotgun apartment, leafing through the stack of poached wallets, one by one. A sharp throb stitched through the front of his skull. He leaned his head against the chipping pink paint of the house's back wall, eyes closed, waiting for the ache to pass. When it began to abate, Isaac rolled a cigarette on his knee, adding a pinch of lavender. Soon floral smoke lofted in ringlets around him.

It wasn't being slammed into a brick wall that had brought on the migraine (though that certainly hadn't helped). The headaches always came when he went too long without performing. It had been that way since he was a boy, as far back as he could remember. The only thing that soothed the pain was to become someone else, even for a little while. Before that afternoon's demonstration on Royal Street, it had been nearly a week and a half since he'd last stood in front of a crowd. Time had slipped by too slyly. It moved as a green fog rising up from the levee, soft and bodiless. A day could easily swell into a week. A week, into a month, lost to liquor and muggy heat and the howls of passing freight trains. But Isaac's hiatuses always caught up with him. A jackhammer in his temple. His hands, shaky. A staccato twitch to his movements. He might become hungry all the time, or not at all. And worst of all, worse even than the migraines, was the restlessness lodged in the hollow beneath his ribs, like a fox burrowing into him with its teeth. That was the true indicator it had been too long. Too long as only one person. Too long as himself.

By the cigarette's end, Isaac had sorted the clump of cash and counted it twice through. A good haul: $415 and change. Enough to pay the month's rent and buy a six-pack of cheap beer for the night. Roughly a third of the money had been given freely. Beyond that, Isaac had skimmed the rest from careless tourists' pockets—Brian's colleagues' among them.

A gratuity. They never donated what he was fully worth, not voluntarily—so he made up for the due. And if those deprived of their vacation money tried to recollect the face of the performer who'd waltzed through them sometime after they'd last palmed their wallets? Usually, they were unable to recall his true face, muddled among all the stray faces he'd tried on for size. Even if he walked by them an hour later, they wouldn't be able to place him. Brian's buddies were an anomaly. He'd gotten sloppy. Sloppy was dangerous.

"Hey man, you coming to the Lovelorn tonight?"

Max, Isaac's roommate, appeared in the doorway.

"Carey Lou's playing, and it's free pool on Saturdays."

Though Max and Isaac had been living together for the better part of two months, their interactions were almost always here, on the back steps of the house. Coming or going. No one sat still for long.

"Might do," Isaac said.

"I'm taking the truck if you want a ride. If I can get the piece of junk to start up, anyway. I had to get Bones and Chris to jump it yesterday."

Max was a short, broad-bellied Australian with strong boxer's shoulders. Using a rusty pocketknife, he spread peanut butter onto a stale heel of bread. A small glob had dropped onto his boot, but he either didn't notice or, more likely, didn't care. Hubcap padded over to lick it off.

Isaac prepared the components of a second cigarette.

"Should warn you, though," Max continued, "I think Nina's started working there. Saw her behind the bar a couple days ago."

"Your point?" Isaac asked without looking up.

"I just thought you'd want to know," Max said.

"I'll see her if I see her. I'm not going to skulk around keeping tabs on her. You shouldn't either. It's not gentlemanly, Max."

"Aw come on, mate, you know that's not it. I only thought you'd want to *know*."

Isaac shrugged.

"All right, Chameleon King." Max shook his head, stuffing the entire hunk of bread into his mouth.

Chameleon King. The moniker had stuck to Isaac years ago and followed him like a shadow. Those who'd just met him assumed it was due to his singular skill as an actor. That was true . . . in part. But those who spent any real time around Isaac knew there was more to it. In honesty, he'd earned the title because he slithered in and out of loyalties as quickly as a chameleon changed its colors.

Max rolled his eyes, speaking through mouthfuls. "I'll save a place on my dance card for you. The chariot leaves at ten."

The call came at eight thirty.

Like all of history's defining actions, it began as a single small movement. Many thousands of miles away, where the clock read eight hours into the future, one person lifted a device and dialed a predetermined series of numbers. The motion became electrical signals. The electrical signals scurried toward the sky, looped past the moon, reverberated off satellites' glossy shells, which were colder than frost. They snapped and blinked into radio signals. Catapulted back toward Earth like invisible asteroids. The signals raced sunbeams. They sliced through pale clouds of Mississippi River water. Needled through wires and over rooftops and through drooping garlands of Spanish moss. And then, miraculously, only moments after the first simple human work of dialing had been enacted, Isaac's phone buzzed in his pocket.

Within an hour, he'd packed a bag and lifted his roommate's truck keys while the Australian was in the shower. Max was here without a visa—he wouldn't report a missing vehicle. It was why Isaac had chosen him as a roommate to begin with. The most useful people were always the ones who had something to lose.

In place of the keys, he left a gleaming train-flattened nickel. Isaac may have been a backstabbing trickster, but he wasn't a thief. That is, he never took something without leaving a token in exchange. Payment... whether the party he did business with ever agreed to the deal or not. The nickel glinted on the table-top like a silver mirror. The engine growled awake. Radio on.

Then, the Chameleon King was gone, northward bound.

CHAPTER TWO

IF ANYTHING EVER HAPPENED to Bellatine's hands, this story would be over before it began. Without her hands—their delicate motions, their deft strength—none of this would be possible. They were woodworkers' hands, able to whittle an ornate little owl into the neck of a spoon or heft a chainsaw through a Douglas fir. These hands were gentle as lace when they needed to be, or strong as iron. They were small, in fitting with Bellatine's general stature, but could muster a vise-strong grip on a jam lid or a torque wrench. The fingernails were often slicked with a gold glitter polish, gnawed and chipping at the edges. The knuckles, slightly over-plumped from cracking and the fingertips calloused from labor. To guess her age by looking at her hands would be futile, as they suggested far more than Bellatine's twenty years. These were her mother's hands, too, and *her* mother's before that, and hers. Heirloom hands, passed down through generations. Hands like these are versatile enough to carry an entire story in their cupped palms.

Luckily, no harm will befall them. Not in this story, at least.

There will be many other sufferings—I can't protect you from that. But I can promise that of all the pains this story holds, none of them belong to Bellatine's hands. Her hands will remain unsullied.

On the third day in September, Bellatine's hands were busy wringing one suspender of her denim overalls like a goose's neck. Her knuckles were white, fidgeting. She was nervous. She could admit that much to herself. Maybe she had no reason to be, but she could feel a long eel of dread swimming laps in her stomach, nonetheless.

The Greyhound toward the Red Hook Marine Terminal was only halfway to its destination. It had paused at a gas station, and Bellatine jostled past rows of carpeted seats and down the steep stairs to the parking lot. She untangled her matted bus hair with her fingers, a jaw-length shingle bob with bangs; she knew the flapper flair of the cut looked incongruous with her slouchy uniform of overalls and striped T-shirt, but she didn't care. Long hair can get caught in power tools, so she kept hers short and sweet.

It was a cool afternoon, the promise of autumn just beginning to puncture the air. She bent over to touch her feet, stretching the tight muscles in her back, sore from hours on the half-empty bus.

Was Isaac already there, at the shipping yard? She hadn't heard from him in four days, when they'd first agreed on a time to meet. Maybe he wasn't even coming. It wouldn't be unlike her brother to vanish without a word and leave her to deal with the shipment on her own. She imagined herself sitting in some estate office, filling out acquisitions paperwork, cursing her brother's absence while signing her name in wet black ink on the package release forms. The anxiety quieted. Wishful thinking, she realized—to not have to deal with Isaac at all. As much of a hassle as it would be on her own, it would be easier. Calmer. Without Isaac, she could at least be the one in control.

But no. He'd be there. There was no chance in hell that Isaac would skip out on a mystery like this. He wouldn't arrive with a sense of duty, no desire to help out with a tedious family chore—it'd be his curiosity that would draw him in. He'd want front-row seats to see whatever was about to be hauled off that barge when it pulled into port.

A few days prior, both Yaga siblings had received an identical call from a man with a thick Eastern European accent. An inheritance lawyer, he'd claimed. Bellatine had assumed it was a scam at first, but when she called home to check, her mom confirmed the information as legitimate.

"Your twice-great-grandmother, my bubbe's mother," Mira, Bellatine's mother, had clarified.

"On your dad's side?" Bellatine asked, pinning the phone between her ear and shoulder to leave her hands free.

"My mom's. What's that noise?"

"I'm at work." She set down the sandpaper and cracked open a tin of mahogany wood stain, dipping in a rag.

"You know, *she* may have been the one who started the surname tradition, where the women passed on the family name rather than the men. Or maybe that was the next generation . . . At any rate, we've always been a stubborn flock, Yaga women. You certainly inherited that much from the family line, Bellatine."

Stubborn was one word for it. It was true—by all accounts, Yaga women were bold and took what they wanted; what they wanted, however, rarely included their own daughters. Though Bellatine had spent years on tour with her family's puppet company growing up, she felt like she barely knew her mother. Sometimes she felt that her mom parented her puppets more closely than her. Mira wasn't cruel, exactly. Just sealed off, like a museum display of a mother enclosed behind a glass cabinet. To be studied and respected, but never played with.

They'd certainly never spoken at length about their family history—or anything else, for that matter. Mira's own mother had died when Bellatine was little, but the few memories she did have of her bubbe had left a cold, chalky impression, rather than one of maternal warmth. Mothers and daughters might share a name in the Yaga line, but that's where the intimacy stopped.

"Do you know anything about this woman? Any idea what might be in her inheritance?"

"I don't have time for this, Bell. Your father and I are supposed to meet with the board at noon, and I'm knee deep in planning the festival. We've been working with a new set painter, an incredible woman from Yemen, but I honestly don't know where in the budget we'll—"

"Just quick, then. Anything."

"When my bubbe came to the United States," Mira continued, making sure to sound put out, "my great-grandmother stayed in Russia. There may have been letters after that, but they never saw her again. I know she was very poor, like my grandparents were poor, so we didn't think she'd bothered to leave a will. What would she have written into it? Seems like we were wrong."

Per stipulations in this will, according to the lawyer, it had been hidden from the family until seventy years from the date of their ancestor's death. As of this month, those seventy years were up. Allegedly, the document had specifically directed that the inheritance be bequeathed to the deceased woman's "youngest living direct descendants." When the estate lawyer had traced the Yaga bloodline, he'd found the youngest members: Bellatine, and her older brother, Isaac.

"No money," the lawyer had insisted. "An heirloom."

"What kind of heirloom?" Bellatine had asked.

"Very large. But I know nothing what inside box, I have not open. The will clearly: no one open but you and your brother. There will be shipment, from Ukraine to New York. You must go New York, receive shipment, early next week. Paperwork wait for you at terminal."

And so, Bellatine had booked a bus from northern Vermont to New York.

Soon, she'd be there. If all went according to plan, the shipment would be waiting. And so would Isaac—her only sibling, whom she'd last seen six years prior, when he'd dropped out of high school to hop trains and chase stories and see America, leaving everything and everyone behind. Even her.

Behind her, the Greyhound growled back to life. She imagined its headlights glowing like nostrils full of golden flame. Great wings unfolding from its metal spine. Her hands tingled, dots of heat humming in her rough fingertips. She reached into her overalls' pocket and gripped a little wooden spoon, pressing her thumb into the dipper, already smooth and worn from touch. *Breathe slow. In, then out,* she told herself. *Count to five.* Her emotions were getting the best of her. She hadn't felt her control on edge like this in a long, long time. But ever since she'd learned that she'd be seeing her brother again, her thoughts had been fragmented, flitting from the past to the future to the past again. She squeezed her fists tighter until her joints cracked. She couldn't let herself get careless. There was work to be done. She turned and climbed back aboard.

Scarlet scaffolding laced over the Red Hook Marine Terminal, hovering above concrete runways in vast, interlocking bridges. It gave the appearance of a massive red spiderweb, woven with steel. Bellatine navigated past car-sized crane hooks, which swung down to hoist shipping containers from barges to the mainland. The containers reminded her of children's building blocks, all orange and green and blue and silver, stacked one atop the next. Across the black harbor waters, the New York City skyline loomed steady, a chrome army of giants keeping watch.

Bellatine nudged past a cluster of longshoremen in hard hats. She followed signs for the freight station, where cargo was stored and unloaded from boxes before being restuffed and transported by train. According to the short, white-whiskered man she'd encountered at the gate, her great-great-grandmother's shipment would be held there for pickup. How she'd manage to transport it afterward was another question—but that was a problem for later. First, she'd need to find out what exactly was in that box.

At just past four, the sun was beginning to weep down toward the horizon, hazing the quay in pale peach-colored light. Bellatine rounded a tall warehouse. There, perched on a stack of wooden pallets, sat Isaac.

He was leaning back with his eyes closed, a cigarette tucked behind his ear. *Asleep,* Bellatine realized. Beside her brother lay a green, metal-framed backpack, stuffed full enough that the flap was pinned down with a bungee cord. A tiny black cat dozed atop the pack, its back rising and falling in a spot of sunlight. Was it Isaac's cat, or did he simply attract strays? The dress suit Isaac wore was filthy, the sleeves rolled up to his elbows. His jacket flopped open to reveal a white T-shirt, torn from the collar to the left armpit. A watch chain dangled from his front pocket, glinting against the setting sun. He looked like a movie villain or the ghost of a 1930s bank robber. Bellatine would have laughed at the spectacle if her stomach weren't suddenly roiling like a school of fish had just hatched inside it.

For a moment, she didn't move. She watched her brother sleep, comparing him to the memory she had carried with her for the past six years, and the few scattered photos she'd seen online. He had sharper edges. New lines etched into his forehead, the corners of his eyes. She sucked in a breath as her gaze fell on his right forearm, where a long red scar snaked around his elbow. He'd changed since she'd seen him. But then again, so had she.

A lick of breeze rose up from the harbor, brushing a curl of Isaac's hair down over one eye. He twitched, lifting a hand to his face. He opened his eyes.

"Well I'll be damned." He sat up straight, looking Bellatine up and down. She froze, a beetle under a microscope. "Tiny, you're not so tiny anymore." A grin split across his face, and he leapt off the pallets, sweeping Bellatine up into a hug. "But kid, you'll always be Tiny to me."

Despite herself, Bellatine beamed into her brother's shoulder. She let herself squeeze him back.

Suddenly, she is seven years old again. She and Isaac are scurrying through the seats of their parents' puppet theater, burgundy silk capes ribboning behind them. Isaac belly flops onto the stage, dragging his sister up after him.

"I claim this ship on behalf of the Yaga family enterprise!" he announces, removing his cape and tying it around a set ladder like a flag. "Your crew is now ours to command." He yanks up one of their father's puppets—a knee-high tailor sitting at a miniature sewing machine. "Do it, Tiny," he whispers, thrusting the puppet into her hands.

Bellatine's palms fill with coal-dark warmth. She focuses on the little tailor. Her heartbeat grows louder, throbbing in her fingertips. More heat. Brighter. Her focus intensifies as a spark needles into his delicate coat, then grips some inner part of the puppet. There. She feels it. A pulse.

A horn from a passing barge jerked Bellatine back into the shipping yard. *No. Enough.* The last thing she wanted was to feel like a child again.

"You're right," she said, pulling back from her brother. "I'm not tiny anymore. It's been six years—a lot's happened, Isaac." It came out colder than she'd intended.

"I bet, I bet." He released his grip on her, setting her firmly on her feet. He seemed uneasy then, unsure of what to say. "Hey, you seem like you're doing great. You been going to school? Carpentry, right?"

"Woodworking. Graduated this past spring, I apprentice for a cabinetmaker now."

"That's good, that's real good . . ."

They lapsed into silence.

The truth was, she *had* been doing well. She'd been surprised at how sweet a life she'd found up north, tinkering in her old teacher Joseph's woodshop during the day, retreating to her apartment at night to drink a few beers with Carrie and Aiden over hands of Bo Potato—the card game they'd made up when they were all in school together. She was happy—or rather, she wasn't unhappy. And wasn't that enough?

Bellatine broke the stalled hush, noticing a pile of books and cigarette butts on the pallet where Isaac had been sleeping.

"How long have you *been* here?" she asked.

"Since last night."

"How'd you get in?"

"Drove the first half. Truck broke down outside Raleigh. Hitched the rest of the way."

"You hitchhiked here? When we had a deadline? Isaac, what if you hadn't been able to get a ride, we'd have missed the pickup."

Isaac shrugged. "Except I did get a ride, and here I am. I beat *you* here, didn't I?"

"Is that your cat?"

His hand flashed in and out of a pocket, emerging with a pen and a crumpled strip of receipt paper. He offered them up.

"What's this?"

"If this is going to be a full interrogation, you might want to take notes."

The doors to the warehouse screeched open, and a tall man in an orange vest squinted out into the lot.

"You two here for the crate from Pivdennyi?"

Bellatine spun on her Chuck Taylors so fast that the rubber squealed against the concrete. The man peered down at a clipboard.

"Bay Eighteen. Follow me."

The box was enormous. A cube twice the height of a standard shipping container and fortified with steel bars. Even in the dusty warehouse they'd been led into, vast enough to be an airplane hangar, the metal crate occupied formidable space—looming at least fifteen feet above them. Its shadow pooled across the cement floor like a gray blanket. Isaac crept forward. The shadow slid over him.

"I'll just need to see some ID, then I can sign her over to you," the dockworker said.

Bellatine had her driver's license at the ready. She'd brought her passport and birth certificate, too, in case they wanted further proof, but the tall man gave her ID one casual glance and nodded, checking something off on his clipboard. Isaac pulled out a worn black billfold and shuffled through it with a blackjack dealer's dexterity. In her periphery, Bellatine glimpsed flashes of at least four driver's licenses, each with a vastly different Isaac pictured—and each with a different name. He handed one to the tall man, who seemed satisfied, making another mark on the clipboard.

"She's all yours." With that, the tall man left, leaving Bellatine and Isaac alone in the dim warehouse.

Isaac approached the crate and grabbed hold of a vertical sliding bolt, thick as his arm. He wrenched it. The lockrods clattered.

"Hold on!" Bellatine started.

"What?" asked Isaac, freezing.

"We don't even know what's in there," she sputtered.

"Well, yeah. That's why I'm gonna open it."

"Don't you think we should have some sort of moment or something? This is the last wish of one of our ancestors, you know?"

Isaac raised an eyebrow. "Should I chant?"

Bellatine flushed. "I don't know. I mean, no."

"Blood sacrifice? Ah, I know, I'll call the rabbi. Hold on, I've got him on speed dial."

"Stop it. Let's at least open it together." She stepped forward, placing a hand on the bolt, next to her brother's. The metal was oddly warm and seemed to buzz a little, as if carrying a subtle electric current. She glanced at Isaac to see if he felt it, too, but he didn't seem to notice.

"Ready?" she asked.

"Tally."

Their grips tightened.

"Kill the lantern . . ." Isaac nodded at her.

"Raise the ghost," she replied automatically. Their family's preshow equivalent to "break a leg." She'd been echoing that call and response since she first learned to speak. When was the last time she'd heard her brother say those words?

They heaved up the lever, unhitching the bar, and then tugged in unison. The hinged door of the shipping container swung open.

For a moment, neither of them said anything. They just stared, their eyes adjusting to the darkness within the box. The darkness gave way. Their vision stretched and cleared.

"Oh my god," Bellatine gasped. "It's . . ."

Isaac finished, "A house."

The house was small, a cottage really. The walls were made of timber, buckling with age. They had been painted white, but years of neglect had left long strips of exposed wood where the wash had peeled. Mud filled the gaps between boards, a sort of mortar mixed with feathers and hay. A low balcony encircled the house, edged with a pike fence made from rough-hewn branches, rushed with barbed wire. Behind the fence, a front door, over which faded a painted swirl of knotted vines, along with a little illustrated menagerie—a tiny gold lion, a crow, a blue rabbit, their heads all bowed toward center. The ornamentation must have been brilliant once, bright as blood and sapphire, but its glory had ebbed with time. Overhead, a turf roof sagged with overgrown weeds and flora, punctuated by a stone chimney. The whole structure seemed soft around the edges, like a great sleeping animal.

As the initial shock wore off, practical worries set in. Bellatine tensed. "How are we going to *move* this thing?"

She needn't have worried. As if in answer, the house began to move itself.

Bellatine and Isaac lurched back in surprise as the house wiggled forward. Isaac grabbed his sister by the arm and dove to the side, ducking behind a forklift. The house continued to move, shimmying from side to side as it squeezed itself out of the shipping container. Then, when fully free of its enclosure, it stood up. The house rose a full story taller, its chimney nearly grazing the warehouse ceiling. It loomed over the Yaga siblings, propped up on two long, yellow chicken legs.

"Nope, no way, I'm out." Bellatine yanked her arm free of Isaac's grip and started marching toward the exit. Isaac didn't follow. Instead, he buckled over at the waist, cackling.

"Stop it," Bellatine snapped. "I'm not doing this. We're going." Outside the warehouse, she could hear barge horns and men's voices and the clanging of metal against asphalt. Regular sounds. Sane sounds. The sounds of business and labor and a functional, dependable world with dependable laws. That was the world she wanted. The world she'd fought to be part of. Not this one.

"Oh, come on," Isaac needled. "*Look* at this thing!" He took a step forward, and the house scuttled backward.

"Hey, easy now," Isaac cooed. He lifted a hand cautiously, as if trying to pet a wild stallion. The house slowed, tilting slightly toward the body below it. "That's it. There you go, it's all right.

I'm just saying hi, I'm not gonna hurt you." Isaac took another step closer, his palm outstretched. Cautiously, the house knelt. Its great knees bent backward. Feathered thighs as thick as oaks bulged under the weight they carried. From her hiding place, Bellatine watched as her brother laid one hand on the front gate of the balcony, then another—and quicker than she could cry out to stop him, he had vaulted over the fence, thinly avoiding the barbed wire, and skidded toward the front door. Flashing a wolf's smile her way, he lifted the metal latch, flung the door open, and vanished inside.

All she wanted to do was run. To leave this place and this monster and the terrible, bright burning that had spiked up in her hands behind. And why shouldn't she? Hadn't Isaac done the same once? Wouldn't he do it again in a heartbeat, if the roles were reversed?

"I'm leaving!" she called out to him. "Goodbye, good luck, Godspeed!" *At least I'm giving that idiot some warning,* she told herself. *More than he afforded me.*

She waited for a response. A chastisement or laugh. Hadn't he been laughing? But only silence and darkness emanated from the gaping door.

"Isaac?" she called out. Nothing. Her stomach clenched. "Isaac?" she called louder. "Are you okay?"

The door slammed shut.

Bellatine's pulse leapt into her throat. She could feel her fear rising in waves. *Come on out, Isaac. Come on.* She waited. Nothing. *Goddamnit.* She spotted a cable coiled beside some machinery, and already regretting it, tied one end around her waist and the other end to a bar on the now-empty shipping container. At least she'd be able to yank herself back out if there were some sort of trap inside. *Or a gullet.*

She approached the house slowly, the way Isaac had, one hand outstretched. It bobbed on its talons. She tried not to gawk at the scaly skin, thick as an elephant's hide, which stretched over the tall golden legs. Nor the beast's haunches slicked with ruddy feathers, each plume as long as Bellatine's arm.

"That's it, come on. Shhh. Good . . . house."

The house dipped down to her level. She gripped the gate, and with a grunt, climbed up onto the porch and crawled toward the door. She didn't trust herself to stay steady on her feet if she stood. *I should knock,* she thought fleetingly, before realizing the madness of the idea. But before she had a chance to, the door creaked open.

CHAPTER THREE

BEFORE I WAS A house, I was a baby chick, cracked loose from an egg. It may be difficult to imagine a strong-walled, thick-roofed structure like me as a hatchling—but it's true. That's how the story goes, anyway, so that's how I'll tell it:

A hen sat on her roost in the dimming light. This hen had no name, no lineage to speak of, no story of her own save for this one I am telling you now. She had been bred for laying and had known nothing save for the small farm where she was raised. The farm was in a Russian shtetl called Gedenkrovka, in what is now Ukraine. It was near spring. The hen heard a goat bray on the edge of the farmland. She shook rain from her feathers. As she sank into the hay's sweet musk, a song came to her, though she, being a hen, did not know what a song was. It was a strange, lilting thing. A tune the farmer had sung as he had combed the henhouse for speckled brown eggs the day before. The words of the song, I'm sorry to say, have been lost to time. You may write your own lyrics if you like. Outside the henhouse, a light rain fell. The hen felt the laying coming on, so she bedded down deep in the hay, and let an egg loose into the world. Thus, I began. And what a beginning!

Can you imagine what the hen thought when she saw me? First, my tiny golden feet cracking through the shell, all as it should be. Then the rest of me: chimney and gate, small wooden doors, windows blue with glass. The hen, my mother, she spooked too easily. She looked at me and didn't see a bird at all. Flapped squawking from the roost, they say, so frightened that she ran right out into the night and straight into the town butcher Reb Leiser's knife. Don't pity me for losing my mother. I'm not sentimental. She wasn't my real mother, my heart mother, anyway. She was just an ordinary bite of poultry.

There are many stories about my origin. This is one of them, but not the only one. People talk. How they talk! What I can tell you for sure is that I was born already running. I'm still running. I don't plan to stop.

The hen was right, of course, to doubt my legitimacy as her child. I've never been a very good bird. I am, however, an exemplary house.

I differ from regular houses in two primary ways:

1. I do not have a foundation. Instead of a foundation, I have two chicken legs, strong and restless as a slingshot.
2. I do not reside in a single static location. I loathe sitting still. If you try to make me sit still, I'll kill you.

Other than these departures from the norm, you'll find me perfectly habitable—as long as my guests are friendly, invited, and do not steal anything from the cupboards.

I have one door, on the front. No back door. I had one once, but it was only used by one woman. When she died, the door died, too.

I have a sod roof, overgrown with alfalfa, vervain, basil, turmeric, gingerroot, yellow squash, heirloom tomatoes. Sprigs of horseradish and thyme. A cluster of purple yams. All a family needs to feed itself and a few visitors. In the sun, the lemongrass lengthens. In the moonlight, smoke blooms from me like dark fistfuls of roses—the great cookstove in my belly always lit, always warm. A porch belts my middle, where one might doze or dangle their legs over the edge to feel the dawn air on their knees. A dried owl talon hangs on a rope beside the door. Tug it, and a deep chime will sound to announce your presence. Knocking is useless. I am too plump. The sound would be swallowed up like a fruit fly into a frog's throat. Tug once if you're a stranger. Twice for a salesman. Thrice for a friend. Tug four times if you are my one true enemy, finally caught up to me.

Have I ever heard four tugs? No. It's not for lack of foes—anyone as strange as I am gathers a bushel of them. But none have ever been polite enough to ring the doorbell. They just try to storm in with torches or rifles, pink-faced as fools. No, when my true enemy arrives, I'll know him by his civil manner. An enemy who bothers to ring the talon fourfold must feel no threat, as he is in no rush, and still makes time for pleasantries. The most dangerous and violent men are the ones who believe they have nothing to fear.

CHAPTER FOUR

IT WASN'T UNHEARD OF.

Rare, yes, but it happened. Buildings petaling with thick, water-resistant scales during floods, or sprouting wings to escape an avalanche. There was a viral video of a Burger King in Ohio that grew a fat, gawking eyeball after a break-in. During wildfire season in California, stories emerged of houses growing gills, families surviving for days in black clouds of smoke, breathing strange, filtered air. Even so—it was surreal to be so close to one of the mutations. Like stepping foot inside an urban legend.

Isaac was reclining in a plaster chair, his feet kicked up on a crate. Paging leisurely through a book, he paused and looked up at his sister.

"Tiny! Come in, how good of you to join."

She was crouched on her hands and knees in the doorway, buzzing with the fury of a matador's bull.

"Going spelunking?" he asked, gesturing to the cable knotted around her hips.

"You asshole," Bellatine spat, rising to her feet. "I thought this thing had *eaten* you." But already, he could see her panic subsiding. Her muscles unstitched. Her shoulders lowered. Hands unclenched.

Hubcap slinked out from behind Isaac's chair and batted at a cobweb on the wall.

"How'd that get here?" Bellatine asked, pointing at the cat.

"She's hard to lose. Trust me, I've tried." Hubcap shook a spiderweb from her claw and skidded back out of sight.

Bellatine unbuckled the cable from her waist and stepped inside.

As soon as Isaac's sister crossed the threshold, a change overtook her. Isaac saw it as clearly as a light bulb illuminating. She softened. Her eyes glanced easily around the room, pausing on small, personal details. A hand-carved mezuzah above the door. A tin kettle on the corner shelf. A tree knot in the beams of the ceiling. It was the same reaction he'd witnessed in every tourist who'd beheld his doppelgänger act. *She recognizes this place.* There was no mistaking it. He could see her entire body relax as the fear that had toothed into her veins melted like warm honey. She loosened into the space with the unmistakable ease of a person returning *home.*

"This is my house." A look of bewilderment spread across her face, as if surprised to hear the words coming from her own mouth.

"Excuse you," Isaac replied. "I believe this is *our* house."

"No." She seemed confused, but not uncertain. Rather, a knowing had settled on Bellatine, which she appeared to flex into like a pair of stiff boots.

"Or, yes, I know it's both of ours. But . . . I don't know, it's like déjà vu. It doesn't look familiar to you?"

It looks like leverage.

"Come on, let's check it out," Isaac said, rising.

"What's that?" asked Bellatine, pointing to the book he'd been holding.

Isaac shrugged, "No idea. They're all in Yiddish." He gestured to a basket stuffed with books beside the open door.

The space they'd first entered into appeared to be a living room. Against one wall stretched a low wood-seated bench, wide enough to seat four people, the armrests made from fired clay. The bench's seat lifted up to reveal a storage compartment, deep as a hope chest, full of moth-bitten wool shawls and cream-colored linens. It was bolted to the floor. The house had no cupboards or cabinets, instead featuring built-in closets sunk into the walls. Some of the inlaid closets were fixed with wooden doors, others open like shelving. All were cluttered with pots and pans, jars of dried herbs long gone brown, canisters of pickled onions and beets. Across from one closet squatted the plaster chair where Isaac had been sitting—it, too, was embedded in the wall.

"It's like poof, she just disappeared," said Bellatine, examining rows of dried lavender their ancestor had suspended by their stems from the rafters. "No one emptied anything out."

The house was fitted with windows of thick, warped glass. The light turned milky as it fell through them, illuminating columns of dust, silver and swirling like smoke. Beyond the living room, a small door led to a second enclosure. Isaac stepped inside. His footfalls seemed deafening. He could almost feel the house flinching as the floorboards creaked, his leather boots clapping against wood. Perhaps Isaac's footsteps were the first noises the room had heard in years. Sound waves rippled out from his heels and washed over the ground. This was the opposite of a lullaby. It was a song of awakening. Of beginnings. He let his steps grow heavier.

This second room contained a tall bureau and two feather beds, side by side, with feather pillows leaning on wooden headboards. A bedroom. Bellatine trailed along, touching the center of the first mattress, where a person's nightly weight had depressed an indent into the feathers. Isaac watched his sister reconnoiter the space. She was touching *everything*, cautious at first, then more firm, as if petting a host of attention-hungry dogs. She dipped through another passageway, running a fingertip up and down the doorframe as she crossed the threshold.

Isaac moved to follow, but then stopped. A wooden ladder led up the side of the wall, vanishing into a small overhead loft. He hoisted himself up, coughing as disturbed dust rose around him. The loft was cluttered with tools and canning jars and crates, but Isaac didn't notice them. He was looking at the ceiling.

A huge painting hovered overhead, like a church fresco. It was circular, slicked directly onto the ceiling boards, and featured similar motifs to the painting that stood over the front door. The same twisting vines, laden with fruits. The same florals and pigments. Both must have been painted by the same artist. As he leaned in for a closer look, Isaac's eye caught on a speckling of odd, crooked berries bloating on the vines. Or no, not berries. What he'd thought were fruits were actually dozens of tiny bodies. They wore long olive coats and peaked caps, rifles strapped to their sides. Soldiers. The vines tightened around them, looped across their throats and wrists and waists, as if the soldiers were prey caught in a hunter's snare. Some lay limp. Others struggled to break loose. One had his mouth wrenched open, a vine snaking past his teeth and, farther down, erupting out his back.

In the painting's center, the vines and soldiers gave way to a bright clearing. Again appeared the lion, crow, and little blue rabbit that had guarded the house's exterior. Beside them stood a cottage on chicken legs. The animals weren't looking at the soldiers, but at one another, their heads once again bowed inward. And there in the heart of the discord, the four figures were dancing.

"Look at this," Bellatine called from below.

Isaac broke his gaze away from the ceiling and climbed back down. Bellatine stood in a bare kitchen. It contained the same built-in closets, plus a washbasin and a countertop for preparing meals. Bellatine leaned over a large cookstove built of clay bricks, her hands outstretched.

"It's still lit!" she said.

Sure enough, the stove emitted a steady heat. Inside, firelight leapt and blinked, licking over a half-burned log. Isaac suspected this fire had been burning for a long, long time.

Bellatine turned to face him. All her visible fear was gone. She bounced on her toes, beaming. She may as well have been wagging her tail like a golden retriever.

"I want this house. I really want this house."

Everything in this world is an exchange. Isaac knew this all too well. To shapeshift into a new person, you had to abandon the person you were. To bullet into a foreign, fresh, thrumming city, you had to turn your back on whatever city you came from. All we're ever doing is bartering one precious thing for another. It's commerce, plain and simple—though Isaac preferred to think of it as a conversation. Life as give-and-take, a listener for every speaker. Without this balance, the universe wouldn't hold together right. It was why Isaac kept a pocketful of train-flattened nickels: the piper must, eternally, be paid. In short—no one gets something for nothing.

"Buy me out," he said.

"What?" Tension snapped back into Bellatine's posture.

"I said, you can buy me out. We both own the house; you want it, I don't. I'll sell you my half."

"How much?"

Isaac looked around the room. A thick layer of dust lay like pale velvet on every surface. The building was simple. Fully furnished, though stained with grit. No, soot. The wood carried evidence of flame damage, black trails smearing parts of the walls. No real structural damage, but there had clearly been a fire here at one point, put out just in time. Perhaps that had been the danger that prompted the house to sprout limbs.

They both knew the aesthetics didn't matter. Whatever unnamable bond hovered between this creature and Tiny, it was beyond monetary worth. Something else was at play here. The house swayed on its legs as if breathing. It was worth the world.

"Whatever I ask, you won't be able to pay it."

"Don't taunt me, Isaac. Make me a reasonable offer."

"I am being reasonable. You just graduated school. You're probably already in the red. You don't have anything to offer me."

"Okay, I'm a bit tight right now. But if I start saving, in two years, maybe three? We can work out a five-year plan, or I can take out a loan."

"Or you could move in right now and own it in full by this time next year. No debts, no loans."

Bellatine hardened. "Why do I feel like you're setting a trap?"

Isaac pulled a nickel from his pocket, absentmindedly twirling it through his fingers.

"You'll pay me your earnings from the tour." The coin caught a shaft of light, ricocheting a spark across the room to land on Bellatine's cheek. She brushed at it like an insect.

"Oh, good. Nonsense declarations. I forgot how much fun you are," she sighed.

"Not nonsense," he said. "You, me, and this place. We're going on tour." Already, a plan was arranging itself, lining up in neat rows like a book of matches ready to combust.

"We're going to convert this house into a theater. Or rather, you are, I can't build shit. *You* have just the skills we need. We'll turn that front balcony into a stage, clean up the inside, make it livable." He leaned forward. "Then we'll go on the road. Book a big tour, march this beast all across the damn country. We'll be like old bards, a traveling medicine show. We'll make bank." He stopped and shot a look at Bellatine. "Or rather—I will. At the end of the tour, I get all the cash. You get the house."

Bellatine grimaced. "Oh, come on, Isaac, I'm not a puppeteer anymore. And look, I have a life. A tour is a big commitment."

"Exactly, kid—you have a life. Either you spend the next however many years saving and paying a mortgage, or you get it all done now, in just one year. We won't get rich, but it'll be enough to buy the house. You have my word; whatever amount we make, that's what I'll sell for. No matter what, I'll earn a hell of a lot more than I make as a busker." *Or a pickpocket,* he thought. "And I want the money soon. I don't want to wait for your five-year plan. I want to get paid."

When was the last time he'd had any sort of savings? Maybe never. For years he'd been riding rails, sleeping under bridges, eating out of dumpsters. Freedom is power—and money can buy a different kind of freedom. He could hear Benji's voice in his head, rebuking him: *With that money, you can pay off your debt to me.*

"Think about it, Tiny. It's a good deal. A great deal."

"What show would we do?" Bellatine asked, her voice soaked in skepticism.

"The Drowning Fool."

She laughed loud enough that the house gave a startled twitch. "You've got to be kidding."

"We already know it. The staging, the lines, the set rigging. We worked it a thousand times. It's ready to go."

The Drowning Fool had been their parents' signature piece. As children, Bellatine and Isaac had toured hundreds of theaters with that show, packing puppets in and out of vinyl road cases, helping run lighting and sound, filling in onstage whenever their mother or father was ill or too weary from travel. They'd watched night after night as the Fool sank below a tulle river, the same beautiful, pre-fated death on loop. After the five hundred and fiftieth performance, a year after Isaac left home, their parents had retired the show in favor of other projects. Wake up the Fool again just to drown him? Cruel, perhaps. But that's what he'd been made for.

"That's it," Isaac announced. "That's my offer."

"Why this?" Bellatine pleaded.

"Because," he said, tossing a wink across the ancient room, "I'm bored."

He was goading her, yes. But he wasn't lying. He'd been growing restless for a while now. New Orleans had been his base for nearly two full months. The last time he'd stayed anywhere that long was when he'd spent a summer at a bread bakers' cult in the Nebraskan flatlands—and that was only because he'd been too broke for bus fare and couldn't get anyone to drive him off the farm. Two months was a few migraines too long. It was time for something new. Time for the wind to turn. And here came his ticket, tap-dancing into his life on a pair of bird legs.

Bellatine grazed her fingertips over the wall, squinting at the ash that smudged off at her touch.

"I'm not agreeing to anything yet. I'll need some time to think about it, see if it's worth my investment." She lifted her chin defiantly.

Bullshit. Isaac knew a bluff when he saw one, and this one was painfully shoddy. He'd have to teach his sister to lie with some subtlety if they were going to travel together. He had her squirming on a fishhook, and she knew it. She was already in.

"The deal's on the table now. You can take it, or not."

"Are you serious, Isaac? I don't even get a few days to think it over?"

"Picture it." He swept his hand through the air, as if revealing an invisible painting. "You're on the front porch in summer. Lemonade in a pitcher, a little something extra splashed in. You're whittling little cutlery or whatever the hell you do. No rent. No landlord. Just you and this arguably cursed residence. The dream RV for haunted Jews. Living easy."

Bellatine's eyes flashed. She had always hated being toyed with. Hated having to play by anyone's rules but her own. And he couldn't blame her—he was the same way. Neither of them liked to be under anyone else's heel. His sister avoided it by making her own rules. Isaac avoided it by living without any.

"The longer you wait, the longer it'll be before this place is all yours."

Still, she said nothing, glancing again around the room as

if looking for a trapdoor to crawl out—away from him. He was getting impatient, and bored of blithe entreaties.

"I won't wait around for you to play house. You already know what you want. You've known exactly what you wanted since you first walked in that door. So don't waste my time."

Bellatine stopped wavering as soon as she heard the cold snap in his tone. It was as if she'd only then realized what was at stake. Not a whim. Not a consideration. A certainty, plain and simple.

"If we do this, I'm Rigs. I'm not a puppeteer anymore."

In its simplest incarnation, *The Drowning Fool* took two people to operate. Both lent their voices to the puppets, but each performer had a starkly different set of physical responsibilities. "Strings" animated the puppets themselves—a term leftover from their parents' early years, when they had performed with marionettes rather than the tetherless, wool-stuffed, wood-and-fabric dolls that had become their specialty. Animating the puppets in a pair of white-gloved hands, Strings planted life into the Fool and his compatriots. "Rigs," the second performer, was tasked with everything else—swooping set pieces in and out, arranging the Tailor's workshop, the Green Woman's bower, punching light and sound cues, and, finally, waving a long ribbon of blue tulle against the stage floor to create the river in which the Fool meets his predictable yet untimely end.

"*Not a puppeteer.* You keep saying that."

"If I say it again, will it sink in? Or is your hair too thick for anything I tell you to reach your brain?"

"The hair's a modern miracle. It can pick up radio signals from thirty miles away."

"That explains this idiotic idea. Your head's full of static."

"This pettiness hardly seems appropriate for a business meeting, Tiny. Which we might consider returning to. Business. You want Rigs, you want me as Strings. I accept those terms."

Bellatine shuffled her feet, like a rabbit shaking its legs loose from a snare. "You'll be in charge of the puppets? I won't need to have anything to do with them?"

"What I'm hearing," Isaac confirmed, "is that *you* want to slog through Rigs, and to leave the *fun* parts to me. I can work with that."

"One year?"

"One year."

Isaac's sister took a deep breath and let it out slow. The little fire in the cookstove brightened, as if in encouragement. She put out her hand.

"Kill the lantern," she said. There was no more hesitation in her voice.

Isaac smiled. He took her hand in his and shook.

"Raise the ghost."

CHAPTER FIVE

THE DRIVER WAS EXHAUSTED. He'd spent ten hours whizzing around Boston, shuttling professors and visiting tech moguls and rich Harvard kids up and down the tangle of one-way streets. Now, his lower spine ached. He'd heard the same radio pop hits cycle through at least three times, prepubescent boy bands with canned voices. He couldn't say he understood the appeal, but his daughters Maggie and Lena were partial to that kind of music, and he liked to be reminded of them on these long driving days.

One more ride, he thought, *then I'll call it.*

As they often did when the hours grew late, the driver's thoughts flicked to "Plan B." The life he'd always told himself he'd flee to if his own fell apart. He'd go to County Kerry over in Ireland, where his people were from. He'd visited once as a young man, seen the house his grandfather had been born in, met a few cousins. One, Kimberly, owned a pub, The Archer's Way. She'd told him then that any time he wanted to, he could come work there.

He hadn't spoken to Kimberly in thirty years. For all he knew, she'd paid a visit to Saint Peter by now. But still, the pub loomed in his mythos like a beacon. He'd live in the little apartment above the bar. Pull foamy draft beer from the oak levers on the countertop, smooth and oiled with age. Maybe he'd change his name—leave bland *Tom* behind with his old life, and go by O'Malley or Tommy Slim, something befitting a publican. His daughters could come, too. And before he'd go, he'd drop a brick on the gas pedal and watch his taxi drive itself into the Charles River.

A man outside Logan Airport waited with a hand raised to traffic. Tom barely got any rides out here anymore, ever since rideshare apps came on the scene—but that didn't keep him from circling the airport like a vulture. Looked like tonight, there'd be a meal for him. He pulled over.

The man wore a peaked, navy-blue cap with a red stripe, tamped over straw-blond hair. The look lent him a military air, particularly when coupled with the long, blue wool dress coat that went down to his ankles. He had on business attire beneath, well tailored and carefully fitted. His pink, narrow face was punctuated by an upturned mouth, balanced atop a scooped chin. The effect made the man appear to be smiling, even when he wasn't.

"South Station please, good fellow," the man said. An accent slid through his speech, plumping the consonants, and lifting the centers of words like questions.

"You got it, *good fella* yourself," Tom chuckled, leaning out the window. "Any luggage?"

"I travel light."

The man dusted off the back seat with a white handkerchief before climbing in, and Tom pulled out into a mess of traffic. A horn blared at their car as the taxi cut in front of a red Honda.

"These goddamn newbies, these rideshare jerks, they don't know what the hell they're doing," Tom griped. "These guys, they think that anyone can drive taxi. You know what I've been doing? I've been driving taxi for twenty years. I was born in this damn city, raised here. These guys, they show up in town and use their damn GPS to get around, looking at their damn phones instead of the road. Goddamn idiots."

"Sounds stressful," the man replied. Outside the window, car horns blared like angry geese.

"Yeah, well, times change I guess. So my kids tell me."

"How old are your children?" the man asked.

Tom gestured at a weathered photo of two rosy, blond girls taped to the dash. They preened at the camera with matching lip-glossed smiles.

"My youngest is fourteen. Oldest is seventeen. They're good girls. Real good girls. This one"—Tom tapped the taller girl in the photograph—"my oldest, she just got into BU. Smart kid, wants to be a, what's she call it, a nutritionist."

"You're a lucky man," the passenger said.

"How 'bout you? Any kids?"

He shook his head. "No, no children. But I try to take care of people, even though I do not have family of my own. I try to keep people safe. It is a frightening world."

Tom snorted. "Sure is. Sure as hell is." He turned left down a narrow cobblestone street. "Hey, where's that accent from, if you don't mind me asking? You flying in from somewhere far?"

"Russia."

"Russia! That *is* far. Tell me, you like it? Even with that commie shit you got over there?"

"It is where my history is. Our histories keep us bound to places, do they not?"

Tom found himself nodding. There was something familiar about the man, though he couldn't quite place it. Could they have met before? Maybe the man was on TV? Or no, he reminded Tom of a photograph he'd seen of his grandfather, standing beside the house Tom had visited in Ireland. Ease washed over him. Being with the man, it felt like being with kin.

"Here, will you take a small toast with me?" the man said. "I have never been to America, and I always raise a toast on new soil." He pulled a small blue bottle from his coat pocket. It looked old, made from frosted glass and engraved with a two-headed eagle, its beaked faces turned outward. "It would honor me for you to join." He craned over the front seat, offering Tom a drink.

Tom frowned. "I shouldn't. I'm on the job, man."

"Yes, of course. I understand," the man said, replacing the stopper in the bottle's mouth. Disappointment laced his voice. Tom didn't want to disappoint this man, this friend, one of his own.

"Aw, hell," Tom conceded, "one shot never laid a man down. Makes the senses sharper if anything."

The man smiled. "We'll toast to your daughters' good health, yes?" He took a sip of the flask to prove his goodwill, swiped the bottle's mouth with his handkerchief, and offered it up. "All clean." He smiled, and the man's smile was clean, too. They'd arrived at their destination. Ahead, the glass walls of South Station rippled green over gray granite steps. The taxi pulled over by the entrance.

"Cheers and welcome, pal." Tom took the flask and downed a swig.

The liquid went down searing, like choking on soot. It poured over itself, down his esophagus, spreading outward into his veins, one thousand small, reaching hands of smoke. Ash spiraled against him from within. It wisped out the cracks between his parted lips.

The driver trembled.

"Your daughters," the passenger said, "they're beautiful girls. It must be frightening as a father, knowing the sort of people who are out there. I bet you meet all manner of dangerous characters, job like this."

Tom nodded. His eyelids fluttered. Drip. Drip. Something else was filtering through his capillaries, burning, spreading. Fear. It crawled up his spine, climbing vertebra by vertebra.

"And university! Exciting," the man continued, "but expensive, I imagine. It must be difficult, especially with your occupation threatened as it is."

"Threatened," muttered the driver. Terror began in a pulse, pumping through his jugular in panicked bursts. A weight had settled on his back, as if a spindly body were perched on it, clinging to him. Motion caught his eye in the rearview mirror—a pale shape just over his shoulder. Not his passenger, who leaned back, an arm cocked nonchalantly on the seat. This was someone—something—else. Tom reached up to grab at the figure, but his hand passed right through it. The shape dispersed and reassembled like mist.

"Exactly. These men who are destroying your taxi business, they're not from here, you say?"

"Not from here . . ." The figure in the mirror solidified. A head. A neck. Arms, reaching around him, taking hold. Its mouth hovered against Tom's ear and a strange static emanated from it, a crackling of flame. Blood pumped in Tom's throat like an alarm sounding. The thing's body swirled with smoke. Its legs roped around his middle.

"Imagine! Imagine if I, a foreigner, came into your city and claimed to do your job better than you. It's outrageous, no?"

Other cars parked around them—taxis and rideshares, passengers bubbling out onto the stone steps.

"They come here," the Russian continued, "to your country. They do not have the experience you have. They do not have the knowledge you have. They probably do not even speak your language. And you, with two young daughters who rely on you!"

"Maggie . . ." droned the driver. "Lena." The weight on his back grew heavier.

"Yes, Maggie and Lena. It is their futures at stake here, no? Their futures these interlopers are stealing. Their educations, their hopes."

Tom's eyes widened. He stared out at the other cars. A block away, a young, brown-skinned rideshare driver in a Red Sox cap helped a woman pull her suitcases from the trunk of his car. The woman reached into her purse for a tip as the man stacked her bags by the roadside. Tom watched through white fog, shaking.

The man in Tom's car yanked the door handle and stepped out, but the driver didn't notice him leave. He had forgotten his passenger entirely. Visions of his daughters overtook him, destitute, begging, their ribs sticking through their skin with hunger. He saw young, foreign men in expensive cars, the entire city funneling into those back seats as Tom scratched at the dust in the road, searching for coins. He saw Plan B, the pub, washed out by flood. There was no Plan B, he realized. There never was. There was only this life, this one, irreplaceable life. The weight on his back dragged heavier, heavier. The creature hummed against his throat.

Tom's knuckles paled as they tightened on the wheel. His foot sank into the gas pedal, grave as a pocket filled with stones. The car engine wheezed. Then the taxi bulleted forward, roaring through traffic, until it exploded against the back of the parked car—the young driver crushed between. The woman with the suitcases screamed.

The man in the wool coat took another sip from his flask. He smiled. He turned and walked toward South Station. He had a train to catch.

Miles away, the wind turned. In the Doña Ana Mountains of New Mexico, one hundred twisting dust devils took howling to the air at once. Outside a Baltimore cemetery, every crabapple on every bough browned to rot and thudded to the soil, perfuming the earth with vinegar. On Frenchmen Street in New Orleans, hundreds of trombones and clarinets choked into sudden silence as if buried alive. And at South Station in Boston, a man walked through tall rotating doors. He tightened his coat against the chill. The driver had offered a small purge, enough to hold the man over, but it was hardly satiating. The man was still eager. His tongue flicked over the singed roof of his mouth. The living house, it was close now. So close. He could feel it—not an ocean away, not a century, but here, on this nation's soil. A final stain, waiting to be cleansed.

As he walked through the building, his shape glinted in the terminal's green windows. If anyone were to have glimpsed this reflection in the instant it scurried over the glass, they would not have seen the reflection of one man, but many—thousands of ashen figures crowded into a single form. The bodies of the mass writhed in the glass, climbing over one another, knotting fists, tearing at one another's skins with their teeth. They stretched, elongating like a winter shadow. But in the violent chaos that had erupted outside the station, no one noticed the man (if he could rightly be called a man), nor his reflection. He continued undisturbed. And it was thus that the Longshadow Man began his work.

CHAPTER SIX

THERE'S A SCENE IN *The Drowning Fool* where the Fool is jour-
neying from town to town telling jokes. One day he arrives in
the biggest city he's ever seen, with tall purple skyscrapers cut
from plywood and flocks of toy motorcars that zoom about
with a snap of Rigs' wrist. The Fool goes to the city hall. He
asks the Mayor if he'd like to hear a joke. The Mayor says, *Yes,
please,* and why don't they have a big party in the Fool's honor,
and at the party, the Fool can tell his joke? So the Fool waits all
day, and by evening, the party is ready. There are balloons, and
a DJ, and a perfect miniature replica of a bounce house with
the Fool's face painted on the side. He's about to start telling
his joke, but the Mayor cuts in. *First, let me honor you by telling my
own favorite joke!* says the Mayor. And the Mayor goes on to tell
the very same joke that the Fool had planned to tell. Then he
continues—telling joke after joke, until he's told every joke the
Fool knows. You'd think the Fool would be humiliated—but
instead, he laughs. He laughs and laughs until he isn't laughing anymore, but sobbing, Strings raising his wooden hands

to his eyes. *I've spent my whole life with these jokes,* cries the Fool, *but never once have I heard them myself. Oh, what jokes! What jokes! What a life I have lived!*

That's how Bellatine felt inside the legged house. Like she was living her present and her future and her past, all at once. Like her own story was being told back to her, floorboard by floorboard.

Together, they'd trotted the house up to the Northeast Kingdom, a wooded region of Vermont just south of the Canadian border. It was where she'd spent the last couple of years, first at woodworking school in Fairfax, then apprenticing at Joseph's shop outside Greensboro, where she helped her old mentor assemble cabinets and repair antique furniture. Once, they'd even been commissioned by a private collector to help restore an armoire that had originally belonged to Napoleon.

She loved the work. Boards and screws were quiet in her hands, materials she could understand, manipulate, shape into whatever forms she wished. The more time she spent in the tool shop, the more she'd felt she could understand how the world around her was put together. Not just understand—inform. By assembling a chair or a dining table or a maple cutting board, she held jurisdiction. The world came together at her command.

Joseph had given her a key to the woodworking shop, granting her twenty-four-hour access to all the tools she'd need. It was the perfect place to convert the house while Isaac loitered downtown. Though her brother was of little help, she didn't mind. Better to have him out of the way. Better to be alone with the house, *her* house, while she could.

Squatting on the kitchen floor, Bellatine brushed her hands on her thighs and devised a plan. She'd start by pulling out the wood with the most burn damage and replacing the ruined beams. Then, with the structure restored, she'd move on to additions.

Palming her hammer's steel weight, she raised it over a singed board. The house creaked, as if from unease.

Her arm fell limp at her side.

This wasn't a chair, a dining table, a cutting board. This house—it was a body.

Inch by inch, Bellatine let her fingers wander over the aged oak, trailing to the edge where one board met the next. She looked closer, examining the lines where the woodwork came together. Her heartbeat skipped in excitement. *No nails.* The next panel was the same, and the next—the wood hovering in place without a single metal fastener. *Of course,* she realized— metal nails would have been too expensive when the house was built. It must be secured entirely through carved joinery: tongue and groove, mortise and tenon, as if the entire structure were a puzzle comprised of thousands of perfectly cut pieces. The build would have required an immense understanding of the material and incredible precision. A masterwork, hiding centuries of craft and technique beneath its whitewashed walls. If Bellatine was going to rebuild this house, she would have to rebuild it *right.*

Taking up her hammer again, Bellatine gently slipped the back end between two boards, readying to pry. She laid her empty hand flat against the singed wall.

May I? she thought, funneling the intention into the house with all the focus she could muster. She waited.

The creaking stopped. The great creature settled, sinking into itself. From the cookstove, the fire let out a small, accepting puff of smoke. And so, Bellatine bent the hammer back.

Nights were serenaded by a table saw's whine. Hours upon hours bent over lengths of pine, birch, spruce, oak—intricate joinery carved anew to lock the boards together. In the after-noons, Bellatine foraged for river clay and moss to refresh the mortar that bound wooden panels into walls. Surfaces replastered and painted, roof weeded, cabinets and solar pan-els and limited electrical wiring installed in cautious mod-ernization. On the porch, velvet curtains were sewn, inky as plums. Barbed wire was snapped loose inch by inch, replaced by little tin lanterns and silk garlands. Bellatine even found an old air popper at a junk sale, affixing it to the side of the house so they could sell striped paper bags of buttered popcorn to their audiences before performances. The exte-rior walls she decorated with chalkboard signs rimmed with red and gold borders. SHOW, TONIGHT! Bright shellac made the front balcony—now the stage—look wet and clean in the autumn sunlight.

As she worked, Bellatine kept a list of the objects she found within the house. She thought herself an archaeologist excavating a dig site. The inventory included, among other treasures:

> Six linen dresses in various colors of stripes and checkers
>   (two child sized, three infant sized, one adult)
> What looked like a cat's leg bone wrapped in red thread,
>   with a sprig of rosemary tucked inside
> A set of silver Sabbath candlesticks
> A horseshoe
> A box of papers and letters, all in Yiddish
> An array of Yiddish books
> A tobacco tin with two human teeth inside
> A man's brimmed wool cap
> A pantry of pickled vegetables (turnips, beets, green
>   beans) brined in yellow vinegar

But it was the macabre mural hidden up in the loft that intrigued Bellatine most—soldiers massacred in writhing vines, the house and its little animal menagerie celebrating in the center. The other remnants suggested her ancestors living gentle, provincial lives, seasoned with folk magic and Kabbalah and familial tradition. But the painting added a sanguinary slant to her twice-great-grandmother's world.

Why was it there? Bellatine wondered. *What did it mean?*

"Do you know about this?" she asked the house accusatorily.

It said nothing.

In the studio, there were certain tools of Joseph's that Bellatine didn't touch. His equal space divider, which zigzagged like an electric eel. His layout square, a triangular ruler for measuring cuts of stock, which looked like a yellow-winged moth fluttering on the workbench. His favorite chisel, which she'd watched the old man whisper to like an accomplice as he marked pieces of cedar with a number two pencil. These tools were all too lively for Bellatine's comfort. It wasn't uncommon for woodworkers to talk to their tools, to treat them almost as if they were alive. There's an intimacy that comes with craftsmanship, not unlike the bond between a cellist and her instrument. In school, Bellatine had seen her classmates anthropomorphize utility knives or even table saws to which they'd grown particularly attached. She was always careful to take note of which tools had been given lives and which hadn't. She needed her instruments silent. Objects as objects. Nothing more.

For the house, she made an exception.

"It looks . . . healthy," Carrie had said when Bellatine brought her friends over to see the house's partial transformation. Nearly six weeks had passed since she and Isaac had convened at the New York port, and already, the progress was immense. The building shivered, as if with pride.

"Oh my god, can it hear me?" asked Carrie, pulling out her phone to snap a selfie with the house in the background. Her buzzed bleached blond hair pricked up almost identically to the house's spiky sod roof.

"I don't know," Bellatine said. "At least, I don't think it understands English."

"Vous êtes une belle maison, mais oui!" Aiden cooed in his Québécois lilt. He scratched a sunburned cheek, awaiting a response. The house ignored him.

"Definitely doesn't speak French," Bellatine said, to Aiden's clear disappointment.

It had taken the better part of that first night back at the marine terminal to crack the code on maneuvering the house. They'd tried yanking on the balconies like a horse's reins, tried tossing pieces of jerky and shiny flat nickels from Isaac's pack in front of it as a lure, attempted simple, old-fashioned yelling. It was only when Isaac gave up to page through another Yiddish book that Bellatine found the winning method. She'd pulled up a translation app on her phone and typed "walk forward" into the dictionary bubble. *"Gey vayter,"* she'd stuttered in Yiddish, more confidently than she felt.

The house shifted. One great knee folded and straightened. Then another. Giant yellow feet thudded on the warehouse floor, and the whole building shook. The cottage tilted like a seesaw, left, right, left, right as the legs carried them forward. Bellatine lost her footing and tumbled onto the floor with a yelp. Isaac sprang over to grab the doorframe for balance, as if readying for an earthquake. The great beast bobbed—and then, it galloped out of the warehouse.

"Thistlefoot—*drey*," she commanded now as Aiden and Carrie looked on. The house turned a full circle like a porcelain ballerina in a music box.

"Guess it only listens to *you*," Aiden pouted.

"What's a thistle foot?" Carrie asked.

"It's what I call it." She didn't elaborate.

The name had come from something her mom had once said: *People in our family, we're born with thistles in our feet. It's why we're always traveling. Because if we stood still, the thistles would prick us.*

"I've told you how I was on tour all the time as a kid, right?"

Carrie swung an arm around Bellatine. "Yes, we all know about your sordid past. And to think, here Aiden and I are, *daring* to address the esteemed puppet heiress of Oregon."

"*Thistlefoot*," Aiden tested. "It's got a spooky creature-y ring to it. Suits the thing."

"I can come by tomorrow and help you insulate," Carrie said. "Yeah, yeah, I know—"

"I don't need your help," Bellatine and Carrie said in unison.

Bellatine stiffened. "Stop asking. I've got this. Really."

"I get it, you don't trust us." Carrie stuck up her nose in feigned offense.

"You know that isn't it," Bellatine insisted.

"She doesn't mistrust us," Aiden said. "She just trusts herself more."

"Our Liberty Bell, always tolls alone."

"For freedom!"

"For sovereignty!"

"For the right to do everything herself and never accept help from her friends who love her!"

Bellatine ignored the taunts. There was nothing wrong with working alone. If you start accepting help, you start to rely on people. If you start to rely on people, you lose your self-sufficiency. If you lose your self-sufficiency, you become little more than a kite in an inconstant wind, at the mercy of whatever storms that blow.

"Mind if I post this pic?" Carrie said, returning to her phone.

"See, *now* you're helping," Bellatine said. "We'll take whatever promo we can get. The more tickets we sell, the easier it'll be for me to get my brother off my back."

"Speaking of your brother," Carrie mumbled, not looking up from her screen. "What's his number?"

Bellatine flashed her a warning look. "Absolutely not."

"We live in the woods. It's him or Aiden at this point, and I'm not fucking Aiden. No offense."

"Offense taken," Aiden said.

"Anyway, his number's useless," Bellatine insisted. "He only has this brick of a flip phone, and he never turns it on. He's impossible to get a hold of."

"Holy shit," Carrie said, thumbing the screen. "Did you guys see this?"

Bellatine was grateful for a change in subject, whatever it might be. "See what?"

"A whole family was killed in Burlington last night in their house. I guess their next-door neighbor did it, some random lady?"

"How'd she do it?" Aiden asked.

"Nice, ghoul."

"Like you aren't curious."

"Hold on I haven't gotten to . . . Oh. Oh, fuck."

"What?"

"She shot them. She shot them in their beds. Kids, too. Then she lit their house on fire to make it look like an accident. It looks like one of the kids hid in the closet, but the fire got him anyway."

To that, Aiden had no immediate response.

"Does it say why?" he asked after a moment, leaning over Carrie's shoulder to look.

"Because she's a psycho, why do you think?"

"I was just wondering about *motive*."

"It . . . I can't tell," Carrie said, scrolling through the article. "Dude, it seems like she doesn't even remember doing it. And

when they picked her up, she was ranting nonsense and clawing at her back, saying something was *on her*."

"Like what?"

Carrie shrugged. "Doesn't say."

"Sounds like those attacks in Boston last week. Remember,
the taxi driver? And the woman who worked at the seafood
place? Wasn't that the same—violent attacks, no memory?"

Bellatine's stomach sank. Her hands cropped up with a sudden, deep itching. Why did all this feel so familiar—not as if
she'd heard it before, but as if she'd dreamt it?

"Zombie apocalypse?" Carrie suggested.

"Alien mind control?" added Aiden.

Bellatine's two friends launched into a debate over who
would win a war, zombies or aliens ("But are we talking modern warfare? Or pre–World War One, feathers-in-caps-nobility-
on-the-battlefield type stuff?"), and just as quickly as it had
come up, the news of the murdered family and the Boston killings faded. It wasn't long before the conversation circled back
around to Bellatine's brother.

"I saw the Waltser kids who live next to Mona's talking to
him yesterday, and they asked him if he was a vampire," Aiden
said.

"A vampire?" said Bellatine, incredulous.

"Let's just say he didn't *dissuade* them."

"I'm afraid to ask what you mean by that."

"They tried to pet that cat that follows him around—he told
them it used to be a kid but asked too many questions."

"Oh good. Perfect. Thrilled he's making friends with the
locals."

Thistlefoot swayed on its hips like a diva. Showing off.
It's probably jealous that Isaac's getting all the attention, Bellatine
mused. Or maybe that was just her.

In the month and a half Isaac had been in Greensboro,
he'd garnered a mythic reputation. He was charming, Bellatine couldn't deny that—but his charm had an arsenic edge

to it. People were afraid of him. They halted their private conversations when he walked by. Avoided eye contact. It's not that he was anything especially ominous to look at, but he carried himself with a dangerous confidence. When he talked to people, it wasn't with the ease of neighborly conversation; it was more like a cat playing with a songbird before the kill.

Bellatine suspected he'd started half the small-town whispers himself: that he was a Rhode Island gangster in witness protection. That he was a tech billionaire, in Greensboro to buy up farmland for a private prison development. That he had recently been released from medical quarantine, a guinea pig for genetic modification. And now, apparently, he was a vampire, too. What truly embarrassed Bellatine was how readily people were willing to swallow the legends. *Don't encourage him,* she wanted to shout at the gossiping old men playing chess at Mona's back counter. She knew Isaac only indulged the rumors because he was bored, lolling around the small town while the show came together. Like everything he did, he would gladly set fire to his own clothes if it meant keeping himself *entertained*. Bellatine just had to make sure the flame didn't spread to her.

"That *thing* he does," Aiden said, "where he mimics people— it's creepy, no?"

Carrie shrugged. "I think it's hot."

"I am *begging* you . . ." Bellatine groaned.

"It's almost too spot on though, right?" Aiden continued. "Eerie. Sort of inhuman."

Bellatine's stomach clenched. Inhuman . . . There was only one Yaga sibling worthy of that accusation. And it wasn't Isaac.

"Maybe he *is* a vampire," Carrie said, perking up.

Whenever she watched her brother interacting with the soft, quiet life she'd worked so hard to build—hanging around Carrie and Aiden, loitering at her apartment, drinking cup after cup of coffee at Mona's while chain-smoking out front—she caught herself grinding her teeth. It was a simple existence, but it was *hers*. It was *normal*. She'd intended for it to stay that way.

But any hope she had for maintaining life as usual shattered on Monday. On Monday, the box arrived.

CHAPTER SEVEN

THEIR PARENTS HAD MAILED it from Oregon—a knee-high black road case with silver buckles. The sight of it made Bellatine's throat close like a fist.

"Our old pals are here," Isaac announced, dropping the case onto the woodshop's cement floor with a smack.

Between endless construction projects, Bellatine had almost managed to forget that the box ever had to arrive at all.

She crossed her arms over her chest. Her hands buzzed. Why had she agreed to this? Isaac unlatched the two large buckles on the front of the case and swung the lid open. Bellatine dug her nails into her palms, the sting grounding her. Inside: the seven puppets from *The Drowning Fool*.

The Fox with the little green vest and the garnet eyes.
The Mayor with the purple sash.
The Tailor at his sewing machine.
The Moon.
The Green Woman with willow arms and legs.

The Girl with No Face.
The Fool in red shoes, black tears etched down his
    wooden cheeks.

The puppets were all roughly a foot and a half tall, hand sewn from cream-colored muslin. They were stuffed with raw sheep's wool, an animal aroma still lingering in the unwashed fleece. Some of the characters had hands or feet or faces of whittled basswood, oiled dark. Others had features painted on in inks the Yagas' mother had mixed herself—dyes made from turmeric, hibiscus, hollyhock, and later (when their parents' homespun fanaticism had mellowed) Kool-Aid packets, stirred into white oil paint. Many of the puppets wore tiny goat-hair toupees and clothes stitched from old lace and thrifted linens. Some even had gemstones for eyes, or sewn into their garments for ornamentation. Amethyst. Tahitian pearl. Tourmaline. Bits of pyrite glinting like gold. Bellatine had forgotten how achingly *beautiful* the puppets were. Each tenderly devised by their mother's needle and paintbrush. The wooden accoutrements bearing thousands of small marks from their father's dedicated carving knife. There in the vinyl road case, the puppets looked like a family of imps, stowed away from faerieland to seek a new life among mortals.

The Green Woman was the most elegant puppet, with velveteen ivy and fiddleheads spooled around her long ankles. The Tailor the most intricate, his glinting needle made from the tip of a porcupine quill. The Girl with No Face was the most haunting, and the Fox the fiercest, his knife-sharp teeth glinting with real bone. But the Fool was the puppet with the most magnetism. Unlike the others, the Fool predated the Yaga family theater. He had begun life as a doll in their mother's childhood collection. Mira had kept him into adulthood, and after adding a fresh coat of paint, a fine new wardrobe, and a series of small wooden rods at the base of the head, mid-back, and elbows where he could be held and animated, the Fool was ready for his new role. The rest of the cast was built up around him, until *The Drowning Fool* was as bold and bodied a myth as any legend before or since.

Quick as a snake, Isaac lifted the Moon from the box and tossed it toward Bellatine. Her reflexes betrayed her, hands raising to catch it. Blind heat surged into her palms, like she'd touched a stovetop. Panic. The Moon fell to the floor.

She's seven years old. "Do it, Tiny," her brother whispers. A heartbeat, a singe, and the Tailor twitches.

Nine years old. "Child, you are a maker of miracles!" Her father, clasping her shoulder. Dim stage lights. The Fox hisses at her, scratches his snout—though no one is holding him.

Bellatine is fourteen. There's dried blood between her fingers. She holds her hands under an ice bath until they ache. *Monster*, echoes a voice in her head, *monster*.

Isaac looked from her to the puppet on the floor. "That's right, Tiny, screw the moon. What's it doing up there all night, anyway, lurking, spying, messing with the tides. You show 'em."

"Sorry," she murmured. "Slipped."

"We'll start rehearsing tomorrow," Isaac said, one of his signature decrees.

Nausea boiled in her stomach. "Tomorrow? I . . . I have to finish insulating tomorrow, it'll take all day. How about Wednesday?"

"Insulate Wednesday. This comes first."

"I'm not ready to start rehearsing," she said, fists clenched.

"We rehearse tomorrow," Isaac repeated. His voice was flat and easy, as if he were stating an inarguable fact.

Wasn't this her town? Her life? Yet Isaac had started calling the shots since day one, back in Red Hook. When her brother decided something, that was that. He was like royalty making a pronouncement, and Bellatine was his subject, expected to bow and take orders.

Isaac drew the other puppets from the box, examining them one by one. The heat in Bellatine's fingertips fizzed hotter.

"This is how you are with people, isn't it?" she snapped. "You strut into other people's lives, decide what's best, and expect everyone to follow along. Sorry, but I'm not part of your fan club. I'm not going to trip over myself to please you."

Isaac didn't look up from the puppet in his hand—the Fox, whose garnet eye dangled loosely from a thread after so many years unused.

"We rehearse tomorrow because it'll be raining. And if you're going to react like that"—he pointed to the Moon, still lying on the floor—"we'd better start you off outside, wet, to keep you cool."

Bellatine's face reddened. He knew then. They'd been so young when Bellatine had started hiding her Embering, she'd hoped her brother had forgotten—chalked up any lingering recollection to a childhood fantasy that faded with age.

"I understand you want time," Isaac continued, "but it isn't going to get better. Our first gig is less than a month away, and you'll need to be able to keep yourself steady by then. I wish we could lounge around like we're on vacation, but we have to start heading south before the season turns, and we can't afford to wait. So we'll start tomorrow. Until then, take Thistlefoot into the woods for the night. Bring the puppets with you. Collect yourself. We'll start at noon."

"I don't need your coddling," she said. "And the puppets won't be an issue. I'm Rigs, remember? They're your problem." But even as she spoke, her words felt hollow. Isaac was right—how was she going to go on this tour if she couldn't even touch the props? Just because she wasn't Strings didn't mean she wouldn't have to be around them all day. What if one got left onstage, or Isaac missed a cue? She'd have to touch them eventually. She felt foolish. They were only dolls. Fabric and wood and paint. She spent all day with hissing table saws and wood burners that could melt her skin clean off, yet she was terrified of a boxful of little sewn puppets.

If she wanted the house sooner rather than later, she had to do this tour. And to do this tour, she had to make her peace with *The Drowning Fool*.

The forest was serene. Slow. A welcome respite. She gathered late-season berries from wild briar patches and foraged chanterelles. It had already begun to rain, and the earth wriggled with red efts—neon salamanders, narrow as splinters. The maples had shed their final leaves, leaving the forest skeletal and stark. Etched into the gray October sky, branches tangled like a highway map. Crows cannonballed through. *That's where we'll be soon,* Bellatine thought, *soaring across maps.*

She'd placed the box of puppets in the center of Thistlefoot's living room. For the first hour, she circled them. She imagined herself a hyena approaching prey. She held the power. Not them.

Wasn't handling the puppets the same as working with wood? All she had to do was apply the same principles. Attend to her breathing. Move slowly and deliberately. Think of the puppet as an object, a tool, no different from a hammer or a table saw. Something to control, not be controlled by. And if she started to feel that black-blue heat creep into her hands? Well . . . she'd dated a guy in high school who'd silently recite the US presidents in his head to help him last longer during sex. Maybe she'd give that a shot.

After first touching the Moon puppet, her hands had screamed for hours. By late afternoon, half mad with residual shame, she'd tumbled through the threshold of her twice-great-grandmother's house, and all symptoms of the Embering had vanished. It was like dousing a fire in cool water. *Which is why I agreed to all this in the first place,* she reminded herself.

Her attachment to the house had come from more than an unexplainable sense of nostalgia. Inside Thistlefoot, her hands were completely . . . still. Almost *chilled.* Even during Bellatine's greatest stretches of control, when seven or eight months would pass between Emberings, her hands never quieted completely. There was always an itch under the surface, humming. More than once she'd woken with her pillow and face smeared red with blood, her fingernails sticky from the half-moon wounds they'd gouged. But in the house, even that constant tingling vanished.

This could be my life, she'd thought, trailing through the cottage's dim rooms, her body cool and quiet and *hers.* Her heart had signed on the dotted line the moment Isaac uttered his offer to sell.

Since returning to Greensboro, she'd started staying in Thistlefoot overnight, spread out on the harder of the two beds. Sometimes she'd climb up into the loft and lie on her back among the clutter, gazing for hours at the mural of the soldiers caught in vines, tracking the loops and twists of each tendril. It was a violent image, but Bellatine found it soothing. While the edges were brutal and fevered, the center where the crow, the rabbit, and the lion danced beside the house was celebratory. Joyful, even. It was a victory painting—triumph over encroaching chaos. When was the last time she'd been able to sleep until morning without the itch in her hands waking her? For the first time in years, she'd arise feeling rested. Rejuvenated.

There were always more tasks to be done. Cotton-draped

scaffolding to erect between the two beds for privacy. Soot to scrub from singed plaster, before hiding the remaining damage beneath mint-green paint. She hollowed out one of the two pantries, installing a composting toilet and a sink with a simple foot pump for dispensing fresh water. Affixed hooks to hang puppets and costumes and backdrops still wet with glue. It felt good to be working. Felt good to know that her labors were leading to something real.

The box of *Drowning Fool* puppets squatted in the living room, a terrible toad. Bellatine breathed slowly, extending her pinkie like she was lifting a teacup in a fancy parlor, and reached out. *In. Out. In. Out. That's it. A little closer.* If there was anywhere to reacclimate herself with the puppets, it was here, in Thistlefoot, where the Embering felt like a far-off creature, a migrating bird flown south for winter.

It's not as if she didn't know how to maintain control. She'd become an expert at quelling the Embering over the past decade. She had hundreds of tricks for grounding herself. *Poplar, maple, redwood, cedar, cherry,* she recited silently. The wood she'd manipulated thousands of times, carved and bent to her will. She reached one hand into her overalls pocket and gripped the small wooden spoon she always kept close. A talisman. But even with her usual protective charms in place, the puppets from *The Drowning Fool* had been such a huge part of her life when her Embering was at its most unmanageable. They carried too many memories with them, too many stories, too many tongues of flame.

She leaned toward the Fool—but stopped herself. He was powerful. He carried so much *pull*. Better to start simpler. Gently, the tip of her pinkie made contact with the little silver Moon. Bellatine held her breath. There was a tiny pop, like a small fuse blowing, and she yanked her hand back fast. No. It was only a branch, tapping the window. *Keep going,* she told herself. She reached out another finger. This time, no sound, but when her fingertip touched the painted fabric she pulled away out of instinct, as if recoiling from a tarantula. She closed her eyes and thought of the real moon, cold and unbothered. How it bloomed and shrank dependably, unaffected by the world's tumult. Poets cried to it, and still, it waxed. Scientists studied it through long telescopes, and still, it waned. *In, out. In, out.* Girls discovered the terrible powers that their bodies were capable of—and yet, the moon rose and fell over the horizon, undisturbed.

Bellatine tried once more. She fixated on the puppet's intricacies, each pale pock and crater, each dark lake—a perfect, careful replica of the actual thing, rendered in silver embroidery. One finger slid against the fabric, then two, until her whole palm was covering the Sea of Tranquility. Her hand remained cold and still as stone, but Bellatine's stomach had other plans. She leapt back from the Moon, rushing to vomit into the sink.

The following morning, the egg yolks in Bellatine's cast iron pan gaped up at her like two golden eyes. She flipped them with a plastic spatula, accidentally breaking one into a leaky wink. This was her favorite time of day—dandelion-tinted light cutting through Thistlefoot's wedged glass windows. No one else awake. The perpetually burning cookstove wafting a smoky warmth throughout the house.

In the corner, the road case of puppets sat abandoned, sealed shut.

"One for me, one for you," Bellatine said, dividing up the eggs. She slid the first onto a piece of toast. The second she tipped into the cookstove.

She'd picked up the habit a few days after moving in—sharing her food with the house. She never did so in front of Isaac or Carrie or Aiden, only when it was just her and Thistlefoot. Half a Kit Kat. A few strawberries. Puffs of buttered popcorn. All fed to the great brick stove. It probably didn't even notice the offerings, or care, but she kept on anyway. It was silly, she knew—but she wanted the house to *like* her. She sang to it while she worked (*If all the young men were hares on the mountain / How many young girls would take guns and go hunting?*) and played klezmer tunes through her Bluetooth speaker, in case it longed for the sounds of home. She plundered her apartment's closet for her old silk prom dress, which she cut into rags, wanting the house to luxuriate in the fabric's soft sweep as she dusted cobwebs and dead ladybugs from the windowsills. She imagined herself as a plover, a bird delicately cleaning between an alligator's teeth. She, a small, flighty creature. The house, a beautiful beast. Each dependent on the other.

This could be my life, her thoughts echoed.

She glanced with dread at the box in the corner. She wasn't ready. Not ready to handle the puppets, to put her fate in the hands of her vagrant brother, to leave her home of more than two years behind . . .

A breeze passed through Thistlefoot, funneling down the chimney and spiraling through the kitchen. It carried with it the scent of baking bread, of wheat fields in bloom, the scent of woodsmoke and apple blossoms and dust as if kicked up by footsteps in some long-ago marketplace. The house rocked, listening to far-off music one hundred years and an ocean away. Bellatine imagined her great-great-grandmother gliding through her home, reading and cooking and birthing her children. Who was she? What loves and sorrows befell her, so long before Bellatine existed? How did she come to befriend this loyal, astonishing creature?

Thistlefoot *would* be Bellatine's life—but only if she went along with Isaac's plan. He didn't need to know she hadn't overcome her block. As Rigs, she could surely avoid touching the puppets—for now.

She picked up her phone and thumbed a quick text.

I'm coming. Let's do this.

The house creaked.

CHAPTER EIGHT

SLIPPING OUT THE BACK door, Isaac left the workshop lights on, giving the illusion that the room remained occupied. He didn't *need* to sneak out. He wasn't sixteen anymore. Yet at every moment, he could feel Bellatine's attention like a cloud of gnats, ever swarming about him. Keeping tabs. Even hiding out in the workshop, where they'd been holding their rehearsals over the past week, he was a moth pinned to corkboard, a specimen under observation. And not the way he liked to be observed, as a character, an illusion, as a lie. She was trying to observe *him*.

Bellatine didn't know Isaac at all. Not anymore. When he'd left home, he was still a kid. Cocky and restless, starving for adventure. Didn't know how to pick a pocket or survive a night in a train yard, stalled and waiting on a ride. Had never shook so hard from cold he thought his teeth might crack. Never been woken up by the cops while sleeping beneath a highway bridge. And most importantly, he'd not yet learned to be possessed by another person, hadn't learned to study the precise quirks of a body and mirror them. He wasn't the Chameleon King, yet. But he may as well let his sister believe she knew him. It would be easier for her to think he was still the boy who'd left—a reckless teenager hunting for thrills.

The tremors were bad today. Hands shaking too hard to be any use with the puppets. His head throbbing like it had been slammed in a door. Whenever he caught his own reflection in the bathroom mirror, his throat filled with bile and he'd down another fistful of Advil. He needed to get out.

It was past ten as he descended the dirt road toward Asylum Bar. The moon cast silver half-light onto his shoulders, whetting his sharp angles, a knife blade of a boy. Isaac took up a stone and threw it into the air, watching bats chase it down, mistaking it for prey. It was a trick he'd learned as a child growing up in Oregon, when he'd do the same with a sneaker, hurled from the giant trampoline in the backyard. In the distance, a coyote yowled, joined by another, then another. There was an untamable quality to the New England woods. A frenzy, frothing rabid at the mouth. Especially now, in October, when the air was tight as a seam, as if Isaac need only exact one firm tug for the whole night to unzip and let some Otherworld leak in. The feral season made his tremors feel less like a sickness and more like fuel. A currency to spend.

Even a quarter mile away, Asylum Bar's echo jostled into the road. Drunken laughter, the snap of an air hockey puck against fiberglass, canned pop music. Same as all those like it, the hallowed dive of dives. It was one of only three bars in town—the other two slick, overpriced cocktail spots catering to "leaf peepers," the New York tourists who came to Vermont to snap foliage photos and throw the word *quaint* around like it was a compliment. Asylum Bar was different. Two-dollar PBR. A tub of pickled eggs on the countertop. Darts in the corner and a lax IDing policy and a perpetually sticky floor. The perfect place to peel out of your skin. Half the people there were already pretending to be someone they weren't.

Isaac drew his thin billfold from his back pocket. He'd run out of busking money weeks ago, but his visit to the bar would rectify that. He flipped through his pack of borrowed driver's licenses, a menu of lives, all delectably inhabitable. Who would he be tonight?

Lenny, a radiologist from two states south, who'd come out to toast the birth of his newborn son?

Jackson, backwoods boy looking to pick a random fight after getting laid off from a job at Goodhue Construction?

Paul, who would already be drunk when he walked in and insist on leading the bar in a rousing off-key rendition of "Sweet Caroline"?

Anyone. He could be anyone. None of those men shook so hard they couldn't light a damn cigarette without dropping the lighter. None of them flinched at the sound of their own name or doubled over with a migraine if they looked too long in a mirror. None of them dreamt of Benji every night. Of his emerald eyes flashing with the stripe of a passing train, his feet dangling over the side of the freight car, guitar on his back. The *tap, tap, tap* of his foot against the trestle. Not one of the men Isaac would shapeshift into tonight remembered what Isaac remembered. They were simple. Easy to become. Easy to satisfy.

"What do you think, Hub?" Isaac peered down at the tiny black cat trotting along beside him. There was a time when it would have aggravated him, to find her trailing him like a comet tail. Back when she'd first started following him, he'd tried everything to lose her. Hopping out of freight yards in the middle of the afternoon while she slept. Ditching her on wide stretches of prairie land, rich with field mice. Giving her to farmers or other travelers or anyone who'd take her. Sometimes she'd even disappear on her own for days or weeks, and he'd think he was finally rid of her. But she always popped back up again. It was like that old folk song, *The cat came back the very next day / The cat came back, they thought it was a goner / But the cat came back; it just couldn't stay away* . . . Eventually, he stopped trying. He'd grown used to her. She was his shadow, constant and lurking.

Hubcap was the nearest thing Isaac had to an anchor. A tether. Most travelers kept an anchoring object with them. A familiar of sorts, part for luck, part for company, part to give them some sense of constancy amid an inconstant way of life. Instruments were most common: banjos, beat-up guitars with holes worn through from picking, clunky accordions in alligator-skin cases. But Isaac had seen all sorts of talismans— raccoon vertebrae on leather cords. Hunting knives. Notebooks with broken spines. Even a mason jar with a goat's heart inside, pickled in whiskey.

When he practiced mimicry, he replaced himself with some- one else. His body shed its Isaacness, its *himness*, and in those moments, there was no Isaac anymore. His personality was wiped clean off him. On occasion, he slipped too far away from himself, and he'd forget who he started as. But then Hubcap would hiss, or dig a claw into the soft pincushion flesh of his ankle, or even just rub up against him, and he'd recognize her. She became a reference to tug him back. A map to lead him home.

There were times when he didn't want to come back, but Hubcap would always mew at him until he couldn't ignore the keening anymore. He'd snap back into himself. But some nights, when the trembling and headaches and restless scrab- bling in his chest grew wild, he couldn't help but wonder what it would be, to disappear entirely . . . to tumble into another life and stay there. Sometimes he thought about leaving her behind one last time and letting himself vanish for good.

Isaac tripped over a pothole in the street, barely righting himself in time, his knees rubbery. The tremors were making him careless. He couldn't afford that. He had to stay focused on what really mattered. The money. And at the end of the day, Isaac's bazaar of characters had one purpose: they all appeared harmless to a bar full of patrons. Every one of them was artfully designed to make a person let down their guard.

"All right, Hub, scatter. I'll see you in a few hours." The cat vanished into the dark, following some invisible rodent heartbeat, just as Isaac arrived at the bar.

Tonight, the Chameleon King was on the job.

⚜

"A round on me—my kid was born today!"

The room cheered as the bartender spread a row of shot glasses across the counter, splashing them full of tequila in one unbroken stream. Isaac paid for them with the fifty-dollar bill he'd swiped from the doorman on his way in.

"Six pounds, five ounces, looks like an alien. A gray, wormy little alien. Most beautiful fuckin' thing I've ever seen. It's wild." He'd broadened his shoulders a bit and tucked down his chin and forehead to tack a few years onto his age, but otherwise Lenny didn't require a huge physical change. It was mostly the nervous excitement that made the man. Fear of fatherhood, relief at a successful delivery. And with Isaac still tremoring, Lenny provided a good excuse for the shakes.

Some of the old hobos Isaac had met riding rails liked to call him a Paul Bunyan: a chronic, yet nonetheless interesting, liar. He didn't hate the term. Lying was reductive, but in a way, all art was a form of lying. Poets hyperbolize. Painters heighten colors, smudge edges. Actors shapeshift. All ways to twist reality in order to tell a deeper, more potent truth. Fact only goes so far. There are a finite number of facts in the universe with which to tell a story. Lies, on the other hand, are limitless.

There were a good twenty people or so at Asylum. Six at the bar counter with Isaac, another five clustered into a booth with red leather seats in the back, two more at the air hockey table, and another pumping quarters into a claw machine, which, as Isaac noted on closer observation, was full of rubber sex toys.

The rest smoked by the doorway out front. Some of them Isaac recognized from Mona's café, or just around town—but they wouldn't recognize him. Not with Lenny draped over him like a new coat. Isaac downed his shot.

"It's Cyndi Lauper!"

A girl a few stools down was leaning over the bar, squinting at a whiteboard that hung above the beer taps. It read: WHAT '80S SINGER COMPARED LOVE TO AN ASTROLOGICAL PHENOMENON? GUESS FOR A FREE DRINK.

The bartender shook his large bald head. "Nope, Bonnie Tyler, 'Total Eclipse of the Heart.' Sorry, sweetheart."

"I'm not your fucking sweetheart. And I think you mean *astronomical*, not astrological, dipshit."

The bartender's jaw tightened, a look that likely preceded kicking somebody out.

The woman wore dark cherry lipstick and had a long, jet-black ponytail erupting from the top of her head. Her consonants carried a Hispanic lilt, her skin brown and honeyed in the bar light. Her left hand (the one enthusiastically pointing at the whiteboard) had the letters *B Y R D* tattooed across the knuckles. Isaac couldn't help but wonder what the right hand said. She was armored in a grimy denim jacket with a patch sewn on the back, baggy black jeans, and a pair of black combat boots. The patch looked hand embroidered, an ornate wreath of morning glories wound around a horse skull. She was easy on the eyes, in a way that might get your teeth knocked in if you looked too long. Isaac briefly considered how badly he needed his teeth anyway.

"Hey, mister." She tempered her words with a smile, sensing that her ejection from the bar might be imminent. "I think I've still earned a free drink. Isn't that how drinking games work? Loser takes a shot?"

"This guy just gave you a free shot," the bartender said, jabbing a thumb at Isaac.

The girl glared. "But see, I've already finished that one."

Before the bartender could respond, another customer appeared, easing himself onto the stool directly beside Isaac. His shoulders blocked the girl from view.

"A vodka, good sir," ordered the man. "Moskovskaya." The bartender raised his eyebrows. This wasn't a top-shelf liquor type of establishment. Isaac smirked into his beer.

The man wore an expensive-looking wool coat along with an antique brimmed cap, and Isaac could see the edge of a fine watch peering out from his sleeve. Someone who didn't belong in this bar. Someone with money.

In movies, pickpocketing scenes always show grubby English orphans returning to their lairs with enough wallets and watches to heave into a cinematic dragon's hoard of a pile. A game of reckless quantity. This wasn't realistic. In Isaac's experience, the craft was more like fishing or hitchhiking. You wait, and you watch, your catch slips by you—and once in a while, if you're lucky, you reel in one big fish, or one good ride, or in tonight's case, you snag one rich guy at a dive bar, his jacket pocket just a few inches away from your elbow.

"How about a Svedka?" asked the bartender.

The man waved a hand. "Yes, fine. When in Rome, do as the locals do, they say, no?" He grinned.

Russian, Isaac noted from the man's accent. What was a wealthy European doing in a rural, health-code-defying townie bar?

If Isaac had been Isaac that night, he might have tried to tease it out of the man. He might even have mentioned his own national connection—the strange inheritance, his personal lineage. His roots weren't something he'd thought of much, before Thistlefoot had arrived. His mom's side was Russian-Jewish, his dad's some Anglo-Scottish amalgamation, making him and Bellatine true-blue American mutts. They hadn't been raised with religion. Instead, they'd practiced holidays their parents invented. Strawberry Palooza, where they'd eat only strawberries for all three meals. Clownuary, when the family theater was free to the public and they threw a big fools' festival. Beach Day, always the coldest day in February, when Isaac's dad would drag a plastic swimming pool into the living room and fill it with packing peanuts and they'd bask all day in their bathing suits drinking lemonade. A traditionless upbringing—or rather, new traditions. Their own traditions. All Isaac really knew about the Russian part of their family history was that they'd arrived as refugees at Ellis Island in the late nineteen-teens, to escape the pogroms on Jewish villages. *Think Fiddler on the Roof,* his mom had said. Young Isaac had thought that meant back then everyone sang instead of talked.

But Isaac was *not* Isaac tonight. Isaac was Lenny. He beamed at the stranger with his proudest, tipsiest smile. "Hey man, you want to hear something crazy? I'm a dad today, my son was born this morning." He swayed a little on his chair, feigning drunkenness. Admittedly, the tequila shot had helped make the motion more convincing.

"*Pozdravlyayu,* friend!" The man clapped Isaac on the back in congratulations, firm enough that Isaac slid half off his stool. "We must have a drink in celebration."

The stranger leaned into Isaac's ear, whispering, "But we'll have only the finest libation, no Svedka for an occasion like this." He winked, drawing a slim blue bottle from his coat pocket while the bartender had his back turned. *Flask in the inner pocket. That means wallet's likely in an outside pocket.* Isaac noted a sort of griffin or multiheaded bird engraved on the front of the bottle. Looked old. *Potentially valuable?*

The man took a swig, then filled Isaac's empty shot glass with clear liquid. "To your new child and making a more perfect world where he may grow and thrive!"

Rising above the stranger's shoulder, the girl with the ponytail caught Isaac's eye with a hard stare. Her red mouth was set in a grim, flat line. Almost imperceptibly, she shook her head. *No.*

Why? Was the stranger trying to drug him? He doubted it, but better to be safe. Isaac lifted his glass. "To the future." He tipped it back, suppressing a shudder as he let the icy liquid slide invisibly down his sleeve. A bitter perfume rose from the dregs at the bottom of the glass—burning hay, thick as ash, muddied with the heady, underlying scent of maggot-ridden meat. Isaac's stomach turned.

The Russian paused, as if in expectation.

"Good . . . stuff." Isaac returned the empty glass to the bar top with a clack.

For the briefest moment, the stranger's mouth ticked down in displeasure, before sliding seamlessly back into civility.

"What do you do, friend? For your labor?"

"I'm a radiologist." He'd stolen that bit from X-ray repairman Brian and his orthodontist cronies. There's inspiration everywhere.

"Ah, so you know how diseased this world is. Your child is born into a strange time, indeed." The man's breath was startlingly hot against Isaac's cheek. It smelled like smoke.

"I suppose." Isaac slid his arm gently against the man's coat, scanning for the lump of a wallet. "Though my job is to focus on the getting well part. Making people healthy again." Smooth pocket. *Damn.* Must be on the other side.

The stranger tilted his head closer. "Not everyone is clean, like you and I are clean. Some people, they are prone to filth. Encourage filth. I do not mean to alarm you, friend. But now that you are a father, you must be careful, yes?" The man wiped his mouth with his hand, sweat beading above his clean-shaven lip.

"You know," the man continued, "I read about this region before I came. There is a great legacy of doctors, here. Medical men who saw a brighter tomorrow. A more perfect humanity. Who created a better land for their own children, through careful biological selection and cultivation."

Isaac's attention sharpened. *He's talking about eugenics.* In the prior century, Vermont had been home to one of the country's most aggressive eugenicist movements, leading to the forced sterilization of hundreds of women. The initiative, officially titled Breeding Better Vermonters, had overwhelmingly targeted poor, disabled, and Native American women, continuing all the way into 1957. He'd learned about the nauseating statistics from an Abenaki girl he'd hopped a few trains with in the Midwest. She'd played the banjo and her mouth had tasted like orange soda.

The stranger carried on, uninterrupted. "The work you do, you must be a talented young man. You could make a clean world for your boy. A clean future. To think, what you could achieve with the diseases in your care. A single syringe of flu. A few cancerous cells, implanted in a body."

What. The. Fuck. Had the stranger actually just suggested to a radiologist that he deliberately spread disease? And what was in that drink that was now soaking through the elbow of Isaac's suit jacket?

The girl with the ponytail hadn't moved from the end of the bar. Her eyes were fixed on a fresh drink in front of her, but Isaac could tell she was listening.

And he was beginning to realize that something else about the man made him uneasy. It was more than his rhetoric, more than the too-slick clothes, the charred breath. The man lacked *tells.* Those signature twitches and mannerisms that made a person who they were. But the stranger—Isaac couldn't grip onto him. No nervous habits, no crooked motions, no mimicable traits, save for his formal, almost antiquated way of speaking. If Isaac were a radar, the man simply didn't show up on the screen. Isaac couldn't have mirrored him if he tried. He slid right off.

The bartender tapped a plastic cup down in front of the stranger, half full of cheap vodka. "Anything else I can get you?"

"Only knowledge," the stranger said.

"Can't promise you that," the bartender scoffed, "unless you want to know about curling at the 1988 Winter Olympics. Then I could probably help you out."

"I was hoping for directions," the Russian said, "to a house that I believe may be near here."

"You got the address?" asked the bartender, sweeping a rag over the counter.

"See," continued the stranger, "here is the mystery. This house doesn't like to sit still."

Once again, Isaac sharpened.

"This house, I've been tracking it from back in Russia. It should not have left our shores. There are very dangerous aspects to this building, matters of national security."

"You're tracking a *house*?" asked the bartender.

The Russian sighed. "As I said, it is no ordinary house. The building is on two legs, talons, like a bird. Have you seen this place?"

The bartender shook his head. "I sure have not. Reminds me though, down by my sister's place in Hartford—a steam pipe burst in this mall, killed a janitor, I think, and the stores sprouted all these creepy mouths. One's right in the *O* of the Old Navy sign. Every now and again the mouths open and steam comes out. It's bizarre, man."

The Russian stood, stepping back from his stool. "This is of no use to me. I am done here." He turned to Isaac. "My great blessings again, on your son, and the world he'll inhabit." He walked away, leaving his Svedka untouched on the bar.

"Canada and Norway," said the bartender.

"Huh?" Isaac's pulse was thudding in his throat.

"1988. They won the gold."

He could still feel the stranger's hot breath. The intoxicating charm of his voice. A paid goon—must be. This wouldn't be the first time some rich schmuck Isaac had fleeced had sent a cutthroat to deliver payback. Whoever it was must have gotten a tip connecting Isaac to the living house, and started tracking from there, making up some government backstory. Isaac was lucky to have been shapeshifting that night; it was a loose disguise, but it must have been enough to throw off whatever descriptions or photos the man had been given. This was why Isaac didn't tie himself to anything flashier than his own skin. Too easy to find.

This year was supposed to be Isaac's windfall. He'd labored long enough, scrambled enough for the bare minimum, hungered enough for so many unreachable yearnings. But with Thistlefoot—he'd finally struck it lucky. A new beginning. The promise of cash, dangling in front of him like a prize from the Asylum Bar's claw machine, nearly close enough to touch. A new kind of freedom. Finally, *finally*, a way to pay his debt. No one was going to take that from him.

Isaac heard the front door swing open and shut as the stranger left. He glanced down to the end of the bar. The girl with the ponytail was gone, too.

Screw rounding up wallets tonight. Isaac spun off his barstool and strode toward the exit. The stoop had cleared out quick, only an empty set of benches strewn with cigarette butts remaining. He'd hoped to find the girl, ask her why she'd warned him against the stranger's drink, see what she knew—but only the wind greeted Isaac as he stepped into the night. Tinny music still leaked from the bar. He'd head along the main road toward town instead of the backwoods way he'd come in, see if he could catch up. Isaac ran a hand through his hair, which had leapt up in the wind like a cloud of alert antennae. He started walking—toward a threat. Toward a question. Toward a coming storm.

CHAPTER NINE

GOOD DAY! FORGIVE MY appearance, my shutters crooked as an old zayde's teeth, my fine walls dripping with paint. I am a work in progress, as are we all, yes? I know, you are trying to hear a story, and I keep interrupting. It is best you know this now: I will shove one story between the gaps of another, and then lop my own tales off before they're done. You may call it vexation. I call it suspense! Does life, too, not progress in this manner? Some lives born unexpectedly, inconveniently—others, ended too soon before the climax is reached. I have watched enough lives begin and end that such storytelling style has become my nature. Would you begrudge an old house its nature? Of course you wouldn't.

I'll tell you what came before. I'll recite it like a folktale. These sorts of memories, they're easier to understand that way. A memory, a true memory, is harsh and full of sharp edges. The facts, they don't always make sense in the ways that we might wish. Things happen that we cannot speak of aloud. These rememberings are prickly like blackberry briar in winter, with no leaves to soften them. And the very worst thing about memory, the deadliest, most brutal part: memory can be forgotten.

But a folktale—a folktale can never be forgotten because it wriggles and rearranges until it sits neatly on the heart. It is fluid and changing, able to adapt to whatever setting it finds itself in. It shifts in the mouth of every teller and adapts to the shape of each listener's ear. The facts can change (place names, the color of a character's woolen coat, the particular flowers in a small, circular garden), but the core remains the same. So, the folktale survives. Assimilates. And with it—so survives the memory.

Another disclaimer: though these events took place over a century ago, I will tell you this story in the present tense, as if it were happening at this very moment. I want you to experience it the way *I* experience it, and for me, the story *is* happening now. It is always happening. That, perhaps, is my curse.

There is a shtetl called Gedenkrovka, in the Smiliansky district of the Cherkasy region of Imperial Russia. That much, at least, is factual. In this village lives a woman. Her name is Baba Yaga, and she lives in a house on chicken legs. The house, it does not remain on one patch of ground for more than a day, but Baba Yaga never has trouble finding her way home. She simply spits on a dry bean and throws it on the ground, and whichever way the bean rolls will lead her to me. A fence of pikes surrounds her house, and upon the pikes are skulls. Every pike is occupied, except for one—that pike is for you. At night, the skulls glow like moons. Were you to approach the house uninvited, the skulls would weep moonmilk down their pale cheeks. They would sing to you in a language you do not speak, but that sounds familiar, so familiar, like a song your mother sang to you when you were young.

Have you heard the story about Baba Yaga's two daughters? She made them out of teeth. Listen:

All autumn, Baba Yaga watches the goyishe neighbor girls playing in the creek bed. She studies how they hold earthworms between their thumb and forefinger, gently so as not to crush them. She studies the odd proportions of a girl. The way a girl's hair darkens when wet with stream water. The bright hunger in a girl's eyes. She takes careful notes in a catskin notebook. She cultivates the yearning that roots in her own body, a lonesomeness as sturdy as an apple tree, the fruit ripening so sweetly it half turns to rot. Her heart fills with the nectar of loneliness, a syrup thick and cloying enough that it replaces the crone's need for food, for water. She teases out her loneliness and stirs it up in a wooden bowl with flour and honey and butter. She rolls out the dough. That dough, she curls into little twists and bakes the twists into rugelach.

The following morning, Baba Yaga approaches the two girls playing in the stream and offers them the pastries she made. The girls accept eagerly. But when the girls bite into the treats, the loneliness is so sticky that their teeth catch in the syrup and will not come free. They gnaw and tug and grind their jaws, but nothing will loosen them. Then, Baba Yaga reaches forward, takes hold of the rugelach lodged in each girl's mouth, and yanks. *Pop!* Out come two teeth, one from each of the two young girls.

Baba Yaga spits on a white bean and throws it on the ground and watches it roll. She scurries back to her house. She soaks the rugelach in rosewater to soften it and free the teeth. Then, she wraps each tooth in wool. Into each bundle she tucks a sprig of rosemary, a copper kopeck, and a drop of her own blood pricked from her fingertip. When night falls, she holds a bundle to each breast, and nurses them.

By daybreak, she has two young daughters. Her eldest daughter, Illa, has long, crow-black hair that falls past her ribs, and hands as strong as metal. She is very smart, and very cruel, and Baba Yaga loves her more than life. Her younger daughter, Malka, is only an infant, still plump and soft as a young rabbit. Her eyes are wet and glossy as river stones, and she weeps all day and all night. Baba Yaga loves her more than the moon, more than death, more than she could ever speak in mortal words.

One evening, a soothsayer comes to my door and rings my owl-talon bell, and he tells Baba Yaga that one of her daughters will not live to see womanhood. Baba Yaga cuts the soothsayer's throat and cooks him in a cast iron pot in the wood-burning oven, and that night, she and her daughters feast. The crone and her children nestle together atop the stove, wrapping themselves in sheepskins, and they sleep.

For a while, they are happy.

CHAPTER TEN

ISAAC HAD TRAVERSED HALF a mile without a lead when headlights erupted into view. They skimmed forward, twin lanterns cutting through the October darkness, and Isaac sashayed toward the road's edge to let the car pass.

Twenty feet away, the lights hovered, disembodied. Isaac squinted, but couldn't see the outline of a vehicle, only something levitating between the lights: a horse's skull. Hollow cavities where the eyes should be. Jagged xylophone of teeth. Bleached jaw. An engine growled. Isaac stepped back, stumbling into a roadside ditch. He hissed as his palms met gravel. The spectral horse rocketed closer, screeching brakes whinnying into the air, light and bone slamming to a halt before him. Moonlight rippled off the road, and Isaac realized why he hadn't been able to see a car.

It was a school bus, spray-painted midnight black. Even the windows were blotted out. The paint job made the bus disappear entirely against the sky—everything, that is, except the blanched horse's skull zip-tied to the front grille.

The door folded open, dispensing two shadowed bodies, and before Isaac could right himself again, the figures descended upon him, each grabbing him by one arm. He bit down hard into the wrist of the person to his right, inspiring a string of curses as one set of hands dropped him. The other figure kicked Isaac's legs out from under him and yanked up his second arm, giving the first person time to reassert their hold. Together, the pair dragged him headfirst into the bus.

Better play along now, then shapeshift my way out when I can. He wasn't strong, but he was smart. That would have to do. It had always been enough in the past.

The scent hit Isaac immediately—chamomile, lemon balm, lavender. Despite himself, he felt his heartbeat calming from the bus' perfume, the herbs soothing his ragged breath. Shoved to his knees, Isaac looked up and was met with a flashlight's glare. He cringed against the burst. Someone grabbed his face hard.

"No passenger." The voice was dismissive, almost relieved.

"Not yet," snapped a harsher voice. This one Isaac recognized. *I'm not your fucking sweetheart.* The girl from the bar.

The flashlight clicked off.

He blinked as his sight readjusted. Taking quick stock of his surroundings, he saw the bus' interior had been hollowed out and built up with plywood. Two sets of bunk beds in the back, opposite each other. A shelf stuffed with paperbacks. Ledges draped with sheepskins and roadkill furs. Fragrant herbs hanging in dried bundles from the ceiling. A cluster of instrument cases leaned against a far wall. This wasn't just a bus—it was a home.

Three human outlines solidified. The girl was crouched in front of him, still gripping his jaw, her black ponytail like a geyser of oil fountaining from her head. She glared into his eyes. Something about her stare reminded Isaac of the way his mom used to shake him down when he got home from a high school party—sniffing his clothes and staring into his dilated pupils to see if he'd been smoking weed.

Inches behind the girl, a second captor peered over, holding a metal camping flashlight in their gloved hand. Isaac couldn't read their gender, but they wore snakelike locs tied back into a knot and a burgundy velvet jacket down to their shins, a rattlesnake's rattle dangling from one ebony ear on a gold chain. They pivoted to whisper something to the girl, and Isaac saw that the back of their coat sported a similar patch as hers—a horse skull, this one stitched over a blazing sun instead of the girl's morning glories.

Off to the side, a third person sat on a cushioned bench. This one was smaller than the other two (though all three seemed roughly Isaac's age) and more delicate, softer, feet tucked invisibly beneath, hands clasped. They wore a copper-colored sweater nearly the same tint as their skin and brown wool pants, united by a pair of suspenders. "Should we tie him up?" The voice—male—was surprisingly gentle, given the inquiry. A jacket bearing a third patch draped over the bench seat—this horse skull laced with a spray of constellations across its forehead.

The girl yanked Isaac's face up so he was looking at her dead-on. "Did you drink it?"

"Nuh," Isaac squeezed out through pinched cheeks. "Mow erlbr."

"Speak up, chump." She removed her hand from his jaw, yanking his hair instead.

Isaac stretched out his mouth, sore from the girl's grip. "I said, my elbow." He shrugged his right shoulder in indication.

She nodded, and the person holding the flashlight knelt to look. "It's wet," they reported.

"You said don't drink it. I didn't. Poured it down my sleeve. I'd be happy to send you the dry-cleaning bill."

The girl let him go. "Take it off."

"Why?"

"I said take off the damn coat. Now."

Isaac stripped his jacket loose, flinching as he moved his arms. He'd have preferred a gentler kidnapping.

"I was hoping I'd run into you," he grinned. "Thanks for the lift." His showman's flare. An easy attitude, intended to disarm. Underneath, he directed his focus to his pulse. *That's right, slow down,* he told it, sucking floral air deeper into his lungs. *Be calm. Climb back into character. Safer not to be yourself.*

As soon as he was halfway free of the coat, Ponytail yanked it away and tossed it to her crony in the velvet coat and locs, ignoring Isaac entirely.

"Think you can sample that?" she asked. Her voice had the timbre of military command.

"*Can I sample . . .*" they mocked. "Darlin', I better not hear you doubting my skills."

"I'm Lenny," Isaac cut in.

"No you're not." She reestablished her grip on his hair. It pinched, not unpleasantly.

"Excuse me?"

The woman scoffed. "I know a liar when I meet one. And to think, I just saved your life."

"Did you?" Isaac kept his voice flat, appraising. "Because from where I sit, it seems like you jumped me, are holding me hostage, and most sadistic of all, took my favorite jacket."

Regardless, he let Lenny wash off him. His gut told him she would yank the veil off whatever he tried to pull anyway. Takes a con to know one.

"My apologies. Let's try that again," Isaac conceded. "My name's Isaac. And you are?"

She gave his hair a sharp tug in her closed fist, Isaac grunting as his neck wrenched back. "I'm a shadow, who can creep through your window as easy as daybreak, whenever I want, wherever you are. So you better be a good little boy. Because if you fuck with us, or are working for that monster, believe me when I say"—she pressed her lips against his temple, a hard kiss—"we will kill you."

Isaac could feel the waxy lipstick print that the threat had left behind. He couldn't help but be reminded of the Black

Spot, that legendary mark pirates dreaded, portending their doom.

"I'm Rummy," the delicate boy in suspenders said. "They're Sparrow," he continued, pointing to their colleague in the long velvet coat, "and she's Shona."

Shona shot Rummy what Isaac was beginning to recognize as her signature glare.

"It's fine, he's safe," Rummy said. Sparrow shrugged, seemingly accepting the character judgment, while Shona's grip on his hair only tightened.

A groan rose from one of the bunks deeper in the bus.

Someone else is back there.

Sparrow and Rummy rushed toward the sound.

"She's awake," Sparrow reported.

"Passenger?" asked Shona.

As if in answer, the commotion in back grew louder. "Rats, they're all rats! Can't you see? They're already here. They're already here! They'll take everything from us!" The voice was frantic as if in a fever, words punctuated by wheezing, hyperventilated breaths.

"Pure-grade, straight-from-hell clinger," Sparrow called forward. "She's smokefed, all right."

"Come," Shona demanded, yanking Isaac after her. "Look."

On the farthest bunk, a woman was tied down against a bare mattress. Her hands and feet had been bound with rope, each knotted to a wooden post. She was writhing, snapping her teeth, muttering, but she didn't seem to care about the four people standing over her. *What is she on?*

Sparrow lit the flashlight again, shining it directly at the woman. That's when Isaac saw her face.

It swirled with white. A gaseous substance—*could it be . . . smoke?*—pressed up from within her, trying to leak out. Wisps escaped her nose and mouth like small, fleeing poltergeists.

Smokefed.

"What do you see?" Sparrow urged.

"She's . . . burning," he said, trying to untangle the image before him.

"That's all?"

"'All'? Isn't that fucking enough?" Isaac snapped.

"He can't see the passenger," Rummy said. "He's clean."

"The *what*?"

"Nothing," Shona said, finally releasing Isaac. "That's what you would have looked like if you'd accepted a drink from that charming gentleman's flask."

The woman on the bed spat at them. "*You people*, I know you, you're here to take what's mine. Well you won't, you never will. I'll die first." She kicked hard, managing to snap the rope pinning her right ankle. The rest of her remained bound.

Shona drew a taser from her back pocket, but Rummy put out a hand to stop her.

"Not necessary," he chided, and laid a hand on the woman's arm. "You'll be okay," he assured her, "we aren't going to hurt you."

She hissed. Sparrow drew a small silver case from a nearby satchel and flipped open the metal buckles. From within, they removed an EpiPen, jabbing it into the restrained woman's thigh. She hushed, eyelids fluttering shut. Asleep.

"I don't think that was an allergic reaction," Isaac said.

"The injection's contents have been . . . modified," Sparrow said. Rummy laid a hand on the woman's hair, stroking it softly, as if she were a child with the flu in need of a little care. Her breathing slowed.

"What's happening to her?" Isaac said. If the Russian had been sent after him, why had he drugged this woman, too? What kind of drug could even cause a symptom like *that*? And what was the "passenger"? This was growing complicated. Isaac hated complicated.

Shona checked the knots around the woman's wrists. "Mercifully, that's none of your business. Just be glad it isn't you. And now you know better than to take candy from strangers."

"I was also taught to steer clear of unmarked vans, but look at me now."

Sparrow returned the EpiPen to its silver case, removing an empty syringe in turn and twirling it with a flourish like a tiny baton before passing it to Rummy. Rummy swept a gentle finger across the woman's arm, searching for a vein, then slid the needle under her skin. Blood flushed into the vial.

Whoever these people were, this clearly wasn't new to them. The terrified seizure. The tethered woman. The smoke. They'd dealt with this before. To them, it was casual.

Rummy placed the cylinder of drawn blood into Sparrow's silver case, beside six or seven identical, full vials. Were they all from this woman? Or had there been others like her? How many people had been kept tied in this bus?

"Do you know her? Where she lives?" Rummy asked Isaac.

Isaac shook his head.

Rummy turned to Shona. "We need to drop her somewhere safe. She'll be through it in another two hours or so."

Clearly Shona was the alpha. It wasn't just her militant air—it was the way the other two turned to her for permission. But Rummy carried power, too. A gentle authority, not of force, but nurture. He was the bandage, Shona the bullet. And Sparrow, though looming enough to be written off as brawn, fizzed with a mad scientist's zest. A zest that was currently being funneled into a frenetic drumbeat, rapped onto the lid of their medical case.

The woman on the bed moaned in her sleep. Whatever she had been drugged with, it was outside Isaac's realm of experience. He'd watched friends collapse from molly laced with fentanyl, had seen heroin overdoses, bad acid trips, a manic break triggered from drinking lighter fluid . . . but he'd never seen anything like that mist, twisting up from the woman's body. Whatever it was, the Russian wasn't selling it. He was deliberately dosing people without their knowledge. Why would he do that while on the job, tracking Isaac? A warped form of entertainment? A side gig? Clearly there was more at play than a simple bounty.

The uncertainty made Isaac squirm. He wasn't used to being on the outside of a secret. The Chameleon King was always one step ahead, maneuvering ten games of chess at once, each move predicted and accounted for. But now, he lagged. The *unknowing* swelled like an over-chewed piece of meat, growing fatter and less manageable the more he gnawed on it.

He hadn't wanted to reveal anything more to these people than necessary—but the truth was, they knew more about what was going on than he did. Information is currency. And as always, you can't get something for nothing. If he wanted to learn about the stranger, then he was going to have to give these bus punks a reason to tell him.

"I don't know where she lives," Isaac said, "but I *have* seen the house on legs."

All heads snapped toward him.

"I've seen it because it's mine. It's my house."

"Where?" demanded Shona.

"Tell me what was in that drink," Isaac shot back.

For a moment, no one spoke. His captors shared a glance. A silent debate, how much to divulge. How much to conceal. Then, the silence cracked. The woman on the bed groaned.

"It triggers a glutamate release," Sparrow said, "and a zippy little echo from the periaqueductal gray. Gets the adrenaline and cortisol feeling feisty. Among . . . other symptoms. But what's in it, exactly, to cause that response . . . That, we're still working on."

"*What* now?" Maybe Isaac shouldn't have been so quick to drop out of chemistry.

Sparrow wiggled their fingers in the air. "A *maaagic* potion."

"Adorable," Shona rebuked. "I'll put it on the grave of your flippant ass if the Longshadow Man kills you."

The Longshadow Man? A shiver scurried down Isaac's spine.

Sparrow swallowed at Shona's admonishment. Isaac recognized the dynamic. This gang had been traveling together far too long, trapped in a tin can.

"The drink makes you panic," Rummy said. "Makes you . . . see things. Heightens and encourages paranoia. In a word—it's fear."

"What's it make you see?"

"People get mistrustful," Shona said, sidestepping the question. "Violent. Their lizard brain kicks in, tells them that not only are they in danger, but their loved ones. Their town, their job, their bank account, whatever they're afraid to lose."

"And he uses that to control them?" Isaac asked.

"More like he's a slingshot, they're the stone," Sparrow said. "The drug makes them . . . easier to aim." They mime-fired a pair of finger guns.

"They get scared, and the Longshadow Man suggests a scapegoat," said Rummy. "A path to safety."

"A path to safety . . ." Isaac trailed off, glancing at the woman tied to the bed. She growled through her teeth, still unconscious. That's what the man had been doing when he talked to "Lenny," planting seeds about spreading illness. He'd tried to use Lenny's infant son as fuel. Something worth protecting—at any cost.

Shona took a rag from her back pocket and shoved it into the sleeping woman's mouth. "They're rabid dogs."

"No," countered Rummy, "they're scared people who've been weaponized and fired in all the wrong directions."

Shona brushed Rummy off, turning to Isaac. "They tend to latch onto anybody who doesn't look or act like them. Strangers, outsiders. Homeless folks. Sometimes it's a race thing. We saw a lady bite the ear clean off a guy in a rival team's basketball jersey. It doesn't take much. Easy to be scared of what you don't know."

"A fight-or-flight response," said Rummy.

"Mostly fight," Shona added. "It stays in the body a few hours, and when they wake up, they don't remember any of it." She cracked her knuckles. Isaac spotted the letters *E R L Y* tattooed across the joints of her right hand to match the *B Y R D* he'd seen on her left hand at the bar. She caught him looking.

"I always get the worm," she leered, launching both middle fingers.

"The key," Rummy said, ignoring the interruption, "is restraining them in time."

The woman on the bed twitched.

"So that's why you're holding her here," Isaac said, "to keep her from hurting anyone until she's come down."

Shona nodded. "We've been tracking him for nearly two months, cleaning up this damn mess. As far as we can tell, that's when he arrived stateside."

Two months . . . Right when the shipment arrived in New York. Isaac cursed silently. He'd let his paranoid ego get in the way of his judgment. The Russian had never been after *him*. He was hunting exactly what he'd claimed to be: Thistlefoot. *Where Bellatine is now.* He blanched. *Unaware. Defenseless.*

"Why do you call him that? The 'Longshadow Man'?" Isaac asked.

His captors shared a glance. Shona snapped a quick, discouraging blink.

"I voted for the 'Milkman,' but I was outranked," Sparrow shrugged. *"Milkman, milkman, take my cup, when my man is away, come fill me on up,"* they sang, bobbing their head to the rhythm.

Shona cast them a disgusted look.

"What? That's classic blues, honey. *I got a baker for bread, got a butcher for chuck, I got a husband for cash, and a milkman to*—oof."

She'd thrust a heap of rope against Sparrow's chest. "Be useful."

Sparrow rolled their eyes and set to retying the woman's freed ankle, humming under their breath as they worked.

So they didn't want Isaac to know. Fine. He could dig that up later—along with whatever the dosed were hallucinating.

"Have you figured out why he's doing all this? Is there a pattern to who he's targeting?"

"Nope, not that we can tell," said Sparrow, finishing a fresh knot.

"But you know what's funny?" Shona said, leaning closer to Isaac. Her tone didn't sound tickled. "What's funny is that wherever he goes, he makes a point to ask about that *house*. So it seems to me that the only common ground, the only discernible pattern . . . is you." She was close enough that Isaac could see each of her individual eyelashes, like rows of black daggers. "Now, why don't you tell me why that might be?"

The herbal perfume of the bus had grown dizzying. The same chamomile, lavender, lemon balm, plus bergamot, valerian . . . *They're all antianxiety plants,* Isaac realized. *They must be using them to keep people sedated. This is a tranquilizer on wheels.*

"Honestly—I have no idea," he said. And it was true.

Shona sighed, "Doll, I'm wearing a clean shirt for the first time in two weeks. Don't make me dirty it with your blood."

Isaac almost smiled, but caught himself just in time. This woman was growing on him. He was threatened often—but rarely with finesse.

"It's no different than any living house, the kind you'd find at a roadside attraction. See for yourself. Turn around, drive half a mile. Left on Birch, right on Redford."

A drive would give him time to think. To formulate a plan.

Shona nodded, an order, and Sparrow slid into the driver's seat, putting the bus in gear. It lurched forward. Herb jars and bones and instrument cases chattered against one another, the room like a panhandler's tin can clattering with coins.

Could Isaac trust anything he'd been told? He knew how to spot physical signs of lying: sideways glances, adjusting vocal levels, over-gesticulating. Shona and her crew hadn't exhibited any. Granted, Shona had called Isaac out when he'd given her a false name, and if she could spot that, she probably knew how to manipulate the tells in herself, too. He'd be a fool to assume she was honest. Who knows—maybe the drugged woman on the bed had nothing to do with the Russian man at all. Isaac hadn't actually seen her interact with the stranger. For all he knew, Shona could be a predator who had drugged the woman herself—and would do the same to Isaac.

But Sparrow and Rummy didn't seem to carry the same knife-glint sharpness as their leader. If they'd been lying, Isaac would have seen it. When they talked about the "Longshadow Man," they'd fully believed what they were saying. These people might not be on Isaac's side, but they definitely weren't on the Russian's. And as Isaac had seen firsthand at the bar, between his sinister conversation with Isaac-as-Lenny and his inquiries about the house, the stranger certainly wasn't a friend of his.

So whose side *was* Shona's gang on? They'd spent the past two months tracking this man—and for what? Altruism? Three kids in a school bus playing vigilante? There was more to it than that.

"Turn here."

A wide left and they reached the driveway's end. Thistlefoot emerged from the dark. It stepped into the glow of the headlights like a starlet taking the spotlight. One goliath leg shuffled toward them, then another.

Shona took in a sharp breath. Rummy stood and even Sparrow half rose from behind the wheel.

Isaac smoothed his hair and tucked his shirt back in, loosened from the manhandling. "Well thanks for the date, but it's past my curfew. Appreciate the lift. Let's do this again sometime."

"Nice try," Shona said, blocking the door. Her eyes were still fixed on the house.

"Tell me—why are you after this guy?" Isaac asked.

She broke her gaze away from Thistlefoot and gave him that hard look. It wasn't purely a glare, Isaac realized. There was something else underneath it, past the malice.

Heartbreak.

"To keep monsters from becoming real."

Only idealists spoke like that. Isaac had shed that sort of rhetoric a long time ago. The monsters—they were already here. And they couldn't be banished.

"I'm sure you've considered," he said, "that this *Longshadow Man* might become more dangerous, more powerful, if he gets his hands on the house."

No one answered. Affirmation enough.

"So you're thinking it's some kind of weapon. In which case, the only safe choice would be to let me go so I can take the thing as far away as possible."

"I'm *thinking*," said Shona, "that the only *safe choice* is to burn down your house."

"Now, we're just being rude." Isaac clicked his tongue.

"We don't mind rude. What we mind are more dead bodies."

A spear of pain lanced through Isaac's skull. "Burn the house down, sure," he said with a shrug. He drew his lighter from the pocket that held his tobacco and tossed it to Shona, quick so she wouldn't see his hand shake. She caught it without breaking eye contact. "Though of course, that could be this Longshadow guy's goal, too. Maybe he isn't trying to weaponize it. Could be a threat to him he wants gone. I'm sure he'd appreciate the helping hands."

Isaac leaned back against a bunk ladder, cocking his elbow on the rung. He willed himself into nonchalance. The ladder absorbed his tremors, hiding them from sight.

In his periphery, Rummy crouched again by the drugged woman. Isaac performed slight alterations to match him—lowering shoulders, softening the eyebrows, lifting his cheeks slightly. The change was too subtle for the naked eye, but Shona's subconscious would catch it. The human brain, it recognizes a friend. It recognizes its comrades and its foes. Shona trusted Rummy. Isaac needed her to trust him, too. A little borrowing, and he'd be able to slip into the part of her that hoards its trust. Trust, a special reserve, the best bottle of wine on a dusty shelf in the cellar of the heart.

"Either he wants the house as a tool or he wants it out of the way. Both are risks to you and whatever you people are fighting for."

A thin layer of Shona's glare yielded. It was working.

"So we use it as bait," Sparrow said, dangling an invisible lure.

Isaac laughed. "Your fearless leader was six feet away from him in the bar tonight, and she didn't catch him."

"There were civilians in the bar," Rummy said. "We don't want casualties."

Shona hooked her thumbs into the front of her jeans. "We can't give him access to the one thing he wants. If it's a weapon, who knows the damage he'd do. If it's a threat to him, it could be enough to take him down and—"

"End this," Rummy said.

"So we kick it here, bait, like I said," Sparrow repeated.

"No," said Shona, "if it *is* a weapon, we can't afford to let him get close. We need to find out which *before* we make our move." She looked Isaac up and down, like a judge at a dog show. "Your house can run?" Shona continued.

"Like Jesse Owens."

"And you can control it?"

Isaac nodded.

Shona grabbed the lever to the folding door and swung it open.

"Get out," she commanded Isaac.

Sparrow threw up their hands. "What, we a party bus? Pop in for a good time and bounce?"

"Pinocchio here can buy us time. That's what we need most."

"Don't love the nickname," Isaac said.

"You sprint that house as far away as you can. We'll stall the Longshadow Man. We can't have him close to it until we figure out why it's so important."

"So we're gonna let the one lead we have disappear?" Sparrow argued.

"Yes," Shona said. "For now."

Rummy nodded. "I'm with Shona."

"Course you are." Sparrow shook their head.

"If you're done with your family squabble, I'd love to stop being kidnapped."

Shona shoved Isaac against the bus wall. His skin pricked awake at the feel of her hands, warm on his chest.

"Don't think for a second that you're free of us. You're only buying us time. A month. Less. Enough to be ready."

She slipped a hand into his pants pocket and Isaac couldn't keep a flush from rising to his cheeks. She pulled out his phone, typed in her digits, and pressed CALL, securing his number, before returning it. "And when we do meet again, I'd suggest you don't get in our way. Or I, personally, will make sure your sweet, lying little heart stops beating."

She stepped back. The exit gaped, an invitation. Isaac wouldn't keep it waiting. He darted down the stairs, turning at the bottom to call back.

"Bring my coat, next time. Cleaned and pressed." He bowed. The door folded shut.

Isaac watched the black glow of the bus shrink into the night. *You'll never see me again,* he vowed.

As soon as they were out of sight, he drew a small plastic vial from his pocket, delicate as a cologne bottle. Removing the screw-on lid, he sniffed the contents within. Burning hay. Rust. That same animal rot. When he'd nabbed it from the silver case, he'd hoped he was grabbing the antidote sedative, insurance in case he came across anyone smokefed again. But it seemed he'd swiped a sample of the poison instead. Just as well. One never knew when a sip of chaos might come in handy.

But for now, it was time for Isaac Yaga to do what he did best. It was time to run.

CHAPTER ELEVEN

BELLATINE SAT IN A tin basin by the cookstove, her knees tucked up to her chin in a soapy bath. She'd already thrice rewarmed the tub with boiling water from the kettle, and her fingertips were amphibiously wrinkled. The thing about a good soak was that she didn't have to work while she was having one. Baths were a neutral zone. If she was dressed and up and active, she had no excuse to avoid tinkering with the house. There was ever more to be done, and the tour was scheduled to start in under two weeks. But there in the quiet steam, a row of peony candles balanced on her locked toolbox, she gave herself permission to rest. Sure, a three-hour bath was cheating . . . but as splinters worked their way out from under her nails, she figured she'd earned it.

Thistlefoot bucked, splashing water from the basin, which extinguished the candles with a wet hiss.

"That wasn't nice!" she scolded.

She still wasn't used to the random tosses and sways of living inside what was essentially an animal. Maybe she'd never get used to it. She imagined it wasn't unlike life at sea, at the mercy of a fervent wave.

"Rapunzel, Rapunzel!" a voice singsonged from below. *Isaac.* She should leave him there to beg. Why was it always her job to tend to him, to labor, to jump at his call like a spaniel fetching a stick?

He called again, the house hopping uneasily from foot to foot. Her bath had transferred almost entirely onto the floor. Bellatine sighed, reluctantly rising from the safe warmth of the tub, and pressed her wet hair in a towel. She pulled on a baggy T-shirt and her overalls, cringing as the denim stuck to her damp skin.

One of the first additions she'd made to the house was affixing a steel-cable ladder to the front balcony, purchased from a company that sold helicopter parts. Turning a handled crank, she watched the ladder dunk into the dark. It wasn't long before she felt the cables go rigid with her brother's weight on the bottom rung. He scrambled upward until he reached the top, tipping himself onto the porch-stage. Isaac's little cat leapt out of his shirt like a magician's rabbit from a hat and rushed into the house.

"You know the prince from Rapunzel ends up dumped in a briar patch and blinded," she said, hauling in the last of the ladder.

Instead of responding, Isaac dangled his legs over the stage edge, slowly rolling a cigarette from a blue pouch of American Spirit tobacco. He was panting, as if he'd been running. His hands shook as he sprinkled in a pinch of dried lavender. He probably hadn't eaten that day, just smoked endless cigarettes and brooded. Some men can't take basic care of themselves without women stepping in to help. Peter Pan syndrome, ever in search of mothering. Well, she wasn't their mother—and even if she were, Mira had never been the nurturing type. Let him shake.

Once Isaac had caught his breath, he smoked in silence, staring forward into the sky.

"Tiny," he said at last, after half the cigarette had transformed into smoke. "We're hitting the road early. We got a gig in Brattleboro for the twenty-eighth. I told them we'd be there."

"The twenty-eighth? Of this month? That's in two days."

"That's right, Nancy Drew. October twenty-eighth on Caesar's calendar, Scorpio season, when the veil between worlds grows thinnest. Two days from now."

Of course. As always, everything was Isaac's decree. With Isaac, there weren't questions. Just announcements. And either you tagged along with whatever he decided or you got left behind.

Bellatine was a hostage. That was the only honest way to describe it. Either she'd abide by Isaac's whims or he wouldn't hold up his end of the bargain. If she even survived a season on the road with him, that is . . .

After a few minutes, Isaac flicked the spent cigarette nub off the stage. Bellatine watched the red pinprick of light fall like a shooting star until it landed, snuffed out by the dark.

"Pack what you need," Isaac said. "We leave tonight."

"A spectacle, a miracle, an abomination! Call it what you will, the Thistlefoot Traveling Theater is here to dazzle and dismay! You don't know it yet, but your life is changing tonight. Do you believe in magic? No? Let us prove you wrong!"

Isaac stood on a park bench hollering like a revival preacher as Bellatine dispensed hand-drawn flyers, photocopied at the library early that morning.

"What's this about?" An older man in a green cap took a flyer, holding it at arm's length to read it through wire-rimmed glasses.

Isaac leaned toward him over Bellatine's shoulder.

"That's right, sir, come see a premonition of your own death!"

Bellatine coughed. "A puppet show, sir, we're performing a puppet show, which has absolutely nothing to do with you or anyone else *dying*." She shot Isaac a withering look.

The bespectacled man shuffled away, confused.

"I'm building mystique," Isaac said.

"You're building a load of crap, and no one here will show up having any idea of what they signed up for."

He winked. "No expectations, only curiosity."

At the intersection a few yards away, a skeleton hung from a traffic light. Three days before Halloween, and Brattleboro, Vermont, was bedecked in macabre splendor—congregations of polyester ghosts holding hands, faux cobwebs drooping like gauzy chandeliers from the barren oaks, pumpkins littering shops' front stoops. Bellatine had never liked the holiday. Too gaudy, too flippant. Gummy coffins and plastic skulls, funerary fun for all ages. Commodifying death was tacky. Disrespectful to those who had known death, or someday would know death—in short, everyone.

Isaac, however, fit right in like another gruesome decoration. An autumnal specter in undertaker chic, black hair and trousers stark against his fair, bony frame. Lifting his arms as he continued to proselytize, he looked like a spider spinning an invisible web.

"Come as you are or come as you aren't! Come with a hungry heart, come with a taste for the impossible, bring your exes to show them what love really looks like. That's right, fates and furies, Thistlefoot awaits you at the devil's crossroad. Sell your soul for one night of wonder. Tonight, and only tonight, the door to the Otherworld is open to you. Won't you step through?"

A woman in a wool shawl took a flyer. Then a handsome young dad on a bicycle, his toddler strapped to his back. Next, a brood of teenagers in sequined tank tops. Bellatine had to give it to Isaac—his carnival barking seemed to be working. Even Bellatine herself had felt seduced by it, at first, as if lulled by a river current. But each time he mentioned the supernatural, she thudded back into her body. Her brother presented it like something desirable, something harmless. Bellatine knew better.

Thistlefoot had carried the Yaga siblings 145 miles south. One hundred forty-five miles from the quiet, measured life Bellatine had constructed in the Northeast Kingdom. She hadn't even been given the chance to say a proper thank-you to Joseph for his generosity over the past year, or hug Carrie and Aiden goodbye, reduced instead to an apologetic text and a promise of postcards. And this, she knew, was only a sliver of the distance that would soon stretch between her and her old life like a tightrope. How long would she be able to pluck on that distance like a harp string, and still hear the sounds of home? When the time came, would she be able to tiptoe along it, back to her old life? Or would the line grow so taut in the coming journey that it would snap altogether . . . ?

Bellatine thrust the last yellow flyer into a passerby's hand. The evening was cold with the scent of coming winter on the air as the Yaga siblings made their way back toward the house.

"What happened to that raggedy jacket you had?" Bellatine asked as Isaac blew warmth into his clasped hands.

He bowed his head piously. "Donated to a toddler trying to sneak into an R-rated movie."

"Wouldn't that be a trench coat? And two toddlers?"

"A trench coat is a couple's disguise. This kid was a lone film buff, just wanting to look his best. Speaking of which . . ." He scanned Main Street's shop fronts, halting at a shimmering window display. "Bingo."

"Where are you—" Bellatine started, but her brother had already darted off, vanishing inside a vintage boutique across the street. He emerged a few minutes later in a crisp tux coat, the swimmingly wide sleeves rolled to his elbows.

"Well?" He spun, the tails fanning out at his waist.

"Did you pay for that?"

Isaac popped up the narrow collar against the wind. "I *always* pay my debts."

She snapped the tag off the hem. "Eighty-two dollars?"

Isaac waved her off. "A suggestion. I paid its worth."

She rolled her eyes. Though Bellatine had her Carhartt jacket with her, she didn't put it on. A toothy shiver passed through her. Good. Stay cold enough, and maybe, just maybe, the first show wouldn't be a disaster.

Li Fen, their host, met them around the bend.

"Oh *interstellar*! I was just about to come looking for you two." Though she must have been at least sixty-five, she bounced as she ran to them as if there were springs coiled into the soles of her bare feet. She wore a blue-splatted painter's smock over a sleeveless floral sundress, and her straight hair was pinned behind her ears with plastic poodle clips. She must have been even colder than Bellatine, but if so, she didn't show it.

"Look at you two peaches! Last time I saw you, Isaac, you were barely a year old. Could it be?"

She hooked her arm through Bellatine's as if they were old friends on their way to a slumber party. "And *you*, last time I saw you, Bellatine, well, it was before you were born, and you were in a dream of mine. I called your mother, and I said, 'Mira, I met your daughter last night.' And your mama, she said, 'I don't have a daughter,' and I said, 'You will!'"

Bellatine smiled. She'd heard stories of her parents performing at Li Fen's theater in Beijing, where Li Fen had run an English-language exchange program for decades, before retiring to Vermont. *If the light fireflies give off could be bottled and compressed into a human being, that's Fen,* her mother had said once. In her presence, it seemed an apt assessment.

"Come on," Fen chirped, "I'll show you where to set up."

They walked down a residential street. Dozens of jack-o'-lanterns winked from the stoops.

"You know, when Isaac called this morning and said you kids were in town early, I was thrilled! I know you weren't supposed to be here until next month, but honestly, the sooner the better. Who knows what could happen in this world if we wait too long, right? We could be dead by next week! We could all be hit by a truck!" She giggled. "Well maybe not all of us—wouldn't that be a coincidence—but hey, it's possible. Do you know how many people are killed by falling gargoyles every year? One moment you're wandering under a cathedral, the next—splat."

"Our pleasure, ma'am, thank you for accommodating," Isaac said.

"This *morning*?" Bellatine pivoted to Isaac, Fen uttering a little squeak as she was pulled along. "I thought you said they were expecting us, and that's why we had to leave early."

"Fen, would you say you were expecting us?" Isaac asked.

"My horoscope did say 'Expect the unexpected' yesterday, and—"

"See, we were expected," Isaac said.

"—it also said eat more pickles. I should eat more pickles. Oh! Here we are."

She'd led them to an empty lot behind Birge Street, beside a row of looming gray factory buildings.

"This used to be the old Estey Organ factory," Fen explained. "They made reed organs and melodeons in the 1800s. It's been empty since the fifties."

The buildings resembled a corridor of giant tombstones, sheathed in slate. The row had a Dickensian quality, as if transplanted from a Victorian slum. Li Fen had chosen the spot for its football-field-sized parking lot out back, hidden from the street, big enough for Thistlefoot and an audience to fit in comfortably.

"Want to see something entirely *uncommon*?" Fen said. She skipped up the low flight of stairs leading to one of the buildings, still dragging Bellatine along by the arm.

"Watch the broken glass, I've been meaning to clean that up." Fen barely looked down as she danced barefoot over a shattered wine bottle on the steps. She slipped a brass key into a deadbolt. The lock clicked open, and she let the three of them into a cavernous room, flicking on the lights.

"Ta da! Pretty interstellar, huh?"

"Interstellar," Bellatine echoed.

The room was full of organs. Tall pipe organs with golden columns vaulting into the eaves. Squat mahogany reed organs with mother-of-pearl inlay. Grand Salon organs with elaborate high tops and electro-pneumatic organs in sleek cases. The wood gleamed marigold under the light bulbs. So many delicate carvings, so many precise corners, meeting perfectly to form geometrical marvels. Bellatine longed to examine them inch by inch, to find out how they were put together.

This was what she loved about woodworking. If you understood the world enough, understood materials and tools and the motions of your own capable body, you could transform a tree into . . . this. A cavern of perfect machines.

To her right, a whoosh of heavy breathing sounded. No, not breathing—Isaac was pumping the bellows of a massive pipe organ, which wheezed as it filled with air. With his other hand, he pressed the keys. The warehouse exploded with sound, like one hundred war brides wailing in unison.

"Welcome to the museum," Fen yelled over the moan. "I volunteer here. Give tours, sweep up, that sort of thing. This is just a small sample of the Estey collection, but pretty glam, right? It's only open on weekends, so we don't have to worry about tourists today."

"This is amazing," Bellatine whispered.

"What?" yelled Fen.

"I said, it's amazing!"

Isaac pounded out the first few notes of "Greensleeves," ignoring the rest of the room.

"*What?*"

"Interstellar!" Bellatine yelled back.

"Oh! Yeah, totally!"

An hour later, they'd docked Thistlefoot in the Estey parking lot and begun to set up for the show. Though Li Fen had locked the factory museum up for the night, Bellatine felt as though she could still hear the organs' howls hanging in the air. A haunting.

"Rigs on deck?" Isaac called.

"Rigs on deck," she replied.

Bellatine emerged from Thistlefoot in all white. Her go-to denim overalls had been replaced with bleached linen trousers and a collared shirt pale as starlight, dotted down the back with alabaster buttons. Typically, Rigs would wear black, allowing her to disappear within the dim theater and create the illusion that the puppets moved all on their own. But performing on Thistlefoot called for a different strategy. With her hazelnut bob covered in a white scarf and spotless tennis shoes on her feet, she was rendered nearly invisible against the whitewashed stucco of the house. The only color: a bright blue sash, draping from shoulder to hip in a brilliant stripe. She'd watched her mother dye this very silk fifteen years ago or more. It must have been one of her earliest memories—the vat of indigo and soda ash, its sulfuric odor bubbling as her mom had stirred the dye with a long wooden stick.

"I thought Rigs was supposed to be invisible?" Bellatine had asked her mother, then.

"She is," she'd replied tersely.

"Then why are you coloring your costume?"

"Because."

"Because *why*?"

Mira relented. "Usually, the audience shouldn't notice what is moving behind the scenes. That's how the magic works. But in *The Drowning Fool*, we make one small exception. A single stripe of river before the river even arrives in the story. Do you know what *premonition* means?"

Bellatine did not, and said as much.

"It means that even before the river comes to swallow the Fool, it is already here." She lifted the wooden stick from the vat, which had gone blue from stirring. "The Fool can't escape it, and neither can the audience, because it's already happening. That is called *fate*. And this color will help remind them of that. Now, leave me be; this is delicate work. Not for a child."

Here, flexing her fingers around her mother's sash, Bellatine felt her own fate catching up to her.

Isaac's costume was no different from his daily garb—his new tailcoat standing out stark as a stain against the wall behind. Strings, in their parents' tradition, always remained visible— a character in his own right, conversing or bickering with the puppets, trying to coerce them to make better choices, which they would ultimately ignore. Beside her, Isaac set each puppet and prop in its designated place on the stage, while Bellatine ran through the light cues one last time. They'd marked Thistlefoot's porch with dozens of gaffer's-tape *X*s. Placement was important. Misplacing a prop even a few inches to the right or left, and Strings would reach blindly to grab a puppet that wasn't there, potentially missing a cue or sullying the pacing.

A motorcycle engine revved a few blocks away, and Thistlefoot twitched, skidding the props out of place. Just when Isaac had returned them all to their rightful homes, Thistlefoot shuffled its feet, and the props scattered further.

"You know what I could go for right now? A big ol' bucket of fried chicken. What do you think, Tiny, doesn't that sound good?"

"Don't taunt it."

"It can't understand a word. Isn't that right, Foghorn Leghorn?"

The house dropped down on its haunches, as if pouting.

In truth, Bellatine thought the house understood more than either of them gave it credit for. Maybe not their words, save for Yiddish commands, but other things. Perhaps she was projecting, but it seemed that when Bellatine was most anxious or the Embering felt closest, the house grew impeccably behaved. *It knows when I'm not feeling well,* she considered. And it knew when to cause trouble.

But there was so much they still didn't know about it. What had it experienced? What did it remember from its life before? It definitely *had* a memory, because as the siblings rehearsed, the house had grown progressively more in time with the show. It would preemptively tip forward on its feathered haunches before the Fool's and the Fox's poker game, so the audience could better see the petite playing cards. It turned slightly to the left when the Mayor gave his speech from his stage-right podium. And as the play neared its conclusion, the house would sink down on its knees to let wind swoop beneath the tulle river and liven it. Or, Bellatine wondered, perhaps it kneeled in mourning for the Fool's passing, akin to removing a hat at a wake.

It was undeniable: Thistlefoot was learning. And if it could learn, it could remember.

As Bellatine knotted a curtain rope around one of the balcony posts, she caught a glimpse of the ground. A crowd of people gaped up at the house, slack-jawed. She almost called to Isaac, said, *We picked a bad spot; folks are already using it for something,* when she recognized the woman in the wool shawl. The dad on the bicycle. Scanning the assembly, she saw half the people there were clutching yellow flyers. These people, they weren't there to use the parking lot for a barbecue or a Frisbee game or a Dairy Farmers of America meet and greet. They were there for the show. This was their audience. This was real now. This was happening.

The seven puppets shimmered in Bellatine's periphery,

each collapsed delicately at its place on the stage. Her hands hummed, as if saying, *Something is coming, and coming soon.*

"Welcome, my ultimate babes, you thieves and lovers, to the greatest show this side of the Mason-Dixon Line . . ."

Whatever warning her hands were offering, it was too late now.

CHAPTER TWELVE

TWICE A WEEK, BABA Yaga goes to the market to sell eggs. The people, they love Baba Yaga's eggs, because inside the shells are not yolks and whites, but small objects the people believed they'd lost. Some eggs contain letters that were never delivered. Some eggs contain silver jewelry. Some eggs contain kopecks. Women come to Baba Yaga when they fear their husbands' gazes have wandered, and split eggs in the dark to reveal their husbands' eyes—or worse—cleanly delivered. The men's wails can be heard for miles. If you're looking for something, and it isn't under the mattress, and it isn't in the garden, and it isn't in the horse cart, then you can bet it's in one of Baba Yaga's eggs. Sometimes you'll buy an egg and crack it open and there will be a tiny dead dog inside, infested with worms. For most, this is a risk worth taking.

The eggs, of course, are mine. They are large, like ostrich eggs, with shells spotted and glossy as baker Reb Berish Yoneih's bald head. How do I lay my eggs? You are crass for asking, and I would be betraying my modesty to answer. All I will say is Baba

Yaga knows to keep my bedroom cupboard closed between the hours of daybreak and noon. After that, chances are there will be an egg inside, waiting. This is true all days but the Sabbath, for though I am but wood and stone, not even I will work on the holy day of rest.

Like all shtetls, the market is Gedenkrovka's heart. Anything you want, the market has it. Little wooden tchotchkes, smoked fish, floral shawls from Kyiv, heaps of fresh and dried fruit, carts full of sweet milk sloshing in aluminum cans. There are trays of buttons, grain stuffed into burlap sacks, pop-up tables stacked with colorful tobacco tins. On occasion, wealthy merchants come in from the city in rubber-wheeled automobiles with trunks full of dyed silk and silver rings, delicate as frost. In the market's center is a well full of clear, cool water, and the stalls circle outward from it like ripples. To the left of Baba Yaga's cart: a blacksmith the neighbors call Bull, so strong he can forge a blade with only one fall of his hammer. To her right: the wine seller, barrels of drink balanced one atop the next in grand, precarious towers that flow more bountifully than the village well water. All around, gossip and haggling and laughter.

Many stories have been told of this market, by many storytellers besides myself. Like any town, Gedenkrovka folds one hundred thousand stories inside it. One hundred thousand joys and sorrows. Marriages and births and deaths. But who am I to care for these? I am only a house, and a house tends only to its own residents. It is Baba Yaga's story I concern myself with, and I suggest you do the same. To let too many stories in—it will undo you. You could not bear it.

One market day, Baba Yaga kisses her daughters goodbye, puts three eggs into her basket, and goes to town. She sets up her table, and on it she spreads a blue cloth and the three speckled brown eggs. Then, she waits.

First comes Bilha, the tavern keeper's wife, dragging her youngest son, Anszel, by the elbow.

"He's lost his glasses," Bilha moans, "and he's blind as a mole without them."

"I looked everywhere!" Anszel says. "Josef took them, I know it. He's always saying how handsome my glasses are, you must have heard him."

Bilha shakes her head. "Looked! 'I *looked*,' he says! But how did he look if he cannot *see*, eh?"

Baba Yaga is glad her daughters are not idiots like Bilha's son. She hands Anszel an egg. He cracks it. Inside, a pair of wire glasses.

"Oy vey!" Bilha cries, and slaps the back of her boy's head. "Not stolen, you lost them. And now my pocketbook pays the price," Bilha grumbles, reaching into her apron. "What is it you want in return, Baba Yaga?"

"No money," Baba Yaga says.

Bilha shakes her head. "*Shmegege*, you think me a *shnorer*, begging something for nothing? You dishonor me."

"No money, but when that barn cat of yours has her next litter of kittens, you'll give me the two latest born." A new pair of catskin slippers would be a fine gift for Illa.

"Very well," Bilha agrees. "So it will be."

For the second egg comes Reb Leiser, the butcher. Leiser has a habit of gambling his four gold teeth away. They are all molars, and it is impossible to chew without them. He drops a thick slab of beef on Baba Yaga's table, and in exchange, she gives him the egg. He opens it and finds four gleaming teeth inside. Leiser sighs in relief.

Through the market's gate, two soldiers enter.

Tell me, how many stories are interrupted by soldiers? Hundreds? Thousands? I, alone, have lived through many. A house's life is longer than a man's life. We squat through one war, then another, then another. Battlefields erupt around us and then quiet. Entrails fertilize the wheat, the apple trees, the rows of fleshy tulips. After a while, it is difficult to separate the memories of each war's army. Are they in red or green or black uniform? Do they wear patches on their right or left arms? In what dialect do they speak death's tongue? I grow weary. I let the ink separating sorrows run. When I tell you the name of *these* soldiers' army, *this* war, I need you to understand—it matters not. It has never mattered. A soldier is a soldier.

Yet you ask, so I tell you—these particular soldiers are Denikin's men, from the tsar's Imperial White Army. In the cities outside Gedenkrovka, Russia is embroiled in civil war. Lenin's Bolsheviks seek power. The White Army opposes them. For months, warnings have trickled between the lips of the tsar's men: *Beware,* they say, *Trotsky is a secret Jew. The Freemasons? Also Jews, conspiring against the state. The Bolsheviks, all Jews, red-eyed with horns tucked under their hair.* Lies? Of course, lies. But what is a lie if not a story? And ah, what power a story has when whispered into the ear of a man with a gun.

As they pass Reb Berish's bakery stall, one soldier, tall with uneven ears, grabs a fresh loaf of challah and rips off a chunk with his teeth. He does not look at Reb Berish. He does not pay for the bread.

At Bull's cart, the second soldier examines an iron hatchet. He looks young enough to sleep in his mother's bed.

"You made these?" he asks the blacksmith.

Bull nods.

"Jews should not have weapons," the soldier says. "Who do you sell these to?"

"They are for wood," Bull says, his low voice wavering. "For firewood, and for beheading chickens."

"Which is it then?" The soldier lifts the hatchet and spins it in his hand like a plaything. "First you say wood, then you say chickens. Next you'll say for the tsar's skull, eh, Jew?"

Bull stutters, "No, never. Never."

The soldier laughs. "I'm *joking,* Blacksmith. Do you know what a joke is?" When he turns from Bull's cart, he does not return the hatchet.

Baba Yaga slips the third egg into her apron, out of sight. Across the market, she catches the widower Haim's eye, the stone carver, to whom she would have delivered the third egg. They both know this is no longer possible. He nods and vanishes into the crowd.

"And what do *you* sell? There's nothing on your table," the tall soldier asks Baba Yaga.

"I can tell you the exact day you will die," Baba Yaga replies. "For a price."

"Crazy old crone," the young soldier scoffs. He hoists his rifle higher on his shoulder. Ammunition bulges in the soldiers' rucksacks. Their bayonets jut out like angry erections eager to spring from their barrels. So aroused by their power, these men. In her apron, Baba Yaga feels the egg grow heavier.

A third soldier approaches. Andrei is his name. Baba Yaga has sold to him before, when he'd sought a brooch his mother had once worn, as a gift for his father. He is wider than the other two, with low eyebrows cocooning over a squashed nose. He pats the young soldier on the back.

"Come, Ivan, join me in a drink," Andrei says jovially. When they turn to leave, Andrei turns back to Baba Yaga, nods. "Excuse my friends," he whispers. "They mean no harm." Then he places two kopecks on her table. "For your troubles."

When Baba Yaga returns home, her daughters are asleep. She does not wake them. Instead, she lifts a loose board on the bedroom floor and cracks the egg into the gap. Five, ten, fifteen, twenty lead bullets fall out. The eggshell, pale with gunpowder. She replaces the board.

From the bedroom, baby Malka cries. She goes to her.

CHAPTER THIRTEEN

BELLATINE, ISAAC, AND LI FEN shared a meal on the organ factory floor. They'd spread out a painter's drop cloth, heaping it with cured meat and brie and a five-pound sack of apples from a nearby orchard. Half the money from the first night's show had gone toward the bounty, the other half into a red Tupperware for savings.

Opening night had gone as smoothly as it could have. Butter smooth. Smooth as a greased floor. The kind of smooth you'd slip right off if you weren't careful.

"Solid work, Tiny." Isaac nodded. He speared a hunk of summer sausage with a pocketknife and held it out to her.

She wanted to say, *What is this, a treat you give a dog after a trick?* Instead, she said, "Thanks. You too." She left his offering dangling midair, cutting off a slice of her own. He shrugged, giving the sliver to Hubcap, who pierced it with two white fangs before vanishing into the maze of pipe organs.

Bellatine's annoyance at departing so abruptly had only festered since their arrival. Why had he pushed her, if, as Fen suggested, it had been Isaac's idea all along to leave early, *not* the behest of a venue, as he'd made it sound? Was it a power play? Had he invented the urgency to establish some initial dominance? Until now, she'd thought of her brother as impulsive, skittish even. Certainly unreliable. But maybe his manipulations were more deliberate than she'd given him credit for.

Hubcap sprang out from behind a melodeon and scampered over Bellatine's shins, toppling her water bottle in the process. She scrambled to dab the spill before it caused any damage. See, *now* came the slipups.

Something had been off. Not a single dropped line the entire night. No fumbled props. The pacing, seamless. The jokes, precise. This wasn't the performance of a rushed, under-rehearsed troupe that hadn't touched the material since childhood. Yes, it had been nearly two months since Thistlefoot had entered into their lives—but most of that time had been spent on repairs. Only nine days had passed since the crate of puppets arrived, fewer spent on actual practice. They should have at least tripped through a few stilted moments—but it had been transcendent. The audience had watched, enraptured, as the puppets moved across the stage, bathed in primrose light from the floods she'd operated from the tech board.

"It shouldn't have run that well," Bellatine said after blotting the last wet spots from her overalls.

"Don't sell yourself short!" Fen exclaimed. "You were incendiary! Totally glowing, both of you, like pregnant ladies."

"I don't *glow*," Isaac scowled.

"Of course you glow! Everyone glows, you just can't always see it. I'm orange. Bellatine's also orange. Isaac, you're lime green."

"I highly doubt that."

"We didn't prepare appropriately," Bellatine continued. "We barely got off book. We should have at least stumbled through a little."

"Oh, sweetheart, you're upset because tonight went too *well?*" Fen asked.

"It felt like a bad omen or something," she said. "All our good luck spent early."

"Superstition! Mark of a true thespian," Isaac said.

"It's not superstition. It's caution."

"Did you know," Fen piped up, "there's one four-leaf clover in every square yard of clover patch, which contains roughly ten thousand total clovers? Last summer I collected one-hundred-twenty-two four-leafers. There's always luck if you're looking!"

"If we get complacent expecting the best, things *will* go wrong. I'd rather be prepared, take preventive measures. Tackle a contingency plan to avoid any mistakes," Bellatine said.

Isaac spoke into the summer sausage like an intercom, "General Yaga, the German artillery—it's too much! They'll break through at any moment. The western front will fall. If only our puppet show had been better rehearsed, goddamnit, this catastrophe could have been avoided!"

"I just want to do this job and be done, okay?"

"Christ, Tiny, this isn't a heist. You're thinking of it wrong. There are going to be bad shows. There *have* to be bad shows. It's how we pay up." He bit into a Honeycrisp, speaking between bites. "Every night, we'll stand up on that stage and absorb people's time, attention, alertness. It isn't balanced, to draw that kind of energy. The stage, it has a way of evening things out. Every once in a while, it will demand *debasement.* A humiliation, to neutralize the scales. Consider it a tax. Tonight, we got lucky. But we won't always, and we *shouldn't* always. Don't question it or you'll curse us." He spit three apple seeds over his shoulder.

"Now who's superstitious?"

"Only bad actors and dead hobos fuck with the fates."

"Says the guy with a black cat following him around."

"A black cat crossing your path signifies the animal is going somewhere," Isaac deadpanned.

"Who is Groucho Marx," Fen said, pressing an invisible *Jeopardy!* buzzer.

"Congratulations, you win five thousand dollars and a block of warm cheese." Isaac passed Fen the brie.

"You remember how this goes," he said, turning back to Bellatine. "Some shows are perfect. Some are a wreck. It's all part of that big cosmic moneybag we keep dipping into. We're paying dues."

Nervous energy crackled inside her. She did remember. She remembered hundreds of shows on the road with their parents. She remembered the Embering, hissing with every step she took. Maybe she *was* superstitious. That's how they were raised—with *The Scottish Play* and chewing thread and fistfuls of salt. Life was uncertain; a little manufactured certainty didn't hurt. But this time, small rituals would only go so far. It couldn't go this well forever. And if something went wrong—*when* something went wrong—was she prepared to face the consequences? Was her brother?

But the next night went just as faultlessly. And the night after that, and after that. They'd decided to stay in Brattleboro for a week and a half, holding nightly performances before continuing south to their next scheduled gig. Some evenings, the crowd was all new faces. Others, familiar visitors appeared, bringing friends along. Somehow, it was all *working*.

Routine set in, and Bellatine's wariness eased. There was one part of this she *had* trained for, after all. Years spent dampening the ebb and singe of her fingertips. Years of calculating and controlling her breath. The circumstances were different now, with Isaac back, and the house, and the old puppets haunting her again—but so what? Even when context changes, the materials that build the world remain constant. Wood. Metal. Fabric. Stone. The puppets were only conglomerates of those same elements. Thistlefoot, too. So far, she hadn't had to handle the puppets at all, and maybe she wouldn't have to. But even if she did—all her years of keeping the Embering at bay had to count for something.

Maybe, just maybe, their early luck hadn't been an ill premonition after all.

"Kill the lantern."

"Raise the ghost."

One week had passed, Halloween come and gone. The red Tupperware had begun to fill. Autumn leaves darkened to amber and floated like feathers to the ground. The air, perfumed with rotting crabapples and damp earth.

On the evening of their eighth show, it rained. Great silver blankets fell sideways, swept in from the coast. Rather than lose a night's earnings to the storm, Li Fen had offered Isaac and Bellatine the Estey Organ Museum as a temporary venue, clearing a makeshift stage in one corner and wreathing it in a clutter of table lamps she'd dragged over from her own home. The building was cold and musty, made all the more gothic by swells of inky storm clouds overhead, but at least it had a roof and a dry floor where an audience could take refuge from the rain.

The motions began as they always did: Isaac entering. The crowd's applause as he bowed low enough that his hair glanced the floorboards. His pithy announcements as Bellatine preset the lighting cues to auto-run. Then, the aluminum thunder sheet, a rag-wrapped mallet dragged down to birth a storm, mingling tonight with the music of true thunder, farther off. Isaac lifted the Fool from his bed.

"Once"—Isaac dipped, lulling the audience into the world of the play—"there was a city like this one, in a world like our own—but without bankers or billionaires or generals. Instead, there was a Fool, who traveled the world telling jokes." He placed one of the Fool's hands onto the puppet's heart, the other to the sky, as if readying to deliver an address. In the background, Bellatine turned a crank, and a panoramic backdrop on a great wooden frame scrolled through painted silhouettes of Rome, Paris, Berlin, New York, Rio, Cairo . . .

"*Why, hello there!*" Isaac said in the Fool's voice. "*What fine friends you all are, to visit me here. You know, I have told jokes to queens and dancing bears and astronauts alike, but I must say, I'd rather be here, spending time with all of you.*" Isaac let the Fool walk across the stage with such ease one might forget Isaac was there at all. "*Have you ever heard my jokes?*" the Fool continued. "*Ah! You have not? Well—I do not mean to brag, but my jokes, they are so funny you need hear them only once before you'll toss your dreams away to spend your whole life hunting for me, desperate to hear them again.*" Bellatine stopped turning the scroll at the Mayor's feast backdrop, where the Fool's first full scene took place. She slipped behind it, taking up a cluster of silver bells.

"*Would you like to hear one such joke?*" the Fool asked the audience.

Murmurs echoed in reply.

"Come on now. Don't insult him; he's traveled all this way to see you," Isaac scolded in his own voice. "Let's try that again—*Would you like to hear a joke?*"

This time, the crowd cheered louder. Bellatine shook the silver bells, and onstage, Isaac whooshed the little Fool onto a pedestal—and the Fool began to speak.

It wasn't long before Bellatine felt a shift. The first irregularities manifested in the lighting cues, firing a few seconds too fast. Then Isaac dropped a line, giving Bellatine less time to preset the hourglass than she was used to. As she scurried across the stage, a snap of lightning made her twitch, and the hourglass slipped out of her hands, cracking on the hardwood. Sand poured free. *Time,* Bellatine thought, *I spilled time.*

Isaac didn't hesitate, miming the missing object with

uncanny precision. His hands seemed to re-form entirely, an invisible hourglass hovering in the empty space between his fingers. *Like watching a potter at the wheel,* Bellatine thought, his hands a mold with infinite potential shapes. She sighed in relief.

Perhaps not all mistakes were portents. Not all mishaps, warnings. Maybe Isaac had saved them.

But half an hour later, the Girl with No Face wasn't in her station. She was supposed to offer the Fool a rose, bow, and receive a joke so sad, she dies.

Instead, Isaac reached blindly into a blank space on the stage and found nothing. He shot Bellatine a look, nodding his head imperceptibly stage right. It was too small a gesture for the audience to read, but enough for her to recognize. A request. No, an *order*.

In the rush of setting the temporary stage, Isaac must have placed the puppet incorrectly. She lay lifeless, back near the entrance. This was Bellatine's job—Rigs was supposed to pick up the slack, smooth out the edges, while Strings kept the audience's attention from straying. But something about the command in his eyes made her blood boil. He knew, he *knew* why she didn't want to touch the puppets. Yet he'd demanded this of her. Not just retrieving the faceless girl; *all* of it. An avalanche of small, invisible power plays. She wasn't a collaborator to him; she was just another puppet. A tool to be tugged and manipulated so he could have his grand adventure, before vanishing again.

Bellatine's hands grew hot, but she didn't notice. She was distracted by her anger. It wound through her like the vines in the soldiers' mural, piercing her belly and erupting out the other side. Fine. She'd bite, be the good servant. She marched to the Girl with No Face.

As soon as she picked the puppet up, Bellatine knew she'd made a grievous mistake. Her hands seared as if they'd caught fire. She tried to let go but couldn't. Her grip atrophied. *No. Not*

*now. Think of snow. Think of whittling a spoon. Think of the mother-
fucking presidents. Washington, Adams, Jefferson, Madison . . .*

But it was too late. The heat swelled. A spark dug into the
Girl with No Face, a small searchlight, frenzied as a smoked-
out hornets' nest. And then—a sound. *Tha-thump.* It was infini-
tesimal to the audience, but to Bellatine it sounded like war
drums.

Tha-thump, tha-thump, tha-thump.

She wanted to slam her hands over her ears, but they were
still fused to the little doll. *Please, let it be my own pulse,* she
prayed, even as she knew it was futile. *Tha-thump, tha-thump.* This
was not her pulse. Hers flapped alongside the sound like an
erratic, terrified bird. *Tha-thump, tha-thump, tha-thump.* No, this
was the steady, waking heartbeat of the Girl with No Face.

The Girl with No Face sat up. She turned her head. She
reached for the Fool, as if yearning toward a sweetheart she
hadn't seen in years. Finally, Bellatine's hands shuddered and
dropped her. The Girl with No Face crawled across the factory
floor, alone—then, she held out a red rose.

CHAPTER FOURTEEN

PERHAPS THERE WAS A time before the Embering, but if so, Bellatine had no memory of it. Nor did she remember the first time it had happened. As a child, it seemed entirely ordinary—so much so that for a long while, she thought everyone could do it. She used to spend hours in her parents' workshop, skimming her hands over the puppets, feeling the shimmer run between them, searching for the delicate drumbeat of a pulse. And when she found it? Steam escaping from a teakettle. A searing heat. A hollering. She would forget where her hands ended and the doll began. *Tha-thump, tha-thump, tha-thump,* the little heartbeat sang. And then—the puppet would wake up.

It wasn't that she could *make* something alive. She didn't think she could insert anything into an object that wasn't, somewhere deep down, already there. What she could do was activate it. Animate it. Tunnel deep into fabric and wood and wire until at the core, she'd locate where the ghost was hidden. She became a paleontologist, hunting a lost creature hovering in ice, each object's soul a frozen specimen waiting to be melted loose. And when that ghost was found, the heat in her hands thawed it until it stretched like a cat into the crevices of its object-body and woke up.

Bellatine did, however, remember the first time she realized there might be something *wrong* with her Embering. She was four years old. She was at Bluefish Park with her mom and Isaac, and it must have been spring, because Bellatine's clothes were wet from trying to catch wriggly black tadpoles in the frog pond. Isaac was playing with Transformers on their blue-checkered picnic blanket. Bellatine reached for one of the toys, all plastic and shiny moving parts. Her hands started to vibrate. She felt the toy start to stir in her grip with that same eager newness as the tadpoles, all its robotic lights blinking. Her mother saw, and yanked it out of her hands with a harshness that startled Bellatine. She'd started to cry.

"That's something we do in *private*," her mother had scolded, "like going potty, or getting dressed. Some things, they aren't for other people to see—understand? Tell me you understand, Bellatine. Do you hear me?"

She nodded. A sense of shame had washed over her so strongly that she'd felt the overwhelming urge to hide, but there was nowhere to go. All she could do was curl up on the blanket, gaudy, unbearably *there*, and pretend to be invisible. It wasn't her mother's words that disturbed her, or even frustration at having the toy taken away. What had alarmed Bellatine was the genuine *fear* in her mother's eyes as she'd looked around the park, one hand on her daughter—praying no one had seen.

After that, Bellatine never again woke a puppet in front of her mother. Isaac, however, still looked on with glee as she animated playfellows in secret from their toys or from puppets around the theater. The little Tailor, who would tell them stories of the old country as he repaired rips in their jeans with his tiny needle and thread. The Fox, who snarled and chased them in endless games of tag. The funny, red-shoed Fool, who told the same five jokes again and again like a jukebox on loop. The dolls never stayed awake longer than a few minutes at a time, stretching in their bodies and looking around at the world like newborns. It was fun, then. She'd felt powerful. And she never had to be alone.

But that was before she knew how dangerous the Embering could really be. Before she knew what horrors her hands were capable of, and how little control she really had. She'd spent years learning to tamp it down, keep it quiet. Years training herself in the careful art of restraint.

Her mother had always regarded her Embering as something to fear, to conceal. Had sewn Bellatine gloves lined with blue freezer gel. Had begun keeping the family's puppets in a pad-locked case, higher than Bellatine's reach. When she bought her daughter toys, they were never dolls or stuffed bears or masks like the ones she gave to Isaac. Only faceless, ghostless objects: puzzles, board games, candle-making kits. If only Bellatine had heeded her mother's worry more strongly. Quit altogether instead of merely hiding. She could have put a stop to it then, before the worst began.

Her father, on the other hand, had taken the opposite approach. Treated her as somehow more than human, the perfect puppeteer. *Your mother and I, we only aspire to gift life to these creatures,* he once told her, *while you, you actually do it. You are evolution at work. The puppeteer of God.* This pedestal filled her with nearly the same humiliation as her mother's scorn. Soon, she began to conceal her talents from him, as well.

Only Isaac saw her power as something . . . neutral. Simply a part of her. Not a holy gift. Not a terrible secret. Just a trait, like any other, on par with her cropped brown hair, her Ping-Pong skills, her crooked bottom teeth. Around her brother, she wasn't a demon nor a saint—she'd just been a *kid*. He'd been her mainstay. Her only grounding force as the fires in her blood grew hotter, closer to combustion.

But then he'd left. No goodbye. No warning. And without

him? It was like a crutch had been pulled out from under her. Like a bullwhip cracking. The sonic boom that follows. A loud gap in the air where he sliced through it, already gone. He hadn't been there when her hands learned to do things that no one, not even her father, could call holy. When she wasn't a girl, anymore, but a monster.

The Girl with No Face raised her red silk rose to the audience. Whatever the crowd's response was, Bellatine didn't hear it. The inside of her head droned. Was she still onstage? Was Isaac there? All she could focus on was the faceless puppet and her flower, standing puppeteer-less on the ground. Flashes of light. Fire. Memory. A cabinet of dolls, the key hidden in her mother's drawer. The stench of rotting flesh. A terrible, creaking howl. *Tha-thump, tha-thump*, that impossible pulse still thudding in her ears.

Bellatine hovered over herself, as if watching a movie version of her own life from far, far away. All around her, Estey organs crouched like goblins. Pipes javelined into the rafters, and even though no one touched the bellows, Bellatine could hear a low, constant hum. *They're alive*, she thought, *everything, everything is alive.*

She tumbled through the crowd and free of the museum. Barreling down the stairs, she slipped on damp concrete. She fell too long toward the ground—a moment, a minute, an hour, a year . . . In her suspension, she imagined her body engulfed in a fire too blazing to be smothered, one hundred firefighters surrounding her. She saw their hoses turning to snakes, writhing in their hands.

Bellatine hit the ground with a crunch. Was it her bones? No, just the broken glass still scattered across the Estey Museum steps. She scrambled to her feet and ran.

Someone, maybe Isaac, called to her, but the voice sounded as if it were moving through a deep, black lake. She tore through the parking lot, looming gray factory buildings casting accusatory shadows over her, a burial shroud. She couldn't distinguish between her feet pounding the asphalt and the thunder overhead and her own pulse sounding inside her like a gavel, *Order, order, order.* Rain bulleted down on her. It burst to steam on contact.

At the far end of the lot, Thistlefoot loomed like a lighthouse, beckoning her to port.

The very first time she'd set foot in the legged house, it had been as though she were a little girl again, before the Embering had grown unruly. It had felt like a sigh. The unfurling that comes over you when you climb into your own bed after weeks away. As if finally, having pressed through every toil and trial, she'd received permission to rest.

Or the promise of rest. If Isaac stayed true to his word.

He won't, a voice groaned within her as she careened toward the cottage. *He'll leave. He always leaves. And when he does, how will you stop him from taking your salvation with him?*

She must have pulled herself up the ladder and through the front door, though she couldn't remember getting there. Somewhere along the way, the white scarf had fallen from her hair, her trousers torn at one knee. She collapsed in the parlor. Immediately, some of the heat lessened. It wasn't unbearable anymore, and she felt herself sinking back into her body. She was on the floor now, pressing a hand to her chest. It came away wet with blood. When had she cut herself? It must have been on the broken glass on the steps, though she hadn't felt it. The red rose still hovered in her vision, a stain, as if she'd stared at an eclipse head-on. She blinked, but it remained—the faceless puppet and her flower. Her obscene, inhuman motion. Bellatine's hands throbbed as if she'd slammed them down on a red stovetop.

Regain control. I must regain control. She fumbled in her pocket for the wooden spoon, her thumb hooking into its curved handle. The first object she'd ever whittled herself. Proof that she could command material to her will, shape it, carve it—not be carved *by* it. *"Cedar, oak, redwood, maple,"* she muttered, a prayer.

Behind her, someone ascended the ladder. *"Loyf,"* barked Isaac's familiar voice. *Run.* She felt the house sway and bolt forward beneath her.

Then, blackness overtook her, and the world was gone.

CHAPTER FIFTEEN

THE LITTLE BOY IN Shona's arms went slack. A moment ago, he'd been writhing, his gaze snapping back and forth between her and Rummy in nauseated panic. Now he softened. An ashen breath escaped his lips. The passenger clinging to his back flickered.

"Shhh, that's right, it's okay, kid." Rummy brushed a hand over the boy's forehead, carefully skirting contact with the passenger. Its misted arms remained noosed around the boy's neck.

Shona and her friends had discovered early on that the spidery creatures that clung to the drugged victims' shoulders were intangible—nothing but billowing silver palls—but they preferred to avoid wafting through them on principle.

Shona tossed a look over her shoulder toward Sparrow, who had the child's father pinned to the ground. His passenger, too, had gone still, while the man's pale eyes undulated like spider sacks about to hatch. Sparrow pinched the man's face. He didn't register the touch.

This was new. Never had the smokefed given up or gone quiet without the help of Sparrow's delectable little sedative syringe. Shona's arm stung where the boy had bitten her, but he was limp now. Despite this, she tightened her grip. The pause wasn't a relaxed calm. The passengers weren't fading yet, weren't relinquishing their hold. They weren't giving up. They were focusing.

In unison, both passengers turned their heads southward. A response to some silent call, a dog whistle a register above the human ear. Shona thought of butterflies with an extra cone in their eyes allowing them to see colors humans have no language nor comprehension for. Craning, the creatures' necks elongated into narrow pillars of smoke. *What do the smoke-eyed see? What speaks to them that is beyond our knowing, beyond our senses?*

Their united gazes lasered past Shona and Rummy and Sparrow, past the black bus idling in a bodega lot, past the rest stop, and onto the highway. There, the milky stares darted along the interstate, southward bound. Past black tar wriggling with mirages of colonial gunpowder. Past old lynching forests where the trees had doubled over, as if to keep a man's feet on the ground. Past hand-hewn crosses beside dented guardrails and bicycles painted white, their wheels eternally spinning. Past endless rememberings, warping the road. The highway, a cemetery for the lost and the restless. A memorial. A circulatory system running through a nation.

As the smoke's sight traveled, the highway barely noticed. These roads were accustomed to the motions of hungry ghosts. Wraiths who have traveled a long way, and still are traveling. They linger behind the living like shadows. Some came shackled in the bottoms of ships, drawn to the stench of despair. Some came disguised as bone combs or little music boxes in young girls' hands, clung to as the girls were pinned to filthy cots in rooms thick with opium. Some came stapled into boys' shoulders or hips returning from battlefields, adopting the shape an arm once took, a missing leg. Others stowed away in more insidious places, still. In blood. In bones. In a genetic code. An inheritance so haunted it altered the very shapes of bodies. Some perched like vultures on soldiers' backs as they drove convoys down Eisenhower's great interstate—a nation's pride, built wide to carry men more quickly to base, more quickly to war, more quickly to glory. What an invention, this web of highways, tying America to America! Laying a path so that no matter how far we flee, there is always an easy trail leading back to the start. There is no leaving the ghosts behind. Not when they can simply hold out a thumb. Wait for a ride.

For ghosts, the highway only runs one way—it drives the past toward the present. Closer and closer to collision.

The passengers' sight darted past semitrucks and gas stations. Rounded off exit 2 from I-91. It turned onto Western Avenue. Again, on Birge Street. It came to a row of slate-covered factory buildings, crooning with the memory of organ song—and at the end of this row, it arrived at a legged house with a girl inside, clutching at her hands. These hands, the smoke remembered them. These hands, the smoke had known them for longer than the girl had lived.

Miles off, the Longshadow Man cast an eye in the same direction. He rose. He tightened his coat. He took one step closer. Then another.

CHAPTER SIXTEEN

ISAAC WAS DREAMING AGAIN.

A boxcar floating in a blue tulle river.

Benji, a resonator guitar on his knee, singing, singing, the song a skyful of crows. The song, a forgetting. The song, a goat's heart in a jar. The song, a thick wedge of brown bread and a stolen bottle of gin. The song, a payphone that rings and rings and no one answers. The song, a truck stop with a dead opossum in the parking lot. Benji's song, part lullaby, part metal grinding against metal.

"What's that you're singing?" Isaac asked.

"Come on, baby boy, you've forgotten that fast? We wrote this one together."

Atop the boxcar, their legs dangled off the edge. Red shoes on both their feet. The Fool's river rising, rising, waved upward by invisible hands.

"Tell me again, about the song," Isaac said. "I can't remember."

"I remember everything," Benji said.

Benji opened his mouth and gravel spilled out. Bus tickets.

Railroad spikes. Scraps of tin. He kept singing. The song screeched, a freight flinging on its brakes.

"Tell me, please," Isaac begged. He stuffed the falling pieces into his pockets, as if to ease the flow of it. Benji's voice rose, his guitar pinging with falling debris.

"This song is for the goners, whose smiles are dust."

The sound grew. The river swelled. Sand and metal spewed from Benji's throat too fast for Isaac to brush away. It covered them. Knee, waist, neck, and then, darkness. Isaac scrambled to escape the avalanche, managing to grab hold of something solid to pull himself over the tide. It dissolved in his hand, wet. An arm, wrenched from the shoulder and decaying. He dropped it, reached for another hold. This, a long bone, tangled in sinew. The pile was full of bodies. Stray limbs bloating. Eyeless faces oozing yellow, the gums pulled back.

Isaac screamed.

"Have you come to bury me?" Benji rasped from beneath.

Outside, the river rose.

He woke to a crash. Hubcap had knocked a stack of books from his bedside table before pouncing on his bare chest and kneading her sharp paws against him. The pricking claws against his sweat-soaked skin yanked him back. Isaac let out a sigh. No sand. No boxcar. No Benji.

Hubcap purred, rubbing her forehead against his chin.

"You're a menace." Isaac tousled the cat's ears.

A rustling came from the other side of the bedroom curtain. *Tiny.* The clatter must have woken her, too.

Isaac rose and tugged on his suit trousers, then drew back the curtain separating their two beds. Bellatine squinted, holding up an arm to block the light.

She must have noticed the house bobbing then, because she craned forward, trying to peer out the hall window.

"Where are we?" she croaked.

"Western Mass. Southward bound."

"How long have I been out?" she asked.

"Two days. Left Vermont without finishing act two, much to the confusion of our paying audience. Fen packed up the gear and met us at the town line."

She groaned but pulled herself upright.

Though he'd done his best to clean his sister up, dried blood remained crusted under her nails and in splotches across her shoulders and neck. He'd been too embarrassed to change her out of her performance clothes so had left them on, white on white.

"How do you feel?"

"Fine, nothing I can't handle." She flinched.

"You look *interstellar*."

Bellatine grunted.

She *did* look uncommonly healthy. Nothing like she'd appeared two days prior, when he'd found her curled on the floor and shaking with fever. Even the typical dark circles under her eyes had faded, replaced by a peachy softness. Though her hazelnut hair was matted from tossing in her sleep, it was glossy and thick, and her freckles seemed to float over a cherry-pink light in her cheeks. She could have passed for fifteen or sixteen years old.

"Did you do this?" Bellatine asked, touching a torn strip of bedsheet wrapped around her shoulder, from her collarbone to her underarm, where Isaac had plucked out a rhombus of broken glass.

He ignored the question. "Quite the parlor trick you pulled back there."

Bellatine wouldn't meet his eye. "It won't happen again."

"I was *going* to suggest—it'd be tally if you could play the littlest resurrectionist every night. If we'd seen the show to the end, I bet your stunt would have pulled in double our normal tips."

"Are you insane?" Bellatine pushed herself up straighter, cringing as the makeshift bandage twisted against her wound. "You saw what happened."

"What I saw was an audience charmed by a clever bit of stage-craft, which they assumed was fixed with wires and pulleys."

Bellatine laughed. "Okay, so you *are* insane. Fantastic."

"I think your talents are an asset to the show. I've always thought that."

Bellatine paused. "You knew this would happen."

"Hell, sure. Didn't you?"

The muscles in her neck set firm, jaw tightening, and by her sides, her hands balled into fists. By the tension in her wrists, Isaac could tell she was driving her nails into her palms. She wanted to hit him. Good. She must be feeling better.

"It's not healthy to keep energy bottled up," he urged. "You should let loose more."

"It *won't* happen again," she repeated, rigid. She reached for a glass of water on the nightstand without taking her eyes from him. "You know, you were talking in your sleep."

"Was I?"

She took a long sip from the glass before returning it to the table.

"Who's Benji?"

A jolt ran through Isaac's bones, hearing the name aloud. Like a ghost had walked through him.

"A friend," Isaac said.

"A friend . . ." Bellatine echoed.

Isaac shoved his hands into his pockets to anchor their sudden trembling. "You're lucky, you know."

Her eyes narrowed.

"It's a valve, isn't it? A tap you open and everything in you that's gone sour or sad or rotten spills out. Every fly or vulture swarming in you. Every bit of sulfur and fear and regret and—"

"You don't know what you're talking about," she interrupted.

"Don't tell me I'm wrong. I can see it in your face."

"It's not a valve, it's a curse."

"You look like you were born five minutes ago. Fresh as a trout."

Bellatine studied him. "Magic cures don't exist."

"But curses do?"

She didn't answer.

Before turning to leave, Isaac tossed a flat silver coin onto his sister's lap.

"A token for your labor."

Bellatine reached out instinctively to grab it. Her hands opened like lilies.

In the kitchen, Isaac fished the last apple out of a sack Li Fen had given them and put the coffee percolator on the ever-burning cookstove. He'd gotten sloppy again. Careless enough to let a needle of visible envy creep loose in front of Tiny. Envy implies lack, which implies want, and if someone knows what you want they can catch you. Leave the door open a crack, and all it would take is a good strong wind to blow it open. He couldn't afford that. Not now, when he was so close to laying his sins to rest.

His phone buzzed in his pocket. He pulled it out, check-ing the caller ID without answering. *Shona.* For a moment, his pulse leapt. The white-eyed woman . . . The strange man in the bar . . . Even in recollection, the Longshadow Man's image slid off Isaac's mind like oil. Nothing to grip onto. To mirror and become, and in doing so, understand. But a whole state and a half had bloated between them by now, with more miles added every minute. He sent the call to voicemail with the flick of a button. He knew full well she wouldn't risk leaving one. What-ever Shona had to say, it wasn't his concern.

Thistlefoot's kitchen was always too hot. Even on cold days, the stove blazed bright enough to make sweat run down the back of his neck. It was a luxury, unending heat. How many nights had he frozen half to death, soaked through and huddled in a train yard as he waited for a southbound? Now he had a roof over his head, a real bed, a fire that never went out. Still, he shivered.

He'd thought the daily performances on tour would ease the headaches, the tremors, but if anything, they'd gotten worse. The craft wasn't right. When he practiced mimicry, he replaced himself, gave himself up to possession, to an alien sort of presence. It was a respite from himself. A kind of temporary dying, as if Isaac were merely a jug poured empty and refilled with a new, sweeter wine. His muscles and sinews were tools to serve him, accessories to his vanishing—and if need be, anchors to tug him back home.

Puppeteering was different. The Yaga puppets didn't exist to serve him. It was quite the reverse. *He* existed as a butler to the creatures in his care. As Strings, without Isaac's motions, his breath, his hands, the puppets had no chance to live. In letting their bodies move, Isaac had to place himself fully in a position of service.

As an actor, he invited other characters to inhabit his own flesh. As a puppeteer, however, the characters didn't possess *him*, but sank instead into the fabric and wood of the dolls. He remained solidly himself, only his own sorry spirit batting around within the cage of his skeleton. Rather than escaping himself, he had to be even *more* grounded in order to serve the puppets well. The roles reversed—he, the anchor. The puppet, the actor. The truth was, he *did* envy what Tiny had. Not the power. Not the enchantment. But a moment, just one passing moment, of release.

The percolator bubbled, and he filled a mug, trying not to spill as his wrists trembled. In the distance, a train howled.

Have you come to bury me?

With a spasm, the cup clattered to the floor.

CHAPTER SEVENTEEN

ISAAC HADN'T RUN AWAY. Not exactly. Running away implied secrecy, planning, bags stuffed with spare socks and bone-handled hunting knives, the stink of desperation. It suggested fleeing *from* something. A famished wolf. A birdcage bolted with an iron padlock. A leash hooked to the throat. But no, when Isaac abandoned his parents' house at seventeen, he wasn't headed away. He was headed *toward*. Driven by restlessness or yearning, toward what, he didn't rightly know—which is exactly why it was so imperative he find out.

Earlier in the afternoon, he'd slid the paperwork to drop out of Bentley High School into the attendance office mail slot. Two hours later, he strolled from the Yaga theater doors with only a fistful of cash, a toothbrush, and a Slim Jim in his pocket. He'd hitched a ride within another hour and was in Portland by sundown.

At the nearest gas station, he bought a gallon jug of water and a marbled composition notebook, along with a burner phone, having left his smartphone behind so he couldn't be tracked. He'd be eighteen in three months—so as long as he could stay under the radar until then, his parents couldn't rein him back in. They'd have their hands full wrangling his sister anyway, who'd spent the last two years competing in the Tween Emo Championships: Door Slamming Edition.

He hadn't packed a bag because he wanted a true-blue, unsullied, hot-from-the-skillet fresh start. No past to weigh him down, no objects haunted with the person he'd been before. He'd build a life from *scratch*, with only his wits and his own body to rely on. How else would he truly know what he was capable of? It was time to see if he could survive in the wild.

Two weeks later, he was in handcuffs, cornered against the side of a cop car.

"Caught this kid trying to buy a hat with my credit card," a portly blond woman exclaimed to a crowd of onlookers. "Thought I'd misplaced my wallet, went to Gumley Brothers to tell my husband, and that's when I saw this thief holding it." She turned to one of the cops. "Get my wallet back from him, please, Officer! He still has it."

Most of the onlookers ogled with a side-eye, pretending to go about their own business as they drank in the gossip like it was a milkshake sipped through a long straw. Isaac squirmed under their judgment. He wished he could teleport out of his skin. He wished he'd never taken the wallet.

Only one figure in the crowd watched head-on, a boy with red hair and boxy red freckles. He wore a once-white T-shirt tucked into a pair of blue jeans, with an olive bandanna tied around his neck, a guitar case slung over one shoulder, a steel-framed backpack over the other. He leaned against a wall, jade eyes sharp as a hawk's.

"Did you check your purse?" the redheaded boy quipped.

The woman glared at him. "Yes."

"It's a big bag, seems a little thing like a wallet could get lost in there, all I'm saying."

"Look, young man—" a cop cautioned.

The officer guarding Isaac fumbled in Isaac's pockets. Isaac swallowed, humiliated. He prayed the cop wouldn't search his boot.

The hands moved down his legs, and Isaac's heart sank.

"Is this it, ma'am?" the cop asked, pulling out a worn leather wallet. Isaac cringed.

"No, no, keep looking, I'm sure he has it!"

No? Confusion washed over him. He *had* put the wallet in his boot. Why would she act like it wasn't hers when it was?

After another moment of manhandling, the cop stepped off.

"That's all that's on him, ma'am. Benjamin Short—that you?"

It took Isaac a moment to register that the officer was talking to him.

"Uh . . ."

"Benjamin, that your name?" The officer squinted at a business card he'd pulled out of the found wallet. Isaac's mind reeled.

Before he could answer, his accuser emitted a piglet-squeal of surprise. She was holding her purse open, and after reaching elbow-deep into the mass, had retrieved a small pink wallet—the same one Isaac had stuffed into his boot only an hour earlier.

"I-I could have sworn . . ." the woman stuttered.

"Ma'am, are you entirely sure this boy robbed you? Is it possible you saw him holding this wallet"—the officer waved the fold he'd pulled from Isaac's boot—"and thought it was yours?"

"I thought . . . I really thought . . ."

And as quickly as it began, it was over. The handcuffs clicked open. The crowd dispersed. People returned to their own lives—

purchasing baubles and soy candles from overpriced boutiques, sighing into cinema seats to escape the new summer heat, eating curly fries from steaming red baskets, glutting their cars heavy with gasoline before disappearing into some other town, some other story. The police car shrank into the distance like a moth, winging out of sight. Isaac was alone.

He rubbed his wrists, still sore from the metal, before he remembered the mystery wallet. He opened it, examining the same business card the policeman had read from minutes earlier. It was written by hand in tight, neat script:

Benjamin Short
Songster, Bard, Time Traveler

The card also included a download link to an album and a mobile cash app for tips. He turned it over. Taped to the back was a flat coppery disk, about twice the size of a penny. It *was* a penny, Isaac realized, but stretched, like those made by novelty coin presser machines—only this one was blank and smooth, as if run over by a train.

"Hey, Fresh, can I get my wallet back?"

The redheaded boy emerged from behind a pillar and crouched down next to him on the curb.

"*Your* wallet?"

"Yeah, my fucking wallet. The one I jammed in your boot when I put that squealer's back in her purse."

"You did that? Why?" Isaac asked, tucking the card back inside and returning the wallet.

"Nah, that's for you," the boy said, handing the business card with the taped penny back to Isaac. "Anyway, they had to find *something* to explain what that lady had seen you holding at the counter. And no offense, baby, but you don't strike me as someone with cash on hand, let alone a glove to put it in." A lilting drawl tugged on the boy's words, like he belonged in a Tennessee Williams play.

"But why any of it? Why help me?"

"May he without sin cast the first fishing line."

"Huh?"

"We got to look out for each other." He winked one green eye.

"We?" Isaac sized up the boy next to him. Close up, he could see dirt caked thick around his collar, grease in his hair. "You mean bums."

"Not bums. Angels." The boy grinned.

Isaac snorted. "Sure. Angels." There was something about this kid Isaac trusted. He couldn't name it—but sitting there together felt natural, easy. And *easy* hadn't been part of his vocabulary lately, not since leaving home.

"You're new on the road, huh, Fresh?"

Isaac hesitated. Again he felt a flush enter his cheeks. Was it that obvious? The last thing he wanted was to come across as a noob, gullible, easy to fleece.

"It's all right to be new, every great song has a first note," the boy said. He extended a hand. "Benji Short."

"Isaac Yaga."

They shook.

"Fresh, can I give you some advice?"

Isaac shrugged.

"Don't be a fucking thief."

Isaac's face ran hot and he yanked his hand back.

"What I mean," the boy tempered, "is take this wallet." He waved it in the air. "Now grab it out of my hand."

"What?"

"Go on, grab it."

Isaac did.

Benji kept his hand frozen in the claw position it had been in a moment before, when it had still held an object.

"See this?" he said, pointing with his other hand to the gap between his fingers where the wallet had been. "This has become a *longing*. A lost space. A black hole. People notice a black a hole, don't they, Fresh? They can feel it, the presence of absence, if you will. You get me?"

Isaac nodded, though he wasn't sure he did.

"All right, now peel that penny off the back of the card there. That's right. Place it here, in my hand."

Isaac put the coin into Benji's still frozen hand. The boy clenched a fist around it, the corner of his mouth ticking up in a conspiratorial smile.

"See?"

"I . . . no. Not really."

"It's not a gap anymore, is it?"

"I guess not."

Benji held up a finger. "Thieves gain by leaving gaps. After a while, though, it gets unbalanced. Nature catches on, tries to right it. That's when bad luck hits. You'll start losing things, your pack, your shoes, or worse, an arm, a fucking leg. But if you leave something in the empty places, even something of no seeming consequence"—Benji tossed the coin back to Isaac— "no black holes. No bad luck. No getting shaken down by the pigs."

"So you're saying," Isaac clarified, "I have to balance the scales or I'll get caught."

"That's it, baby. What goes around comes ring-around-the-fucking-rosy. Hey, you got a cigarette?"

Isaac didn't. He'd been considering taking up smoking. Now he wished he already had.

"You a poet?" Benji asked, nodding at Isaac's notebook, still pinned under his arm.

Isaac shook his head. "Naw. Just a journal."

"But you're a troubadour. An artist. I can see it right . . . here." Benji tapped Isaac's forehead, between the eyes.

"I'm an actor," Isaac said.

"An actor! Even better. You'll learn to use that."

There was an assured wisdom to the way the boy spoke, though he looked even younger than Isaac, barely sixteen. Maybe he *was* an angel.

"You play that thing?" Isaac asked, nodding to the guitar Benji had laid down on the curb beside him.

"I play it, it plays me, who can fucking say? You know, in Celtic lore, there's a faerie called the leanan sídhe. You heard of her?"

"No, sorry," Isaac said, to his deep regret. He wanted to be able to say yes, to show this kid that he knew *something* worth knowing, fresh though he was.

Benji leaned in, campfire flickering in his voice. "She's invisible to everyone except for one artist. And to him, she's the most beautiful woman he's ever seen. She lights a fire in him, he falls in love. Everything he writes, or paints, or sings—it's all for her. And the passion makes it brilliant. Genius even."

"Like a muse," Isaac said.

"A bit like a muse," Benji considered. "More like the crossroads demon you'd sell your soul to in exchange for killer piano chops or to be the most famous plastic surgeon in LA, until it circles back to collect. Because, see"—Benji brushed a fly off his cheek—"as the artist yearns for the leanan sídhe, and makes his art, and yearns again, that fire in him burns brighter and brighter, until eventually, it burns him up from the inside out and kills him. They say it's why artists and poets die young.

"Now, tell me." Benji pressed in closer, his absinthe eyes glowing like fireflies. "Do you reckon that story's true?"

Finally, a question Isaac knew the answer to.

"All stories are true."

Benji leaned back, satisfied.

"Why's your card say you're a time traveler?" Isaac asked.

"You try singing a song from three hundred years ago and tell me that's not time travel. Fuck, I need a drink. You want a beer? On me."

"Sure."

As Isaac stood up, he almost tripped over a scrawny black kitten. He narrowly regained his balance.

Benji's face lit up. "My shadow! Fresh, meet my familiar,

Hubcap Short, American rat catcher." The kitten pressed against Benji's legs, purring.

And so, side by side, two boys and one slim black cat walked through the golden light of sunset. They didn't walk away from where they'd started. No, not away. Only toward.

CHAPTER EIGHTEEN

I HEARD YOU HAVE been inquiring after me, at the synagogue, at the pharmacy, at the town hall, asking if you can trust what I tell you. So you do not believe I was born from a hen? Bah! Trust. It is a meaningless word, precious only to *kibitzers* who think all business is their business. I reserve the right to lie to you outright and often—and we must always make use of our rights, lest they vanish from neglect.

So perhaps I was not born from a hen. Have you heard this one then?

There was a forest of old-growth pines. The canopy above, so thick no light showed through. The bed of brush below, so soft a newborn fawn could sleep for many days and nights without stirring. These trees, they inhaled one century, exhaled the next. These trees, they bent in gale and blizzard, but have never fallen, not one single tree in all the great wood. Then, the lumbermen came.

The lumbermen were dressed as soldiers. (I say this as a caution, to remind you that I tell a story, and not a fact. In a story, when a man intends harm, he always arrives dressed as a soldier, whether he is a soldier or not.) The lumbermen found the tallest tree in the forest, and they lifted their great saws to its belly like they were butchering a hog. The tree fell.

There was a family of crows living within that great pine. When the tree fell, the birds were killed. Their ghosts tried to fly out, but got caught in the trunk, squawking. The wood was cut and planed and stacked. It was sold for a fair price to a woman and her two daughters, who used it to build a house. But all the while, the crows' ghosts flapped inside the lumber, spoiling workmen's nails with their beaks, rotting the boards with dung, sickening the men, who coughed up feathers in their sleep. Many quit. Others grew too ill or frightened to work. But at last, after many months, the house was complete. From the floor, two birds' feet erupted. I was born running, already knowing how it feels to die.

Is this birth story more satisfactory than the last? You probably appreciate how this origin mentions a woman and her two daughters. *Ah,* you think, *I know this family!* And you will use that proof to make sense of the rest. I'd advise against drawing conclusions. It could have been any mother and daughters. It could have been any house, any birds. In all likeliness, I'm lying to you still.

But if it is *memory* you want, so be it, I will give you one.

If you are born in Gedenkrovka, you will likely die in Gedenkrovka, and if you die in Gedenkrovka, Haim will be the man to carve your headstone. Do you remember the stonecutter, Haim? Baba Yaga was to give him her third egg at market, an egg full of bullets, before the soldiers came. Yes, now you recall.

All are equal under Haim's chisel. Be you rabbi or shoemaker, Haim attends to your stone with utmost care. He labors for days, transforming what was once jagged, immovable marble into tendrils of curling vine, blooming violets, songbirds pluming in their bowers, fruit-bearing trees heavy with pomegranates. Below, in Hebrew, he engraves an epitaph heralding you as a profound interpreter of the Word of God, a Doer of Good, a Blessed Memory—your life's small, faulty actions transmuted into feats of glory.

There has been talk of wrecked shtetls in other parts of Russia, where every last resident has been driven out or slaughtered by Cossacks. In these hollow once-towns, tombstones are stolen from the earth and used to pave roads. The White Army marches over them without looking down.

When Haim carves your grave marker, he makes his cuts deep, so the images poke out sharp and abundant. Try to lay a road with Haim's stones, and it will trip an army to its knees.

When Baba Yaga next goes to market, she stops at the stonecutter's house first. His lost bullets are in her pocket, and she keeps having to hush them, for they will not shut up.

"Reb Haim," she calls through the door, "take your bullets, they talk all night and keep my daughters awake. I am an egg seller, not a boardinghouse."

He seizes her by the arm and pulls her into the shop.

"Are you mad, Baba Yaga?" Haim whispers. "To speak aloud of ammunitions where anyone might overhear you?"

"They will overhear the bullets before overhearing me," she says.

Haim scrunches up his forehead. He believes bullets cannot speak. He is wrong.

"Whatever you found in your egg, it does not belong to me," Haim insists.

"The bullets claim otherwise," Baba Yaga replies.

She unties her apron and pours its contents out upon the stonecutter's table. *Clack, clack, clack,* say the bullets as they fall.

Then she lifts a carving pick from the table and presses the point into her palm. Haim yanks it away from her, dismayed, before a wound is pricked. Baba Yaga rolls her eyes before reaching down into her undergarments to retrieve a smear of monthly blood, which she wipes onto one of the bullets. As soon as the blood touches it, the bullet begins to speak.

It speaks of revolution. Of small rooms where bookbinders and students gather, their voices low and certain. It speaks of the Bolsheviks, of an empire falling, of power gained and lost. It speaks of the blood that has been spilled and the blood that shall be. It speaks of the body it will one day be lodged in, a soldier in Denikin's army. It speaks of pogroms and of Jews gathering in defiance, like a secret pulse beneath Gedenkrovka. It speaks the stonecutter's name.

"So you see why my daughters are having trouble sleeping," Baba Yaga chides. "This is not a fitting lullaby for any child, Reb Haim."

Haim places his palms on the table. He becomes focused, the way a chisel becomes focused when set to a task. "Did you hear," he says, "the news from Korostyshev? Gentile farmers, they lynched a Jewish man and his son. Sixteen years old. And the tsar's soldiers, there to keep order, they claim—they looked the other way as the man begged for his son's life."

"I know what goes on," Baba Yaga grunts.

"You know a great many things, don't you, Baba Yaga? You always have your little ways of knowing."

"I listen."

The stonecutter nods. "And what if you could use this knowing for good? You could help us. Help your people. There is a resistance, a gathering of Jews who seek to—"

Baba Yaga raises a hand and tiny stitches of red thread seal shut the stonecutter's mouth. "I do not care for the squabbling of men. I care for my daughters. That is all."

Haim meets her eye. Her irises, nearly as black as the pupils within them.

"I protect them well on my own. You will not speak to me of

this again, Reb Haim." Baba Yaga's stare is a carved stone. The bullets on the table are bright and heavy as moons. They wait. They dream of a pulled trigger.

The stitches through the stonecutter's lips will dissolve . . . in time.

I'll admit, I considered telling this story differently. In another telling, perhaps Baba Yaga joins the resistance and I lay egg after egg, fat with lead. Perhaps she and the stonecutter become lovers. It would not have been impossible—Baba Yaga has taken lovers before. One, a golem she built from clay. One, a maggot-heavy carcass of a black bear, sweet with rot. One, a traveling merchant, whom she bedded the way a mantis would, ending in devouring. Forgive us! Gossiping like yentas. But oh, what lovers she has had! Baba Yaga is a creature of hunger. Baba Yaga, with her daughters born from rugelach and rosewater and teeth. Baba Yaga, glutton and giver of secrets.

Listen, did you know that when moths are reborn from the cocoon as winged beasts, they have no mouths? As caterpillars they feast on green leaves, plump themselves into morsels, hide away in pale silk, and then reemerge to never eat again. Imagine! To live with all your hunger behind you. Our Baba Yaga is no moth. She is built of one thousand open mouths, and they are always wet at the jaw.

In this telling, Baba Yaga does not join the whispering bullets. She does not tuck into back rooms where maps and pamphlets flutter like severed wings upon tabletops, nor does she tuck into the stonecutter's bed. Instead, she takes care of her own, as she has always done. She and Reb Haim never speak again. At least, not while he is alive.

Though Baba Yaga has had many lovers, she only has two sweethearts—Illa and Malka. Lovers are for eating. Sweethearts are for pressing a cool cloth to their foreheads when a fever spikes and whispering, *Hush now, darling, sleep. Sleep.*

CHAPTER NINETEEN

LI FEN BOLTED THE final latch on the Estey Museum door, turning the brass key with a heavy click. It was one of her favorite sounds—evoking completion, like a ribbon being knotted atop a paper-wrapped box. Another day come to its end.

It had been a good day. Most days were—if you set the intention for goodness. Fen held intention in high esteem. That was the role of the artist, after all: to see the world not only as it was, but as it could be. An empty stage (only wood and curtains and renter's debts) could become a forest inhabited by nine-headed birds and wise goats able to tell truth from lies. A canvas could become a lake, moony with magic toads, or a sky tangled with dragons. Surely, a day was the same. A blank page to fill with whatever made the imagination buzz. So yes, she *could* have taken today as simply another long stretch of aching hours giving tours to sticky-fingered schoolchildren with short-tempered teachers. But what was the fun in that? No—today, she had led small, growing minds through a labyrinth of sounds and sights. She had planted tiny pipe organs in their chests that would oompah-pah in their dreams.

Li Fen pocketed the key and made her way down the steps to the parking lot. She softened in the evening air. *A good day,* she told herself, a mantra.

A clatter rang out from the alley between the nearest two factory buildings.

"Hello?" she called, her voice cartwheeling off the looming slate.

Something moved in the shadows, and Fen's breath caught in her chest. *Intention.* That's what it all came down to. You could choose to be afraid or choose to be curious. She took a step forward.

The shadow shifted.

"Hello?"

With a rattle, a fat raccoon tumbled off a metal trash bin, and Fen giggled with relief.

What an odd-looking fellow, with hands like a tiny man and that plump waddle. They didn't have raccoons where she'd grown up, a few hours outside Shenzhen, nor in Beijing, where she'd run her theater. Occasionally she forgot just how different things were here—and then she'd see a strange creature like that, almost mythical in its otherness.

Of course, it wasn't the only reminder. The residents of the small New England town had their own ways of reminding her. Rude questions about her heritage. Mocking her accent or pulling their eyes into slants with their fingers. Certain moments made Fen want to buy the first ticket home, and damn the work she did here, the art she made, the community she had built for and with these people. But an artist sees the world not as it is. She sees its potential. And so, when the brash couple on the morning tour that day had asked whether anyone *local* might be available as their guide instead, Fen merely smiled, and complimented the lovely tulip brooch pinned to the woman's lapel. *Intention.*

The raccoon scampered off into the bushes, and Fen fished through her purse for her car keys, coming up with nothing but loose coins and lip balm. No keys. She sighed, envisioning the green glass cup on the ticket counter where she'd last placed them—and where they almost certainly still lay. One of the drawbacks of the artist's gift: sometimes you're so busy seeing the world as it could be, you forget to keep track of the one you're in. Turning back toward the museum, she bounced up the cement stairs. Just as she was about to slide the brass key back into the deadbolt, she heard another clatter. It was louder this time. Too loud, surely, for a raccoon . . . She spun, squinting into the alleyway.

"Is someone there?" Again, Li Fen took a step forward. Then another.

A man emerged from the darkness.

He moved oddly, like a jerky silent film skipping between stills. As he passed under the light of a streetlamp, she saw that one of his legs was badly twisted, his trouser torn, but he leaned on it like he didn't notice. His back was hunched, as if bearing a great weight.

"Sir, are you all right?" Her pulse quickened—but if this man needed help, she would help him. *Intention.*

He lurched closer, wheezing.

The man was of medium height, and older than Fen—perhaps seventy—with thinning white hair tied back in a ponytail. She recognized him. He'd been in the audience for Mira's kids' final show, the one hosted inside the museum just before they'd left in a hurry. While some of the audience had been ornery, demanding their money back, this man had been easy and polite. He'd even offered to donate extra to help quiet some of the more demanding customers.

"Sir?" Fen stepped down from the stairs and approached him, slowly. A breeze sliced through the night, strangely warm for autumn. "Do you need help? Can I call someone?"

The man stumbled, landing on his twisted leg, and Fen reached out to catch him. His shirt was wet. *Blood.*

A cold fear slipped into Fen's veins, but she pushed it away. This man needed help, fast. She had to stay clearheaded. "I'll

call an ambulance. Can you tell me what happened? Did someone hurt you?"

His head snapped up. Fen gasped. His skin . . . it shifted,
as though a brushfire were writhing beneath. His veins had
risen to the surface, but without the dark blue black of blood—
instead, the man's face was rivered in pure white, as if his capillaries had been hollowed and filled with smoke. White wisps
seeped from between his lips and rose from his eyes like gaseous tears. She stared, transfixed, as he bared his teeth to emit
a low, animal growl. Startled, Fen let go—but before she could
pull away, the man snapped up a hand and seized her by the
throat.

It was a sweet little cup—the green glass where her car keys
waited patiently on the ticket booth counter. She'd gotten it
from her brother, part of a set he'd received on his wedding day.
The handle had cracked off, and he'd been about to toss it away
when Fen had rescued it from the rubbish. It only needed a
new life; for someone to see its potential. Would it miss her, her
little cup, after all this was over? Would someone else adopt it?
Or would it be thrown away? Lost to a trash heap somewhere,
where no one would hold it again? *Like my body will be.* Her
vision blurred from lack of air. Her sight, speckling with green
light. She could almost feel the cold weight of her car keys—as
if in some other dimension, some other version of her life, she
hadn't forgotten them at all, but had plucked them out of the
green cup and pressed them into her hand as she'd made her
way safely back to her Subaru . . . They seemed so solid, so present, the teeth digging into her skin.

No—what she felt was real. The brass museum key, still
grasped between her fingers.

Li Fen choked, panicked, in the man's grip. He squeezed and
her eyes watered as she felt her windpipe bruise. Her hands
fumbled. The key, sharp and glinting in her fist. Then, she
drove the metal teeth into the man's wrist with all the strength
she could conjure. He dropped her with a howl. Li Fen ran.

Down the alley. Up the museum stairs. *Please,* she prayed, shoving the key toward the lock. She was moving too fast, the first two attempts scraping past the opening without catching. *Please. You will open. You* will *open.* Intention . . .

The door swung free and Fen tore inside—slamming it shut behind her.

She stood paralyzed, staring at the locked door. Then, a bang sounded as the man slammed against it from the other side. *Thud. Thud.* Fen clasped her hands over her mouth. Though the building was old, the metal door had been put in only last year. It rattled under his weight but held. *Thud. Thud. Thud.* She wasn't sure how long she stood there, listening to the drumbeat of his body pounding against the door. Eventually, it slowed. *Thud.* A pause. *Thud.* Fen was shaking. She tasted rust—she'd been biting her tongue.

"Are you well, *sudarynya?*"

Fen yelped and spun. Another man stood mere feet away, beside a tall reed organ with pink and mahogany columns. He wore a long wool coat and a brimmed hat, his posture upright but relaxed. He leaned an elbow on the antique instrument— then, noticing the dust, frowned and wiped off his sleeve.

"Who are you?" she demanded, thrusting the key out in front of her. A pitiful weapon.

"Me? I am here to clean."

To clean . . . Fen could have wept with relief. *A janitor.* He must have come in the back entrance after she'd closed up. She hadn't seen him before, but there was a rotating cast of volunteers who kept the museum running, and she never could keep track of them all.

"You seem distressed." His voice was velvety, a calming hum. It didn't sound like the other Vermonters she knew, thick instead with unfamiliar intonation. Another immigrant, like her.

"Y-yes," she croaked, and her hands flew to her throat in pain. Her larynx throbbed from the attack.

"Shhh." He crossed the room to her, seeming almost to glide rather than walk. It was so the opposite of the lurching, stilted movements of the man outside that she couldn't help but feel comforted by the contrast alone. "You have had a fright, no?"

Fen nodded. The man was close enough now to see the lines in his face—or rather, the lack thereof. His skin was smooth and glowing, as if warmed from within. He had an easy smile. The sort of smile you could trust. Already, she felt the adrenaline hush inside her. Outside, the thudding had stopped. Safe. She was safe. Thank goodness this man was here.

"T-there was a m—" Fen gagged, crumpling into a wounded cough. The bruises must be swelling. She could barely breathe.

"Quiet now, *mechtatel'nitsa*. Save your voice."

The man put a hand on her back and she focused on his warmth. *See, even in darkness, there are kind people. For every one who seeks harm, there's one who seeks good. Believe in goodness, and the good will come.*

Intention.

Another cough jolted through her.

"Here." The man's free hand slipped into his coat, reappearing with a small blue bottle. It was made of frosted glass, like her little green cup. He unstopped the cork with a thumb, and a strange perfume lifted from the vial. Hay and dust, like the farms from back home in late summer. And something else beneath it . . . a sharp, ashen stench, like burning hair. Fen's stomach turned, and she swallowed to settle it, bursting into another fit of coughs when she did.

"Drink." The man lifted the bottle to her lips, and she sipped gratefully, lifting a hand to steady it. Her fingers traced a raised shape on the bottle, some insignia. She focused on the gentle grooves. Symmetry, like spread wings. The aching in her windpipe calmed. But her heart—her heart galloped loose from its stirrup, bolting.

The room went white.

Thud. Thud. Thud. A knocking.

He'd returned. The man from outside. He would come. He would kill her.

Smoke crawled from her stomach up her spine as if she were

a staircase. One step. Then another. Her shoulders buckled with fear. A shifting pressure settled there, as firm as if someone were crouched on her back.

She would never see her home again. Never see her brother and his wife and their new grandchild. She would never take her keys from the little green cup and feel the engine rev, never leave this place, not now, not ever again.

She looked up at the man in the wool coat. He seemed to glow like a low moon, golden light upon his skin. A beacon in the dark. Safety. He reached down. She took his hand.

"Come."

Thud. Thud. Thud. Thud.

She stood and the man led her. They crossed the antechamber and ducked through the halls. Past towering pipes trembling with silence. Along rows of dead melodeons and upright pump organs. All Fen could see was fog, hazy and blanched, creeping in from every corner, every wall. She clasped the hand as if it were a rope dangled over a cliff's edge. A lifeline. They reached the second showroom, dark save for the white smoke tendriling before Fen's eyes. Another scent filled the air—different from the bottle's burnt rot. Different from the pinched smell of fear. Sweet and pungent. She squeezed the man tighter, glancing down for reassurance—and a wail boiled in her throat. She was clasping a hand, yes—but beyond the wrist, where the hem of the coat sleeve should have been, was only roiling smoke, elongating. The pale arm went on and on. It snaked through the room, stretching ten, twenty feet long, and vanished back around the far corner from where they'd come, out of sight. Refracted in the fumes, she could somehow see its continuation even around the bend, stretching farther, farther, until at last it reached the man's body all the way back at the entryway door. He smiled. Turned the latch. *Thud thud. Thud thud.* The door creaked open and the man outside staggered through. A gaunt creature crouched on the man's back, the same color as the terrible arm—and at once, Li Fen felt the weight on her own shoulders intensify. Knees jabbed into her back. She moaned. The hand holding hers let go—leaving something solid in its wake.

There was a box of matches in her palm. Red and worn at the edges, foreign black lettering inked over the back. A hot breeze pressed over her shoulder, lifting the room's strange scent into the air—gasoline. Liquid pooled around her feet, thick and shimmering.

"I know it was here," a tilted voice hissed in her ear. (Was someone behind her? Or had the voice scurried up the length of the long arm?) "The monstrosity. I know you saw it, helped it. But do not worry. Soon, no one will be left to remember. You will be absolved."

Down the hall, she heard the smoke-veined attacker from outside stumbling close, his twisted leg cracking beneath the weight of the shadow on his back.

She closed her eyes. She would free herself. She would not be taken by a rabid stranger. She would write her own story. Fen's fingers fumbled over the matchbook, flipping it open. She ripped a match free and dragged it against the striker. Once. Twice. On the third scrape, it caught. The flame crackled awake.

Intention.

Li Fen let the match fall.

CHAPTER TWENTY

A PUNK HOUSE IN Amherst where they were paid fifty crumpled dollars and a bag of weed. Three town libraries and a private elementary school on the Cape. An arts collective built into an abandoned zipper factory in central Connecticut, slated for demolition. A birthday party for a wealthy professor in his manicured garden. Show after show, town after town, until they all began to blend together.

It had been three and a half weeks since their opening show in Brattleboro, and each day brought a new, eager audience. Every night, the stage flickered with the glow of pink paper lanterns, the fragrance of buttered popcorn and wet velvet, gathered voices floating up like bells.

Bellatine crouched on one knee on the stage, cutting through a stack of plywood with a handsaw. Normally, she'd use the circular saw, quick and electric, but she wanted to feel her body working. Her arm strained as it heaved the teeth back and forth, back and forth, her calloused hands mercifully mute against the handle.

Since waking the Girl with No Face, it had taken twice the work it normally did for Bellatine to keep her hands under control. If she took her focus off them for even a moment, she could feel the Embering begin to pop up like a demonic game of whack-a-mole. The lapse had reminded her body of what it was capable—but she would force it into forgetting again. She'd done it before. Here, in a public park outside Newark, at least the air was cool enough to bite. Foliage sifted down all around her as maples relinquished their color. Leaves fell like one thousand small, flaming hands.

A ribbon of giggles and lavender smoke wafted up from the ground below. Bellatine watched Isaac cavort with two women at least twice his age, who clearly wanted to sleep with him or adopt him or both. He coaxed a silver coin from behind each of their ears, batting his eyelashes like twin cabaret fans. To the right, a conspiracy of children examined an anthill on hands and knees, while their parents half looked on, catching up with neighbors and friends or gawking up and down the house's long legs like Miss America judges.

This was the postshow audience mingle, in full swing. She rarely took part in the ritual. The chatter exhausted her: endless questions of how long they'd been on the road, where they were coming from or going toward, minutiae about the house or the play or the little wood-and-fabric puppets. Well intentioned, all, but it left Bellatine feeling like a vampire had tapped and drained her into a cocktail shaker. Leave the schmoozing to her brother.

"Right back to work, huh?"

Bellatine sighed. Looked like she wouldn't be escaping the Inquisition after all.

The young man who'd called to her from below had to crane his neck up to do so, holding one hand to his forehead to squint against the sun. Bellatine assessed his trucker cap and denim jacket, the blond beard trimmed close to the sharp of his chin. From her heightened angle, she could peek at the edge of his clavicle under the collar of his shirt.

"Back to work?" he repeated, as if she hadn't heard him.

Already regretting it, Bellatine trilled a command at Thistlefoot to lower her down until the man's eye level hit her shoes.

"Hey there," she acknowledged, keeping one eye on her work.

"Great show, really awesome stuff."

"Thanks for coming."

"Planning a funeral for a family of elves?" the guy asked, nodding at one of the seven small, lidless boxes Bellatine had assembled.

"You caught me."

"I've heard they prefer a Viking burial."

He waited for a laugh. He didn't get one.

"What are they for?"

Bellatine yanked the saw free and wiped sweat from her forehead with the back of her wrist.

"There's a bin to hold each puppet," she explained. "They'll be affixed to the stage with Velcro where each puppet is pre-set. That way, if our stage moves or bucks during a performance, the puppets stay in place. But with the Velcro, we can remove the boxes for a flat stage when not in use."

The man contemplated this. "Why not Velcro the puppets to the floor directly?"

"Too easy."

In reality, she'd thought of that already, but it would have meant holding the puppets to sew the Velcro on. And that wasn't an option.

"Anyway, I just wanted to say thanks for a great show. And I don't know when you're hitting the road again, but if you want something to do later, there's this party in a warehouse off Montrose. It's sci-fi themed, but you don't need a costume. You should come." The man fidgeted with the hem of his sleeve.

Bellatine imagined herself in a tinfoil crown, low lights strobing over a cement dance floor. She saw herself melting into a bevy of strangers, saw herself closing her eyes, jumping to the throb of the bass. Drinking mysterious green punch from a plastic bowl. Pressing against this man, whose name she didn't even know, skin hot through the thin fabric of his shirt. She saw her hair whipping into the air as the music thrashed louder, louder. Saw herself dancing.

Then, her hands spiked with black heat, and she jolted back into the sunlit park.

"Can't tonight. But thanks."

The wood handle of the saw charred in her hand. She pushed the Embering down, down, down.

She turned, opened the front door, and strode into the house. As soon as the door closed behind her, she punched a hole into the plaster wall.

Bellatine wasn't sure how long she lay faceup on her bed, staring at the ceiling. At the organ factory show, she'd been so distracted by her anger at Isaac that she'd let him become a priority. Petty annoyance. It had led to disaster. The Embering was wily—and if it saw a gap to fill, a moment when her head was turned, it would take over. Her attention *had* to stay on keeping the Embering at bay. Always. Carrie and Aiden used to tease her for her stoicism, for holding them at arm's length. But they had no idea. The few instances when she'd almost slipped up around them, she'd managed to snuff it out just in time. If they'd seen her . . . really seen her? There would have been no more teasing. No more anything. They wouldn't have stayed by her side at all.

Bellatine sat up. Lying down was useless. She should give her hands something to do. Leaving the bed, she climbed up the ladder to the loft where she'd stored her spare tools. Being inside Thistlefoot transformed the sting into a faraway ache, like a fading burn balmed by aloe. But even long after her hands went numb, even after she heard Isaac yip at the house to move and she felt the sailing-ship sway of Thistlefoot's footsteps southward, the anger remained.

In the loft, the mural on the ceiling stared at her. Those four figures—the house, the lion, the crow, the hare—dancing while vines ravaged an army of soldiers. Bellatine couldn't help but envy the dancers. Their joy, undiluted and unbridled, even in the midst of chaos. Maybe they'd even been the chaos' cause . . . Would she ever be able to loosen like that, to revel and hoot and dance and not care what madness unraveled around her? Ever be able to let her attention wander, even for a moment, from her curse? She was tired of tamping herself down. Tired of all of it.

"Hey."

Bellatine startled, thumping her head on a ceiling beam. Isaac stood at the base of the ladder, a cup of coffee in hand. He'd grown paler with each day they'd been on the road, and unsteady on his feet. What would you call legged-house-induced nausea? Not seasick or airsick or motion sick . . . Homesick? Liquid sloshed over the mug's rim.

"And I thought I was the dramatic one." He glanced back at the hole she'd pounded into the wall.

"How were your adoring fans?" she asked, descending.

Isaac held up a twenty-dollar bill. "Friendly."

"So you stole that."

"I don't steal. I trade."

Bellatine scoffed. "One of these days, you'll *trade* yourself right into prison."

She bit her cheek to keep from saying more. She had to stop blaming Isaac. After all, hadn't it been blame and the anger alongside it that had caused her Embering to relapse? She couldn't *afford* to blame him anymore. Not for dragging her on this trip—she'd agreed to that herself. Not even for leaving. Not for the fact that he'd almost certainly leave again. Motion was in his nature. To be angry with him for disappearing would be like punishing a goose for migrating. It was her own foolishness that made her cringe, looking back. Naïveté. Without Isaac's flight, back when they were young, she never would have learned the most important truth about the world: you should only ever rely on yourself. If you put too much of your own well-being in anyone else's hands? Well, you forfeit your right to complain about loss of control.

She was glad Isaac never asked her if she needed help. She would have said no.

"Let's spend it at a diner tonight," Isaac said, still brandishing the twenty dollars. "This is Jersey, after all."

Bellatine hesitated. But her stomach was growling at the thought of a big plate of fries and a burger in a chrome truckstop diner. That was all she wanted. Normal stuff, cheap greasy food, a jukebox of eighties pop songs. And there, in the house, her hands gone entirely quiet, she could imagine it: being normal. That's the gift the house could give her—as long as she never strayed far from it, never left it for long. Not now. Not tomorrow. Not for the rest of her life.

There's a scene in *The Drowning Fool* where the Fool goes to the Tailor. He wants a new shirt made of fine cream-colored linen and the brightest, strongest thread and round blue buttons. He wants to look like a Puppet of Importance, and a new shirt with these attributes should do just the trick.

The Tailor obliges. Behind the stage curtain, Rigs gives a *zip, zip, zip* on a kazoo and Strings lifts the Tailor's tiny foot up and down, up and down on a tiny pedal. The tiny sewing machine rattles, with buttons made from bottle caps squeaking and clicking and glinting with motion until the shirt is done.

When the Fool puts on his new shirt, the Fool is outraged. *There are four very large holes in this shirt!* the Fool insists.

The Tailor is highly embarrassed, for he prides himself on his detail and craftsmanship and the flawless fabrics with which he makes his clothes. He apologizes, and asks the Fool to point out the holes, and he'll fix them. *You won't even need to take off the shirt,* he tells the Fool, *I'll mend it where you stand.*

Here! And here! And here and here, too! cries the Fool.

But, sir, says the Tailor, *those are—*

Sew them up, or I'll tell everyone I know never to patronize this shop again! the Fool insists. He feels very commanding saying this, and very much like a Puppet of Importance indeed.

The Tailor sews. It must be working, the Fool thinks, because the more the Tailor sews, the more important the Fool feels.

When the Tailor finishes sewing, the shirt has no holes at all. No hole at the head. No two holes at the arms. No hole at the waist. And the Fool has been sewn inside.

CHAPTER TWENTY-ONE

"HERE Y'ARE, ONE CHEESEBURGER for the lady, and one curly fries with a glass of merlot for you."

The waitress plunked two plates down onto paper place mats, along with a red wine filled audaciously to the brim. Bellatine cast a skeptical glance at Isaac's meal. He raised his glass in toast.

"May there always be wine, may there always be smokes, may the jesters be kings and the kings become jokes."

"Say, you come up with that? I like that," the waitress said, hand cocked on her hip.

Isaac made a few quick alterations to his posture. He furrowed his brow to add wrinkles and drooped the left side of his lip, a remnant of a bygone stroke. Why not.

"My ol' man," he said, "used to say that before a drink. 'Course, he wasn't no king, and the bottle made a joke of him in the end. Pappy was a long hauler, like me."

Already, he felt his headache ease. Their reflections gleamed in the chrome by the rotating pie case. Tiny looked like a child in her overalls, feet barely reaching the floor below the red vinyl diner stools.

"This one—" He turned to Bellatine. "What you say your name was again, kid? Ah, never mind, don't tell me." He turned back to the waitress. "Picked her up at the on-ramp to 95. Been seeing more and more of these runaways lately. Says she's going to a place called Swallow's Perch, you know how to get there?"

The waitress frowned. "Never heard of it. But you should call your folks, little lady," she said to Bellatine. "They're probably worried about you." She skittered away to attend to other patrons.

"Why do you do that?" Bellatine asked him.

"Do what?"

"You're a compulsive liar."

He popped a fry into his mouth, chasing it with a gulp of wine. "We're all acting, all the time. We have different selves for different people, different circumstances. You play one part for me, another part for your friends back north, another for Mira and Dad, and another altogether when you're alone."

"I don't think so. I'm just me."

"Even now—your posture, your attitude, the volume of your voice, it's all tailored for a public restaurant with certain etiquette. The only difference between you and me is that I'm willing to have a little fun."

"Whatever." Bellatine tucked into her burger. She bit into the meat like a tiger at a kill, barely swallowing before ripping off more. He was glad to see her hungry. Isaac had hardly seen her eat in the two weeks since Brattleboro, save for a handful of potato chips here and there.

His phone vibrated on the counter where he'd stacked it atop his near-empty billfold and a dwindling booklet of rolling papers. It buzzed twice. Three times.

"You gonna get that?"

He snapped it up without answering and turned off the ringer, a glimpse at the external screen confirming his assumption: Shona. He slipped the phone away, into his pocket.

"Who was that?" Bellatine asked, poaching a curly fry off his plate.

"Nobody. A guy who runs one of the theaters we're playing at in Atlanta next month. I'll call him later."

"You got fifty cents?" There was ketchup smeared on her chin.

"What for?"

"Gambling debts."

"Now you're getting it. What's your backstory—were you raised by Vegas card counters? Did you gamble the family farm away trying to save your ailing mother?"

She heaved a sigh, unamused.

Isaac fished two quarters from his pocket. "Don't spend it all at once."

Bellatine hopped down from her stool and headed for the jukebox. She *was* acting. And more than normal. He could see it. Even when she was teasing him, or stealing fries off his plate, or, like now, flipping through the jukebox offerings, she wasn't relaxed. She was playing at nonchalance. Her shoulders remained knit close to her ears, her jaw tense. And though her face was messy, she'd been careful to keep her hands pristine as she ate, wiping away any stray salt or grease with a napkin as soon as it landed. She was clinging to a life raft.

The jukebox rattled with sound and pink neon.

> *"Once upon a time, I had a little money*
> *Government burglars took it*
> *Long before—"*

A headache speared through Isaac's skull.

"Hey, this isn't the song I picked," Bellatine griped, smacking the side of the jukebox.

> *"Blame it on Cain*
> *Don't blame it on me . . ."*

Isaac chugged the rest of his wine, remembering.

"*Blame it on Cain / Don't blame it on me,*" the bar radio blared. One beer had become three, which became six, which became the whip-poor-will call of morning, and still, Isaac and Benji remained in each other's company. Benji taught Isaac refrains from old ballads—songs in which girls' skeletons are carved into fiddles, and men shapeshift into lions and bars of hot iron and swans. They sang and told jokes well into the afternoon. Come nightfall, they got drunk again on cheap forties and stayed up until another round of dew had soaked through their filthy clothes.

Benji sang for drink money, while Isaac practiced skimming extra from spectators' pockets. He was always careful to leave a flat coin or a playing card or a piece of gum in its place. Soon, he started experimenting with his skills as an actor, using it to make himself seem more trustworthy or less noticeable. Once the boys made enough to call it quits, they'd buy more booze and a pack of cigarettes (Isaac coughing his way through, until he didn't). Then they'd wander off, Isaac almost sober by then, Benji droop-eyed and slurring, to find some dry corner in which to sleep. A few days into this ritual, the pair had reached an unspoken understanding: This was how it would be from now on. The two of them.

Benji had grown up in Arkansas, a ward of the state since he was three years old. Both his parents addicts, he'd come into the world shaking. He didn't blame them. His father had gotten hooked on morphine after losing a leg in Afghanistan. His mother was the latest in a long line of self-medicating schizophrenics, traceable four generations back. Suffering was in Benji's bloodline. As for Benji himself, he'd been shuffled in and out of nineteen foster homes before his fourteenth birthday, and by then, he'd already learned more than any child should about survival.

He taught himself to scrounge up a good, hearty meal from garbage scraps at the Hollard house, where they often forgot to feed him for two or three days at a time. He learned to fight at the McHall house, where he was the smallest of ten kids sharing a single bedroom, and which would be the cause of his removal from at least eight houses thereafter. He learned a little gin helped him sleep through anything—breaking dishes, weeping, piercing screams—at the Pennington house, and how to dress a wound at the Tam house, and how to make no sound at all when it was time to be invisible and immortal and small, like the palmetto bugs who lived in the sink at the Lowell house.

And he learned other things, too, softer things: The Newberg house taught him to read books three times his grade level. The Poole house taught him to whistle so birds would whistle back—chickadees and mourning doves and terns.

And finally, when he'd arrived in the cool, blue room at the Abidi house with his one allotted trash bag full of clothes, his heart had pattered like rain on tin at the sight of a beat-up acoustic guitar, leaned against the wall, waiting for him. When he touched the strings, they spoke as if speaking only to him. The metal made his hands smell like blood, like he was a god of war, an ancient, feral creature.

After that, everything he touched was a song. He wasn't a troubled, abandoned kid chewed up by a ramshackle legal system. He was a tragic hero, a mythic bard traversing an endless stream of unfamiliar lands. He spent hundreds of hours with his headphones on, sounding out the notes of traveler songs and old ballads, voices that sang of hardship and suffering and loneliness, always the loneliness, but in a fashion that sounded romantic somehow. As if to be unwanted and untethered was something beautiful. Something true.

Two months later, when social services came for him yet again, he left his trash bag of clothes behind. He took the guitar instead.

The night after they rehomed him for the twentieth time, he ran away. They surely looked for him, but Benji couldn't help but think they mustn't have looked very hard. That was two years ago. He'd been alone since then. Until now.

"So you've got two types: your highballs and your junk trains. Highballs are fast, top-priority freighters that get where they're going direct. Junk trains, those are what's called *general mani-fest*. Slow, lower priority, for cargo that's not in any hurry."

The two boys were crouched in the Portland freight yard, waiting. Benji had staked out a spot in a grove of trees a good hundred yards from the rail office, and farther still from the bull yard, which swarmed with train cops. But now that they were here, and hidden, and safe as they were going to get, Benji insisted Isaac pick his first train himself, like a lioness letting her cub hunt its first meal.

"So what's better, highball or general whatever?" Isaac asked.

"Junk trains are safer, but you can end up stranded in the middle of the fucking desert for days if they pull over to let a highball take the track. Which could be fine, if you don't have a girl or a gig waiting for you at the other end. But if you have somewhere to be, highballs are more sure to get you there."

The crossing sign flashed red as a freight howled into the lot.

Isaac gave Benji an inquisitive glance as a row of cars halted mere feet away from them. Benji shook his head.

"Coal bins. If there's already coal in there, they might decide to dump it, and we could get sucked in. If it's empty, they might fill it, and we'd get buried."

"So how can I tell what's rideable?"

"All trains are rideable, baby. Some are just more likely to send you riding the Westbound than others."

"Riding the Westbound?"

"Heading to that big rock candy mountain in the sky." He drew a sharp finger across his throat.

"Oh." Isaac gritted his teeth. The train rattled onward, a great dragon whipping its tail through the dust. It screeched against the track, snaking as if the cars went on forever.

"So how can you tell what kind of train it is?" Isaac asked.

"The kind of cars they drag, mostly," Benji said, pulling a half-smoked cigarette from behind his ear. "Highballs have a few junk cars, but are mostly fifty-threes, forty-eights, forties, piggybacks, which is like a semitruck trailer on a flatbed. Then you've got pig with a skirt, which is the same, but with flaps on the sides. Autoracks, double-stacks, a few suicides . . ."

"Suicides?"

"They're like numbered cars, but suicides don't have floors. Just open-bottomed to the tracks."

"Got it. So also not ideal."

"Correct. Anyway, junk trains have your lumber racks, your grainers, which carry sand or dry concrete or any other dry good that can flow, then there's oil tankers, gondolas, which are basically big buckets, and of course, good ol' fashioned box-cars. Junk trains never have piggybacks, autoracks, or double-stacks."

An SUV drove by, and Benji yanked Isaac flat onto the ground. Fear spiked into Isaac's throat.

"Another lesson—always keep an eye out for SUVs. That's what the bulls drive," Benji whispered. Headlights skimmed through the trees, casting shuddering shadows over the two hidden boys. Sweat gathered at the base of Isaac's spine and the train howled, loud enough that Isaac could feel it in the back of his throat. By the time they were in the clear, the end of the train was in sight. It heaved to a stop.

Isaac's seeking eyes flicked over car after car. He wanted to pick right. He wanted to show Benji that it hadn't been a mistake to bring him along, that he could be a quick study, an asset. The sleepy train croaked, settling into its weight.

"How about that one?" Isaac pointed to a car shaped like a Campbell's Soup can.

Benji grinned, "Fresh, you've found us a grainer Cadillac."

"Is that . . . good?"

"That, baby boy, is the luxury dream ride of hobos every-where. No riding dirty faced for us tonight. The perfect car." He clapped Isaac on the back, and Isaac couldn't help but feel a twinge of pride.

Slinging his guitar and pack over his shoulder, Benji trilled a wren call through his teeth. Hubcap pounced out from the underbrush, and Benji scooped her under one arm.

"Fresh's first train," he cooed at Isaac. "You ready to get the fuck out of Oregon?"

"Tally," Isaac confirmed, trying out the word he'd read in a book about Depression-era hobos and their rail slang. It tasted good and strong on his tongue. Benji may as well have sewn wings onto Isaac's back, for all the freedom he felt.

They slinked through waves of tall grass to the grainer.

"First, one last debt to pay," said Benji. He crouched to his knees, and Isaac's breath went jagged as his new friend knelt under the train's belly. The steel track shimmered with heat as the boy laid a row of coins onto the rail, pressed pennies not yet born.

"Ride fare," he said, standing back up. "But don't you ever fucking do what I just did. I'm immortal. You're not. Not yet."

"But you won't be here to pick 'em back up after pressing," Isaac said, already mourning the loss of the precious, sacrificed coins.

Benji cast an eye at the summer-sick moon. "You always meet twice, Fresh. Every person, you'll see again one day. Every inch of earth, you'll step on later. Every coin comes back around. Maybe in the next year, maybe the next life."

A ladder seemed to manifest out of the darkness, hovering just above them. The great train groaned, a Jurassic beast.

"After you." Benji bowed.

Isaac hoisted himself onto the ladder. Below him, Benji fol-lowed one-handed, holding Hubcap with the other.

At the top, they found themselves on a small porch, shielded from the wind. The cat scampered out of sight.

"She knows these rigs better than I do. Probably hunting for the foxhole, spoiled little shit," Benji said.

The train grunted back to life and began to chug forward, picking up speed. Isaac peered down toward the earth. The ground seemed impossibly far away, and it moved like water as the train pulled out from the yard. He was overcome with the stink of oil, of metal, the screeching of the freight against the track, the splitting howl of the train's whistle. They'd entered a new world.

Benji fished a rattle can of blue paint from his pack. He shook it, then sprayed a figure eight onto the steel wall, each loop containing one of his initials.

"That your tag?" Isaac asked.

Benji nodded at his handiwork. "Hourglass. Infinity. And a whole load of BS—that's me." He tossed the can to Isaac.

Before he'd taken time to think, his arm was already moving, the paint falling in sheets onto the wall. A lantern, with a simple ghost inside.

Benji studied the mark. "You believe in ghosts, Fresh?"

Isaac shrugged. "Depends on your definition of a ghost."

"Well, what would you call *me*?"

"An angel." Isaac grinned, nudging Benji with an elbow.

Benji smiled back. "Same thing, really. You'll feel it soon. You'll move from one town to another to another, barely leaving a trace. People will remember only the essence of you, not your name, or your face fully—you'll be mist, a flash of light, someone they won't be sure was ever there at all. Maybe you'll leave them humming a song they don't recall learning. Maybe a splash of blood in the sink, or an eyelash on a pillowcase. And before you know it, you'll realize you've become more ghost than human. Every town a wall you walk right through."

The train erupted in a mournful moan.

"Why'd you choose it?" Benji asked, nodding at the spray-painted ghost caged in the lantern.

"A little something from home," Isaac said.

The train gained speed.

"Wherever you draw that, baby—that *is* your home."

Behind them, the city fell away.

The song crooned as the jukebox shuddered with electric notes. Isaac's sharp knees shook under the table. He was glad Bellatine's back was still turned as she fiddled with the croaking machine. *It's just a song,* he urged himself. *Nothing's changed.* Iced coconut cakes boasting frosty sugar peaks still spun in the carousel display. The counter was still littered with cumulous arrays of crumpled napkins. Salt and pepper shakers remained steadfast knights, guarding plastic jelly pods. *And I'm still here, too, Fresh,* a familiar voice whistled in his ear. The sharp scratching of claws within Isaac's heart began to dig deep. *Go.*

Isaac floated out of the diner booth and across the restaurant, sliding through the glass doors toward the parking lot. The jukebox's song leaked through the walls. He rubbed his temples, trying to stave off the headache he knew was coming. Each thud of a foot on the pavement, an affirmation that he was still moving, still living, still capable of placing distance between himself and all that sought to follow him.

At a gas station across the street, Isaac bought a packet of tobacco and a new sleeve of rolling papers. Some glittery pop number played over the radio, and he let it stitch him back together like the Tailor's thread before returning outside. He'd been holding his breath, he realized. He exhaled with a rasp. Across the way, Thistlefoot wobbled on one leg, the other trying to scratch at its ankle, the position making it look clownishly like an amateur yogi. *Take a breath, baby, take a breath.* He pushed the past away.

Bellatine rounded the corner at a sprint. Her eyes flashed between him and the house with visible relief.

"Where the hell are you going?" she panted.

"Stepped out for a smoke," Isaac lied, as if his feet weren't bidding him even now to run and keep on running.

"I thought . . ." She hesitated. "Never mind."

The waitress huffed after them, waiving their bill. "Nice try, you two, but that grub ain't coming out of my paycheck today. Cough it up."

"Eat and run, Tiny? I'm impressed."

"H-hold on, we'll pay," Bellatine stuttered. "Isaac, you got that twenty bucks?"

He held up the fresh sleeve of tobacco. "Sorry, darlin', just spent the bulk of it. Can you get this one?"

Bellatine thrummed with anger and fished out her wallet. "Can you take card?"

The waitress harrumphed. "I suppose you'll want to tip in well-wishes, too." She relented, accepting Tiny's debit card and running it through a handheld reader. The machine hummed, spitting out a paper ribbon.

"I apologize. I wasn't leaving, just stepping out, swear," Tiny entreated as she signed the receipt. "Really, I'm not that kind of person."

She wants to prove she's nothing like you, Benji's voice clacked inside his head.

Thistlefoot's feathers bristled in impatience. The waitress turned on her heel, returning to the gleaming restaurant.

"Come on," Isaac said, already heading for the ladder. "Let's go."

But Bellatine didn't follow. She had paused to check her phone. Now she stood frozen, a hand over her mouth. Isaac stalled.

"What?"

His sister didn't answer, eyes fixed on the screen.

"*What?*"

"There was a fire," she muttered, "at the Estey factory."

"Well damn, we got out of dodge just in time, eh? Last thing we need is to get wrapped up in some small-town arson investiga—"

"Isaac." Her voice, hollow as a well.

His stomach dropped. "What is it?"

"Fen is dead."

The cheerful, floral-clad woman padded barefoot through Isaac's memory. She was holding an apple. Cracked it in half with her hands. Took a bite. Smiled.

"Who . . . who told you that?"

"Mom just texted me."

"Where did *she* hear it? Maybe you misunderstood. She wouldn't *text* you something like that, she'd *call*. You can't have all the informa—"

"*Isaac*," Bellatine breathed. "I'm telling you what I know. And it says here that there was a fire, and Li Fen passed away."

"I . . ." He trailed off.

Bellatine sighed, brow knit. "Yeah."

For a moment, Isaac recalled the flicker of smoke rising from the restrained woman in the black school bus. *She's burning,* he'd said when Shona had asked him what he saw. He shook his head to banish the thought—pushing the worry of a connection far into a padded lockbox, too deep to touch.

Isaac whistled between his teeth and Thistlefoot turned.

"Let's go," he said. "Nightfall's coming on soon."

They ascended the ladder in silence.

A day's drive north, Shona crouched in the back of her bus and pressed her ear to a voicemail. *"Estaré bien, mija,"* her father's voice promised. *"The guards say they'll let me go home to you soon."* Her lips moved in unconscious echo, mirroring the recording she'd listened to a hundred times before. She tried not to think of the cold cement floor of the detention center, the chain-link cages. Another sort of haunting.

Awake in his bunk, Rummy couldn't stop thinking about the smokefed. Their panic bubbled in his body like tar. He could feel their hatred and their lack. Their desperate reaching, staticky with fear. The shadows heavy on their backs. And he could feel the people they had been. Sweethearts and brothers and daughters—people who loved, who were loved. *You're such an empathetic child,* his aunties had always told him. *It's very sweet, the way you seem to feel what other people feel, as if it were happening to you.* Sometimes it didn't feel sweet. Sometimes bearing other people's hearts felt less like a kindness and more like a poltergeist.

Sparrow dreamt of home. Of church ladies in their finest Sunday hats, frothing with satin carnations and mesh veils specked with faux pearls. The whole congregation singing together, *Oh! What a salvation is this / That Christ liveth in me,* with Miss Bess on piano. The pews were soft and glossy in the dream, and the congregation smiled at Sparrow, and called Sparrow by name, this name, the one Sparrow chose. In the dream church, Sparrow was wearing a tuxedo tailcoat and top hat with a silk dress underneath, just like they had to the prom, but this time, their mother wasn't crying. *So, praise the Christ of truth and grace / His Spirit dwelleth in me.* Home as it could have been—no more than a phantom.

Bellatine washed her hands in a tin basin as Thistlefoot carried her, scrubbing every speck of dirt from under her nails as if water could rinse off memory.

Isaac couldn't get the jukebox's song out of his head. It played on loop, Benji humming along as they swayed at the bar, the boys' cheeks pink with liquor.

Li Fen's bones sifted with the ash of a dozen antique organs. Wind sang over the metal pipes, lofting her into the air.

All across America, people shut their eyes, hoping their recollections might vanish upon the next glance. When they opened them, the specters remained. The Longshadow Man raised a glass.

It is impossible to take a step without walking through a ghost. Every memory creates one. Every version of ourselves leaves a shadow self behind. Every regret and every promise and every touch of skin against skin. The living houses of San

Francisco know this—arms gripping the hem of the San Andreas Fault since 1906. The death fields around Wounded Knee know this, where every blade of grass and weed and briar is poison to the touch. The Tallahatchie River knows, gone bone dry the day Emmett Till was pulled from the waters. The Triangle Shirtwaist Factory knows, and Columbine High School knows, and Ford's Theatre knows—with their leviathan eyes, their mouths that lick familiar air and sigh. The land, inch by inch, brick by brick, is alive with remembering.

Across an ocean and one hundred years away, an army awaits its orders. It undulates like a single mass, but if you look closely, you can see it is made of men, living men, each of whom has a name and a story, each of whom has his own ghosts following him. When these men crest the hill toward Gedenkrovka, they become ghostmakers. In the barrel of each gun, a haunting waiting to fly.

CHAPTER TWENTY-TWO

ALL DAY, LITTLE ILLA plays in the town square, and all night, Baba Yaga yanks out the knots in her daughter's hair with a bone comb. Though her scalp bleeds with the pulling, Illa never cries.

"You must never allow a knot in your hair, bubbala, for that is how men will try to control you. Think how sailors tie knots to leash the wind. Think how tailors at their wool tie knots to keep the fabric bound. Men, they tie knots into everything they wish to tame."

"I *know*, Mama." Illa sighs, and glares at baby Malka from the corner of her eye. "Maybe I'll tie *you* into a knot and then you'll have to be my servant and do whatever I say," she tells her sister. She grins her wolf's grin. Malka hiccups.

Baba Yaga collects the knots she pulls from Illa's hair and weaves them into a rope. Every night after combing, she adds more to the rope until it grows long enough to wrap around her middle five times over.

"If a man ever seeks to tie you, you can hang him with this,"

Baba Yaga says, placing the rope into a wooden box. They stow the box on the shelf in the kitchen for safekeeping.

As you may imagine, the Yaga family are the subject of much local whispering. For one, there are no men. With no scholar in yeshiva to study the Talmud, surely it must be a lesser home, further from God. With no papa, surely Baba Yaga's daughters were born in disgrace. Plus, whenever Baba Yaga gives tzedakah, her offerings of charity tend to be more trouble than good: a loaned goat whose milk is pink with blood, or a shawl so rough it leaves blisters. At market, her neighbors are polite and make their business dealings quickly, and that is that. Baba Yaga, she prefers being disliked. It means people leave her and her daughters be. They fend for their own. It is safer this way. A little loneliness? They can handle loneliness. Now death, that's a tsuris. None of them lie in ditches like the Miroshniks' son, accused of colluding with the Bolsheviks, or dangle from trees like skinny Zurach Vasserman after refusing to cobble a Cossack's boots. Reb Haim has not etched Baba Yaga and her daughters' names into a headstone yet. Yes, it is better to be alone.

Baby Malka has no hair, save for thin milkweed wisps, nor teeth, nor useful skills. Baba Yaga feeds her on custard and goat cream and spoonfuls of plump weevils.

"When you are older, you will be fat and strong and unknottable," she whispers, rocking the child against one knee. She dreams of her daughters taking lovers to the forest and leaving them there. She dreams of her daughters reaching fearlessly down a wolverine's throat to cut out its liver for supper. She dreams of the day her daughters will bury her. She dreams of them singing songs so sad that Denikin's soldiers weep and wedge their rifle barrels beneath their own chins, kneeling in the tall grasses. So many beautiful, terrible, wonderful things her daughters will do.

CHAPTER TWENTY-THREE

COME MIDNIGHT, THE THISTLEFOOT Traveling Theater had made it another two hundred miles south. What would have taken under four hours driving took closer to ten in the lumbering house. It galumphed slowly, a big rig chugging step by step. The house never seemed to get tired, but it did get distracted. More than once it deviated from the path to chase down a stray dog or ogle at a flashing billboard. It liked yellow things—sunflower fields and crossing signs, goldenrod sports cars with roll-back rooftops. How it could even *see* the color yellow was beyond Bellatine, but despite her instinct to wrench back floorboards and hunt for clockwork, she knew that some questions might simply not have answers.

And with other questions, she wasn't sure she wanted an answer. *Whatever happened here before,* she told herself, *it doesn't matter. This house and I—we belong to each other now.* Even so, she couldn't help but fixate on the kitchen walls, where singe marks still hid beneath coats of fresh mint-green paint. *Burns . . . fire . . . Li Fen.* A shock of sadness passed through her like electricity.

"Walmart or junkyard?" Bellatine asked Isaac from her perch on the sod roof, where she was pulling radishes for pickling. He was lounging on the stage, wrapped in one of their twice-great-grandmother's floral shawls and shuffling a pack of cards. It was the nightly question before bedding down. Either they parked in a superstore lot, serenaded by security's footsteps and rattling carts, or they settled into some overgrown dump.

"We're near Baltimore, yeah?" Isaac asked.

"Mm-hmm."

Her brother grinned. "I'll do you one better."

The curling wrought iron gate was padlocked when they arrived, but Isaac urged the house around back instead, to a rock wall topped with chain-link. Thistlefoot stepped over it like it was nothing more than a fallen log. At first, Bellatine thought they'd entered into an arboretum or even a private estate—so manicured were the shrubs and gardens. Then the moon slid out from behind a cloud, revealing hundreds of polished stones.

A cemetery. It stretched on as far as Bellatine could see, webs of frost turning the tombstones into gems with a million tiny, glinting facets. Thistlefoot followed a meandering loop of concrete paths, wide enough for a truck to heave through. Mausoleums punctuating either side of the trail seemed to bow to them as they passed. Graves jutted from the earth in jagged, haphazard rows with none of Arlington's military precision, merely an hour's drive south. Stones tilted forward or back, some cracked at the base and half swallowed by turf. Some were arranged not in lines, but in spiraling rings like gothic crop circles. They passed a stone dog, asleep on a stone pillow. A granite goblet overflowing with chiseled water. A life-sized girl wrought in cold white rock, her arms eternally outstretched. One stone appeared to have a full-sized Ouija board carved into the face. Another, which Isaac pointed to as they passed, bore the name of John Wilkes Booth.

He couldn't possibly think they were *sleeping* here? Especially after the macabre news about Li Fen . . .

Isaac must have sensed her hesitation. "Scared?" he asked with a wink.

"No," she insisted, her voice pricking up higher than she would have liked.

"Don't worry, ghosts love me. We'll all be playing Texas hold 'em together before the night's out."

Ghosts. Bellatine would have traded her left leg to have ghosts be the height of her worries. What a luxury, to fear something bodiless, only memory and fog. An enemy you couldn't touch. Who couldn't touch you. She huffed out a puff of visible breath, which crystallized in the frigid air.

All around, Bellatine could feel the gravestones pulsate. Even though she couldn't see them all, shrouded in wild grapevines or blocked by obelisks, she could *sense* them. Statues carved in the shapes of lost loves, of the Virgin Mary, of buckled, weeping angels. Her hands yearned to brush a thumb over their lips, their eyelids, to feel their lashes flutter open. Why must her hands always seek to betray her? Her fingertips chattered with one another, harmonizing into terrible songs that called out to the stones, and the stones called back. But worse even than the statues, worse than giant golems waiting to be woken, was what lay beneath.

Thistlefoot lowered itself down with a great heave, tucking its feet invisibly underneath to roost. A few downy feathers puffed loose and wafted through the graveyard on a night breeze.

"We'll be noticed here," Bellatine protested. "They must have a night watch."

"Who's going to come across an entire *building* and think it isn't supposed to be there?" Isaac said. "They'll assume we're a groundskeeper's shack."

Each hair on her body prickled, her skin hot. The night air felt claustrophobic, as if she were pressed up against every lifeless, humanoid shape in the boneyard. A cursed, crowded nightclub where Bellatine was the featured dancer.

Isaac swung a leg over the side of the stage, using a beveled headstone as a stepstool. Hubcap jumped down after, purring. They moved almost identically.

"Where you going?"

Isaac shrugged. "Thought I'd take up a side hustle as a grave robber. I hear Burke and Hare-ing is where the big money is."

"Can't you give a straight answer about *anything*?" Her hands itched. Her temper's fuse burned close to the quick. "What if I need to find you? What if we have to leave fast and I don't know where you are?"

"We won't need to leave, I told you, the night guard won't—"

"Not the night guard, I don't give a shit about the guards."

"What kind of emergency are you anticipating that I can't go on a fucking walk for half an hour? Jesus, kid, drop the leash."

"Leash? We're working together, we're living together; asking you for basic accountability and professionalism isn't a *leash*. I wouldn't have to monitor you like a toddler if you had any dependability at all."

"Bellatine, you sound ridiculous." His voice was completely calm, which infuriated her all the more. It was another manipulation, another performance—if he remained unperturbed while she appeared aggravated, it automatically made her the hysterical one. The unreasonable one.

"Or come along," he offered. "If you can't bear to let me out of your sight, join me, let's walk."

"No."

"No?"

"I can't."

Isaac scoffed. "You can't. Okay, so you won't chaperone me, to protect my *delicate sensibilities*. But I can't go on my own. Charming. You're even more uptight tonight than usual. Is this about Fen? I know it's tragic, Tiny, but—"

"It's not about Fen. I said can't, not won't. Another time, maybe. Not here."

"Not here?" He looked around. "It's the statues, isn't it? God, Tiny, it doesn't matter to me, there's nothing wrong—"

"You don't understand."

"What's she going to do," Isaac said, nodding at the carved-stone girl with the outstretched arms, "wake up and curtsy me to death?"

"This *place*, it's not the *statues*," Bellatine snapped before clamping her mouth shut. But already, she could tell she'd said too much.

Realization spread across Isaac's face in a pale sheet. Another cloud shifted, and moonlight poured an immutable silence between them. For a moment, he only stared.

"The bodies," he said, when he finally spoke. "You can animate the bodies."

Bile rose up in Bellatine's throat. Her hands itched as all through the cemetery, thousands of invisible strings tugged on them to reach, to reach, to touch.

"Of course," Isaac muttered, more to himself than to her. He seemed frenzied now, like a scientist stumbling upon a groundbreaking formula. "Of course. They're shaped like living things but aren't alive—just like dolls. Of course you could wake them up."

Bellatine turned toward the door. She couldn't talk about this. She should go inside, where it was safe, where everything was quiet and nothing was burning and the dead weren't tugging, tugging, tugging.

"Wait!" Isaac called after her. But already, she'd slipped into the house and bolted the door.

She could hear him demanding to be let in. She ignored him. He wanted to go out on his own? Fine. She didn't want him here anymore. The thought of him knowing and looking at her with that knowing as if each glance were an affirmation of her monstrosity—no. He could stay on the porch a while. An hour. A day. Forever.

As always, crossing Thistlefoot's threshold brought instant relief. The swarming sensation abated. But while the house could fix her body, it did nothing for her mind. She peeled off her clothes and shoes, then pulled on a pair of jogging shorts and an oversized T-shirt riddled with holes. The fabric was soft and breezy, and she tried to focus on each cotton fiber against her skin—the opposite of rough-hewn rock. Of jagged bone. She flopped down onto her bed. She sealed her eyes shut.

As soon as she did, her eyelids became a cinema screen. Stone creatures crawled across the void. Angels winged over her like monstrous wasps. And from deep, deep in the ground echoed the sound of scratching.

She'd been fourteen. She was walking back from soccer practice when she'd seen it, tangled on the roadside three blocks from home. No one else around to bear witness but the neon ball she dribbled at the toes of her cleats. The deer—it lay on its side, its legs stiff and straight, its head craned up as if begging. It had been split open by a passing car, half gone to rot. The carcass had bloated at the belly and flies swarmed at the gash like pilgrims dipping bottles into the waters of life. The creature was too still. Stiller even than the rocks, the tarmac— a misplaced stillness, a stillness that shouldn't have been there at all. Bellatine's hands, they'd felt a hunger then, unlike anything she knew how to hold. She set her soccer bag down in the street. *You can help her,* her hands had said. *She wants you to help her. Look how smooth the hide. How kind the slope of the snout, pleading for mercy.* Bellatine's hands had pulled her toward the animal. An awful stink like spilled propane surrounded them. A red stain on the rumble strip. A neck bent wrong. She watched her fingers open like ferns as she reached out to touch the deer's cheek. If she could only stroke the bristled fur, the softened muscle, perhaps she could remind the deer of what it was—an animal, with hungers of its own. Not an object. Not death. Her hands had become a famine, hot with want. If any cars passed by, she hadn't known. She wouldn't have heard them. All she could see, hear, smell, taste was the yearning, strung taut as a bowstring between her and the ruined beast. Bellatine traced the animal's face, from its eye to its lip, small sparks of heat trembling through her. The flesh was too soft, puttied with decay, but she kept pressing. One of her fingers tore a hole in the cheek and fell through, then another. She didn't stop. She pressed her hand in all the way to the teeth. Slid her knuckles into its mouth and drew them out wet. Stroked the throat. The eyes, gone. The eyelids, gone. Still, the yearning. The stillness. Bellatine pressed both palms against the doe's open belly. She kept pressing until she'd sunk in up to her elbows. *Keep reaching,* said her hands, *there is so much more to hold.*

When the animal awoke, she awoke braying. It wasn't the sort of sound an animal was supposed to make. It sounded like a stick being trilled along a chain-link fence, the rattle of something outside our world begging to be let in. Bellatine's hands, they wanted to throw open the gate. They wanted to press through the deer and into somewhere else. The deer lurched and its body fell away from its body. Its flesh opened along invisible seams. Bone pushed out. It tried to move toward Bellatine, but its legs were frozen with rigor mortis, its feet chewed off by scavengers. As it struggled, a rope of something pink and glistening tumbled out of its stomach, and as it did, Bellatine's hands slid out, too.

As soon as the contact broke, Bellatine cannonballed back into herself. Revulsion shot through her. She stumbled back. The deer bucked toward her again, that *tap, tap, tap* croaking in its throat as if saying, *Let me through, let me through, let me through.* Her arms were black-blooded, writhing with larvae. The deer continued screaming.

"Shut up!" Bellatine choked. "Please, shut up!" But it only keened louder.

How long would it go on? The sound was unendurable. She had never applied her Embering to a body before. Were the rules the same? What if it didn't go back to sleep? And even if it did—a quarter hour of convulsion, of death's anguish stretched out second by second—it would be a century of suffering.

The doe's mouth was open, and Bellatine could see down its throat. There was nothing but darkness.

She lifted her foot over its head and brought her leg down hard. Her spiked cleats split through skin and collided with the skull. She stomped down again, bone cracking, then again and again until at last, the doe fell silent.

Bellatine fell back, shuddering with sobs. The horror of her monstrosity descended on her like a coffin lid. She had dragged a soul out of the Other Side—and made it relive the agony of its own violent death. She'd forced it to die twice.

That night, she doused her hands in bleach until they'd blistered.

Thistlefoot shifted on its perch and Bellatine sat up.

She couldn't fall asleep like this.

In the kitchen, she swung open cupboard after cupboard, unsure of what she was even looking for—a distraction, a comfort. She found a half-eaten Snickers bar that she gnawed on as she crouched to root through the herb pantry in the hall. She ran her fingertips over rows of glass jars—basil, bay leaf, nettle. Her twice-great-grandmother had probably picked and dried most of these herself. Some remnants of the woman's hands still lived in those herbs, the stems broken or twisted from her touch, the petals indented from where she'd pressed a thumb. Do our hands ever truly die? Ever truly go quiet? How long does their impact endure, long after the rest of our bodies have vanished?

Reaching deep into the shelf to examine a jarful of what looked like pickled beets, Bellatine's wrist brushed up against something soft. She jumped. A dead mouse? No. Peeking in, she found a cotton handkerchief tied into a small bundle. Pulling it out into the light, she recognized the cloth. It was one of Isaac's bandannas, which perpetually drooped from his back pocket like an old dog's tongue. She unknotted the kerchief and opened it up. *Well, hello there.*

Inside was a plastic vial, roughly the size of a nips bottle. It was shaped a little like a test tube and bore no label, though liquid sloshed within. So Isaac had been hiding liquor back here. Unsurprising. She unscrewed the cap, the scent of burning hay mixed with something dark and pungent spiriting from the bottle's mouth. Bellatine gagged, shutting her eyes against the vapor. How very like her brother, to hoard rotten moonshine he'd probably stolen off a hitchhiker. *Uptight*, was she? Well, fuck him.

"L'chaim," she toasted, raising the little bottle in the air. Then, she pressed the vial to her lips and drank.

The liquid plummeted down her throat, passing her esophagus, sliding below her lungs, her liver, her stomach. It webbed out into her blood. The room swayed with pale light. Her pupils shivered and shrank. Smoke needled through her veins and outward, ascending her spine, where it grew arms. Legs. The smoke crawled atop her shoulders and took its perch. A wild, twisting panic leapt awake in her stomach. Could there have been something wrong with the liquor in the little bottle? No, no, the beverage was fine. It was *her* that was wrong. It had always been her. A burning weight bore down on her shoulders and her fist tightened around the drink. She felt her fingers dig into the plastic. Her hands.

She looked down at them. They were hideous. Gnarled, evil objects. Weapons. As long as she was bound to them, she would never be safe. She would never know rest.

With sudden certainty, Bellatine rose to her feet. She returned to the kitchen. Her hands, they could cause nothing but horror. But she could fix that. She could save herself. The room undulated. Everything was white, even the fire in the ever-burning hearth beside her, the corners of her vision smudging with fog. She dragged her toolbox out from under the sink and unlatched it. On top, a small bow saw, its serrated teeth fuzzy in her wide, smoke-tinged gaze. She seized it and turned toward the kitchen counter. Then, she laid her left hand, still clutching the vial for solidity, onto a cutting board. She lowered the saw, laying it gently against the line where her hand met the arm. With a sharp tug, the skin on the back of her wrist bloomed open like a wet, red mouth. A second pull, and she would hit bone. Over her shoulder, a vaporous form nodded.

"Tiny, come on, let me in!"

Isaac was pounding on the door. *Isaac.* Her heartbeat accelerated. Isaac, he *knew*. He knew what she was, what she could do. He knew the unearthly transgression she was capable of. What if he told someone? What if he used it to blackmail her, to exert even more power over her than he'd already held? Or worst of all, what if he coerced her into laying her hands upon rotting flesh, forcing it to stir? The pounding grew louder.

Bellatine spun toward the door, the saw still tight in her grip. Blood flowed freely from her wrist, but she didn't notice. She'd forgotten the cutting board, her hands, their terrors. Isaac was the threat now. It was Isaac who had to pay, had to be dealt with, so that she could be safe.

She walked to the door and unbolted the latch.

"Look, I wouldn't have brought you here if—" Isaac stopped short when he spied the empty vial in his sister's fist.

She lunged. He sidestepped, quick as a cat, and Bellatine tumbled onto her knees. She sprang back up, then lunged again, the saw hissing past Isaac's left shoulder as he ducked nimbly out of harm's way.

He held up his hands. "Tiny, stop. You're not yourself. Easy, kiddo, take a breath."

She didn't want to hurt her brother, she didn't—but if she stopped, he would kill her. She'd never been more certain of anything. Either he'd end her here on this stage or he'd betray her secret to the world and she'd be ruined. No, this was her only option. Smoke wafted from her wounded wrist. She ran at him.

And at once, she was flying. Isaac had leapt off the stage's edge, landing on the sod with a soft thud and rolling to the side. Bellatine, expecting to collide with a body, met only empty air. Her balance faltered. She fell. Hitting the earth, she felt the wind slam out of her. The bottle and the saw tumbled from her grasp. Isaac was a shadow in the night.

Above her, Thistlefoot swayed, looming, a mutant, a beast. *One last stain,* a voice whispered, its attention fixed on the house. *One last stain before it's clean.* Something wriggled inside her brain. An interloping presence. Bellatine's throat tightened. She wasn't the only person looking out from behind her eyes. Someone—some*thing*—else was there, too, seeing what she saw. She—they—looked upon Thistlefoot and a mirage flickered through the graveyard. A village overlaid atop the landscape like a translucent film. Horse-drawn carts wedged between headstones. Stalls and shops blotted out mausoleums. Other houses appeared. A man walked through the village, tumbleweeds trailing at his heels. He wore a long coat, a peaked cap. Or no, not one man—the figure warped and refracted into smoke, becoming many men in stark military uniforms. There were other people, too, civilians, who scattered as soldiers approached. In the gossamer vision, Thistlefoot looked different—reverted to its state before Bellatine's alterations. Barbed wire, cracking whitewash . . . In the window, she could have sworn she saw three round faces, peering down. The phantom town blinked like a dying light bulb and snuffed out. That's when she heard the ground begin to moan.

Beneath the earth, hundreds of bodies begged for her. *Touch us. Hold us. Wake us.*

Her hands went hot—not the dark coal-black heat she was accustomed to, but a white heat, a bright, blinding scorch. Everything was wrong. The world. The earth. The living and the dead. Her own body. Through her feet, Bellatine could feel the corpses yearning. The weight on her back pulled at her, pressing her toward the soil. She stumbled, slamming into a gravestone. She was being dragged down, her body sinking toward the grave. *No. They can't have me.* She careened backward, tripping over another tombstone. As she fell, she reached out into darkness for whatever life raft would have her—and caught hold of the carved-stone girl.

Her hands sparked. Heat flowed out of her and into the stone. The white pall leaked from her vision, was sucked into her veins, through her arms, into her wrists, and out her hands. The choking tightness lessened. The more her Embering blazed, the more it burned the terror from her body, like a fever driving sickness out. Hotter and hotter, the heaviness lifted, until at last, it was gone.

Someone squeezed Bellatine's hand. The grip was soft and cool. She looked up. A girl in a blue dress kneeled on a stone pedestal. Her blond curls bounced in the moonlight. Their eyes met.

Then, the girl screamed.

CHAPTER TWENTY-FOUR

"WHAT WAS IN THIS BOTTLE?"

Though she'd fired the question at her brother, Bellatine's eyes fell neither on him nor upon the empty plastic vial balanced in the center of the kitchen table, midway between the two siblings. Instead, she watched the pacing girl in the periwinkle Victorian dress. Up the hall. Down the hall. Up the hall. Down the hall.

Tiny's skin, Isaac noted again, lacked even the slightest smokefed remnants, though it had been white swirled, giving off a *Here's Johnny* flair less than an hour prior. She glowed with health as if she'd spent the day primping at a luxury spa with cucumber slices patted over her eyes. If what Rummy had said was true, it should have taken hours for the effects to wear off, with total memory loss. But Bellatine must have been altered for only a few minutes, snapping back as soon as she woke the stone girl. And by the look of shame she wore, Isaac would venture she remembered everything.

Isaac spun his chair around backward and sat splay-legged

with his elbows cocked on the top slat. In his periphery, he, too, could glimpse the girl in the blue dress, who alternated between hacking out sobs and giggling like a kookaburra. She wiggled her fingers open and shut and tugged on her cheeks in the mirror, as she'd been doing without pause ever since they'd brought her inside.

Perched on her own wooden chair, Bellatine squeezed her knees to her chest as if trying to physically press herself together.

"Why did you take—" Isaac started.

"No," Bellatine interrupted. "No. I asked a question. You answer it."

"Questions!" the girl in the blue dress exclaimed in manic glee. "Answers! I can answer a question *and* ask it! With my mouth, and my tongue inside my mouth, and oh, how oddly it feels waggling there, *waggling*, what a strange word, have you *ever—*"

"Shut up," Isaac and Bellatine said in unison.

"Well, isn't that rude! The reverend would never approve," she huffed before returning to her pacing.

"The bottle," Bellatine repeated.

"The *bottle*," stalled Isaac.

"Bahhh-tulll," the girl in blue relished before bursting into tears again.

"Or if you prefer," Bellatine said, "I'll go get the saw and finish what I started."

Isaac knew she meant it as a threat to him, but he couldn't help flicking a glance at her wrist, rag-wrapped, already soaked dark. Blood pooled on the cutting board behind her. She caught him looking and tucked her arm out of sight.

"You owe me an answer," she whispered.

Owe. A debt. The kind that couldn't be bought with pressed nickels.

"Fine. But it's a bit of a tall tale."

Bellatine glared. "Regale me."

He told her about meeting the Longshadow Man in Asylum

Bar. About tipping the drink down his sleeve and overhearing the man ask after Thistlefoot and later, the frothing woman with smoking, vengeful eyes. When the part of the story with the black bus arrived, he flashed over it quickly, mentioning Sparrow's sedative cocktail and Rummy's description of the strange man's patterns. He flicked casually past Shona. Why, he wasn't sure. But that part of the memory felt like his and his alone.

After he finished, Bellatine sat with the information in silence, picking absently at the fabric around her wrist before finally responding.

"We're being tracked," she said. "We're being *tracked*, and you've *known*, and you didn't tell me."

"It wasn't relevant," Isaac asserted.

Bellatine let out a cold laugh. In the far hall, the new girl giggled back, slipping into uncontrolled hiccupping.

He doubled down. "We're miles away. Let him chase us. Let him run himself ragged. It's not our concern."

Isaac had been sought after dozens of times—by cops, by loose-walleted strangers seeking retribution, by girls whose beds he'd slipped from before daybreak. And he'd never been caught. How other people chose to spend their time in his wake had nothing to do with him.

Bellatine met his eye for the first time since they'd returned to the house, the stone girl in tow. He was surprised by the conviction in her stare.

"What if this has something to do with Fen?"

"Come on, Tiny, not everything is connected."

"Did you even *bother* to think that you were putting people in danger? That if we're being followed, wherever we go, our pursuers will go? Everyone at our shows, everyone who hosted us, who invited us into their communities—we've placed them right in harm's way. And *you*, you put them, put *me*, in that position without knowledge or consent."

He rubbed his neck. "I thought it would be easier this way."

Bellatine leaned forward and took up the empty bottle, turning it between her fingers. "When I was under, when I was 'smokefed' or whatever you call it, I saw something. Or rather, something saw me. Saw *through* me."

"What do you mean?"

"There was someone else in my head. And there was this weight on my back, like a person was clinging to me. But I could feel it inside me, too, like I was a telescope and it was peering through my eyes from a distance. Then it was gone."

"You were tripping. That stuff makes you crazy."

Bellatine shook her head. "I'm telling you."

"Oh, come on," Isaac's groused. But underneath, he felt his stomach drop.

"It saw our house. And Isaac, this thing, it sure isn't looking for a summer home in the country. It wants Thistlefoot dead."

"When you say *thing* . . ."

"It's not a person. I can't explain it. It's . . . it's something else." Bellatine gritted her teeth. "I think it knows where we are."

Isaac stood up.

"I need to make a call. Deal with her." He pointed to the tombstone girl, who had begun curiously unlacing the front of her bodice and peeking inside in dismay.

"You've been dodging me."

"Swell to hear your voice, too, Shona. You're taking good care of my favorite jacket, I trust. Miss me?"

"You bet, whenever I knee a smokefed motherfucker in the dick, I wish it was you."

"It's nice to be thought of."

She'd answered after only one ring. Despite any faux venom in her voice, the horse-skull crew had certainly been hoping to hear from him.

"What do you want, Chameleon King?"

Isaac hesitated. She knew his sobriquet.

Shona caught the delay. "The Longshadow Man isn't the only one doing his research on you."

"Learn anything that tickled you?"

"A history of petty larceny, impersonating police and military officials, a string of pissed coconspirators who claim you duped them out of a share, and yet not a single charge or arrest. Well, except for a bounty on you in northern Idaho for stealing a gold pig."

"Gold-plated," Isaac corrected. "Unfortunately worth far less than the trouble. And that wasn't me, that was"—Isaac pinched his voice into a Midwestern lilt—"Lyle Lundberg, from the commemorative hog restoration coalition."

"Adorable."

"Not my finest, granted. One of these days, I'll give you a real show."

"God willing I'm killed in action first. Did you call for a reason, or to waste my time? Where are you?"

"Baltimore. He's found us."

"You've seen him?"

"Well . . . not exactly."

He'd have to tell the story selectively. Shona shouldn't know about Tiny's abilities. Especially not now, since he'd learned there was so much more to her power than simply making a porcelain doll pirouette on command. If Shona knew she could burn through the Longshadow's poison, they'd want to jam her full of syringes and drain her dry to find an antidote. Isaac needed her on the road. He still had a tour to finish. For Benji's sake . . .

And if anyone found out about Bellatine's *other* ability? That her animation power extended beyond fabric, beyond wood, and into organic bone and muscle? No. Shona didn't need to know any of that.

"I traded a sample out of Sparrow's case when I was in the bus and—"

"Stole," Shona cut in.

"I left a nickel."

"We noticed. You're a little freak, aren't you?"

"A businessman."

"Sure y'are."

"Well my sister found the stuff, was feeling a bit parched, and . . . let's just say it's been a lively evening at chez Yaga."

"She drank it?"

"She drank it."

"Your sis, she's not quite as sharp as you, is she?"

"So you think I'm sharp?"

Silence.

Isaac cleared his throat. "Anyway. I'm going to need you to suspend your disbelief with me for a second . . . She's on the other side now, no major damage, but . . . when she was under, she says she felt someone else in her head with her. I think being smokefed connects back to the Longshadow Man somehow. Have you seen anything like that before? Where he's known something he shouldn't have? Something he might have learned by popping into his victims' heads?"

"A psychic connection?" The line fell silent. He could hear her breathing. Was she mulling through recent encounters? Deciding which information to divulge . . . ? Isaac hated talking on the phone. No musculature to study for tension or ease. No facial giveaways preempting what a person might say or do. Just a disembodied voice severed from context. It made him uneasy, as if he were maneuvering a labyrinth with a blindfold on.

The voice theoretically attached to Shona returned. "The smokefed are open to *suggestion*, sure, but aren't controlled. He triggers them by talking. If there were a full psychic link, he wouldn't have to make verbal suggestions." She hesitated. "But it would stand to reason he could receive certain . . . information." No dismissal or surprise at the outlandish notion. She'd known, then, that the Longshadow Man was more than met the eye. That aspects of him were capable of transcending the laws of the physical world.

"Shona, back in your bus, y'all talked about a *passenger*. That I couldn't 'see the passenger.' What did that mean?"

A crash came from the kitchen, followed by a startled squeal. Bellatine's voice wafted through the wall, "Stop touching things! Jesus Christ, sit *down*." The stone girl whimpered.

"We shouldn't talk about this over the phone," Shona said. "But, Isaac . . ."

An involuntary shiver passed through him—was that the first time he'd heard his real name in Shona's mouth? Her dark painted lips fluttered through his thoughts, a cruel winged insect. He swatted them away like a gnat.

"We're coming to you," she continued. "First, dig up whatever you can about the house's history. Where it came from, how it was used before you got it. Anything that could help us understand why it's a target."

"It gathered dust in a Ukrainian warehouse for the last seventy years."

"Then before that. As far back as you can go."

Before . . . Could whatever was following them be that old? How much *did* Shona know about the Longshadow Man?

Her urgent voice pulled him back. "You need to find somewhere safe to lie low. Somewhere you can hide in plain sight, where the house won't stand out enough for people to notice. When you land, send us a pin drop and we'll meet you there."

Isaac cringed. He knew just the place—a city where phantasmagoria glistened nightly in the streets, haloed in auras of lilac smoke. Where a legged house would blend easily among towering headdresses dripping with beads and story-tall carnival floats and flaming pyres. He hadn't expected to return so soon.

"Shona, baby," he said, "you're gonna love New Orleans."

CHAPTER TWENTY-FIVE

"I NEED TO MAKE a call," Isaac said. "Deal with her."

He pointed at the statue Bellatine had awoken, then slipped away, vanishing into the bedroom. She heard her brother ascend the loft ladder with a creak.

Bellatine hadn't taken her eyes off the stone girl, not since their first moment of contact. "Stop that," she snapped as the girl tugged at the laces of her bodice.

"Did you know there's more *me* inside here?" The girl unfastened the top of her corset and peeked down the front.

She was young, a bit younger than Bellatine, with a peachy flush leaking through the silvery sheen of her formerly granite skin. Ringlets of gold hair bounced past her shoulders, some pinned atop her head in a pillowy bun. The girl's face was heart shaped and smooth, baby fat still softening her cheekbones, and she was dressed in an ankle-length tailored dress that fit snugly over her plump figure. Nothing so regal as a ball gown or party dress, it was made from simple blue linen with plush gathers at the shoulders, lace peeping over the neckline. *The sort of dress a person would be buried in,* Bellatine thought before she could stop herself.

Leaning to gawk in the mirror, the girl knocked a jar of dried flowers onto the floor, which shattered with a crash.

"Stop touching things! Jesus Christ, *sit down.*" Bellatine was surprised at the harshness in her tone. The girl's eyes went wide and moony.

"Yes, miss." She flopped cross-legged on the floor, her hands clasped softly in her lap. Tears stained her cheeks.

Bellatine bit the inside of her lip to steady herself. "I'm sorry. I've just had a long night. And so have you. Come on, let's go get you ready." She made certain not to brush up against the girl as she passed into the bedroom and toward the parlor. The stone girl whimpered, but trailed loyally behind.

"Get me ready for what? Is there to be a funeral today?"

"Ready to go back to sleep."

It had been nearly an hour since the Embering had plummeted into the granite statue. Typically, an Embered object remained sentient for fifteen minutes at most, often less. Bellatine wasn't surprised that this had extended longer. The power she'd felt in the cemetery had been unlike any she'd known before. Heightened by smokefed fear, she had felt like she'd held an entire sun in each hand, blazing. But it *must* be nearly time now. An hour was too long.

"Follow me," Bellatine beckoned. She hopped down from the stage onto the spongy turf of the boneyard, shivering as soon as her feet met grass. She expected to feel a tug set in, but her hands stayed cool. The cemetery contained nothing but monuments and wind. No phantom village. No begging dead. No yearning.

The girl-statue tottered clumsily after. She moved like a toddler, still unsure of how her limbs connected to her body.

"Climb on." Bellatine patted the empty pedestal that had held the stone girl an hour prior. "That's right, up you go."

Faltering, the girl slipped. Unconsciously, Bellatine thrust her arms out in support, and the girl sank against her. The moment seemed to hover out of time—the girl's cool chest pressed against Bellatine's own, the thudding of two distinct pulses as if one were the echo of the other. Bellatine's fingers dimpled into the girl's fleshy waist where she'd caught her. She could see tiny goose bumps ripple over the silvery skin. Then the moment broke. With a gasp, Bellatine shoved the stone girl away.

A cackle erupted from the stone girl before she clamped a hand over her mouth, startled by her own boisterousness. "I'm sorry," she said. "It's only such a funny, squishy feeling."

Bellatine averted her eyes. "Just get up on the block." The girl obliged, this time with success.

1:54 a.m. 1:57 a.m. 2:00 a.m. Bellatine glanced at her phone once, then again and again. An hour had well passed now. The girl squirmed on her perch.

"Is something supposed . . . to happen?" she whispered.

"Yes. Keep waiting." Bellatine ignored the needle of dread puncturing her stomach lining. She mustn't linger on the time. Mustn't notice the striking humanlike softness of the stone girl, the forget-me-not fabric wrinkling, the stray blond hairs escaping from their flawless ringlets. Mustn't dwell on how very *different* this Embering had felt, her smokefed blood magnifying the blaze. She mustn't consider the possibility that the girl was awake for good.

Bellatine pressed a hand to her ribs in worry. Still, a memory of the girl's cool touch lingered.

The girl squirmed impatiently on the pedestal, her dangling heels bouncing against the words carved into the front:

WINIFRED A. HADLEY
17 YEARS
D. NOVEMBER 23 1884

"Winifred," Bellatine said, "is that your name?"

The girl sat up straighter on her post, squaring her shoulders for a schoolhouse-worthy recitation. "I am the memory of Winifred Hadley, stricken with typhoid fever while attending school, soon terminating in fatal lung trouble. The funeral was presided over by Reverend W. L. Miller. The grave was lined with flowers, sent by her m-many—" the girl stuttered, then began again: "Sent by *my* many devoted friends. The sudden death will be received with universal sorrow. *O beloved, soar away unto eternal rest. To mourn her beauty evermore, the pious and the blessed.*"

The closing remarks, Bellatine noted, were quoted from the epitaph carved into the pedestal's base.

"I'm sorry," Bellatine said. "It must have been an awful way to die."

The girl nodded somberly. "Yes, yes it surely was. Everett always said so."

"Who's Everett?"

"My betrothed," the girl sighed. "Oh, he was a beautiful mourner. He brought me white orchids every day for a year. He studied cartography at the university and used to sit here at my feet and tell me of all the wonderful places in the world that we would have gone together. He was very good at weeping, you know. Some people are hideous when they cry, or dishonest. Some only cry for show and stop sniffling as soon as the other mourners leave. But not Everett. Sometimes he cried himself to sleep right in the grass, only woken by morning dew."

This boy must be half a century in the grave himself, by now.

Behind them, Thistlefoot's door creaked open. The house ruffled as Isaac stepped onto the porch, a cigarette drooping from his lips.

"All aboard. Time to go."

"What do you mean?" Bellatine asked. "Where are we going?"

"Out of dodge."

"Which means . . . ?"

Isaac shrugged. "Do you want the bastard who knocked around in your head to catch up to us, or don't you?"

"We have to wait a little longer," Bellatine protested, looking to the stone girl. "She has to go back to normal first."

"No time. Leave her."

"I can't leave her!"

"Then bring her."

"There's no way—"

Isaac turned his back on them and cleared off the porch, readying to launch. His oversized dress coat flapped in the wind, his hair sweeping back, ringed with smoke. Bellatine scoffed. As always, her brother looked like he'd been hired to play Nonchalant Highwayman #3 in a B movie.

"*Shtey uf,*" he commanded.

The house stood up.

"What a funny bird!" the stone girl chirped, and Thistlefoot preened.

"*Greyt,*" Isaac yipped.

"Damn it," Bellatine cursed under her breath. She was under no illusion that Isaac would wait for her. At any moment, the house would bolt forward.

"Come on," she said, grabbing the girl's arm and yanking her off the platform. The girl dutifully kept pace as Bellatine ran ahead, catching the cable ladder just before the house lifted a foot toward its first step. She thrust the metal rung into the stone girl's hand.

"Climb," she instructed. "Hand over hand. That's it."

Shakily, the girl ascended. Bellatine followed behind.

The ladder swayed with each footfall. A whistle of night wind swirled against Bellatine's neck like the touch of an icy wing. At last, they pulled themselves panting onto the deck.

Isaac crouched to meet them. He put out a hand, helping the stone girl to her feet. The statue took Isaac in, calmed enough from her initial awakening panic to study him with full attention for the first time.

"Are you coming from a funeral?" she asked earnestly, pointing to his dark threads in all their pallbearer chic. Bellatine smothered a laugh. He winked at her. She was startled to feel a tulip of lightness sprout in her—here, bombarded with danger, a stalker on their trail, her hands defying her. And yet, the lightness remained.

"Guess you're with us now, kid," Isaac said to the stone girl. She curtsied.

"Don't get attached," Bellatine cautioned. "She'll be a lawn ornament by morning."

Isaac sized the girl up. "Somehow I doubt that."

In truth—so did Bellatine.

"To whom do we owe the pleasure?" Isaac postured. "My apologies for foregoing proper introductions before. We had . . . shit to deal with."

"I am the memory of Winifred Hadley, stricken with typhoid fever while—"

"Winnie," Isaac grinned. "Fantastic. Welcome to the team."

CHAPTER TWENTY-SIX

IN APRIL, A BOY delivering newspapers discovers hidden weaponry and communist pamphlets in Haim the stonecutter's studio.

In May, *pogromtshiki* hang Haim from the tree behind his workshop. It is an old apple tree, with twisting branches that reach out at odd, crooked angles. The trunk is narrow, but it is strong, the bark velveted in moss. This tree has not borne fruit for many years. Today is different.

One soldier laughs. "The Jew is an ugly apple. He isn't ripe enough to pick."

When the soldiers leave, Haim's sister's boy tries to cut him down, but the rope won't sever. With every drag of a knife, the rope hardens—first into leather. Then into steel cable. Then into a gleaming diamond chain, which snaps every blade from its handle. There can be no mourner's Kaddish. No burial. After seven shiva-less days and nights, only a skeleton remains.

Everyone avoids Haim the stonecutter's workshop after that, and the terrible tree with the terrible rope and the terrible shape dangling from it. Everyone, that is, except for Baba Yaga.

"Good morning, Reb Skeleton," Baba Yaga says to Haim's bones each week as she passes for market.

"Good morning, Baba Yaga," say the stonecutter's bones, feet not touching the ground.

Sometimes she has Illa and Malka with her as she travels. Illa likes to place hollyhock blossoms between the skeleton's toes.

One day, the skeleton asks Baba Yaga for a favor.

"Baba Yaga," the skeleton says. "I have been in this tree for sixty days now and sixty nights, and have grown tired of the view. My neck is sore at this angle, and I wish to see the world. Would you be so kind as to cut me down?"

"Reb Skeleton," says Baba Yaga, "everyone knows that you hang on an unbreakable rope. Why do you ask me such a thing?"

"Feh!" says the skeleton. "Are your daughters not born from teeth? Does your house not walk on chicken feet? If anyone can cut the unbreakable rope, it is you. If you agree to free me, I will do any three favors you ask of me before I go on my way. I swear it."

This, Baba Yaga likes the sound of very much.

"Very well," she says. "I'll cut you down. But let me tell you your first task: It is my daughters' birthday soon. In life, you were a wonderful artist, Reb Skeleton, and I trust that skill has not left you in death. You will paint a mural over the front door of my home to honor my littlest daughter who is small as a hare, my older daughter who is cruel as a crow, and myself."

Reb Skeleton is baffled. "But Baba Yaga, I was a grave cutter—my art was for the dead. It is not befitting to create art like this for the living."

"The dead do not see their own tombstones," Baba Yaga insists. "All art is for the living, and so too shall this be. Will you agree to it, or shall I leave you here so the birds may build nests in your ribs?"

Reb Skeleton agrees.

And so that night, Baba Yaga returns with a long pair of scissors. The scissors are glossy as snow. At the hinge where the two blades meet is a raised rose, and the grips are encircled with silver thorns like barbed wire, so no one but Baba Yaga can bear to hold them. *Snip!* She cuts Reb Skeleton free from the noose, easy as that.

By morning, a beautiful painting hovers over my front door.

The next day, Baba Yaga finds Reb Skeleton leaning against the lip of the town well. He is wearing a new suit and a fine hat and a pair of shiny leather shoes.

"Reb Skeleton, death looks well on you, I see—but you are not free yet. You still have two tasks you must do for me."

"I remember, Baba Yaga," says Reb Skeleton. "What shall you have me do tonight?"

"My eldest," says Baba Yaga, "she has begun playing a game called the Orchard, in which she is dangling from an apple tree and all the apples are sweet and ripe and though she is hungry, she cannot eat them, for she is dead. Neither of my daughters have slept the night through since the *pogromtshiki* strung you up. You will make another painting for them. One upon the ceiling to help them sleep, where the soldiers are ruined and my daughters are happy."

"Very well," says Reb Skeleton. "But you can tell your eldest daughter that when you are dead, you no longer want apples, nor honey, nor matzo. You only want to be less dead."

Still, by morning, a beautiful, terrible mural extends across my ceiling, shimmering with scarlet and gold and emerald paint. Vines emerge from men's ears and mouths, curling in elegant ringlets. When Illa and Malka scramble into the attic and lie beneath it, two wet dollops of paint fall. Drip, onto one girl's cheek. Drip, onto the other. The paint leaves dimples that never fade, no matter the scrubbing, which emerge whenever they smile.

"Baba Yaga!" Reb Skeleton cries. "Today I will do my final

task, and then I will be free! Tell me, what is it I can do for you?"

Baba Yaga gives Reb Skeleton the scissors she had used to cut him down. The blades glint like bright little fish in the dawn light.

"Tonight, you will slit the throats of every soldier in the White Army, and every Cossack, and every *pogromtshik* peasant who would take up a torch. And when that is all done, you will return home and kill each of the men who killed you," Baba Yaga says.

Reb Skeleton is furious. "But Baba Yaga, this will take a century! How am I to know freedom?"

"Good Haim, bringer of death," she says, "you *are* freedom."

This, as always, is only one version of the memory. Funny, how truth changes in the telling. How a person becomes a myth, how a myth becomes a hero. Do not mistake Baba Yaga for the hero of my stories. She is not. She is not the villain, either. She is only a woman. Sometimes, one cannot know until retelling what was right and what was wrong. Sometimes, we cannot know until it is too late the significance of a man who becomes an apple who becomes a skeleton.

In another version, when soldiers hang the stonecutter from the tree behind his workshop, Baba Yaga does not cut him down. Instead, she crouches in my belly and holds her daughters close. She rocks, for sitting still is no different than death. She sings, for that is what the living do. In the lullaby, a promise of safety she cannot keep. Her voice, clean as rain.

Then, she boils water on the stove and gives Malka a bath. She slices up an apple for Illa. She scrubs down the kitchen table and puts out bait for the mice. This is what people do, during war. The same tasks as always. What, you believe you would behave differently, should death come to your village?

No. The wood still needs to be chopped and dried for winter. The children still must be put to bed. The floors swept. Life is always just life.

Baba Yaga closes my shutters. The world stays out. In here, the living continue to do what they will. They laugh. They take their meals. They turn away.

Forgive them.

CHAPTER TWENTY-SEVEN

ISAAC YAGA SQUIRMED WITH regret as soon as Thistlefoot plodded across the Louisiana state line, but he buried his unease in the poker deck he was shuffling. Once, twice, again, the cards sifted into one another, purring like a hummingbird's wings.

Benji had taught him to read tarot with a regular pack like this. He'd said he liked the banality, the way fortunes weren't tucked away in a velvet-lined box, but piled behind a bar counter, sticky with spilled drinks. Oracles that could unveil your future one minute and deal a blackjack hand the next. Isaac plucked a card from the pack. Nine of spades. *Depression, anxiety, nightmares.*

"If you don't like your fortune," Benji used to say, "change it."

Isaac pulled another card. Six of hearts. *Memory, nostalgia, old friendship resumed.* He liked that even less.

Returning to a city mere months after leaving . . . the notion chafed against Isaac like sandpaper. Too close. Too soon. Too many of his own footprints still lingering in the southern soil.

Bad blood that barely had a chance to ease its boil to a simmer. They'd be able to hide from the Longshadow Man, but who else would find Isaac in the meantime? He could already hear the calliope's call wafting off the Mississippi River; whether it rose with the hymn of a welcome or a warning, he couldn't be certain. *You always meet twice.*

Bellatine found him with his legs dangling over the roof, worrying the corner of the six of hearts against his bottom lip. From the stage below, she waved her phone at him.

"I heard from Mira."

Isaac's attention perked. "Mom have anything new on our favorite four-walled Rockette?"

"She doesn't know anything else about the history. Just what we already had. And even if she did, she was *not* in a chatty mood. As always."

His brief hope flagged.

Digging into Thistlefoot's origin was proving more complicated than he'd expected. The shipping documents marked its journey from Pivdennyi, one of the leading Black Sea ports out of Ukraine, but prior to that there was little record. The will that entitled Isaac and Bellatine to the house in the first place had been notarized in Kyiv, but apparently their twice-great-grandmother had only moved there in her later years, retiring to the eastern part of the city. All they knew was that she'd spent her childhood and most of her adult life in a shtetl somewhere near a river. Which township, however, had been lost to time and bad bookkeeping.

Bellatine snorted.

"What?"

"I just imagined the Rockettes with backward-bending legs . . ." She attempted a haphazard high-kick.

Tiny had been wisecracking constantly since Baltimore. It didn't suit her. The clumsy levity was a cover-up, a deflection. Ever since leaving Maryland, the *unsaid* had dangled like a mobile between the siblings, twisting and refracting in the

November air, staying barely aloft. Isaac wasn't going to be the one to break its balance. He wouldn't ask. Not of the dead. Not of what a broken body becomes when woken. Of what violations and miracles his sister had surely performed. The confession wriggled on Bellatine's tongue—he could see it, pursing her lips, pressing at the corners of her mouth. It was as if her throat were full of wasps, and she insisted on keeping them sealed inside her. Good. Isaac didn't need to know. Any use he'd once had for bringing back the dead was long behind him.

Isaac pressed a finger to his temple and focused on the muscles in his jaw, his eyebrows, his neck. One by one, he flipped invisible switches, willing them to relax. If Tiny noticed any tension, she'd assume it was about her, and that would only put the household more on edge than it already was.

"Izzy! Belly! Lunch!" Winifred called to them out the open window.

"Those nicknames better not stick," Bellatine sighed.

Winnie had become a small mercy, her newborn chaos a welcome and constant interruption.

"You let her cook?"

"*Let* is a strong word."

"*It's getting cold!*"

"*Cook* is also a strong word."

Winifred had laid two places at the table, each with a plate, a fork, and a knife. On Bellatine's plate were six peanut M&M's. On Isaac's, a loose pile of tobacco.

"You like it?" she asked, batting her lashes. Over a century without a digestive system seemed to have left Winnie with a thoroughly interpretive concept of *eating*.

"My favorite meal, how'd you know?" he said, sliding into his seat. Hubcap trilled and leapt into his lap.

Isaac expected Bellatine to roll her eyes and fix herself a sandwich, but instead, she sat down, balanced an M&M on her fork, and popped it into her mouth. Winnie beamed proudly. With every affirmation she received from Bellatine, the gray sheen beneath the girl's skin brightened one shade silkier. It was as if Tiny's very presence, moment by moment, made Winifred more alive. And though his sister would never admit it, Isaac could tell the effect was reciprocal.

"What are you having?" Isaac asked.

Winifred balked. "*Me?*" She tugged at the hem of the striped tee she'd borrowed from Bellatine, which she filled out much more sumptuously than its owner. The linen dress had been dunked in a pail to be washed.

"I don't think she can—" Bellatine cautioned before Isaac waved her off.

"You have a mouth—do you have guts?"

"Guts?"

Isaac snagged an M&M off his sister's plate and offered it up. "Here. Try this."

The stone girl placed the candy gingerly onto her tongue, closed her mouth, and waited.

A smile played at Bellatine's lips. "You have to chew it. Like this," she exhibited, clacking her teeth.

Winifred followed suit and the sugared shell cracked. Her eyes went wide. Then she dove across the table, grabbed the remainder of Bellatine's sweets, and stuffed them into her mouth.

"Whoa!" Tiny yelped.

Winifred chewed manically, a beam splitting from cheek to cheek. "They're like . . . little planets! With secrets inside them that I get to open up! And it feels . . . it feels very nice." She stared at Isaac and Bellatine, agape. "Humans experience this every day, and act like it's nothing?"

"Wait till you try mozzarella sticks," Isaac said with gravity.

"Hold on," Bellatine said, smothering a laugh. She slid out of her seat and dashed over to the pantry, returning with a wedge of pumpkin bread wrapped in brown crepe paper from— where had that bakery been? Charlotte? Atlanta? It had grown hard to keep track.

Winifred received the bread like a holy sacrament, then shoveled it into her mouth with both hands.

"Guess she doesn't need to breathe," Tiny muttered.

"Ifts wondrlf," Winifred choked out. "Lrk a"—the girl gulped—"cloud."

"You've created a monster," Isaac whispered. And it was only then that Tiny's smile fell.

Though the stone girl was certainly odd, Isaac was impressed by her adaptiveness. Often, he'd catch her mimicking Bellatine's movements as she made a bed or caulked a leaky window or laced up her Chucks. And she seemed to have picked up the rest from watching a century of mourners and dog-toting joggers and bored teens cavorting through the cemetery. She'd had more training studying and memorizing human behavior than Isaac would in a lifetime. With each task, her entire body became fully engaged. She would flop down on her back and lift a leg in the air to straighten her stockings or dunk a whole thumb into a pot of water to test if it was boiling. A ladybug would land on her wrist, and all her attention would zero in on that one small spot. It was as if, in feeling these senses all anew, every inch of her body were an eye ready to spring open.

Then the light would shift, and the strange silver skin would become strikingly evident. Or she'd go hours without blinking, as if it were a conscious chore she could easily become distracted from and forget. She would eat until the food was gone, never growing full—yet could also fast all day without her energy flagging. Sometimes she sat so still Isaac wondered if she'd slipped back into granite, but then she'd spot a field of wildflowers out the window and leap up, pressing her hands to the glass in wonder. And there she hovered: a razor's edge dividing her between human and stone.

Thistlefoot rattled to a halt, plates skidding across the dining table. Bellatine grabbed hers with both hands while Isaac watched his teeter on the table's edge before nudging it back. He rolled a cigarette from the tobacco on his plate and tucked it behind his ear.

A low, whistling song slipped in through the open windows. The calliope, notes clear and sprightly as a carousel jingle, pierced by the howl of the steamboat's bellows. Bellatine and Winnie turned to the window. The song wasn't in Isaac's memory this time. It was real. They'd made it to New Orleans.

Hank's was just as he'd left it. Through the glass, he could see shelves sagging with plastic vodka bottles. An ever-hissing fryer of battered fish. A case of lottery tickets and novelty lighters on the cashier's counter. Out front, a group of crust punks in tattered brown vests crouched by the entrance, passing around a forty of malt liquor. They ignored two blond men in salmon polos and khakis who glanced down in disdain while stepping gingerly through them. The driveway was full, half of lemon-colored sports cars with out-of-state plates, half of junkers with garbage bags duct-taped over the windows. Ah, Hank's. The great equalizer, haven to all dawn and midnight creatures.

"Come on," Isaac beckoned, leading Bellatine and Winnie through the crowded lot. He recognized one of the crusties lounging on the stoop from his busking days in Minneapolis, but the kid didn't notice him back. Who knows what version of himself Isaac had been playing the week he'd met the guy. Clearly someone unlinkable to the one he was embodying now.

"Isaac, young man, how you living? You back in town?" Someone clapped him on the shoulder. An old dark-skinned man leaning on a cane. He rattled a tin coin cup in one hand. His left leg was missing beneath the knee.

"Justus, baby, good to see you. Rolled in just now. You taking care of yourself?"

The old man nodded, rubbing his jaw. "Can't afford my pills no more, they put me off my health care. My joints have been creaking and croaking like Christ's cross in the wind for weeks."

"Sorry to hear that, friend."

"Say, you got a smoke?"

Isaac handed Justus the cigarette from behind his ear and lit it for him. As he held the lighter up, Isaac noticed that his own trembling was, at least for now, mercifully still.

"Take it easy," Isaac said, patting the man on the heart. As he did, he invisibly slipped ten dollars into Justus' shirt pocket. "Don't let those government crooks keep you down."

"Aright, God bless." The old man bid him goodbye and hobbled away toward the yellow sports cars, whose owners would be sure to have heavy pockets. Isaac knew it was the poorest who always gave the most, folks who knew how it was, while the rich kept their wallets sealed tight—but you still had to try.

Isaac led Bellatine and Winifred through the swinging glass doors into the convenience store. Hank's was a go-to hub, but there was little chance of running into anyone else he knew today. Though it was well past noon, his people would be in bed still, sleeping off the sorrows they'd tried to drown the night before.

Bellatine and Winnie stocked up on candy and gallon jugs of water, while Isaac had Miss Jeannie behind the cook counter stuff a white paper bag full of fried chicken and biscuits. In the shop's fluorescent light, Tiny looked sallow and small. The rosy glow that had flooded her after waking Winifred had already begun to fade, and her hands once again balled into white-knuckled fists at her sides. Her lips tight, shoulders knotting. Isaac recognized this. The toll a body endures when neglected. When forbidden to enact the sacred duty for which it was built. When Isaac didn't act, the shakes came. When Bellatine wasn't Embering, she hardened, grew jagged at the edges, paled. She was so bent on withholding life from the inanimate shapes around her, she withheld it from herself, too. She turned herself to stone.

As they went up to pay, a flash of neon-pink paper caught Isaac's eye from the linoleum floor. He snatched it up and flipped it over. A screen-printed flyer etched in black and gold:

LANTERN PARADE

YOU KNOW WHERE
YOU KNOW WHY

HAT PIN BRASS BAND / THE HARVEST MOONS
10 P.M.

"What's that?" Bellatine asked, sidling up beside him, her arms full of water jugs. Winifred trailed dutifully behind.

"A good omen," Isaac said. He thrust the flyer at Bellatine. "And a personal invitation from the Hank's floor to you."

"A funeral?" Winifred asked, perking up.

"A party," Isaac corrected.

"I want to become *drunk*. I want to be the drunkest girl alive," Winnie announced, tipping up her chin like nobility.

Isaac raised an eyebrow.

"What?" she shrugged. "People have thrown parties near my tomb over the past century. I know what the *living* do."

"We're not going to a party," Bellatine countered. "We're supposed to be lying low."

"It's not *just* a party," Isaac said, "it's a parade."

His sister hoisted the plastic gallons up onto the register stand with a thud and slapped down a twenty-dollar bill. Her chin barely crested the counter. "Whatever it is, I'm not going."

"Come on," Isaac said, "a little parade never hurt anyone."

Winnie tore open a bag of peanut M&M's, a dozen more of the yellow packets hoarded in the front of her dress. "Remember in 1918 when that Philadelphia parade killed forty-five hundred with the Spanish flu? A few of them were interred near me."

"What about you?" Isaac asked the peroxide-blond cashier. "If the cosmos called, what would you say?"

"The *cosmos* called me to move to United States," she scowled. "Back home, I was hairdresser for celebrities. I own salon for movie stars. Good life. Now I work red-eye shift selling bottom-shelf tequila for seven-fifty an hour."

"Neither of you are helping," Isaac said, swinging a thumb between Winnie and the cashier. Bellatine handed the flyer back to him without looking at it. He folded it up and pocketed it. For later.

They ate their bounty on the rock pile by the train tracks. It had been one of Isaac's favorite haunts when he'd lived there, a heap of railroad ballast where kids shot beer cans with BB guns and smoked weed in the shadow of a rusted-out water tower. And at only a few blocks north of the river, this neighborhood was no stranger to living houses. Isaac hadn't been there for the floods of Katrina, but most folks in this area had. They'd seen whole streets sprout gills when the levee broke. To a people who'd watched their city learn to swim, a house on bird legs wouldn't be worth a blink.

Bellatine picked up a stick and sloughed off the bark with her pocketknife while Winnie plowed through her third bag of M&M's. Isaac laid a row of nickels on the rail and waited. So much of life on the bum was waiting. Waiting with a thumb out to hitch a ride in the rain. Waiting in the train yard for dawn. Waiting for a dollar to be thrown in the tip jar. Waiting for time itself to decide, at last, to move forward and take you with it. And now, waiting for Shona. Or the Longshadow Man. Whoever found them first.

Bellatine kept glancing over her shoulder, in their house's direction. One great yellow toe peeked out from behind a row of shotgun houses. It scratched at a dead rat in the road before yanking back out of sight.

Tiny squirmed. "We shouldn't leave Thistle unsupervised."

"She's a wanted goon," Isaac said, nodding with exaggerated concern. "With a price on her roof."

Bellatine craned around again to look. "I should check in, see if it needs anything."

"Like what, a pedicure?"

She ignored him, stuffing a biscuit into her pocket. Isaac suspected his sister wouldn't be the one eating it—he'd caught her shoveling rations into the cookstove before. Shona thought *he* was eccentric . . . wait till she met the rest of the troupe.

A train's whistle groaned over the rocks. Isaac swallowed. He dug his heels into the dirt for grounding as a tremor moved through him, the way a breeze moves through wheatgrass, rippling. When he'd been younger, that sound had made him feel light, eternal, like a poison-tipped dart in midair. Like the country was a red carpet rolling out at his and Benji's feet. But all that was before.

The freighters here in Louisiana chugged by heavy and molasses-easy, steel gators lazing on the bank of the bayou. So different from northern trains, which bulleted past each stop fast enough that trying to catch one on the fly could break your neck from whiplash alone. Moving fast gets you where you're going. But moving slow gets you there alive. Sometimes.

Isaac shook his head. Don't think about the past. Plus, he didn't need to be weighing the old scales again. A side effect of never sitting still: life existed in a state of constant comparison. One city held up beside another. Boise or Tulsa. Great Northern or Southern Pacific line. Busking Harvard Square in Boston or Union in New York. Some part of him—a secret, weary voice hidden deep down—wondered if all his motion came from a place of yearning to be still. That maybe, the more small lives he tumbled through, the sooner he'd find one worth keeping. But with this long on the road, would he even know it if he saw it? Perhaps he'd already passed it by, driven on by that endless headache, that scratching in his chest. Stopping wasn't an option. And it never would be.

The train spat Isaac's nickels out into the gravel. They gleamed like small moons.

Winifred picked one up, then yelped. She dropped it.

"They're hot at first," Isaac cautioned. "Friction, it heats up the metal."

Winifred examined her fingertips. "It feels strange."

Bellatine reached for Winnie's hand. "You have to be more careful. That feeling means you've touched something that can hurt you." Isaac couldn't help but note the tenderness with which his sister leaned over the stone girl's burn, blew on it gently.

"So my skin can listen. And metal can talk. How marvelous!" Winnie reached up a finger and brushed Bellatine's lip. "I can hear your skin, too, when I touch it."

Tiny's cheeks reddened. She pulled away.

"By the way," Bellatine said, tightening into formality, "I emailed the Ukrainian embassy to see if they have any suggestions on where Thistlefoot was before Kyiv. Did you call the inheritance lawyer?"

"Me?" Isaac frowned.

"Yes, you," Bellatine said, "like I asked you to five times already."

"See, there's your problem. Try asking less."

She looked ready to punch him.

"Dif is why everyfing should haf an epitaph," Winifred tutted through a new mouthful of chocolate. She swallowed. "'*Dearly Beloved*' . . . like a letter from the past. All the information you need."

Bellatine perked up. "A letter! Oh, I'm an idiot." She palmed her forehead.

"I ain't arguing," Isaac said.

She continued unfazed. "There was all this junk up in the loft when we moved in, remember? I cleared some out, but most of it's still up there. Including a crate full of papers. I'm pretty sure there are *letters* in there. If any of them predate Kyiv, we might be able to find an address. Or more." Pulling herself up from the rock pile, she snapped her pocketknife shut and dusted off her overalls. Winnie, too, hopped up to follow.

"Are you coming or what?" Bellatine asked, Isaac's midday laze unbroken.

He stretched like a cat. "I'm not done with my lunch yet."

She grabbed him by the arm with a yank. "Uh-uh."

Back in the house, Bellatine dragged the heavy wooden crate from the loft singlehandedly.

"Well looks like my help here isn't needed after all," Isaac said, starting again for the door.

Bellatine dumped the contents onto the living room floor. Isaac's curiosity took hold as dust rose up in a purple cloud. Dispersing, a pile of documents remained.

"So much for a day off," he sighed.

"As long as there's work"—Bellatine grunted, shaking loose the last leaves of paper—"there's no such thing as a day off."

They sorted through the papers one by one.

Winifred visibly shivered as she ran a thumb over an onion-skin page. "Like moth wings." It crinkled at her touch, and she delighted at the sound.

Isaac squinted closer. "They're . . . in Yiddish."

"Nothing slips by you," Bellatine said.

"Tally, kid, I've got a knack for these things."

Pages upon pages of delicate midnight ink coalesced into rows of Hebrew characters. Based on the shapes and insignia stamped onto the pages, most of the documents looked like standard bookkeeping forms—bank statements or handwritten store receipts or tattered calendar pages, the edges yellowed with age. But the inaccessibility of the language made each one seem mystical. Fed with possibility. What looked like a simple lending record might actually be a recipe. A spell. A confession.

Bellatine snatched something out of the pile. "Look!"

It was a parcel of envelopes tied in twine. She slipped one from the pack and thumbed it open, revealing a crisply folded letter. Squeezed above the salutation was a date, written in English: *June 3, 1925. New York.*

"Hmm, 1925 . . . If we're looking for *origin* origins, it's probably a few years late, but she'd have been alive. The timing almost fits," Bellatine said, swatting a mosquito from her neck.

"But New York? Fairly certain there isn't a New York, Russia."

"So the letter was sent overseas to Thistlefoot from someone in the United States . . ." Bellatine examined the back of the envelope. "No address."

"How can there be an address for a house that won't stand still?" Isaac said.

Something small and white fell from the envelope's mouth and clattered onto the floor.

Isaac squinted. "Is that . . . a tooth?"

His sister picked it up, pinching it between two fingers. "It's a bean."

"Naturally. Classic . . . postal bean. Glad we cleared that up."

Winifred dug into another envelope, retrieving a small glossy square, and handed it over. Isaac found three pairs of eyes staring up at him. It was a black-and-white photograph with a thin scrawl of English script underneath: *Malka, mother, and I. 1919.* A woman in a white blouse and floor-length wool skirt stood at the forefront, dark hair coiffed atop her head. She wasn't old, no more than thirty-five or so, yet there was a hardness in her eyes that suggested more than her years' fair share. She balanced a pudgy-cheeked baby on one hip, who reached a blurry hand toward the camera. At the woman's side stood a young girl, eight or nine years old, with wild raven hair and sharp features, a doll wedged under her arm.

"That girl looks *just* like you!" Bellatine exclaimed. It was striking—the same crooked nose, lean frame, the same inky spark of mischief behind the eyes. This must be how others felt when he shapeshifted into them. Their own faces mirrored in another's. Their own story hijacked and told back to them. It wasn't a comfortable feeling. It left Isaac with the uncanny impression that not only was he looking at the girl, but the girl was looking back.

Bellatine moved her finger to the adult woman. "And she looks kind of like me, don't you think? In the mouth, at least?"

"What's that?" Winifred asked, pointing to a background shape in the top right corner of the photograph. Bellatine pulled out her phone to shine more light on the image. Behind the figures squatted a building. Whitewashed walls. Sod roof. A veranda threshed in barbed wire. Three tiny animals painted above the front door. There were no legs, at least not yet—but there was no mistaking it. Thistlefoot.

Isaac and Bellatine's eyes met over the glossy photo.

"We need to know what these letters say."

Bellatine cracked her knuckles. "This'll take forever to translate. I guess we start by decoding each individual character? Then once we do that, we can type the English letters into the translator app."

"Or," Isaac countered, "we read it in Yiddish."

"Oh, have you been studying up?" She rolled her eyes.

"No. But I know someone who has been."

Bellatine paused. "Someone *here*?"

"Yes, ma'am. Snap Piernes. Runs a local ephemera collection out of an old warehouse on Saint Claude, but he did a spell at rabbinical school before dropping out and moving to NOLA. So he can read Yiddish *and* is used to messing with old documents."

"So we stop by the warehouse," Bellatine said.

Isaac shook his head in dismissal. "Doubt he'll be in. That place goes dark for weeks, it's mostly storage." A grin began to cut across his face.

"Dare I ask why you're smiling?" Bellatine tested.

"I'm *smiling* because while I don't know where Snap is now, I know *exactly* where he'll be tonight. Wouldn't miss it." Isaac reached into his pocket for the pink flyer. *Lantern Parade. You know where. You know why.*

CHAPTER TWENTY-EIGHT

THE FOUR BOYS SLINKED through Old East Baltimore, streetlamps lighting behind them as if the night itself were in pursuit. Ahead: a looming iron gate flanked by wet stone. First one boy, then another, slipped through the bars butter-slick, scurrying like salamanders into the shadows. The third hesitated.

"Hurry up, slug, or you'll get us caught!" Ronan, the fourth boy, whispered from behind, giving Percy a shove. Percy flinched.

They were the Barclay Street crew, raised up together in the same tenement six blocks north from where they now stood, mischief kings of Lafayette Middle School—and tonight, they were on the prowl.

Luke bounced on his toes beyond the gate, his new green Nikes squeaking against the sod like eager mice. His twin brother, Connor, kept watch, scouting ahead. Through the arch's black rungs, Percy could see hundreds of gravestones, pale as cornsilk in the low light. He shivered. Gates existed for a reason. For safety. For keeping the dead and living in their place.

"Dude, come *on*," Ronan prodded.

What's worse—ghosts, or being branded a coward?

"I'm . . . going," Percy huffed. He hoisted the backpack full of firecrackers higher on his shoulder, squeezed all the air from his lungs, and wedged himself between the widest bars. He wasn't little like the twins, twice their width and a foot taller, and getting through took effort. Metal jabbed into his stomach. His shirt snagged on a metal hook, ripping as he tumbled to the ground on the other side.

"S-sorry." He struggled up, brushing gravel from his palms.

Ronan crawled in behind him.

"You ready?" Connor said.

Percy nodded.

From across the graveyard, a flickering glow appeared, as if from a single candle. Voices tittered over the stones.

Luke's eyes flashed. "Let's do this."

Before Percy could catch his breath, the twins had darted off into Green Mount Cemetery, vanishing behind tombstones. Ronan snapped his fingers and bolted after, leaving Percy to make pace behind.

Keisha had told Jordan and Jordan had told Tan and Tan had told Luke that some of the girls from their class were going to sneak into the graveyard after dark to do some kind of witchy thing.

"Sounds dumb," Connor had said, after Luke told the other three.

Sounds dangerous, thought Percy, knowing better than to say it aloud. There was a code among the Barclay Street kids: *never* be the wimp.

"Sounds like we should scare them," grinned Ronan. And when Ronan made a plan, the rest of the boys followed.

Percy panted, jogging after his friends. He felt cumbersome, exposed, too looming to dart invisibly through the stones like his friends could. Afraid to trail behind, he pushed himself faster. His foot landed on an uneven patch of sod and twisted beneath him. Percy went down with a yelp.

"Jesus, again?" Connor groaned.

Percy had landed in a rough, hollow ditch. Panic shot through him—was it a newly dug *grave*? No—the dip was far too shallow, and altogether the wrong shape. As he pulled himself up, he saw that the hole wasn't dug, but imprinted, as if stamped into the earth by something large and heavy. The edges zigzagged in broad stripes, making the indentation resemble the footprint of a giant bird. Something soft swept against his leg. He picked it up. A long, downy feather.

"Never leave a man behind." Ronan smirked, stooping down to extend a hand.

Percy took it. He stuffed the feather into his pocket, running his fingers over the silken strands as he scrambled back on his feet.

Limping on, he cast a final glance over his shoulder. The footprint filled with shadow, swallowed by the night.

Soon, they'd reached a portioned-off cluster of graves tucked away from the rest so they could prepare without being seen. Here, the stones were different from the others—older, chiseled with vines and feathers. Atop some, visitors had left smooth, palm-sized stones. The boys gathered at an obelisk, the base large enough for all four to crouch behind.

"Do you think," Connor whispered, "they're gonna be naked?"

Ronan slapped the back of his head. "Fuckin' idiot, why would they be naked?"

Connor shrugged. "Like in that movie, where at the end all the witches dance around the fire and that girl is there, and she takes all her clothes off."

"They're not gonna be naked."

"Could be."

Ronan plopped down a paper bag, pulling out four plastic masks they'd bought half off at Spirit Halloween, translucent with painted mustaches and eyebrows forming an eerie double face when the boys put them on. The elastic snapped against the back of Percy's shaved head as he adjusted it. It felt different, having a mask to hide behind. Like having someone else in charge of his body. Someone braver. He could do this. Tonight, *tonight*, he wasn't gonna be the wimp.

Percy unzipped his backpack.

"Zdraviya zhelayu," a man's voice said through the dark.

Percy yanked his head up so fast it cracked against the stone behind him. His friends stiffened.

"Shit," Luke said, "someone's out th—"

Connor thrust a hand over his brother's mouth.

From the other side of the obelisk, slow, steady footsteps crunched along the walkway. Were they coming closer? Percy couldn't tell. His gaze flicked to his open backpack. A flash of red paper. The firecrackers' wicks poking out the top. It was bad enough that they'd broken in after hours, but if he were caught with those . . . Kids his age had been banished to juvie for less. Percy's boldness left him. He wished his mask could make him invisible. His ears rang with fear.

No, not fear. There was a strange fizzing in the air, like in his mom's old Ford where the radio only played static. The footsteps mingled with the sound. And now it was certain: they were approaching.

"What do we do?" Percy whispered, low as he could muster.

"I am glad that you asked," the man said. The boys jumped. He stood right in front of them, tall and sinewy, backed by gray light. He wore a long coat that rippled like smoke, though there was no wind.

Ronan stepped forward, cocky as ever, hands on his hips. "Can we help you?"

Percy shifted, blocking his backpack and the firecrackers with his body. Sometimes it helped to be big.

The man smiled. "So eager to be of service. The sign of a fine soldier."

"L-look man, we're just heading home," Connor stuttered from behind Ronan. "It's the shortcut, and we were—"

"Yeah, cutting through," Luke said, "to get home."

The man surveyed the graveyard.

"Looking for someone?" Ronan said, lifting his chin. Why did he have to be so confrontational all the time? Percy started to shrink further against the stone, but stopped himself. *Tonight, I'm not the wimp.*

"I am tracking my fate. Great footsteps, crushed in time. You touched that fate—I can tell from the soil on your knees, the softness in your pocket." The stranger's smile, now aimed at Percy, widened. "And so it is that you have crushed your own footsteps into time, which I must acknowledge. There can only be so many footsteps in one story, you see. So many witnesses."

The man's voice was solid, like the stone at Percy's back. The sound of static had risen. There was a crackling beneath it, like sticks breaking. No, like fire, licking up a wall. Percy glanced around. Nothing. *Where was it coming from?*

The man pulled something from his coat and Ronan stepped back, wary.

"I do not mean to startle," said the stranger. "It is only an offering, in goodwill."

It was a glass bottle, black blue, stopped with a cork to contain the liquid sloshing inside. The man held it out. *"Za vstrechu,"* he said, hoisting the drink, then took a swig.

"What's he saying?" Luke muttered.

"A toast," Percy said. *"To our meeting."*

"How'd you know that?" Connor asked.

How *had* he known? The man's voice was familiar to him, like a song he'd listened to on repeat, learned by heart. The stranger tilted the bottle toward Ronan.

"Well, my friend?"

Ronan hesitated. Almost as if he were . . . Percy balked. *No.* Impossible. Ronan had never been afraid of anything in his life. He was the troublemaker of troublemakers, reckless to a fault. Percy had once seen him jump off the highest bleacher at the football field just to prove he could. Yet the look of worry on his face was undeniable. Percy almost laughed—he *was* afraid. For once, *Ronan* was the wimp!

An idea came to Percy then, erupting in him like a firecracker.

This was it. His chance to prove himself, once and for all. Tonight, he would show the others that he was braver than all of them.

Percy stepped forward. He clenched his fists. "I'll have some."

Ronan's forehead furrowed. "Hey, man, I don't know if that's—"

Percy snatched the bottle and took a deep, fearless swig. The liquid was warm and smoky. It tasted like courage.

And then, all he saw was white.

"Yo." Ronan touched his shoulder. "You okay?" But Percy barely heard him through the static. It was wafting off the stranger in waves. That flame-like hiss, but now it clamored with the click of rifles. Horses' hooves thudding against earth. Wailing.

"You are a brave young soldier," the stranger said.

Brave. Yes. Yes. King of the Barclay Street crew. His heart thundered in his broad chest. Adrenaline jolted through him like electricity. Like he was charging into war.

"Your small friends, can they boast the same?"

His friends . . . His fist tightened on the bottle. They'd always thought they were better than him. That he wasn't man enough. They wanted to keep him down so they could feel strong. His shoulders bowed with new weight, but he barely felt it through the tightening of his muscles. Percy turned. They *were* small. Smaller than him. Weaker.

"Dude, what's wrong with you?" Ronan squinted. He spun on the stranger. "What did you do to hi—"

The stranger stepped back. From over Percy's shoulder, a crackling voice whispered in his ear, hot as coals. And Percy listened.

White smoke swirled among him and his friends, thick as cream.

I am the king. I won't be pushed aside. I won't be made small. I am the strongest of all of us.

And they will know.

Percy charged, barreling into Ronan's stomach. The boy fell back against the monument with a moan.

"Good soldier," the man hummed, his voice like a chorus of voices climbing over one another, tangling to be heard. "Is it not time to take what is yours?"

What's mine. Take what's mine.

Percy didn't feel the twins at his sides, trying to pry him off. Only the squeeze of the weight on his back. Only the strain of his muscles, coming into their strength. The feel of hair gripped in his fist, a face pulled back, the blue bottle still gripped in his other hand. To be weak was to die. Percy knew that now. He slammed his enemy's head into the tombstone with a wet crack. The bottle spilled in the tumult. A vapor rose, tendriling around the boys. A perfume of burning hay. Ash. Animal rot. It filled their lungs. Crawled onto their backs. Three long, pale creatures took hold, their smoke-built limbs tightening. Three sets of corneas filled with smoke, visions smudging with white haze. The fourth set, slack and unseeing on the stone, dark blood pooling.

I'm not weak. They will never see me as weak again.

Percy had never felt so good.

Across the cemetery, the lone candle flickered. Girls' laughter floated on the breeze. The boys and their passengers lifted their heads. They sniffed the air. *We will take what is ours.*

The Longshadow Man was already gone.

CHAPTER TWENTY-NINE

THIS MUST BE WHAT *death feels like.*

The notion came to Bellatine easily, a simple fact more than a theory. *Soft death, anyway—purgatory, a hovering, eternal place.*

They were gathered in a grove of live oaks deep within the swamp. The trees were ancient, their boughs so long they drooped like hooked elbows onto the ground. A brassy moan of tuning instruments droned through the branches, melding with whispers. In the darkness, Bellatine could only make out the rough outlines of human forms—smudged shapes that moved and tittered in clusters as more and more bodies gathered. Fifty? Seventy? A hundred? Spanish moss dripped from above— *As if the trees' souls are falling out,* Bellatine thought.

Before seeking the Lantern Parade, Isaac had insisted they stop at Dollar General for supplies. LED lights. A frothing garland of fake peonies. A palette of face paint. "If you want to blend in, you have to stand out," he'd said, rouging two scarlet circles over his whitened cheeks, along with exaggerated black teardrops beneath each eye like the Drowning Fool. He wrestled a pink flower crown over his swarm of hair. Bellatine had begrudgingly painted blue stars on her cheeks and hearts on Winnie's, dabbed with silver glitter.

They parked Thistlefoot a mile away, obscured by a stand of magnolias. Isaac had sworn he remembered where the entrance was, and he had—an invisible trailhead marked only by a single flickering votive in a glass jar, hanging from a cypress branch. Though the last burn of twilight had pinched out an hour ago, they'd felt their way along a trail of boot prints and chained-up bicycles until they'd arrived at the meeting place.

It had been nearly half an hour now of lingering, invisible and sightless in the wood. Bellatine couldn't shake the feeling of *afterlife*, a single moment in perpetuity. It was the same feeling she'd had as a child in the Yaga theater, just before curtains opened. The playhouse plunged in darkness. An audience of held breaths. Time dangling in suspension . . . And in that instant, anything, *anything* could come next.

"What are we waiting for?" Bellatine whispered to her brother.

"Soon," was his only reply.

How will we ever find Snap Piernes here?

A trumpet pierced the dusk. All the muddled night sounds coalesced and sharpened, the whispering snuffed out and replaced by a long, reverberating chord. A brass band started up.

"*Now*," Isaac said. He flipped on his LED lights, which were coiled inside a white linen bindle on the end of a stick. The parcel glowed over his shoulder like a cotton moon. Kneeling, he activated a flashing bauble tied to Hubcap's tail, who'd been weaving between their feet the whole walk over. Bellatine and Winnie followed suit, flipping the plastic switches illuminating their own lights—Bellatine's snaking around her head in a gold halo, Winnie's braided into her hair. But they weren't the only ones. All throughout the swamp, beacons ignited. There were round paper lanterns seeping blue glow; a crown pointed in wax taper candles licked with real fire; a parasol full of glittering stars. As the forest lit up, the smudged shadows brightened as well: people. Hundreds of people now, laughing and flicking open lighters, crackling like static. Beside her, Bellatine heard Winifred gasp.

The parade began. The brass band took the lead like the head of a giant serpent. Rhythm hot and rugged, cornets trilling ragtime.

"Come on, kid." Isaac prodded her arm. She hadn't realized she'd been standing still, the procession flowing past her like a tide.

"How will we know Piernes when we see him?" she called to her brother over the trombone.

"You won't! I will. *You're* going to have fun." He thrust something into her hand, wrapped in a paper bag. "It's whiskey, not poison. Promise." She could have sworn she saw him wink, though his face was ensconced in shadow. Before Bellatine could stop him, Isaac darted away, swallowed by the crowd. The blinking light on Hubcap's tail bobbed along behind, then vanished.

Fuck. If Isaac was good at anything, it was disappearing. She could swim through the mass all she wanted—she wasn't going to find him till he wanted to be found. She gritted her teeth and turned to Winnie to deliver the bad news—but her words caught in her throat.

Pale silver light settled on Winifred as if her skin itself were lit from the inside. Her eyes were wide, multicolored sparks dancing in tears that clung to her lashes. "It's *beautiful*," she sighed, her voice like a small bird.

Yes, Bellatine realized. It was.

Her stomach twisted against the swell of joy. *I can't afford distraction. I can't afford to slip up again.* Her fingertips prickled with nervous heat. She squeezed her eyes shut. Through her eyelids, she could still see pale auras ebbing in pinks and lilacs and glowworm greens. She tried to smother the yearning part of her, the lantern deep in her chest growing warmer and warmer, but it only brightened. She was so tired. Tired of holding on. Tired of holding back.

Then, a chilled hand laced into hers and the heat in her palms vanished. Her eyes sprang open—Winnie's smile was lit like a torch. Whatever secret door Bellatine had been pushing, pushing, pushing shut within herself flew wide. The world was effulgent, built of light. The parade swept them forward.

Winnie tugged them deeper into the crowd until Bellatine couldn't tell where the cavalcade began and ended. The girls wove through apparitions: a woman in a hoop skirt stitched with smoldering roses. A masked owl carrying a candelabrum. A man juggling suns. All the while, the music wailed fat and golden through the treetops. Hundreds of celestial bodies promenaded in time to the beat. Light and heat and flame everywhere—but Bellatine's hand was cool in Winifred's grasp.

They marched on. Through the wood. Over a small plywood bridge above a creek. Past a lagoon, where lanterns' reflections rippled in the water like a second procession trailing alongside their own. Snippets of conversation tangled into one another and snapped off mid-thought. A yip sounded, and two dogs bolted past Bellatine's legs, lights dangling from their collars. She teetered, brushing against a six-foot-tall jellyfish glowing with phosphorescence, and yanked away for fear of waking it. Winnie grabbed the whiskey Isaac had given them, uncapped the cheap plastic bottle with her teeth, and took a deep swig. She sputtered, her nose wrinkled. After coming up for air she laughed a belly laugh like church bells.

"I'm living. I'm *living*," Winifred sang, more to herself, Bellatine thought, than to her.

After a while, the ragtime slowed. The music grew mournful and languorous, Baltic dirges heavy with minor notes. How long had they been walking? An hour? Two? Ten? Her feet had been sore, but she'd walked through it until they were numb. Again, she felt the weightlessness of the afterlife. Time had passed over them. Daylight might never come. No clocks anymore, save for a euphonium's grunt. No coming or going, only *continuing.* Silk gowns flowing like water. Torches hissing in the dark. Bellatine's own body shifting, intangible. She was fog. Signal smoke. The only thing grounding her was Winifred's hand, knotted solid and certain in her own.

Eventually, they reached a break in the trees, followed by an open field. The music stopped, replaced by chatter and laughter as the band set down their instruments and passed around a joint. Figures broke off from the parade and formed clumps, friends finding one another and settling in the tall grass. Bellatine and Winnie flopped down on a mop of weeds. From where they sat, they could see the entire congregation, spread around them like squares on a gem-encrusted quilt. The spectacle reminded her of summers in Vermont, when fireflies claimed the cow field behind Joseph's workshop as a breeding ground. Come sundown, the entire pasture would blink with thousands of small lights, as if the sky had been laid upon the earth, pricked with constellations.

Bellatine knew she should let go of Winifred's hand. *She isn't a person,* she reminded herself. *She's a mistake. My mistake. This isn't real.* But nothing about tonight felt real—and wasn't that the magic of it? She didn't want to let go. Not yet.

The two sat close enough that Bellatine could feel Winifred's ribs expand and contract with each breath. *So she* does *breathe. That's real.* Or was it? The girl's chest rose and fell in time with Bellatine's own, as if following along. Winifred's gaze followed a man clad in a raccoon costume as he kissed a fox-woman, each with diamonds of light jeweled in their whiskers and the tips of their ears.

"What was it like?" Bellatine asked, interrupting Winifred's trance. "Before. Before you woke up." She uncapped the whiskey bottle one-handed and took a clumsy sip. It burned her throat, but not an Embering burn. More like the warmth of a lantern.

Winnie shrugged. "Oh, it was awfully dull. Nothing like your life."

Bellatine scoffed. "My life?"

"You've seen so much of the world! It must be exciting."

"I haven't. And it's not." *Not when I can help it.*

"All I've ever done is stand still." She sighed. "I watched people. And clouds. Animals, too. I watched trees grow." She plucked a wildflower from the ground and worked it into her yellow braid, which still shone with plastic light. "And before that, well, there was the funeral. And Everett, and the bouquets, and a woman, her—*my* mother, all in black. But through it all, I just . . . watched."

Bellatine nodded. "And before all that? Before you were Winifred?"

Winnie's forehead wrinkled. "I am the memory of Winifred Hadley, stricken with—"

"I know. I know you are. But was there anything before Everett, and the flowers, and your mother?" She passed Winnie the bottle. "With us, people I mean, we start small and get bigger. But with you, it must have been the opposite. You started as part of the earth and were carved down, I imagine. Do you remember that?"

Winifred's gaze slid over the field and beyond. Her next words seemed to struggle out of her.

"Before Winifred Hadley . . ." She turned to Bellatine, uncertain. "Are you sure I'm allowed to remember that?"

Bellatine raised her eyebrows, surprised. "Memories aren't things you are or aren't allowed to have. They're either inside you or they're not."

Winifred fell silent. Bellatine chewed her lip—she hadn't meant to offend. Who knows what statues find offensive anyway.

Winnie took a swig from the plastic bottle, followed by a deep, heavy breath. "I remember . . . molten. Red and boiling. There was rain. I didn't have a word for it, then, but now I know, that's what it was. A thousand years of rain." She took another sip from the bottle. "It's strange. Words, they never belonged to me. I heard people talking but it glided right through me. Then when you woke me up, it was as if I'd known the names for things all along. Isn't that funny?"

Bellatine accepted the bottle as Winifred passed it back. Already the world was feeling fuzzy and sweet.

"After the rain," Winnie continued, "these giant sheets of ice sliced through me, like big slugs crawling on the earth. They were so heavy, it was almost unbearable. And you have to understand, time, it didn't work for me then like it does now. It lasted forever, like . . ."

"Like tonight," Bellatine said, a glowing paper heron winging past them, roped to a man on wooden stilts.

"Like tonight." Winnie nodded.

"Then what?"

"Men came. They were so *delicate*; I'd never seen anything so fragile. I couldn't believe creatures that mortal and *smooshy* could break through me, but they did. First, explosions. Then pickaxes. There was a wagon and hauling songs as they carried me. And the *me*, I was different suddenly. Smaller. *Separate*. Before, I was part of . . . so much more.

"I remember the chisel, tapping against my cheek." She brushed a finger against Bellatine's as if the memory belonged to both of them now. "Things have always happened *to* me. Around me. I've watched the living, I've learned from them. But I've never joined them. Not until now."

Neither have I, Bellatine thought. The world swirled around her, and yet, her hands remained calm and silent.

Winnie snapped another flower at the stem. "Feel this!"

Hastily, Bellatine brushed her fingers over petals. It was smooth and waxy, and Bellatine's skin tingled in the flower's wake.

"Isn't that the softest thing you've ever felt?"

Bellatine tried to think of a poetic response, but instead fumbled out an "I guess so."

Winifred laughed. "You aren't paying attention! Come on, close your eyes and *feel* it." Winifred pressed the flower to the spot on Bellatine's cheek she'd moments ago touched.

This time, Bellatine put all her focus onto the point where the petals met her skin—and on Winifred's cool fingertips beyond. Winnie smelled good, garden soil and lemon rind with a hint of dew. The point of contact tickled. A shiver passed through her. She pulled back.

"So?"

"It's pretty soft," Bellatine mumbled. She downed more of the terrible whiskey, and her nerves went slack and bubbly as it hit her stomach.

Winifred graced the flower over her own bottom lip and beamed. "For me, it's like everything in the world is a conversation. Every time something touches me, it feels like that part of me wakes up all over again to listen." She surveyed the meadow, her gaze flicking from lantern to lantern.

"I suppose I have seen a lot, even in the past century. Masses of weeping women in black veils, and children lined up in neat rows, and so many somber priests all wrapped in raincoats. There was a lot of talk about the *proper* way to behave in the cemetery. Don't step on a grave. Don't talk too loud. Don't eat or drink or climb on the stones. But you know what, Bell? All those people making all those rules—they got it wrong. That's not respect. You know the only real way to respect people whose lives are over? Or those like me, whose lives never even began?"

"How?" Bellatine breathed. She wanted to know. She wanted to learn everything. Somehow, she'd dismissed Winifred as ditzy, frivolous, airy. But she was wrong. This was an ancient being. She was a part of the planet itself.

Winifred's eyes lit up. "You prove to them that you aren't wasting yours."

Bellatine's heart pounded against her sternum. Maybe Winnie could hear it.

"There were kids, sometimes. Teenagers. They used to sneak into the graveyard after dark. They'd climb over gravestones and hold fake séances and set off firecrackers and . . . and"—her voice dipped low—"they did other things, too, there in the dark. Things the priests would never have approved of. But *they* got it right. They knew that the real difference between being alive and dead, it's this." Winifred held up the flower. "It's *feeling* things, *tasting, smelling. That's* being awake. It's the only thing that matters, Bell. The only thing people really have. But I've never . . ." Bellatine felt the hand in hers squeeze tighter. "I've never been *part* of it."

Winifred grabbed the bottle back, tipped it back to her lips, and chugged, before revealing her teeth in a wild beam. "I think I'm drunk!" she exclaimed. "Come, I have to tell you a secret." She turned, pressing her forehead conspiratorially to Bellatine's. "I *like* living. I want to live *more. I want all of it.*"

A ringlet of Winifred's hair fell loose and brushed against Bellatine's face. Winnie's breath carried hints of spirits and honey. Bellatine's own breath hitched. Yearning reared up deep in her belly like a wild horse. Not the Embering's call, but something else. Something nectared and sugary. She wanted to tumble into this girl, like diving into a lake. She wanted to feel her lips, not stone, not death, but real, dabbed with fading lipstick, a grain of glitter caught in the corner of her mouth. She wanted to unlace that freshly washed linen dress, to trace her collarbone, her chest, her hips. She wanted, for once in her life, to use her hands for something soft. Something good.

Bellatine untangled her fingers from Winifred's. For a moment, the absence was terrible. An error. Then, she pressed a hand to the small of Winifred's back, her fingers tightening around a fistful of fabric. The girl shivered. Her lips parted. She pulled closer.

A heavy peach moon rose over the field's crest. Bellatine didn't remember the moon being full tonight, but somehow it made sense that it was now. The original lantern. It slipped pearly light though Winifred's hair. The moon bobbed nearer. It grew arms. Legs. A body.

"If it isn't the lotus eaters," Isaac said. Bellatine dropped her arm from Winnie's back and jerked away. The round, glowing orb of Isaac's bindle swung jauntily over his shoulder. He stumbled, flopping down next to them on the ground. "Sorry to interrupt." He flicked a glance between the two women. "But I'm *bored.*"

The world grew rigid again. Whatever intoxication had seized Bellatine suddenly seemed miles away.

"Did you find Piernes?"

Isaac waved a hand. "He's around."

"Where?"

"*Around.*" He grabbed the whiskey and finished off the bottle. His peony crown drooped crookedly over one ear and someone else's purple lipstick was smeared over his mouth.

"You're drunk."

"We're not drunks," Isaac slurred, "we are *angels.*" He propped himself up on his elbows. "What do you think, Winnie? The world ain't bad, is it?"

"It's marvelous! There's so much to see and touch and—"

"I *bet*, doll. I bet." He nudged Bellatine with an elbow.

"Piernes," she demanded. "Now."

Isaac sighed, then scanned the meadow. "There." He gestured to a glowing green snake hovering vertically in the air. Bellatine squinted. It was wrapped around an arm, which attached at the shoulder to a tall Black man with a shaved head, limbs lean and narrow as a skeleton.

Bellatine marched across the field. Her vision smudged at the edges from the whiskey, but she was steady on her feet. Her lungs filled. Her lungs emptied. This was right. A task needing to be done, and all her attention set on completing it.

"Mr. Piernes?" She extended a hand.

The tall man turned. He took her hand in his, but instead of shaking it, he bent and kissed her knuckles. "How might I help you, little sprite?" Bellatine retracted her arm, wiping the wet residue on the leg of her overalls.

Snap Piernes wore a pine-green coat and matching trousers, with a frilled undershirt unbuttoned to the base of his ribs and a pair of white gloves. He looked to be nearing forty, his face highlighted by a waxed spiral mustache thin enough to have been drawn in pencil. He would surely have been considered luxurious by any nineteenth-century dandy. To Bellatine's surprise, what she'd assumed to be merely a coil of green lights mimicking a snake's shape turned out to trail the spine of an actual snake—a python, tightened around Piernes' left arm.

"I'm told you can read Yiddish," Bellatine said.

"Yiddish, Hebrew, German, Latin, French, Haitian Creole, and"—he stroked a finger along the python's head—"ancient Mesopotamian."

Bellatine stifled a scoff. No wonder Isaac liked the scene here. It was a theater of posturing.

"I need help translating a letter or two, and I was told you're the person to ask. Old family stuff." She drew the parcel from her pocket and held it out. "Here, it's—"

"This is a *party*, darling. Visit me during working hours." The snake flicked its forked tongue.

"Snap, old boy!" Isaac called, promenading toward them. Winnie's arm was hooked through his. A stab of heat shot into Bellatine's hands.

"*Thrilling*," Snap muttered under his breath. He leaned toward Bellatine. "Ever meet a wolf spider? Its bite can kill." He nodded in Isaac's direction.

"I see you've met my little sister," Isaac said, slinging his free arm over her.

Snap reassessed Bellatine. He took a step back. "Charmed."

"Doubtful. She isn't famed for her savoir vivre."

"A family curse, it appears."

Isaac released the women and clapped his hands together, ignoring the slight. "So you'll do us this quick favor." A command, not a question.

Snap Piernes laughed. "*Favor.* From Latin's *favēre*, meaning *to offer goodwill. To cherish*, even. Tragically, I neither like nor cherish you, so an offer of goodwill would be disingenuous of me. I, dissimilar to some, try to remain sincere."

Friends the world round, her brother.

Isaac drew out his ancient phone and flipped it open. Slowly, he dialed a series of digits, then held it to his ear. He smiled, holding up a finger for quiet.

"You rapacious, stingy cocksuckers," he slurred into the mouthpiece. Something was off about his voice. He sounded twice as inebriated as he had a moment ago—but the inflection and pitch had also modulated. "Do you have any *idea* the rare collection I'm working with? The *inestimable* worth of"—he hiccupped—"of . . . of the . . . the expertise I bring to your sagging, moth-bitten institution? And you call this a *donation*? With all due regard, gag on your pittance and on my . . ." The final words garbled into mumbling.

Piernes went rigid. "What is this?"

Bellatine's ears pricked with paradox. It was Snap Piernes' voice. Isaac had mimicked it with uncanny accuracy—each vocal dip and intonation, the precise harmonics, the cadence of the words . . . tilted with a whiskeyed flourish.

A robotic voice chimed from the receiver. *"If you are satisfied with your voicemail, press one. To erase and rerecord, press two."*

Isaac held the phone aloft like a gun with the safety off. "The Louisiana Antiquarian Institute. They made their annual donation to your archive this week, yes? Generous of them, singlehandedly keeping your operations funded. Too bad their contribution was a tad slimmer around the waist this year." Isaac clicked his tongue. *"Frustrating."*

Piernes tossed his head with forced nonchalance. "They'll know it's an impostor. I'll tell them."

"Good idea. They definitely won't assume you drank yourself blind after receiving a disappointing check and awoke with no memory of filing this . . . humble complaint."

"Please make a selection. If you're satisfied with your message, press one."

Snap's nostrils flared. "I'll lose my funding. The archive relies on—"

Isaac wiggled his fingers and the phone twirled through them like an ace of spades in a magic act. Snap sucked in a sharp breath. "I may have misspoken, a moment ago," Isaac said. "The Chameleon King doesn't call for favors. He calls for payment. My apologies if I was unclear."

The man sagged, then reached out his hand to Bellatine, his eyes downcast. "The letters." She passed over the pile.

"See, easy," Isaac said.

"You can't expect me to translate this entire collection." Snap blanched, assessing the stack.

"Look for anything of interest," Isaac directed. "Here." He removed a crumpled sheet of blank paper and a ballpoint pen from his coat pocket, handing both to Snap.

Piernes leafed through the pages, scanning the contents one by one. He shook his head. "Most of these are nothing. Drivel. Menial descriptions of working at a clothing factory. General pleasantries." He frowned, hesitating over one yellowed paper. "I suppose this one has a bit more *personality*."

"Write," Isaac demanded.

Piernes bent over the sheet, his eyes flicking back and forth between the letter and his hand as he scribbled by lantern light. Over the hill, the music kicked up again. The trumpet skirled a march and the rest of the brass band followed.

"Quickly," Isaac prodded. Throughout the meadow, revelers began to re-form into an undulating river, lamp-fed beasts and wonders tightening into a line like the golden zipper of a chrysalis. Snap rushed the pen across the page. Finally, just as the procession began to move, he sat back and handed Isaac the handwritten document along with the originals, which Isaac slipped into his coat.

"A pleasure, as ever, Mister Yaga," he hissed to Isaac through his teeth. "Now, I believe it's your turn."

Isaac made a show of pressing a button on his keypad.

"Thank you. Your message has been sent."

Piernes' face froze in horror.

"That was for saying you didn't cherish me." Isaac tipped his floral crown, grinned, and spun on his heel to rejoin the parade.

Bellatine and Winnie scurried after.

"Why did you do that?"

"We needed the letter, we got the letter."

"But you didn't have to send the voicemail! His funding, it'll be—"

"His funding will be fine. Oh, here, you have a missed call." He tossed something Bellatine's way and she caught it, fumbling—her phone. A little yellow envelope in the screen's corner signaled a new voicemail. It was from Isaac.

"How did you get this?" she asked, palming her empty pocket.

Isaac shrugged. "Had to make sure it was on silent."

"You . . . never called them," she realized aloud.

"This may come as a shock to you," Isaac said, "but I don't know the Louisiana Antiquarian Institute's number by heart."

"You're a schmuck, you know that?"

Isaac curtsied, lifting an invisible skirt hem. "You flatter me."

Winifred's footing lurched as Hubcap pounced in front, but Bellatine steadied her before she could trip. She blushed at the contact, thankful for the dark.

"How'd you know about the donation check?" Bellatine asked.

"Overheard him griping about it to someone back at the trailhead. Always listen for whiners, Tiny. A complaint is a map to a person's weakness."

"You spotted him back at base and didn't shake him down till now?"

"And miss the festivities?"

Bellatine could see the corner of the translated letter peeking out from Isaac's coat. In the gleam of a thousand lanterns, the paper seemed to emit its own feverish glow. A star with its own gravity. Its own orbiting planets. Bellatine. Isaac. Thistlefoot. Winifred, too. Their twice-great-grandmother, and those who came after. The Longshadow Man. All circling. Tightening. All linked by invisible strings, like a box of marionettes grown knotted. She could feel the letter's pull, its weight, reaching through time, through blood, tugging them closer and closer, nearer and nearer to collision.

A bulbous papier-mâché turtle galumphed through the crowd. Its glitter-slicked shell smacked into Isaac, and a man's head popped out from within.

"Sorry about that, mate, I'm a bit—" He stopped short.

Isaac flinched infinitesimally. "Max, buddy, it's been a while." He thudded two firm pats against the wide costume.

"Isaac. *Isaac.* Do you have— I mean—" Max bumbled. "Not to put you out, but my truck, you know— Do you have— Christ, what I'm trying to ask is if—"

A sleek-boned redhead emerged beside the turtle. She had glow-in-the-dark stars dangling from her earlobes and a sequined fanny pack bounced on one hip. When she saw Isaac, her eyes widened. If Isaac, too, was surprised, he hid it well.

"Nina," he said with a small bow.

As he rose, Nina slapped him across the face.

"You fuckhead. Where's Max's car?" she said, taking the turtle's hand.

Isaac rubbed his cheekbone. He flashed a glance at the duo's entwined fingers and for a moment, Bellatine saw something like hurt flicker in his eyes—but it was gone as soon as it appeared.

The turtle's voice warbled high and unsure. "Man, I'm sure you had your reasons, you know? It was an emergency, right?"

The redheaded girl shook her head. "He stole your fucking truck, Max. Screw his *reasons.*"

"She's right. Bad reasons." Isaac nodded.

Max opened and closed his mouth like a fish.

"But you're welcome to it!" Isaac continued. "Should be somewhere on the roadside in North Carolina if they didn't scrap it yet." Bellatine felt Isaac nudge her with a foot. A signal.

"Delightful to see you both. Nina, radiant as ever. Max, love the new look." The redhead stepped forward just as a ten-foot centipede wriggled near on wooden poles. Isaac hooked an arm through Bellatine's. Bellatine grabbed Winnie. With a yank, Isaac had pulled the trio behind the enormous insect, and within a moment, they were lost again in the crowd. Nina and Max may as well have been mirages, scattered by the wind.

This was how Isaac lived. Part of your life one moment, gone the next, and taking what he wanted. Bellatine hadn't seen his vanishings from this angle before, hadn't seen what became of Isaac *after* disappearing. When she was young, she used to imagine he hadn't left at all, but rather had become something . . . else. Scattered rain on her windowsill. A bank of gray fog in the middle school parking lot. The whistle of a train, fading in the distance. Not a brother who'd abandoned her. A presence, rather than an absence. But here he was. Solid. Breathing. Winging through the crowd with the conviction of a falcon on the hunt. From Isaac's perspective, Max and Nina were the fog, now, thin and bodiless enough to walk right through. Like they'd never existed. Was that how he'd thought of her, too?

"Who were those people?" Winnie asked, casting a look over her shoulder. "They seemed rather displeased with you."

"Out of sight and into the frying pan," Isaac said.

"Are you having a stroke?" Bellatine side-eyed.

"Something a buddy of mine used to say, that's all." Isaac brushed his lapels as if shaking off a ghost and stumbled onward.

Beside her, Winifred was touching Bellatine's palm again, slowly dragging a finger up and down the delicate skin of her wrist. Bellatine closed her eyes. She felt the stone girl slide behind her, felt Winnie's lips graze the back of her neck. A small sigh escaped her. And for a moment, a single, suspended moment, she forgot to hold herself together.

As soon as she did, her hands screeched with heat. They vibrated in the company of the many masks, glowing puppets, papier-mâché creatures with lantern eyes, begging to be woken. She saw the roadside deer in her mind's eye. Heard its death-bray. *No.*

She spun, shoving Winifred away.

"I'm sorry." She shook her head. "I can't. This is a mistake."

She sprinted ahead to catch up with her brother. Her nails cut half-moons into her palms. Her heart thudded in time to the drums.

CHAPTER THIRTY

Dearest Mother,

Yes, yes, it is naïve of me to keep sending you letters. Eleven have gone unanswered now. What satisfaction it will be when this one makes an even dozen! Perhaps you've created a calendar of them, one jaunty rejection per month to hang on your bedroom wall. Or perhaps these aren't reaching you at all.

How am I supposed to contact an address that refuses to stand still? No matter. I keep trying.

Mama, America is a filthy country. I walk home each night after I finish at the factory, and as I walk, I peer in windows. Dozens of women, men, children, crammed into rooms the size of dinner plates. Tangled sheets, yellow light like jaundice. And outside, no one greets each other. It is even common to find Jews hawking wares from pushcarts—on Sabbath! Here, no day is holy. Here, every day is for laboring. America makes a shiksa of me. My hair, you would not believe it, but it has blanched almost white from leaning over the steam vat where we dye the men's shirts. I'm sixteen going on a hundred.

I have only two solaces:

One—I have convinced the foreman's little son that I am a demon (as he believes all Jews are) and that if he does not bring me bits of stationery and ribbon and chocolate bonbons from his father's office, I will eat him.

Two—Ice cream! I'd never had ice cream until this spring. It's marvelous. It's sweet and cold and you can buy it from a cart on Hester Street for fifteen cents. If I save up, I can have a dish with two scoops each month. So far, I have had vanilla and chocolate ripple. Next month I will try strawberry.

Mama, I miss you. Sometimes I imagine coating my letters in glue, so that when you touch them, they stick to you and you cannot toss them aside. Messy, but worth the trouble. Sometimes I imagine walking all the way to Long Island and sneaking into the hangar where they keep old Jenny planes on display from the war. I'd climb into the cockpit and my hands would find all the right levers and there I'd be, in the sky, headed home. Can you imagine? Your little bird, airborne at last!

But I know these are only fantasies. Even if I were to find my way to you, there is no home for me there. Gedenkrovka is gone.

I have been seeing the soldiers again. They appear in my sleep, and their reflections flicker in place of my own when I look into a basin of water or a shopwindow. Sometimes I see green Jews coming fresh off the boat, children bundled to their breasts and dragging their boxes and valises and copper pots behind them, and my heart becomes a wasp in my chest. There in the clusters, I see the soldiers' faces. Sometimes they look like the young one by the river. Other times like the short one with the harelip who killed Reb Haim. Others look only like a torch, burning. But then I blink, and they vanish. It is only a new crop of immigrants, like me, fleeing one sourness for another. Weariness hangs off them like a tallis.

In my dreams, a soldier sits on my chest and drops lit matches into my mouth. I refuse to swallow and spit the fire back at him. But Mama—sometimes I want to let the dybbuk take me and be done with it. Perhaps I am mad. If so, there are worse fates for women. I would be happy to lose my senses. Then I would no longer have to see the world as it is. I would no longer have to remember what happened to us.

Look at me, writing frankly under the assumption you'll never read this. Where has my hope gone?

Mama, someday I hope you eat ice cream from a silver cup. I would include some in this letter, but it would not keep well in a paper envelope. Until we find each other again, I will continue to haunt you. For the both of us.

> *Your crow,*
> *Illa*

Longing draped over the words like a burial shroud, and it was all Isaac could do to keep the veil from settling on him, too. He zeroed in on the letter's anger instead, its bite.

"She's a bit of a fiend," he said, reading it through for the second time that morning. "I like her."

"You had to get it from somewhere." Bellatine grunted, reaffixing a loose bookshelf to the living room wall. She slammed a hammer against a flathead nail. Isaac cringed.

"Mercy, kid, mercy." He pressed his hands together into a mantis' prayer, head throbbing.

"Hard work"—*bang*—"is the best"—*bang*—"remedy."

"If you're into self-flagellation. Quit it, you're tenderizing my brain like a chicken cutlet."

The text was sinking in more concretely this morning than it had the evening prior, now that his booze-sponged skull had spent the night wringing out. He'd have to coax the remaining screws out of his temples later with a greasy meal and a jug of coffee, but this was the sort of headache he could handle. Beneath it lingered satisfaction from the previous night's bout of shapeshifting. Being back to his craft, even for a few moments, had made him feel quick and deadly as a rapier.

Bellatine pounded a final nail into the shelf, then slid the hammer back into her tool belt.

"What happened to the *no nails, historical integrity* shit?"

"The furniture can have nails. Just not the building itself.

Here, fix this." She nudged the Fox puppet, whose trousers had come unstitched at the seam, toward him with a toe.

"So Illa's our great-grandmother, yeah? Mom's bubbe?" Isaac clarified, pricking a strand of gold thread through the miniature garments. Hubcap stalked over like a panther and pounced at the string.

Bellatine nodded. "Right, so the mother she's writing to, that's who left us the house. This lady." She slid Isaac the black-and-white photo of the three Yagas. "And this one"—she tapped the little girl who looked like Isaac—"that's Illa, our future letter writer. She immigrated here at twelve years old, presumably to live with an uncle in New York. And as far as I can figure, she and her mother never saw each other again."

The three faces peered up from the past. There was a talon's sharpness to young Illa, but she still had a child's spark in her eyes. None of the haunting the writer of the letter seemed to bear. What had happened to this girl in the time between the camera's flashbulb exploding and her pen landing on that sheet of paper? Whatever divided the two Illas, it was more than an ocean.

"Did Mom tell you all this?"

Bellatine snorted. "Have you ever heard Mom say a word about our family?"

"Sure. There were those stories about the Vilna Troupe, that Yiddish theatre company. She had an aunt and uncle who joined up with them at some point, I remember, because she said that's what inspired her to become a puppeteer."

Bellatine stiffened. "She never told me stories." A bloated silence padded the room.

"I must have forced her to, refused to sleep otherwise," he lied. He'd been away from home so long, he'd forgotten the glossy, cage-like distance erected between Tiny and their mother. Whether it had started before or after his sister's Embering had begun, he couldn't remember, but it had been a noticeable presence. A silent Elijah at the dinner table.

"I learned this all through some online sleuthing before you woke up," Bellatine continued, pushing past. "Couldn't find much on the shtetl she referenced—Gedenkrovka. Seemed like a barely there sort of town. But I did find mention of a pogrom in December 1919, enforced by the official Russian army. Pretty much wiped out or displaced the whole Jewish population."

"*Gedenkrovka.*" Isaac tested the village's name in his mouth. It felt clumsy and serrated, the sounds struggling to settle on his tongue. Strange that, to generations of his blood, this word must have tasted familiar. Tasted like belonging.

"I also found an Illa Yaga in the Ellis Island immigration records," Bellatine said, "dated 1922, headed to a legal guardian, Amos, who was already a citizen. And from what I could squeeze from the inheritance lawyer—who *I* called, by the way, since you clearly weren't doing it—Illa's mother only inhabited this place for a few more years after that, into the mid-twenties, before she retired it into that warehouse in Kyiv—where it was held until it came to us."

Isaac raised an eyebrow.

"Like I said"—his sister rattled the shelf to test its sturdiness—"hard work."

Winifred tiptoed into the parlor, flounced down on the clay bench, and took to occupying herself with a striped baggie of show popcorn in uncharacteristic silence. The bottom half of her blue dress was stiff with mud from the parade, but she didn't seem to notice.

Bellatine looked away, suddenly fascinated by her handiwork.

"Left in 1922," Isaac considered. "So not too long after the Russian Civil War, World War One . . . and she would have been there for the pogrom." He snapped the gold thread in his teeth, finishing off the Fox's repairs. "It's a lot to survive. I can see why Illa's family sent her to America."

"*Our* family," his sister corrected.

"I like the part about the ice cream," Winnie muttered. "I've never had ice cream."

Bellatine ignored her. "Would explain why she was hallucinating soldiers."

Ghosts. That's what Benji would have called those mirages. But Benji called most everything ghosts: Fellow travelers. Ex-sweethearts. Towns he missed. Smoke from a campfire. The sorrows that followed you long after you'd walked away . . .

"Maybe it explains the mural in the loft, too," Bellatine extrapolated, jabbing a thumb toward the bedroom.

"Like a macabre commemoration? Seems like a funny bit of memorabilia." Isaac tipped onto his back, his spine elongating against the hardwood floor. "Any of this could have put the house under enough strain to sprout a nice pair of gams. But I still don't see what any of this has a damn thing to do with our own personal Terminator."

Bellatine tightened her jaw. "We keep digging. This is solvable."

"We'll go back to Snap with more papers."

"I think you burned that bridge to the ground," Bellatine said.

"What, ol' Snap? Nah." Isaac waved her off. "He'll come around with a little sweet talking. There's another party tonight, a bonfire at the End of the World by the levee." He nudged Winifred with an elbow. "It'll be fun."

"No," Bellatine and Winnie said in unison. Winnie busied herself with scratching Hubcap behind the ears. Tiny tested the sturdiness of the bookshelf. Again.

"You two seemed like you were having a grand time last night," Isaac prodded. He shouldn't push his sister, but the dead-end bust of the letter had left him restless and itching for trouble.

"It was a mistake," Bellatine stressed. "We shouldn't have left Thistlefoot for that long. This is no time for distractions."

Winifred nodded vigorously. "Distractions." She was working hard to keep her eyes down. Away from Bellatine. *If you have to work to ignore someone, it usually means you want the opposite.* Winifred patted Hubcap more vigorously. The cat whined.

"Speaking of which," Bellatine said. "There's a leak in the kitchen ceiling I should fix before the next rain, best to do it now." She stomped out without another glance at either of them.

Of all the emotions he'd played spectator to in his career, guilt was his least favorite. It has a dense, oily quality, like a kalamata olive with the pit still in it. The few times he'd made the mistake of shapeshifting into someone blatantly guilt ridden, he'd found himself hunting for a shower after, as if scalding water might slough the sensation off. Guilt was a useless emotion. It didn't right wrongs. Didn't undo what was done. All it did was weigh a person down.

"Don't let her get to you," Isaac said to Winifred. "She just hates a good time. Some friendly company would do her good, if you catch my drift."

"It's not right," she whispered. "My head wasn't clear."

"If it's because you're both gals, times have changed since—"

"I have a fiancé!" Winnie blurted, covering her face with her hands.

"What?"

"Everett, my betrothed."

"Oh. Jesus, kid . . ."

"I could never betray him. We made vows, he told me—"

"You are not engaged to this *Everett* person," Isaac interrupted. "For one, I don't think it's legal to marry a rock in the state of Maryland. Two, the guy's definitely dead. And three, you are *not* the girl Everett was in love with."

"He came to me every day! He told me we would—"

"Tell me this," Isaac said. "What did he say when he proposed?"

"I . . ." She wrinkled her nose. "I can't . . ."

"How about your first date?"

Her eyes lit up. "He said we went to the gardens and—"

"No," Isaac sighed. "Not *he said*. What do *you* remember? What did the sky look like that day? What was he wearing? Were the gardens full of tulips or poppies?"

"They . . ." She huffed in frustration. "It was too long ago, I can't remember."

"You can't remember because you *weren't there*. *She* was."

"Who?"

"Winifred Hadley."

"*Yes*, that's me," Winnie said, exasperated.

Isaac shook his head. "I know a thing or two about doppelgängers. When you look like someone else, when you take on someone else's image, it's easy to think you're them. But you're not. You aren't the Hadley girl; you were just carved to look like her. And her? The girl who Everett loved, and who loved him? She's in a box. Dust. Dead and gone." He grabbed Winnie's hand—and jabbed it with the sewing needle.

"Ow!" Winnie yelped.

"See? *You* aren't dust. You're fucking alive."

Winifred stared at her palm. She opened her mouth. But before she could utter a response, a chime sounded in three sharp rings.

Bellatine rushed back into the parlor.

All of them stared at the bell above the door.

"Are you getting that?" Bellatine asked Isaac, sounding not entirely confident that she wanted to know who was on the other side.

"You'd think *I* was the golem around here, doing your bidding, O *master*," Isaac sighed, peeling himself up from the floor and heading for the latch.

"Thistlefoot's not a—"

"I meant her." Isaac indicated Winnie. In truth, the stone girl seemed as far as you could get from the mindless, mythical servant—but he couldn't miss the chance to take a dig at his sister. Bellatine's eyes widened.

Isaac flung the door open and grinned. "The dry cleaner makes deliveries! What service. So where's my jacket?"

"Keeping it. Makes me look dapper." Shona shoved past him into the parlor, Isaac's suit collar poking out from beneath her denim. "Look at this place! Quaint as shit. You got any food? There's got to be what, little almond teacakes and hand-churned butter all up in this place." She stopped short when she noticed Bellatine by the bookshelf. "You're the sister?"

"Who the hell are you?" Bellatine asked.

So maybe he should have informed Tiny that he'd invited the Longshadow hunters to help them. But better to ask for forgiveness than permission.

Isaac cleared his throat. "Shona, meet my little sis, Bellatine Yaga. And this"—he gestured to the plaster love seat—"is our friend Winnie. Winnie, Tiny—meet Shona." He considered patting her on the shoulder but thought better of it. Too much like petting a scorpion. "The woman who had me kidnapped, tied up, and interrogated in the back of a moving vehicle. I've invited her and her friends to stay a while."

"Are you kidding me?" Bellatine growled.

Behind them, Rummy and Sparrow hovered in the doorway.

"Here." Rummy extended a messy bouquet of wildflowers to Bellatine. "Thanks for having us."

She stared at the blossoms and crossed her arms. Rummy began to step forward, but cringed, holding a hand to his chest. Bellatine frowned.

"*They* should be thanking *us*," Shona cut in.

"*Thank you* for gracing us with your *humble* presence and expertise." Isaac took the flowers, an array of goldenrod and roadside primrose tied with a scrap of string, and stepped aside to let them in. Sparrow followed, but Rummy held back.

"I'm good right here, actually," he gulped, returning to the doorway.

"What are you, a vampire? Do you require a formal invitation?"

"Just a little under the weather. Could use the fresh air." He gave an apologetic smile.

"Ha! Killer," Sparrow exclaimed, running a finger down the wall. "Inorganic matter, fused to the organic." They popped a notebook and golf pencil from their pocket and started scribbling. "Do you think the entire house shifted on a genetic level when the legs grew? Or was it more like a tumor? I'd love to take some samples if—"

"No samples," Bellatine snapped, her arms still padlocked across her chest.

The crew had arrived clad just as Isaac had remembered—ragged and rough, Sparrow looming in a shin-length burgundy smoking jacket, Rummy in newsboy suspenders and wool, Shona in studs and combat boots, caustic as a razor blade. All three sported their signature horse-skull patches, and Isaac watched as his sister's gaze flicked from patch to patch.

"You people in some kind of cult?" she asked, pointing to the nearest one. "What is that?"

From the doorway, Rummy snorted.

"You never heard of the Duskbreaker Band?" Sparrow said with mock offense. "The sweetest end times folk-swing junket you'll ever have the pleasure to dance to."

Isaac recollected the instruments scattered around the black bus, stuffed into battered travel cases.

"You're a band," Isaac said.

"Were," Shona cut in. "Before we got caught up in this mess."

"As long as there's gas in the engine and hair on the fiddle bow, we're still a damn band," Sparrow argued.

"Let me make sure I've got this straight," Bellatine said, annunciating a little too violently for comfort. "You called in a string trio to be our big bad army?"

"I play accordion." Rummy raised his hand from the porch. "Not strings."

Bellatine's eyes turned to daggers.

"You mind?" Shona asked, plucking the bag of popcorn away from Winnie without waiting for permission. She stuffed a fistful into her face. "So," she said through mouthfuls, "what did you find for us?"

"Slow down and take a load off, doll," Isaac said, "you just got here."

The scent of chamomile and sweat wafted off Shona in a dusty cloud, with the tranquilizing allure of a Venus flytrap. *It wouldn't be so bad to be a fly . . .*

Shona scowled.

"Excuse me," Bellatine said. She crossed the room, taking Isaac by the arm. "I need to talk to my brother." She tugged him toward the bedroom, slamming the door behind them.

"We had this under control."

Isaac raised an eyebrow. "Did we?"

"I don't trust them."

"Aw, you're learning!" He patted her on the head and she withered. "Listen, we don't have to trust them. But trust *me*, they'll be useful to have around. Your enemy's enemy is worth two in the bush."

"That's not the—"

"Leave them to take care of the Longshadow Man, while we ride easy."

"This is so typical of you," she scoffed. "Palming the problem off on someone else. Have you ever taken responsibility for anything in your life?"

"That stings," he said, bringing the fist holding the flowers to his heart. He'd meant to say it with humor, but he was surprised to hear his voice slip out with an earnest twinge.

She's right, Benji's voice echoed in his head, *you're a duty-less coward,* and Isaac closed his eyes, pushing the haunting away.

"I do want to *palm it off*—on people who have been tracking and studying this guy for months. Why not leave the dirty work to the pros and go on our merry way?" Isaac sighed. "Look, kid. Not to harp on the point, but five days ago you were doing a hell of a Linda Blair impression. We're in over our nearly spinning heads."

Isaac expected another argument, but it didn't come.

Bellatine groaned. She dug the heels of her hands into her eyes. "Fine. You're right."

He tucked his melancholic lapse away, out of sight. "What was that? Couldn't hear you over my cardiac arrest."

"We *are* in over our heads. I mean Jesus, I've never been *stalked* before. Let alone by . . . by . . . we don't even know what!" A sudden magpie cackle burst out of her. "All I wanted was some affordable real estate."

"I hear hell is nice this time of year."

Bellatine's manic laugh faded into a gulp. She jabbed a finger in his face. "If they stay, you keep them out of my way."

"If the queen decrees it."

She ignored him, a skill she'd grown deeply proficient in over the nearly three months since they'd reunited at the Red Hook shipping terminal, especially these four weeks on the road. Bellatine unlatched the bedroom door. Without another glance, she returned to the parlor and the houseguests.

A piece of popcorn sailed across the room and bounced off Sparrow's forehead, landing in a pile of kernels at their feet.

"Damn! Try again."

Shona launched another and Sparrow dove, this time catching it in their mouth. Winifred whooped.

"You," Bellatine barked at Sparrow with a general's command. "Pick those up. You"—she spun on Rummy, who still hovered in the doorway—"thank you for the flowers. They're beautiful. Isaac, put them in water, they're going to wilt. And you"—she pointed at Shona—"sit down and tell us everything you know."

"What about me?" Winnie asked.

But Bellatine pretended not to hear.

The six of them settled in the common room to debrief.

"Move over, Pinocchio." Shona shoved him, splaying her legs across the entire clay bench and relegating Isaac to perch like a crow on the seat's arm beside her.

"I like it when you order me around." Isaac winked. Shona sneered in disgust.

Sparrow bounced on their feet, darting off in one direction or another to examine a floorboard, a corner table, a windowpane. Rummy had plopped down cross-legged, remaining just outside the door. Bellatine insisted on standing. She'd positioned herself as far from Winifred as possible. The stone girl had dragged in a chair from the kitchen and draped herself across it like a rag doll.

Isaac passed around the letter. "You told us to look into the past. It's not much, but we got a town name where we think the house originated and a bit of history."

Digging the last popcorn dregs from the bottom of the bag, Shona wiped her salt-dusted hand on her jeans. "History?"

"This village, it was wiped out by pogroms in the late nineteen-teens."

"What's 'pogroms'?"

"Oy vey," Isaac tsked. "What *do* they teach young people in school these days?"

"Let's see . . . Columbus was a hero, the Civil War fixed racism, and, oh"—Shona tightened her ponytail—"you can get pregnant from giving a blow job."

"God bless America," Bellatine muttered.

"They were organized massacres, right?" Rummy interjected, thumbing his suspenders. "Against Jews in Eastern Europe?"

"Tally," said Isaac. "Ten points for Oliver Twist, here. The tsar's authorities would enter Jewish towns, ruffle feathers, throw bricks through windows, torch a few shops. But they'd also rile up local Christian farmers, convince them the Jews were a threat, and then turn a blind eye or even aid when the action escalated."

Shona scowled. "By escalated, you mean killings."

He nodded. "Whatever gave Thistlefoot here its illustrious tap dancing career might be linked to that, or to one of the two nearby wars during that same time—World War One and the Russian Civil War."

"And you think whatever happened to animate the house might explain why someone would want to destroy it?" said Rummy.

"Well that we're not sure about. But it's all we've got."

"And there are more of these?" Shona held up the letter. She'd popped a toothpick between her teeth, and Isaac tried not to fixate on the plush line it indented in her lip.

"Well, yes, but as far we know, they don't contain anything salacious. Though there's still a crate full of legal papers we could dig through."

Shona gave a decisive nod. "So we get more translated."

" 'We'?" Bellatine snorted.

Isaac suspected the notion of accepting help from strangers was, to Tiny, an intimacy akin to letting Shona hand-feed her peeled grapes in the bathtub. A fate that, granted, some would accept eagerly.

"Back in that bar where I met the Longshadow Man, he implied he was with the Russian government. That Thistle-foot had been some kind of contraband export. Could there be truth to that?"

Shona shook her head. "That's bunk. An easy cover—gives him a quick air of authority so people go along. I know a government rat when I see one, and he's not it."

"How do you know?"

"I know."

"Enough," Bellatine cut in, stuffing her hands into her pockets. "You've heard what we have. Now it's your turn, and it seems to me we still haven't addressed the most important question. First thing's first. What is he?"

"We've told you already, we don't know who he—"

"I didn't say who," Bellatine snapped. "I said *what*."

The distinction hadn't been lost on Isaac. In fact, he realized he'd been thinking within that same framework since the day he'd met the Russian in the wool coat. At Asylum Bar, Isaac had been unable to possess him, sliding off his oily presentation. Even the dullest people on Earth had their own blinking pattern, nervous twitch, vocal stain leftover from childhood, some subtle handhold of identity to latch onto and mimic. But the

Longshadow Man hadn't. Isaac had known, deep down, what Bellatine fearlessly insinuated now—even if he hadn't admitted it to himself before. Hadn't *wanted* to admit it. Humans Isaac could deal with. He could con a priest out of his robes if the price was right. He *knew* humans because he'd *been* many of them. But whatever the Longshadow Man was? It left that same feeling in Isaac as the disembodied voice of a telephone call. No safe grip. No ladder to cling to when the train sped up.

"We know plenty about what he *isn't*," Rummy offered with forced optimism.

"He's not a jelly doughnut," Sparrow contributed.

"The question is, is he a man," Isaac said, low. Aloud, the words rang with brutal finality.

"Well, let's see here . . ." Sparrow said. "You know anyone who can rearrange his molecules into a vapor? Sometimes, you'd be looking right at him—"

"And he'd flicker like a match about to snuff out," Rummy finished.

"Or make fire from nothing," Sparrow cut back in. "Conjure heat right out of his *hands*."

Bellatine's body tensed. It was barely a flash, but Shona caught it. Her eyes narrowed.

"And then," Rummy said, "there are the passengers . . ."

That word again.

"*You* know, you'd have felt one during your little bender," Shona aimed at Bellatine, who in turn shot Isaac a *what did you tell them?* glare that could cut glass.

"Felt what?" Winifred said.

"So." Sparrow clapped their hands. "A person drinks from the Longshadow Man's bottle, right? Step one. Big mistake. The liquid turns to smoke. It appears to travel intravenously. Eventually, some of it seeps back out, through the pores, the eyes, the mouth. And then, well—long story short: smoke demons. Poof. They're playing piggyback."

"What Sparrow means," Rummy said, "is that the smoke, it

mimics a humanoid form, then crawls onto a victim's back and takes hold. The smokefed become hosts."

Hadn't Bellatine described feeling a weight on her shoulders when she was under? Something grabbing her? But no—Isaac had been there, and he certainly hadn't seen any sort of *creature* on his sister's back.

"Lanky, creepy fuckers," Shona said. "Real clingers."

"You can only see the passengers," Sparrow explained, "if you've been dosed before. Sort of the way viral exposure builds immunity. Except instead of being immune to a disease, you can see eldritch horrors wrapped around people's necks . . ."

"It's how we knew for sure that you were clean," Shona said to Isaac. "When we met you in the bus. You couldn't see the passenger on that woman tied up in back."

"And you didn't have one yourself," Rummy said.

"So *you* can see them?" Bellatine asked the visitors.

Shona nodded.

"You've been poisoned, then?"

"It became clear that the smokefed had information we lacked," Shona said, "and that seeing things from their perspective might help clarify our goals."

"I developed a diluted cocktail we self-injected—just enough to clue us in, not enough to tip us over the edge," said Sparrow. They slipped their chemists' case from their smoking jacket and flipped it open. "Which reminds me"—they drew out a syringe and flicked the needle—"happy to share with the rest of you who haven't been exposed. Anyone care to see what goes bump in the night?"

Isaac reared back. "No thanks, baby. Ignorance is bliss."

Sparrow sighed. "Ain't that the truth."

"It isn't strictly necessary," Shona said. "Passengers can't be touched or killed, so they aren't the target. The Longshadow Man is."

"But Longshadow and these creatures," Bellatine said. "How are they connected?"

"We think they're, in a way, parts of the same entity," Rummy said.

"When the passengers unlatch, after the smokefeed wears off," Shona said, "they return to him. Into him."

"Into him?"

"We've seen them crawl back, seep into his body. They seem to be *of* him. From him."

"Even though they come from the bottle?" Winifred asked. "I'm confused."

"In folklore, that sort of blend isn't so unheard of, actually," Rummy tempered. "My mother used to warn me about pretas. Hungry ghosts. Like our guy, they were humanoid and often intangible, but also had a food and drink connection. Though pretas would never give *away* a drink. They're beggars."

"There's a legend the real old hobos used to whisper about, back in my rail days," Isaac recalled. "The 'Black Bottle'—they said that if a tramp ended up in the hospital, a nurse would give them what they claimed was medicine. But it was poison—intended to weed out the poor."

"Good ol' American health care," Sparrow cooed, pressing their hands together in mock prayer.

"Lesson number one," Shona said, "no more drinking out of unmarked bottles. That means you, chica." She tilted her chin at Bellatine. Bellatine glowered.

"The smokefed always remind me of people speaking in tongues, back home in Mississippi at the First Pentecostal," Sparrow said. "One lady would take up hollering, then the next, and pretty soon you had a whole roomful of people wearing freshly polished shoes and yelling gibberish."

They traded lore and monsters, rumors and myths, trying to line up the Longshadow Man and his passengers with something, anything familiar. An entity with a name. A history. A weakness. But none of the stories were quite right. And even the grisliest beasts of lore hunted *people*—not houses.

But the Longshadow Man didn't need a name to set one foot upon the earth, then another. Why a name when you can have fire, flickering within impossible flesh? Why a name when you can have an army made of smoke? Why a name when others will gladly hand theirs over to you? Sacrifices. Offerings. Libations. Who needs a name when you can have prey instead?

"Tell me," the Longshadow Man said, leaning over the bar counter. "What is troubling you, *devushka?*"

The bartender frowned. She wrung a rag dry in her fists. "Ran into someone I hoped I wouldn't see again last night, that's all."

The creature nodded. "Some memories are like plagues, better left untouched lest they spread." He lifted a blue bottle. Took a sip. Offered it up. "To remembering only what we wish. May only the true stories survive."

The bartender snorted. "*I'm* serving the drinks here."

"Very well . . ." He began to slip the bottle back into his coat.

"Wait—" She reached out her hand. "Screw it."

Nina took a deep swig.

Not far off, the steamboat's calliope sang its slow, sugared song.

CHAPTER THIRTY-ONE

SURELY YOU HAVE HEARD of the Ziz—that great bird of Psalms, king of all flying things. So tall is he that his feet rest on the ocean floor while his head blocks out the sun. His wings so large that, when unfurled, they darken the sky blacker than the three days of night Moses gave unto Egypt. Legend says that after a thousand years of flight, the Ziz decided to roost upon the earth to lay one single egg—and the patch of land he chose was Gedenkrovka. The shell was thicker than a temple wall, and even all Gedenkrovka's oxen together could not drag it for all its weight. The egg was too large for any nest. It rolled loose and broke, and when it did, so much liquid burst forth that it drowned thirty seders. When the flood abated, there I was: shivering and feathered. The child of royalty.

Well, my most gullible friend? I will admit, I hope you take a liking to that origin, if any. It would do my old rafters good to be treated as a king's heir! No need to worry for my ego; for each story in which I am born to a tsar, there is another in which I wriggle like a golem from the mud—and so it must be, to stay humble before God.

One morning, long after I was born of hens or beasts or felled forests, Baba Yaga awakens to a frigid house. An ice demon must have come in the night. Pesky things, running rampant in late November. He had trailed his bony finger along my windowsills and my doorframe and along each blade of grass jutting from the roof.

"Mother," says baby Malka, "I am terribly cold, won't you be so kind as to fetch me a blanket?"

"Did you hear that, Illa?" Baba Yaga cries. "Our little Malka has spoken her first words! A blanket she wants and a blanket she shall have—the finest blanket in Gedenkrovka, fit for a small queen."

And so Baba Yaga spits into the air, and the liquid freezes solid and plops to the ground in the shape of a small iced toad. "Go tell my friends that baby Malka has spoken her first words," she tells the toad. "And that I plan to weave her a beautiful shawl in celebration."

The toad hops away.

Now, gentile children are born with the *sudzhenitsy* to guide them—those three spirits who huddle over an infant's crib and whisper the babe's lifelong fate aloud for all to hear. For the chosen people, however, our little ones must settle for whatever luck brings them, day by day. Or, in the case of Baba Yaga's two daughters, whatever favors the three horsemen choose to bestow.

An hour later, just as the morning sun has leaked buttercup yellow through the sky, the Dawn Horseman arrives. Baba Yaga welcomes her friend with tea and honey and buttery poppy seed hamantaschen. Of course, the Dawn Horseman does not eat, for the Dawn Horseman has no stomach nor mouth nor throat, only reins and light—but her white horse devours the offerings with gratitude. The Dawn Horseman has brought a gift, as Baba Yaga knew she would. This gift, it is wrapped in thin paper delicate as gosling feathers and tied with hitching rope. Baba Yaga stows it away for later, still sealed.

What is that? You ask what is inside the wrapping? Interrupt me again and the answer will be bubkes. I can change the story like *that*, you know, add or take away as my mood strikes me. What if there was going to be something glorious inside that parcel, so wonderful it would have given this entire tale a happy ending—but to teach you a lesson, I decided to switch it out? Wouldn't you be sorry then?

But here you go: Baba Yaga decides to open the gift after all. Inside the package is a striped yellow karakurt spider, the most poisonous in all of Rus, coiled on a spool of silken thread. Dewdrops cling to the strands and shimmer as Baba Yaga winds a length of web around her finger to test its strength. Satisfied, she pinches the spider's thorax between her calloused fingers, and the small creature writhes. The tighter she squeezes, the more webbing it expels, until there is one mile of silk, which Illa collects in a wooden pail below.

Is that what the gift contained before you asked? Who am I to say?

At any rate, Baba Yaga thanks the Dawn Horseman for her offering, and bids her friend goodbye.

That afternoon, the Day Horseman arrives on a red horse, bearing a gift wrapped in animal skins. (Quiet *now*, aren't you, little mouse? No more questions, I see.) Inside this parcel is a bowlful of crushed purple cherries, warm from curing in the sunlight. Baba Yaga dips a pinkie into the juice, and tastes it, and it stains her teeth bloodred, so she knows it is good. She lets the Day Horseman's red horse drink a sip from the bowl, too, and bids her friend farewell.

That evening, after the sun had slipped beneath the horizon, the Midnight Horseman comes calling upon his black horse.

He offers Baba Yaga a loom built from the ribs of a soldier. It is a sturdy loom and tall, and it is not wrapped in anything but the living soldier himself, whom Baba Yaga unpeels beginning with the clothes, then the skin, then muscle. She feeds the wrappings to the Midnight Horseman's sleek black horse, and the horse is glad.

With that, the Midnight Horseman turns and gallops off toward the moon.

Baba Yaga dyes the spider silk in the crushed cherries until it turns a blushing peony pink, and then she warps the bone loom and weaves and weaves and weaves half the night through. She weaves until her hands bleed, and she can no longer tell what of the silk is cherry-pinked and what is mother's-blood-pinked, but she doesn't mind. At last, as another morning breaks over Gedenkrovka and the Dawn Horseman's steed whinnies miles off, Baba Yaga is done.

"Malka," she says, "I have made you the blanket you have asked for, and all our friends have helped. They are very proud of you for speaking."

Malka coos, for she has forgotten again how to speak—but this doesn't bother Baba Yaga. There will be plenty of time for Malka to speak again. A whole life ahead of her, for making demands of horses and men, for wrapping layer upon layer of this world around her shoulders. Baba Yaga swaddles little Malka in the blanket, and rocks her on her knee as Illa prepares a breakfast of peaches and cake. Today, all is well. Today, they will ignore the bad news from Smela, three villages away. It is not their bad news. Not their dead to mourn.

I feel I owe you an apology. I am not accustomed to such words, but I was not honest with you. I am often dishonest, but there is a right and a wrong kind of lying. I told you that within the Dawn Horseman's gift might have hidden a sweet, good ending to this story. I'm afraid that was a lie. I do not want you to think that what comes after is your fault. I do not want you to think that the ending could have been changed. It is not your fault. It is not your fault. It is not mine, nor Baba Yaga's, nor her daughters', nor Haim's, nor any of the market sellers' faults. It is not our fault. Please, please remember, when the time for remembering comes. The fault, I beg you, I beg you, the fault is not our own.

CHAPTER THIRTY-TWO

BELLATINE DESCENDED THE LADDER to the ground. The house had grown stifling with people. Strategizing had devolved into bickering, which devolved further into hands of poker around the kitchen table as the midday sun began to age. The abrasive woman, Shona, split a metallic cackle down through the floorboards as she presumably won another hand. Something thudded—maybe Isaac had flung his chair over. Again. He was a terrible loser.

Bellatine's feet landed on the gravel. They'd parked Thistlefoot back beside the train tracks, nestled among the mounds of railroad ballast where they'd eaten their lunch the day before. The stone heaps obscured most of the house from sight, while the rail flanked their eastern side, marked by oft-passing trains. Whenever one chugged through, all the jars and windows rattled.

"What do you think, *bashert*?" she said, running a hand over one of Thistlefoot's ankles. The skin was rough and calloused, hard as tanned leather. How many lands had these feet wandered? How much more running would they be forced to endure?

"It's an amazing creature," a quiet voice said from the rock pile behind her.

She jumped.

"Sorry," the voice said, "I didn't mean to startle you." It belonged to the third interloper, the slight, olive-skinned man with suspenders.

"It's fine. I just . . . I thought I was alone. It's Rummy, right?"

Rummy nodded. "Alone . . . Now there's something you don't get a lot of when you live in a bus with two other people."

Bellatine smiled. "I know the feeling."

In front of him, he'd stacked a small cairn from the rock pile's ballast. He lifted another stone, and squinting for balance, placed it on top. It teetered precariously.

Rummy seemed different from his companions. He had a sweet demeanor, mild with a kind face. Nothing like that brash woman with the tattoos, or the bizarre mad scientist who wouldn't stop treating Thistlefoot like some kind of test subject.

"Why do you put up with those jerks?" Bellatine asked.

Rummy smiled. "Not one for small talk, are you?"

She shrugged. "It's a waste of time. Say what you mean or don't say anything."

"They're not so bad," Rummy said. "Sure, Sparrow can get excited, and Shona—"

"She's an asshole," Bellatine blurted.

"Eh, she's all right. You have to get to know her."

Bellatine had plenty on her task list for the week—fixing a roof leak, repainting the kitchen, sending a postcard to Carrie and Aiden, escaping a supernatural stalker. Getting to know Shona was unlikely to make the cut.

"She was raised to be a fighter," Rummy said. "Her dad, back in Mexico—he was a Zapatista and a union organizer." Rummy placed another stone on his tower. "But the government started catching on to him, so he smuggled the family into the States when Shona was a kid. Kept up his work from here." The stones clicked against each other as another was added. "A few years ago, though, he was pulled over with a taillight out. And because he was undocumented, they deported him. He disappeared after that. No one knows what happened to him."

"That's horrible," Bellatine said, softening.

More scuffling floated down from the chaotic houseguests above.

"I thought you'd want to know," Rummy followed. "Why she's doing this, I mean. Why she's in this fight." He thumbed his suspenders. "We'd played a show and were heading back to the bus when we saw, well, we weren't sure then what we saw, not at first—but we knew it wasn't right. Shona, she wasn't raised to see injustice and let it go. If she sees something *wrong*, she follows it. She fixes it. For him."

"And you agreed to help?"

"Of course. We're family."

Bellatine sighed, conceding. "I guess that's pretty fucking noble."

"Now"—Rummy pointed at her—"don't tell her I told you all this, or she'll kill me. I mean it."

Bellatine smiled. "Deal." She thrust out a hand.

Rummy twitched, knocking the cairn to rubble. "Sorry." He shrank back. "Stay there. If you don't mind."

She froze.

"Just . . . I can't shake your hand."

Bellatine's ears got hot. He'd reacted the same way at the door when he'd first arrived. "Do you have some kind of problem with me?"

"I apologize," Rummy said, sucking in a breath.

"Seriously. I don't even know you and you're treating me like a leper."

"It's nothing personal."

Bellatine's stomach tightened. He knew. He *knew*. And he was afraid of her.

"That rat," Bellatine seethed. "What did Isaac tell you about me?"

"Hey, no." Rummy held up his hands in mediation. "Nothing, he didn't tell us anything. I can just . . . I'm different. I can read people. Sense what they're feeling. It's extra sensitive right now because I've been using it to track down the smokefed. I can feel their fear, it's like hearing a dog whistle."

"And you feel me?" Bellatine said. She felt her walls rising again, stacking around her like Rummy's stone tower.

"Yeah," he said. "I can tell you're different, too, like me. Special. I can't see how, or what you can do, but there's definitely some ability you have that other people don't, right? It's okay, you don't have to tell me. You just feel . . . I don't know. Heavy. Like something's pulling on you. It's intense, that's all. It's a little too loud for me when you get close. But please don't be offended, it's not a bad thing."

What had become of that other world she'd cultivated? The world of logic, where a foundation was laid from concrete, not from bone? Where the only things following her were her student loans? Where her friends were builders and carpenters, people who worked with their hands and labored well, who slept easily at night? What was this new world of monsters and heart-readers and living statues? *Puppeteer of God,* echoed her father's voice. *Your life will always be extraordinary.* Perhaps she'd been a fool to think this hadn't been her world, all along.

She took a step back. Rummy let out a breath.

"You've always been able to do this?" she asked.

"Mm . . ." He chewed his cheek. "It started when I hit puberty. But my mom and my aunt had it, too. It's how they escaped Cambodia during the genocide. They could feel when someone was close and what their intentions were. Helped them know when to hide. When to run. So it's sort of responsible for me being born, I suppose." Rummy snatched up a new stone, turned it over. "Yours is hereditary, too, huh?"

Bellatine floundered. "No. I mean, I don't think so. I've never asked." It hadn't occurred to her before, that she might not have been the first to experience the Embering. Surely her mother would have told her if she'd known. But what about before that? What of Illa, of little Malka and their mother? What of her zayde's side? Or her father's family, a whole separate web of longings and losses and triumphs, births and deaths? Bellatine dipped back under the house to stroke Thistlefoot's leg. The house creaked happily. "I guess I don't know."

"I meant your brother," Rummy said. "It's different than yours. Not as"—he smiled apologetically—"noisy. But it's there."

"What?" Bellatine balked. "No. If you mean the creepy way he copies people, that's just acting. He's been practicing since we were kids."

Rummy shrugged. "Sometimes the things we're most encouraged to perfect are the gifts we have from the start."

"Exactly," Bellatine said through her teeth. "He has a *gift*. What I have . . . it's the opposite."

"You sure about that?"

Bellatine bristled, and she could tell from Rummy's discomforted posture that he felt her annoyance. For a moment, they hovered in silence, staring up at the great feathered haunches of the house.

"It's wild, isn't it," Rummy said, "how there are all these stories that played out before we even existed. And their residue is all around us, all the time, but we don't even know it. Sometimes I wonder how much of me is my own, you know?"

Bellatine snorted. "Isaac jokes that he's quick at packing a suitcase because as Jews, we evolved to be ready to run."

"He might be right," Rummy said.

Bellatine chewed the inside of her cheek. "Do you really think my brother is . . . is . . . like us? Different?"

"He sure isn't like everyone else."

Music wafted down from above—fiddle and banjo, Shona's sandpaper voice crooning words too muffled in the breeze for Bellatine to make out. The others must have made their way out to the porch, dirt kicking through the floorboards toward

Bellatine and Rummy like dark snow. Isaac's feet dangled over the edge, one toe tapping to the rhythm.

"As soon as I met him, I felt that we could trust him." Rummy said. "And I felt what he'd lost."

"What do you mean, what he'd—"

"Hey!" Isaac popped his head over the edge of the porch, a cigarette pinched between his lips. "You joining the party or what?"

"It seems our precious solitude is ended," Rummy said, hopping up. He tipped his cap. "It's been a pleasure chatting with you, Miss Yaga." He took the ladder in hand and began to climb.

"Wait," she turned, craning up at Rummy on the rungs above her. "Have you ever tried to find a cure? To your abilities?"

Rummy's eyes creased in the corners. "Why would I want a cure for who I am?"

The music was messy. Notes scratched against one another, grinding off bits of dust, careening out the instruments clumsy and haphazard. Rummy's accordion oompah-pah'd a silty, nightly tune from some future sundown, while Shona's banjo plinked bright dandelion notes from a weedy morning of yesteryear. Tugged between these two chronologies, Sparrow's fiddle screeched so hot and real that both extremes were pulled here, into the glaring present. But the music couldn't distract Bellatine from remembering the terrible interloper that had squirmed into her head on the night she'd drunk from the plastic vial. The unnatural weight on her back, pushing her down toward the graves. If anything, the apocalyptic song made the threat feel all the more immediate. She'd never felt hate and determination linked with such precision. Even now, it bittered the back of her tongue, a burnt aftertaste. Was this what Rummy experienced whenever he was near the smokefed? Fear pressing into him as real and tangible as a flavor, a smell, an accordion's wail? Bellatine felt the late afternoon sharpen with each draw of the fiddle bow. The edges of the world, firming, making her hyperaware of the solid points where her knees, tucked under her, ground into the slats of the stage. She trailed her fingers over the wood. *I'll protect you.*

Beside her, Winifred tapped her thighs, each pat landing precisely in time to the rhythm as if she were a finely wound clock. Could Winnie feel it, too? The *here-ness* of it all?

At the thought of Winifred, Bellatine's mind stumbled back to the previous night. Though the Lantern Parade, too, had been augmented by music and strangers, it had felt the opposite of this. Rather than feeling *more* real, the night had undulated like a mirage. The edges smudged and feathered. Whatever had shimmered between her and Winifred then—had it, too, been only a trick of the light? A dream, brought on by whiskey and the bayou's charm? Had it been real at all?

Something Isaac had said earlier had been gnawing at her for hours. He'd made a glib remark about Winifred being a golem, bound to her master's bidding. Bellatine had heard golem legends. Beings conjured from red clay, Hebrew carved into their foreheads wrenching them awake. In the old stories, golems were bound to their creator's whims. If a golem's maker bid them to labor over a hayfield, they labored. If they were bid to protect a city, they protected a city. Bid to love . . . and a golem had no choice but to love. She had never thought of her Embering as the making of golems, but how else could she describe it? She lays her hands on stone and the stone speaks. And what comes next? The stone follows. When she takes the stone's hand, the stone squeezes back. When she bows toward the stone, runs her hand down the stone's spine . . . what choice does the stone have but to lean into the touch?

What if every spark, every smile, every gentle flirtation from Winnie had been nothing but obligation?

The song ended on a dissonant note, and Sparrow laughed, sawing the bow over the highest string in a dramatic trill.

"This one we learned from some friends in Nebraska," Shona said, cranking the tuning pegs on her banjo. "Imagine the world's over, and this is the only song left." She strummed the strings, even further out of tune now than they were before.

"Close your eyes," Rummy crooned, "imagine the end."

"Or," Shona followed, "the beginning."

Bellatine kept her eyes open. Beside her, Winnie did exactly as she was told.

"Winnie." She craned over, whispering into the stone girl's ear. She didn't respond, and Bellatine prayed she was being ignored. She said the name again, and this time, Winifred looked up, her eyes glossy. For a moment, Bellatine forgot what she'd meant to say, but regained herself. "I'm thirsty. Go grab me the water jug," she ordered.

Say no, she prayed. *Tell me to get it myself.* But Winifred only nodded, stood, and vanished into the house. A moment later, she returned dutifully with a gallon jug of water. As Bellatine brought it to her mouth to drink, she deliberately spilled some onto her lap.

"Winnie, grab me a towel."

She was gone in an instant, returning with a hand towel before the water even had a chance to soak through.

"Better?" Winifred smiled.

"Yes, thank you," Bellatine said—but the words tasted like ash in her mouth.

An egret swooped overhead, its wings wide and glossy as a kite, but Bellatine didn't register it. She was struggling to steady her breath. That moment at the parade when she'd pressed her hand to the small of the granite girl's back, leaned in . . . Bellatine's stomach clenched. The closeness she'd felt—she'd invented it. Worse, she'd *imposed* it. She liked feeling in control, but this—this was the wrong kind. It was puppetry.

What did Rummy feel when he stood near Winifred? Human loyalty? Forced obedience? Or worst of all, would he sense nothing inside Winnie at all—the silence of stone?

The music slipped into a slow, haunted waltz. It dripped with ornamentation, Rummy's accordion sinking like a ladle in rosewater, Sparrow's fiddle trilling birdsong, Shona's banjo conjuring the sway of old-growth trees, ancient things like the ones she and Isaac had grown up around in the northwestern woodlands.

Bellatine startled, feeling a hand slip down her arm.

"Dance with me?" Winifred asked.

"I'm . . . not right now." Bellatine pulled her arm back. She stood, darting away into the safety of Thistlefoot, where none of her yearnings could find her.

She'd hoped to be alone, but Isaac was slumped at the kitchen table, the heels of his hands pressed against his eyes.

"What's wrong?"

Isaac jerked up and leaned nonchalantly back. He tossed her one of his signature winks, slick enough to make her blood curdle, and locked his fingers behind his head, his elbows jutted out to the side like a fancy Thanksgiving hat.

"Nothing going, baby. Copacetic."

Whatever worries he'd been sagging under a moment ago, he'd hidden them well. What was it Rummy had said? *I felt what he'd lost.*

Bellatine sat down across from him. "Listen, when we've sorted this all out, I want to go back up to Baltimore."

"Baltimore? If this is about the gig we missed when you went all Jonestown"—he tipped an imaginary bottle to his lips—"don't worry about it. We were only gonna play for tips that night anyway."

"It's not the gig. We need to take Winifred back."

Isaac wrinkled his forehead. "She asked for that?"

"No, but—"

"Mm. An executive decision."

"I think it's best. I'll find a way to . . . fix her. And even if I can't, she doesn't belong with us."

Isaac whistled. "I must have really interrupted something last night. I've waltzed out on plenty of girls in my day, but I must say, Medusa, I've never tried the turn-'em-to-stone maneuver to evade the morning-after chitchat. Inspiring."

"That's not how it is," she replied coolly. "We're not . . ." Not what? She took a breath. "We're not friends."

Isaac studied her. She felt like she'd been shut in a CAT scan machine, his eyes boring through her with mechanical precision. It made her squirm in her seat.

"Tally," he said at last. "You're not. You're Dr. Frankenstein. She's the creature. When someone *makes* you, is responsible for everything you are . . . there's no breaking away from that. Hell, you brought her to life just by touching her. One touch. When you took her hand, I saw it, you burned through that poison like it was nothing. I don't know what you think that girl is to you, but you're right—she sure isn't your goddamn friend. She's your fate."

Winifred's laughter pealed in from the porch. It passed through Bellatine like a sickness.

"You don't know what you're talking about."

He appraised her, his hands still cocked behind his head. "You sure do love to make yourself miserable, don't you?"

"And you like making everyone *else* miserable."

Isaac's lupine grin ticked up in the corner of his mouth. "Why be wretched alone when you can turn it into a party?"

A *party* . . . Bellatine's jaw clenched. "I can't just waltz around like the world's a candy store to stuff my pockets from. I'm not like you."

He raised an eyebrow. "Would you want to be?"

She paused. Another kind of yearning cropped up in her. To let go . . . Take what she wanted. Not give a damn about anything. It tasted like relief. She cast her eyes to the floor. "Maybe."

"No, kiddo." Isaac snapped up a poker deck abandoned on the table and gave it a shuffle. "I wouldn't recommend it to my worst enemy, frankly. But you might want to take a stab at being *you*."

"I don't know what you mean."

"Sure you do."

"No. I don't."

"You have all this power," he said. She started to open her mouth in protest, but he pushed ahead. "The kind of power people search a lifetime to touch even a sliver of. And I don't mean power like presidents and country club boys, not the kind of power that gets used to keep other people down. I mean *real* power. Power to make something beautiful happen. And Jesus, you're stubborn as a brick and a control freak, but that's great. That's you. You can use that. You're *capable*. But you're wasting all that capability and stubbornness on tamping yourself down. On being someone you're not."

What she wanted to say was *What's inside me, it's not beauty. It's not power. It's an abomination. And if I ever did let myself go, that's all you'd be able to see me as.* But she didn't.

He offered her the cards, fanning them out facedown like a peacock's tail. The backs sported a gilded oval with a midnight-colored steam engine in the center, ink muted from handling.

"Pick one."

"Why?"

"Just pick."

She reached for a card on the left with a frayed corner, but at the last moment reconsidered, flicking her fingers to one in the center, tucked almost invisibly beneath another. She slid it out from the pack.

"For someone whose whole thing is pretending to be people he's not, you sure have a lot of opinions," she sniped.

Isaac's grin returned. "Touché." He pointed to the card in her hand. "What do you got?"

She turned it over. Six of hearts.

"Huh. Funny," Isaac mused.

"What?"

"That's the same card I pulled the other day. Memory and nostalgia. The past leaking into the present."

"Is that bad?"

Isaac tossed up a hand. "Good, bad . . . Is there such a distinction?"

Bellatine rubbed a thumb over the worn red ink of the hearts, and despite herself a frail laugh seeped out. "Do you ever think about how there are people who just live regular day-to-day lives without being racked with existential dread? Like my friends back north. They wake up. They go to work. They watch TV. They aren't in the past or the future, they're like, right now. And they feel *fine*. Wild, right?"

"Sounds like bullshit if you ask me," Isaac said, shuffling the remaining cards before abandoning them on the table. "Going one hour without considering my teeming and immutable ennui?" He feigned a yawn. "How dull."

"Can you imagine?"

"No, ma'am."

"Listen . . ." Bellatine said. "Have you ever wondered if that impressions thing you do, the way you shift—if maybe it's not natural, either?"

Isaac gathered the deck and gave it a new shuffle. "It's the most natural thing in the world."

"What if . . . ? What if it's . . . it's . . . *off*, too?"

Isaac shrugged. "Never thought about it. Don't care."

"How can you not care?"

"Easy. Like this." He shut his eyes, snapped his fingers, and reopened them. "Gone."

Bellatine snorted. "Right, *easy*."

Music crept under the door and spiraled through the room, leaving vibrations in its wake. Thistlefoot swayed back and forth to the rhythm, but Bellatine didn't notice. The house's motions had grown impalpable to her, like her own breath.

"Hey, Isaac . . ."

"Yes, Medusa?"

She narrowed her eyes.

"Sorry. Yes, *Bellatine*, dear sister o' mine, first of her name."

"It's been all right. Getting to know you, I mean. It's kind of nice to have a brother again."

A pang of self-consciousness set in as soon as she said it, and she glanced back down at the six of hearts, desperate for something productive to do with her hands.

"Hey," Isaac said, his voice surprisingly firm.

She looked back up.

Isaac's shoulders were squared right toward her, all his attention locked on her like a spotlight. The directness made her nervous. But the energy catching her there was warm, solid.

"You've *always* had a brother."

That's when the windows exploded.

CHAPTER THIRTY-THREE

WHEN GLASS IS FORGED, raw materials are heated to 2,400 degrees Fahrenheit. What was once sand or limestone or soda ash morphs into liquid light, molten and malleable. There, it can be shaped. Twisted into paperweight swans with translucent beaks. Long-necked lilac vases. Arched mirrors backed with silver foil. As it cools, thermal tension becomes trapped within the glass. It presses against its enclosure like a caged animal, snarling to be set loose. It strains and pushes, tonguing the glossy walls, waiting for a crack, a nick, a jagged fissure for it to scurry along, expand, and break free.

When the first stone erupted through Thistlefoot's kitchen window, glass shattered like a firework.

Bellatine froze. The stone soared across the room in slow motion, a veil of crystalline splinters trailing behind. It was a foreign comet. A strange bride dripping a daggered lace train.

The house reared up. A pile of books crashed to the ground. A dish slid off the table and broke as another stone rocketed through the room. Then another, and another. They bulleted into the house from all directions, mineral and glass blooming in shrapnel chrysanthemums. Bellatine dove under the table for cover. She felt every hit against Thistlefoot like a bullet to her own body.

"Shhh, *shefele*, you'll be all right," she hummed, pressing her palms to the floor. She could feel the house's fear bubbling from the boards. She wanted to soothe the house, to stretch so wide her arms could wrap around it like wings, to keep it safe. Gravel exploded against the far wall. Thistlefoot convulsed.

One last stain, echoed a far-off voice, lodged deep in white-hot flashes of memory.

Isaac slammed his back against the wall, out of the line of fire. When he tried to look out the window at the unseen assailants, a rock whizzed close enough to his face that he could feel the wind of it lift his hair. *Rude.*

Was it Max, taking payback for his lifted truck? Isaac's former roommate hardly had the chutzpah for revenge, but Nina had always been a sparkplug—lest Isaac forget the time she'd left him handcuffed to her bedpost for nearly two hours as she went on a date with another guy. She could have sweet-talked Max into a little trouble, easy. Or maybe it was Snap, though Isaac couldn't envision him adopting the brash inelegance of chucking rocks. If Isaac were honest with himself, there were plenty of dupes in this town who'd be happy for the chance to take a swing at him.

But this was no casual retaliation. Hundreds of projectiles torpedoed against the house. Isaac ducked as another hailstorm of stones exploded through the ruined window.

"The bastard found us," Shona growled, barreling in with Sparrow close behind. She wiped a smear of blood from her chin with the back of her hand.

Isaac didn't bother asking who. He already knew the answer.

"Milkman, milkman, take my cup, when my man is away, come—" *Thwack.* "Home run, baby!"

Sparrow was brandishing a hardbacked book like a baseball bat, slugging stone after stone back out the window. Over the clatter, Bellatine heard a bus engine roar—Rummy must have felt this coming and clambered inside the vehicle just in time. Isaac and Shona were attempting to block the windows with whatever they could find.

Where was Winnie?

Bellatine's stomach flew into her throat. The girl was her responsibility. It was her own carelessness that had woken Winifred. Her fault she was here, in danger. Bellatine scurried out from under the safety of the kitchen table. She flinched as Sparrow's makeshift bat whooshed by her face, colliding with a stone inches away from her nose.

"Thanks," she wheezed.

"Call me Babe Ruth." A rock cracked Sparrow in the shoulder, and they hissed, spinning back toward the window. Bellatine ran.

In the bedroom, curtains had been torn to ribbons. Their beds were dark with dust. She kept running. "Winifred!" Nothing—only the thunder of rocks against wood. Thistlefoot was thrashing so hard Bellatine couldn't balance on her feet, so she resorted to crawling, her palms and knees stinging on glass shards. *She's outside,* she realized with a pang, rounding the corner to the empty living room. Why wasn't Thistlefoot leaving? *"Loyf!"* Bellatine screamed. *Run!* But the house only whipped from side to side without taking a step.

Isaac flipped the table on its end and barricaded a larger window while Shona braced a baking pan over the smaller window by the washbasin. The house jerked and she slipped, her head bouncing off the counter with a crack. Blood pooled where she landed. Flames reflected in the rose-black liquid.

Isaac stared transfixed at the inferno twisting within the pool of Shona's blood, a violent cinema. Had something in the house caught fire? But no—it was only mirroring the cookstove. The ever-burning hearth had kicked up wild, as if stoked with lighter fluid, but the fire was contained. Was this Thistlefoot's heartbeat, rising to a panic? Heat surged through the air, making the airborne stones seem to wobble in visible waves.

Shona groaned.

"Come on, kid, fun's over." Isaac roped an arm around her waist and dragged her into the bathroom, latching the door shut behind them. He flicked on a solar lamp drilled to the wall, casting a green pall over the windowless room. Jars of soaps and shampoos rattled against one another as the house tossed. Rocks pelted the door but didn't break through. They were safe. He dug out his handkerchief and pressed it to Shona's head.

"You all right, early bird?"

She slumped against the sink's basin, eyes closed. Loosened chunks of hair escaped from her ponytail and clung to her face, sticky and dark.

On the shelf behind them, Isaac spotted a jar of rubbing alcohol. He uncapped it, dunking his handkerchief in before dabbing it back over Shona's wound.

"Here, dollface, catch a whiff of this." He held the open vial under her nose. Shona coughed, but it seemed to do the trick. Her eyes bolted open.

"Atta girl." Another round of collisions rattled outside.

"Where . . . where are we?" she slurred.

"Hidden away till this all blows over. Or we're tucked into our casket, depending on the outcome."

She pulled herself upright, shoving away the rag Isaac had pressed again to her bleeding head. "We need to be out there."

"You're probably concussed. And I, personally, prefer my skin firmly attached to my body."

Shona sneered. "You're worse than a liar. You're a fucking coward."

"Sorry I don't want to be biblically stoned to death."

"My friends are out there," she spat. "Your sister ran right into the fray."

His sister.

He was so used to only having himself to look out for. When things went sour, he could always bail. Vanish. Shapeshift. He wasn't used to having to keep track of anyone else. Not for a long time. Not since . . .

Selfishness. It's how you killed me, Benji murmured in his head. *And now you'll kill her, too.*

Outside, the grind of rock against plaster muddled together with a distant yowl. A train was coming. Isaac felt a tremor pass through him like an earthquake. He willed himself to breathe. To budge. To twist into someone else—the sort of person who wouldn't hide, wouldn't vanish, but fight. The kind of man who wouldn't leave the people he loved to die.

But not a single muscle in his body would move.

"Get out of my way." Shona kicked the door open and, half blinded by blood, ran back into the whirling cloud of stones.

Why wouldn't Thistlefoot run? Bellatine craned her head out the broken living room window—and saw why. The house was surrounded. A swarm of fifty people encircled them: men, women, even children. Bellatine's breath stalled in her throat. A figure crouched on each person's back, pale as milk. Ropey bands of smoke ensnared their hosts, shadow-built limbs, needle-sharp elbows, crooked knees. Misted fingers dug deep, slipping into the shoulders on which the creatures perched. The shapes rippled in the wind. The people didn't seem to register them, though they hunched as if bearing a great burden. Meanwhile, human hands flashed from the ground to the air, a hundred small, grasping catapults. Among them, familiar faces—the formerly turtle-clad man from the Lantern Parade and the woman who'd slapped Isaac. The cashier from Hank's. And strangers, dozens and dozens of strangers. The mob was pulling ballast from the rock pile and throwing it at the house, fistful after fistful of ammunition. Even from twenty feet above, Bellatine could see their faces—pale as cracked eggshells, veined with swirling white. The smoke whispered in their ears.

An oblong lump struck the turtle in the head and he flopped down.

Winifred's voice whooped from above. *The roof.*

Bellatine scanned her surroundings for something to use as a shield, settling on the hinged seat of the clay bench. It took a few yanks, but she was able to crack the board free of its fixings. Throwing open the front door, she burst out, one hand holding the board lengthwise to cover her, the other gripping Thistlefoot. The house lurched but Bellatine held fast. "Please, sweet one," she whispered, a benediction, "hold still. I'll replace your windows and hang a jasmine wreath on your door when this is done. I'll sweep every morning and every night. Please. Help me get to her." The house seemed to calm. As Bellatine scrambled up toward the roof, another object soared at the attackers from above. *Was that . . . a potato?* She heard a thud. Someone below groaned.

Halfway to the roof, the stones striking her shield hushed. She must be out of range, too high for the smokefed to throw. Whimpering with relief, she scrambled the rest of the way up.

Winnie was balanced atop the roof, legs locked around the chimney to keep steady. Woodsmoke billowed from the flue, surrounding her with purple gunpowder haze. With both hands, she was digging potatoes from the turf roof and hurling them, one after another. The house resumed its thrashing, and it was all Bellatine could do to keep her grip. *She'll fall,* she thought with a lurch as Winifred raked through the sod for more ammunition.

"Get down from there!" she commanded.

Winnie didn't even look at her, just lobbed another spud overboard. Her face was set in determination.

"I just got here!" Winnie bellowed. "I'm not going back."

"Get down!"

"No," Winifred hollered. "I like being alive. I like being awake. And I intend to stay that way."

No. She'd said *no.* And if she could say no to this, if she really was driven by her own longings, did that mean . . . ? Bellatine's heart flipped within her chest.

Winnie's nails were crusted with dirt. Not grave dirt—garden soil, teeming with life. She let her weapon fly.

The walls around Isaac closed in.

Without you, Fresh, Benji said, *I would still be singing. Do you like my song now? Let's teach your sister to sing harmony, now wouldn't that be nice.*

He had to move. Tiny was only twenty. No damn street smarts. Practically a child.

Just a year older than Benji had been.

He'd simply do what he did best—warp one muscle, then another, until he'd regained himself. Start small. One foot. *That's it. You are a machine. You are levers and pulleys.*

The train's howl surged.

When you leave a gap, Benji rasped, *the cosmos balances itself. And boy-o, what a gap you tore when you let me die.*

Isaac squeezed his eyes shut. The rattler's whistle filled his head until nothing else was left. Isaac sank to his knees. He buried his head in his trembling hands.

A portly old man grunted up a grapefruit-sized boulder and reared back. Bellatine pelted a turnip at the smoky thing on his back, but the vegetable passed right through its head.

"They aren't solid," she remembered aloud.

"What?" Winifred shouted. Beside her, the stone girl wound up like a pitcher and let loose a yam. It struck the man square between the eyes. He stumbled, the rock dropping. The creature riding him shuddered.

"The passengers!"

"What do you *mean*?"

Of course—Winifred couldn't see them. Only Bellatine could, vestiges of the Longshadow poison aiding—or cursing—her sight.

Winnie chucked another root overboard. It collided with a rock in midair precision, knocking it back against the woman who'd thrown it.

"Where'd you *learn* that?"

Winnie blushed. "It's part of the earth. It . . . makes sense to me."

One mighty throw sent a stone spiraling all the way up to them, and Bellatine ducked. Winifred caught it in her bare palm. Easy. As if it were a starling returning home to the nest.

Rocks cracked against Sparrow's book-bat from where they'd taken up their post on the stage below. On the other side of the mob, the black bus idled. Rummy had made his way to the vehicle's roof. He hoisted up a speckled, rectangular object, and strapped it over his chest. At first, Bellatine thought with alarm that it might be a bomb. But then he began to pull on the sides. A melody squeezed out. *You've got to be kidding me.* His accordion.

"What is he *doing*?" Bellatine screamed down toward the stage.

"Music," Sparrow said, their book cracking against another rock. "It passes through the amygdala."

"The what?" Bellatine shouted back.

"The amygdala, it's the part of the brain"—*crack*—"that processes fear. So it can interrupt"—*crack*—"that fight-or-flight signal."

The tune spiraled and dipped, intermingling with the aria of an approaching train. A bereft song, tinted with lost love and wilting summers, rose petals and longing. A few of the smokefed seemed to waver, forgetting the stones in their fists. Some of the shadow beings grew hazy, diffusing. *It's working,* Bellatine thought with amazement. Others swayed to the inhalation and exhalation of the instrument's bellows. The crowd began to thin. But it wasn't enough. There were still too many people with lips pulled back over wet teeth, ridden like horses by spectral jockeys. Too many frothing like sick foxes, famished for a kill.

Potatoes and waltzes . . . some army.

Some of the smokefed had spilled onto the tracks but hadn't yet noticed the approaching freighter. Its whistle blared, begging the path to clear. *To clear* . . . Bellatine almost wept with relief. The mob would have to move to avoid being struck. They'd clear the way—and leave a hole in the ranks. If the attackers took even a few clumsy moments to regroup after the train's passing, Thistlefoot would have an out. They'd only have a fleeting instant to tear across the tracks before the mob filled the rupture like sutures in a wound, but if she made sure Thistlefoot was ready, it could work.

The train would arrive in thirty seconds. Twenty. Fifteen. Bellatine held her breath, her fists buried in the overgrown rooftop.

"*Greyt,*" she whispered. *Ready.*

Ten seconds. Five.

Accordion notes tangled into the train's deafening whistle.

Three seconds. Two.

Just as she'd predicted, the smokefed began to scatter. But in doing so, they pressed closer to Thistlefoot. Some scrambled up to catch hold of its feet. The house kicked, and bodies flew, but there were more behind them. Always more. They swarmed the house's ankles, digging in with teeth and nails and sharp stones, whipping off their belts to tether themselves on. Their shadow riders, carried along.

The freighter arrived. As effortlessly as carving a spoonful from a bowl of cream, the engine swept through the hailstorm of rocks. How long did it take the train to pass? Five minutes? An hour? A lifetime? Bellatine could feel each puncture, each stab that Thistlefoot endured. *Patience.* She gritted her teeth. *Patience.* Eventually, the final car was in sight. *"It's time,"* she whispered to Thistlefoot in Yiddish. The caboose sucked out of sight, leaving a gleaming, pulled-tooth gap in its wake. *"Loyf!"* The house ran. Bellatine found herself flung asunder toward the roof's edge, but a firm, familiar hand caught her. She held tight to Winifred as Thistlefoot galloped on. The smokefed followed, sprinting behind. With each lift of a great yellow leg, Bellatine could see bodies clinging to the talons, refusing to shake loose.

Careening down Saint Claude, Thistlefoot thundered past cars, forcing them onto sidewalks with their horns blaring. One smokefed man scrambled onto a truck's hood and slammed his fist through the windshield. A bicyclist zipped past, her jaw dropped open at the spectacle. Behind, Bellatine heard a bus engine rev awake as Rummy slammed into gear and pivoted down a side route, drawing some of the crowd. Thistlefoot forged ahead. Streets flashed past—Clouet, Piety, Pauline. Ahead, a great steel drawbridge craned over a tributary of the Mississippi. It split in the center and began to rise.

"Come on," she whispered to Thistlefoot. *"Faster."* If the bridge rose before they got there, they'd be trapped. They had to make it past. Yet Thistlefoot was slowing. More frothing, smoke-wrapped bodies had flung themselves onto the house's legs. They clung like burrs, weighing down each step.

"Get them off," Bellatine shouted down to Sparrow. They

nodded, then swung a leg over the balcony and descended out of sight. The drawbridge moaned, rising higher.

One great foot clanged onto the steel bridge, then another. Sparrow must be succeeding, because the house was moving faster, lighter, ascending toward the bridge's crest, where a gap had already formed between the two separating halves. As they neared the top, Thistlefoot hesitated. It was too wide to step over, growing wider every moment. *How do you say "jump" in Yiddish?* Bellatine opened her mouth, language stalling on her tongue.

And yet—Thistlefoot leapt into the air.

Breath hoisted in Isaac's lungs as he felt gravity abandon him. The house was airborne, lurching, Isaac lifting, too, as his feet rose off the slatted floor. For a moment, time stopped. Every second, tortured, lashed to the rack and stretched violently beyond its limit. Thistlefoot dangled, suspended. Isaac closed his eyes and felt it—weightlessness. Absolution. And then— a crash.

He buckled, crumpling to his knees. A teeth-rattling thud shook from floor to chimney. Part of the bathroom wall had cracked in the landing, and it left a gap in the plaster just wide enough for Isaac to peer through, staring back at the direction they'd come. They'd landed on the other side of the river. Their pursuers had scrambled up the lifting bridge's sharp incline, hands bloodied and reaching. Teeth gnashed. One body pushed to the front of the crowd. She loosed a fierce howl, smoke curling around her lips.

Nina.

Nina, whatever you're doing, stop. Stop.

Though the words thundered in his head, Isaac's lips wouldn't move. He could only watch as his old sweetheart scuttled up the steel bridge. She hoisted herself onto the lip—and then, she leapt.

"No!" He heard Tiny scream from above. His own cry seemed to rise from everywhere but his own throat. The bridge moaned like an injured bear, lifting higher. The mob undulated as if it were one great form, a wave bending at the waist, as one by one the smokefed followed, flinging themselves off the drawbridge—and plummeted into the rocky waters below.

Isaac fell back from the wall. He shut his eyes tight.

A mob has no ears to call to, only a single mouth, yelling.

A mob has no hands to hold, only a single finger, pointing.

A mob has no head, only a single body, guideless, acting as it will.

The smokefed fell. These people, they weren't monsters. In a few hours they would have awoken, clouded vision crisping back into place. They'd have gone home to their families. Baked bread. Petted their dogs. Watched TV. They were no different from Bellatine herself. And she still had a saw-blade scab crusted over her wrist to prove it.

The odor of bile and blood rose on the wind. Bellatine knelt, pressed her cheek to the roof. Wet hay and rain, a sweet, simple perfume. *"Loyf,"* she begged again. *"Loyf!"*

Thistlefoot ran. Away from the glittering city. Away from the ruined bodies, twisted into nightmarish contortions in the river. Away from the final stone's reach. Gone.

It was over.

After a few minutes, Isaac figured they'd been running long enough to be safe. Outside the bathroom, he could still hear disorder. There were surely wounds to tend, head counts to make. Shona's growl seeped from the living room, along with Sparrow's relieved moan. After a while, a bus engine growled alongside the steady thud of Thistlefoot's feet striking the earth, having caught up via a tangle of circuitous, potholed streets. Someone opened the front door, and Isaac heard Winnie's delicate footsteps, with Tiny's behind her. *Thank God.* She was safe.

She would be better off without him.

When it seemed the hallway was clear, he tipped open the door and slipped out. He dragged the table away from the kitchen window, careful not to let the wood squeal as it skidded on the floor.

After brushing what broken glass he could from the frame, Isaac swung one leg over the windowsill, then another. The ground swayed beneath him, but it wasn't all that far down. If he positioned his left shoulder at a forty-degree angle with the earth and tucked in his knees, he would land unharmed.

He drew a coin from his pocket, smooth and lustrous as a scarab. "Travel fare," he said to the house, and gingerly slid the train-flattened nickel onto the sill, heads up. Then, Isaac took a deep breath and let himself fall. *Was this what Nina had felt, in the moments before . . . ?* The landing thudded into his lungs—but he was unharmed.

As he brushed himself off, a small black cat padded over dubiously, stopping to lick an inky paw.

"Beat it," Isaac rasped. "Stop trailing me. I'm done." Hubcap rubbed against his shin. He shoved her away with a foot and she pressed back in, mewing. When he took a step, she followed. He knew better by now than to keep trying to lose her. Wherever he went, whoever he became, the shadow would follow.

Thistlefoot stomped onward, heedless, shrinking. Benji flickered in his head. *Did you think it would be different this time?* Enough of Isaac Yaga. That character had worn out its welcome in this body. He wasn't a wry antihero, rakishly lovable. Wasn't a clever trickster hunting for luck. He was a fuckup. A bum. Good for nothing. Good for no one.

It was time to become someone new. He rolled and lit a lavender cigarette, taking a long, heavy drag.

In the distance he heard Tiny call his name, just as the legged house vanished under the curving horizon. The man who had been Isaac turned away. He walked in the opposite direction. Before long, it would be as if he'd never been there at all.

CHAPTER THIRTY-FOUR

THERE'S A SCENE IN *The Drowning Fool* where the Fool befriends the Moon. They meet at a cardboard bus stop inked with miniature arrivals and departures, and spend the evening hat shopping. It's a comedic scene. Rigs makes a great show of the hats all wobbling on their shelves, hoping to be picked, and the audience always laughs when the Moon can't decide which part of itself is the top of its head and which the bottom. The Moon buys a bowler hat made of red felt, and the Fool buys a sparkly top hat, the sort a tap dancer might wear in a big Ziegfeld revue. Then, the Fool and the Moon go for a late-night stroll along the boardwalk, where a Zoltar machine tells their fortunes and they eat fried dough and ride the Tilt-A-Whirl until the Moon is so dizzy the tides go askew.

Each day, the Moon grows a bit smaller (a sleight of hand involving a black velvet panel that pulls inch by inch over the Moon's face). The Fool doesn't notice, until one day, the Fool knocks on the Moon's door and the Moon isn't home. The next day, the Fool tries again—but no luck. Poof. The Moon is gone.

Two weeks later, the Fool runs into the Moon at a clambake. *Where have you been?* asks the Fool.

Gone, says the Moon.

Gone where? asks the Fool.

Not here, says the Moon. *I come and go; it's how I was made. Marvelous, no?*

The Fool does not find this marvelous. The Fool puts a bell jar over the Moon. *There!* he says. *Now we can go hat shopping forever.*

But with the Moon sealed behind glass, it can't reach the oceans. The waters go rabid without supervision. Now it's the waters buying hats and sloshing over the boardwalk and flooding the cinema. The Fool, he walks by the river and can't fathom how wild and rapid it has grown.

You can imagine what happens next.

The silver coin on the windowsill was all Bellatine needed to know. He hadn't been kidnapped. Not injured, nor fallen. Not massacred in the frenzy as the smokefed had been. Her brother had paused. Pulled a nickel from his pocket, shined it with a thumb, placed it in the center of the sill as gently as one would lay a penny over the eyes of the dead. Perhaps he'd tossed a last, cruel wink into the shattered room. And then, he'd left.

It had happened as it always had. As it always would, soon as the going got tough. But this time, she wouldn't drown herself missing him. This time, she wouldn't be the fool.

Bellatine threw the coin from the open window. She began gathering some of the larger pieces of glass into a pile. There was work to be done.

A hand grabbed her fiercely by the arm, and Bellatine jolted.

"What fucking game are you playing with us?" Shona hissed, squeezing tighter.

"What do you mean?" Was Shona accusing her of inviting the attack? Or of helping Isaac run away? "It wasn't my fault. He left. He always leaves."

"Shut up." Shona yanked her through the kitchen door into the bedroom.

The room was unrecognizable, shattered and torn. The floor gleamed with broken glass and splintered wood, the curtain that had bisected the beds in tatters. At first, Bellatine thought the room was empty—until she spotted Sparrow's bulky legs dangling from the opening to the loft.

"What are you doing up there?"

"We were looking for a broom," Shona said. "But instead we found this." She pushed Bellatine at the ladder, and the two of them ascended, joining Sparrow above.

They were staring at the ceiling. The vine strung with ruined soldiers seemed to blend in with the house's destruction, as if the painting's chaos had merely expanded its borders. Thistlefoot, the lion, the crow, and the hare still caroused in the center, despite it all.

Bellatine squinted. "I don't understand."

"It's him," Sparrow said.

"Who?"

"*The Longshadow Man.*" Sparrow pointed. Their finger landed on one of the small soldiers being tormented by briar. Bellatine squeezed in for a closer look. As her eyes trailed from body to body, soldier to soldier, death to death, she realized they all shared the same face. It was smooth with a sharp jawline, and even in its various agonies, its mouth was upturned slightly in an eternal smile.

"You told us you'd never met him," Shona said, a threat lacing her words.

"I haven't."

"Then how did you manage to paint a dozen tiny fucking Longshadows on your ceiling, like some kind of shrine?"

"I *didn't.*"

Shona's eyes narrowed. "Isaac. He's met him. This is his, isn't it? Is he working for him? Is that why he left—to go help the enemy? I should have known, I should have *seen* it."

Bellatine shook her head. "He didn't paint it either. It was here when we moved in. Look." She reached for her pocket and Shona snapped back as if expecting a weapon. Slowly, Bellatine slipped out the old photo of the woman and her two daughters. "Here." She pointed at the tiny house in the background and the painting above the door with the same trio of animals. "See? Same artist, clearly. The paintings must have been here for at least a hundred years."

"But your brother still danced off somewhere," Sparrow pressed.

"Isaac *isn't* helping the Longshadow Man."

"How do you know?" Shona growled.

"Because Isaac doesn't help anyone but himself."

Briefly, a twinge cut through the rage sharpening Shona's face. It looked almost like hurt—but it vanished too quickly to be sure.

Three sets of eyes floated back up to the ceiling. The tiny soldiers writhed, frozen among the thorns.

"It's him," Shona insisted. "I'd recognize that creep anywhere. That's who's following you."

Thistlefoot creaked. Whatever the Longshadow Man was, Thistlefoot already knew him. And her twice-great-grandmother had known him, too. They'd been in this dance for a long, long time. As the colorful characters reveled in the painting's center, Bellatine's stomach sank. It wasn't a commemorative painting recollecting a victory. It wasn't a guilty conscience's stain. The painting was a wish. A talisman. The painting was a prayer—someday, it begged, someday we'll escape. Someday, we will dance.

"What is it?" Sparrow asked.

The mural rippled with shadow. Bellatine swallowed hard.

"It's a warning."

By the time they'd finished bandaging their wounds and clearing the bulk of the wreckage, exhaustion had rooted in Bellatine like a weed. For one brief moment, Thistlefoot had slowed to let the Duskbreakers descend the cable ladder and rejoin Rummy in their bus, but otherwise, they marched on. There was no slowing down. Not anymore. Yet all Bellatine wanted was to collapse, burst to dust, sift into the floorboards of this old house and stay there. She dropped into one of the surviving kitchen chairs, massaging knots from the back of her neck.

A blue shape floated in from the parlor, but upon seeing her stopped and turned away. Bellatine froze. For the first time since the Lantern Parade, she realized, they were alone.

I told her to get down and she told me no.

"Wait."

Winifred turned.

"I'm . . . I'm sorry," Bellatine said, rising.

"For what?" She met Bellatine's eyes, unwavering.

"I doubted you. I was wrong."

Winnie shrugged. "Doubt is human."

Bellatine nodded. Gentle warmth prickled in her stomach. "So, it seems, are you."

"Not quite."

Silence.

"Look, the other night, at the parade—" Bellatine started.

"It's all right," Winifred said. "We were carried away—the music and the lights. You made your desires quite clear. I won't press again."

Bellatine's breath quivered. "It's not about what I desire."

Winifred twisted a yellow curl between her fingers. "Isn't it?"

There had been so much suffering. Death, spilled over river stones. A demon growing nearer. Bellatine's own body, which had fed her nothing but betrayal since she was a girl. And now, one more of her brother's abandonments. It was all too much. The fortress in her, having so long kept her yearnings at bay, groaned under the weight. A tower crumbled. Light leaked through.

"I need you to say it. Without my prompting," Bellatine said.

"Say what?"

"What do you want from me, Winifred?"

Winifred paused. Her gaze slid sideways as if consulting some distant memory, a forgotten duty that may or may not have ever been hers to begin with. But she lifted her head. Her stare, certain. "Everything."

Bellatine's legs seemed to pull her forward then of their own volition, like a predetermined fate had set her body in motion. In three strides, she erased the distance between them. And then, they were kissing. There was nothing doubtful here, no hesitance as Bellatine pressed Winnie up against the wall, Winnie's fists planting themselves in her hair. Her mouth was cold and sweet. She lifted her hands to stroke the stone girl's face, then faltered. Her hands . . . But before she could pull back, Winifred had taken Bellatine's finger in her mouth. She gasped. A mischievous spark played in Winnie's eyes. She bit down lightly.

Winifred slid the denim straps from Bellatine's shoulders, yanking her cotton tee over her head. Bellatine fumbled at the skirt of the blue dress. For a moment, she was lost, swimming through curtains of fabric—and then, contact. The stone girl's thigh, plump and soft. Bellatine slid her hand higher, and a sigh escaped Winifred's lips. Heat surged through Bellatine in response. It rose and fell in waves, turning to shivers as Winifred cupped her chest in her hands. Bellatine craned her mouth up to kiss her.

Winifred pulled back.

"What?" Bellatine's heart thudded. Had she misread the signs? Did Winnie already regret this?

She looked up into the stone girl's—no, the *girl's*—eyes, bracing for another abandonment.

But Winifred only beamed, her smile bright as starlight.

She grabbed Bellatine's hand and pulled. Away from the wall. Through the doorway. Below the loft, as if the dangers hidden above were nothing. Across floorboards, creaking with Thistle-foot's steps, and into the bedroom. Toward the bed.

And for once, Bellatine let herself follow.

CHAPTER THIRTY-FIVE

"ANYONE WHO DON'T BELIEVE in ghosts must never have seen this place," Benji said, the wind combing back his red hair greaser-sleek. "Look out there and tell me this country ain't haunted."

A bone-pale dust devil lifted out of the ivory sand. It swirled alongside the highball train as if dancing, and Benji strummed "Tennessee Waltz" on his wood-worn guitar. "Hey there, Lady in White," he hooted. "Lookin' real pretty in your wedding dress." The dust devil spiraled away into the twilit desert.

It was the last hot night in August. After three days on and off the Sunset Line, the boys had made it as far into New Mexico as the Doña Ana Mountains, their clothes sticky with sweat and slapped fleas. This was Isaac's favorite kind of night. He and Ben watching the stars come out of hiding, America at their feet, summer air whizzing past them as if the breeze herself couldn't catch up. Even after three years, he wasn't tired of this.

Three years. On the road, time wasn't time. Not a straight

line, like a railroad track. It bloated and shrank, twisted in on itself until it felt as if he and Benji existed outside it altogether. They'd descended the Grand Canyon in a blizzard, mule drivers at their heels. Watched a lunar eclipse over the shacks of Slab City while coyotes howled through the old artillery range. They'd busked from New York to San Francisco, hitched through forty-three of the fifty states, been yanked off trains in five, managing to slip out of the bulls' clutches through charm and dumb luck every time. Seen sunsets so wide and golden you'd think someone had cracked open the sky like an egg into a skillet. Isaac had lived a thousand lives. Benji, a thousand ballads.

"Hey, Fresh, let's play a game," Benji crooned over the squeal of the train on the rail.

"Sure, what you got?"

"You think of a song, any song—think real hard, now. I'm gonna read your mind and sing it."

Isaac chuckled. "Godspeed, baby. Isn't gonna work."

"It will, it will, the devil is in the D string." He strummed a major chord.

"All right. I got one."

Benji closed his eyes, tapping his toe to a phantom rhythm. "There she is. *There* she is." He started to pluck out a tinny Hank Williams tune, skipping to his favorite verse.

> *"If it was rainin' gold, I wouldn't stand a chance*
> *I wouldn't have a pocket in my patched-up pants . . ."*

"Nah, not it. Your bust, what do I win?" Isaac said.

Benji grinned. "But you're thinking of it now, aren't you?"

"Doesn't count, it's not what I *was* thinking."

"*Was.* You know there ain't no *was.* Only right now."

Isaac smiled. "Sure, slick. Only right now."

Another dust devil spun up from the desert. The sands stretched on as far as they could see, silky and bleached as baby powder. Isaac felt like they'd left Earth behind altogether and ridden a train right up onto the moon. He snatched a cigarette from behind his ear, and after three attempts to shield a match against the wind, finally got it lit.

"Pass me a smokestack, will you?" Benji asked, tucking his guitar away next to Hubcap, who was curled, sleeping, in the hard case.

"Here." Isaac plucked the lit smoke from his mouth and passed it over. "I'll roll another."

"Always the gentleman, Fresh."

Benji hopped up and looped an arm around the ladder that ran up the backside of the autorack. He leaned out over the endless blanched hills. Smoke haloed him in silver before scattering. A shooting star zipped overhead and vanished beyond the horizon.

"You see that?" Benji shouted. "Bring us a lucky br—"

But whatever kind of luck was coming, Isaac never found out.

Perhaps there was a rock on the rail. Perhaps cargo shifted in the wheel well, lumber settling. Or perhaps that shooting star decided to lend them a different sort of fate.

The train bucked and Benji's grip on the ladder slipped. Their eyes met. Isaac froze for one panicked moment—then shot a hand toward his friend, grasping empty air as the boy lost hold. Benji fell. The wind swallowed his cry of surprise, and he was sucked beneath the grinding wheels of the great chrome beast. Gone.

Isaac screamed his friend's name until he was hoarse. He tried to jump off, but the train was moving too fast. Hank Williams and the "Tennessee Waltz" played in fevered loops in his head.

Surely Benji had managed to avoid the wheels, had rolled sideways to safety and was sweet-talking one of those dust-devil ghosts right now. Maybe he was clinging to the bottom of the train, and a bull would rough him up when they got to

El Paso. It would become a story they'd tell later to some pretty brunettes in a cheap bar. Maybe . . .

It took two days for Isaac to make it back. He walked the rails for a week more, until he was so sunburned and thirsty he thought the vultures were heckling him. His hope eroded with the dunes, the search morphing from rescue to recovery to vigil. The landscape undulated. It wore a different face each time he looked at it, shifted by wind. Whatever fragments had remained of a boy's ruined body were surely blanketed in sand by now or had been carried off by scavengers, lost to the great southwestern expanse. A crosstie instead of a cross for his tombstone. Isaac never found him.

Every night when Isaac closed his eyes, he was back on that train. In one fantasy, he didn't lend Benji a smoke, so the boy never got up to dangle on the ladder. In another, he'd grabbed the back of Benji's shirt as he fell, and Ben had written a song about it called "Close Call Blues." In another, Isaac caught his arm, another, his hair, and Benji had snapped at him for pulling a chunk out of his signature scarlet mop. In one reverie, Benji still died, only for Isaac to squeeze a wish from that shooting star so fervid that Ben reappeared, unharmed and whistling a tune he'd picked up in the afterlife. Though the memory took a thousand shapes, a thousand salvations, one aspect stayed the same: in every version, Isaac didn't hesitate.

A couple weeks later, starved gaunt, Isaac pawned Benji's guitar at a junk shop in Fort Stockton. He gave Hubcap to the girl who worked the laundromat there—but it wasn't long before Benji's sharp-toothed shadow tracked him down. He tried to lose her in Fort Worth and Shreveport and Jackson, but she kept turning up, mewing him awake or dropping a dead songbird on his pack. After a while, Isaac gave in and let the mangy cat stay.

And the rest of Benji? What of the electric, hollering static of him? What of the part where memory and loss and yearning are stored? Surely, they were still out there somewhere—gone to wherever the forsaken are banished. Wandering burnt-out Alabama plantations, the fields rancid with enslaved sorrow.

Across tracks built by Chinese rail workers, shot en masse come payday to save a dime. Into full-plotted cemeteries behind Indian boarding schools and beneath the shadows of burning crosses, white hoods peaked like snowcapped mountains. Over the grounds of Manzanar and potter's fields glutted with migrant peach pickers. Who gets remembered in the great American experiment? Who is forgotten? What becomes of those whose names are dust? *Tell me this country ain't haunted.*

When Isaac had finally given up, collapsing on the curb at a truck stop charging station with his phone in his fist, he'd realized there was no one to call. Benji had no family to moan in mourning. No mother to fall to her knees like a war widow. No father to bellow his son's name. The boy had left this world like he'd entered it—invisible. Abandoned. A no-name kid born in a cradle of needles, without a single lingering footprint to prove he'd ever been alive at all.

Isaac remained at the truck stop for hours. Semitrailers wheezed in and out, hauling through on their way to nowhere. A lone crow pecked at a candy wrapper. Fifty feet off in the lot, a trucker pumped diesel, one hand on the nozzle, the other on his hip. Isaac watched him with a curator's precision. He noted the out-toed splay of the man's boots. The pacing of his shoulders lifting and falling with breath. The upturn of his mouth as he thought about a girl in some other city, or a hot bath, or an old joke. Isaac felt himself turn to liquid. Re-form and solidify. He'd played the mimic before, had acted his way into pockets across the country—but this was different. This time, once he'd become the trucker, he let the role sink all the way down until there was no Isaac left underneath. Weight evaporated from his shoulders, relinquishing him. He unspooled. Gone was the final memory of Benji's face. Gone, all the hands of cards they'd played, the rackets they'd run, the miles they'd treaded. Gone was the boy who'd let his friend die. Only the Chameleon King remained.

––––––––––

Over the years, once memories of the Sunset Line had gone threadbare from picking, Isaac often wondered what would have happened had he found Benji's body. He imagined it pristine and dusted with starlit sand, laid out like a gunned-down highwayman. He'd close his best friend's eyes. Kiss his forehead. Sing their favorite songs as he buried him. He'd say goodbye.

CHAPTER THIRTY-SIX

BELLATINE AWOKE WITH THE sensation that something wasn't right.

Without opening her eyes, she could hear murmuring, paired with a soft, crinkling rustle. Perhaps that's what had woken her, her brother turning in the next bed over. For a blissful moment, she hovered suspended in the space between sleep and waking. A realm of no memory, no past nor looming present, only the sway of Thistlefoot lumbering west.

Isaac isn't here.

The day's events careened back into her like a tire iron to the ribs. Isaac was gone. That was Winnie humming in her sleep, curled around her in the twin bed. Her blue funeral dress discarded on the floor. The rustle came from the ruined windows, taped over with garbage bags. She remembered the *sft, sft, sft* of a broom clearing debris. The cold sting of ice against each bruise. Those spindly *things* crouched on the smokefed's backs. They'd been attacked, and they'd escaped—and she'd watched the life shriek out of a dozen human beings as the smokefed plummeted from the bridge. Seeing their deaths had been like watching a film in reverse. Movements jerky, unnatural. Instead of reaching into an object to seek the spark of a ghost and wake it, she'd seen ghosts ripped loose and discarded. The opposite of what her hands knew to be possible.

A bell chimed softly from the entry room.

It wasn't Winifred's murmuring that had woken her, nor plastic flapping against the whitewashed walls. It was the doorbell.

One.

Two.

Was the wind tugging the owl-talon ringer? Or was one of the Duskbreaker crew trying to get her attention? The politeness of knocking seemed far from their style . . . Plus, she could hear the low rumble of their bus engine chugging along behind.

Three.

It was a soft chime, low and echoing as breath blowing over the mouth of an empty bottle. Thistlefoot's floorboards whined. The house continued limping along, as bid, but tension seeped from the walls. A shiver trembled from the foundation up to the ceiling, and Bellatine could hear Winnie's teeth chatter, her cheek soft against Bellatine's shoulder. *The house is frightened.*

Four.

Bellatine untangled herself from Winifred and rose, tugging on a nightshirt and sweats. She crossed the threshold. The darkness in the foyer was so complete she felt she might walk forever and never reach the door. A void with no edges, no limits. Only her body drifting through space, the ache of her sore muscles the only thing grounding her. The *ring, ring, ring* of the bell.

A rectangular zipper of light emerged ahead, streetlights shoving into the cracks where the front door met the frame. She knew where the latch was even in the dark. She'd put it there herself, a cast iron bolt she'd salvaged from an old barn.

Her hands remembered the drill humming, her finger on the trigger as she'd screwed the pieces in fast. How long ago it seemed now.

Her hand rose. It fell on the fastened lock, thumbing the hammer-forged pockmarks in the metal, the grooves where it met wood. Then, she slid the rod free with a click. The door swung open.

"Hello, Miss Yaga," the man said. He held a brimmed general's cap to his chest and bowed. "May I come in?" Above him, the mezuzah on the doorframe turned, slowly, and faced the wall.

His voice was familiar. It was like the one she'd heard in her head in Winifred's cemetery—but more than that. This voice, she'd known it longer. Her blood had known this voice for generations, echoing back years before her birth. This voice, it had been following her for a century.

They were sitting in the parlor. She didn't remember him entering, nor did she remember settling on the clay bench, the man seated in a wicker chair across from her. Where had the chair come from? She didn't recognize it, but it clearly belonged there. So did the small mahogany table between them and the samovar atop it, painted with red and blue flowers. One of the long white-smoke creatures hovered beside them. It reached forward and turned a valve on the silver faucet. Steaming liquid gushed into a silver-handled cup, which once filled, it placed in front of Bellatine.

"Do not worry," the Longshadow Man said, flicking a dismissive hand at the brew. "It's only tea. I am a civil man, seeking a civil conversation."

Bellatine drew in the steam but did not drink. She tried not to look at the ghostly servant. The tea was fragrant with herbs, a tinge of rosewater and honey underneath.

"I've come to apologize," the Longshadow Man said, tipping his head. A second cup appeared in his hand, which the creature filled for him.

Somehow his words seemed to sit on the inside of her skull, like they had when she was under the smokefed spell. "You aren't here," she said. "This is a dream."

"You are right and you are wrong, as people often are in their assumptions. Is my body here with your body? No. But neither am I a dream. You and I, we have a secret, don't we? A little connection, like a telephone line. So *here I am*." He drew his words out like stretched taffy. "Calling."

A moth fluttered around the samovar, drawn by the warmth. It landed in the visitor's cup. She watched it struggle, its wings growing wet and sticky before vanishing into dark liquid.

"And now," he continued, "we are blessed with the luxury of solitude. How refreshing, to have the young chameleon gone. We are finally free to enjoy each other's company without . . . interruption. So generous of him, to afford us this time together."

"Solitude?" Bellatine allowed herself a glance at the smoke creature. Its arms were so long the knuckles scraped the floor.

"Ah. Yes. They can be distracting. My apologies, your comfort is my priority." The Longshadow Man opened the left side of his coat with a nod and the creature slipped against him, wafting to his chest like a candle blown out. The smoke seeped through his clothes and into his body. Gone.

"You sent those people," Bellatine said. Her voice sounded far away, as if rising through water. "You poisoned them. You hurt us."

A silver spoon festooned in silver vines appeared in the man's hand. "Yes, that display was much more *messy* than I would have liked, and for that I am truly sorry." He wrinkled his nose with distaste. "But sometimes a message must be sent, no?" He stirred his tea counterclockwise, the spoon clicking against the side of the cup. "You must understand, I am here to complete a task. A tidying, if you will. A bed nearly made, with only one corner still to be tucked in. You, a woman of order, of logic, can surely appreciate."

A final stain, Bellatine remembered.

"I only wished to talk, *malyshka,* to explain that I am a righteous man with a righteous mission. But you ran from me, and so I sent my attendants to discourage further stubbornness. Don't you wish for what I wish for—an unblemished world? A safe world?"

The man lifted his cup to his thin lips. He drank. The room flickered. The windows, which a moment ago had been blacked out with night and plastic, now glared with unhindered daylight. Outside, Bellatine glimpsed what looked like a market town, not unlike the mirage she'd witnessed in the cemetery. Hadn't they been passing through expansive oil fields only moments ago? She'd seen the lamplit hammerhead of a pumpjack rising and falling in the distance when she'd opened the door to let the man in. Now, whitewashed cottages surrounded them. The roofs of the buildings were ravished by flames. Tumbleweeds, consumed by fire, churned like infernal wheels across the earth. Farther, a tree, where several dark shapes swung from the branches. She blinked. The images vanished back to midnight—but the scent of smoke lingered.

Bellatine's thoughts flashed to Li Fen. Reed organs, collapsing into ash.

"Ah, yes." The Longshadow Man affirmed. He sifted through her thoughts, plucking up scraps. "Unblemished worlds, they do require sacrifice."

You killed her . . .

"Have you ever heard of serotinous plants?" the man asked, dabbing his mouth spotless with a handkerchief. "It occurs among conifers, eucalypti in the southern hemisphere, some flowering *Macadamia.* These plants, they tuck their seeds within cones sealed tight with resin. And there they remain locked— until!" He snapped his fingers and a small spark appeared as if he were holding a lit match. "Fire!" Thistlefoot shuffled uneasily beneath them. "When the cones burn, they release their seeds. These seeds sprout, root, grow, and thrive. But only once the cone is *incinerated*." He waved his fingers and the light snuffed out. "We do not have these plants in Russia, the climate is too cold and wet. But fabulous, no? An organism God designed to live better when burned. You see, sometimes, what may be mistaken for destruction is necessary for the good of the land. This house—you should think of it as one such cone. The final cone, the very *last*, in fact, from a whole village full, all burned so the larger plant, my Russia, might thrive. It would not do to leave a job incomplete, yes? For the good of what grows in fertile soil."

He stood, folding the napkin corner to corner, then again, precise. "I trust we understand each other. Next time I come calling, no more running. Then, we can meet in the flesh. I look forward to such festivities."

"What are you?" Bellatine asked. She had meant to make her voice strong and unmovable as oak, but it slipped out small.

"Nyet, child, I am no *what*," said the man. His words seemed to echo not only in her head, then, but in every corner of the house. She could hear it in the rafters and the walls, sliding along doorframes and up from cracks between the floorboards; heard it crackling within the pantries and licking up from within her own veins, where it felt familiar, a known terror. "I am not a what," he repeated. "I am a *when*."

When Bellatine blinked again, the table with the samovar, the wicker chair, and the strange man with the long wool coat were gone.

CHAPTER THIRTY-SEVEN

DO NOT BE A fool. There exists no such thing as ghosts of the dead.

But, little house, you will say, *what of the dark shadows our mothers have warned us about? Agras bas Mahlas dancing on the roof? Mazzikin causing rifles to misfire and poisoning well water? Alukah taking a daily blood meal at horses' throats?*

And to you I will say, you do not listen! These are *demons,* not ghosts. There are demons among us, that much is certain! You need only look out my windows, and you'll see them. But a ghost of the dead? Peer through the glass as long as you like. You won't find one.

But, little house, you say, *what of Shaul HaMelech, who, with the help of a witch, conjures Shmuel HaNavi's spirit to defeat the Philistines? Can the Torah lie?*

Feh! It was a trick, as all witches are tricksters. No miracle. There are plenty of miracles in this world and the next, but dead men wandering beside the living is not among them. Any rabbi could tell you that.

But, little house, you say, *what of dybbukim who cling to our backs, who make us convulse with seizures and writhe with migraines all day, all night? Are they not real?*

To this I will say, your questions give me headaches of my own, does this make you a dybbuk? And I do not even have a head.

But, little house, you say, *what is a memory if not a ghost?*

There lives a woman in the shtetl of Gedenkrovka, the region of Cherkasy, the Empire of Russia. The gentiles on the outskirts of the town, they believe this woman is a demon, for she lives in a house unlike all other houses. They say she can make a child from a tooth. They say she feeds these children noodle soup brothed with lost travelers' bones. *Do not go near Baba Yaga's hut or she will put a candle in your skull and make a lantern of you,* they say. The Jews in the market, they do not care if she is a witch or a cucumber so long as she is not a shiksa and so long as she brings healthy eggs to sell and so long as she keeps her daughters from biting the other children. The Jews, they have heard their people called "demon" before. They learned to stop listening.

You are remembering this story as I tell it, are you not? Is this not a haunting, a story that is told and told and will not hush in the telling? A story already inside your ears, even before I speak?

Have you heard the one about Baba Yaga and the Longshadow Man?

One morning, Baba Yaga goes to town, leaving Illa behind to care for Malka. When she arrives at the market, she finds the village empty. When she goes to the grocery, there is no one to sell her peas and pickling jars. When she goes to the milliner, the hats are gossiping among themselves, alone. When she goes to the butcher, the floor is too clean, no blood at all. Then, as she makes her way toward the synagogue, she spots a lone man lingering by the village well.

"Pardon me, stranger," Baba Yaga says, "can you tell me where everyone has gone? I hope it isn't some high holiday and I've forgotten to go to shul . . ."

The stranger tips his brimmed hat and smiles. "Why yes, today is a holiday. It is the first day of the end."

Baba Yaga has no time for riddles and no time for strange men, so she turns to continue on her way.

"Wait," says the man. "Let me accompany you to the synagogue."

"I am perfectly happy to walk myself," Baba Yaga replies, and she begins to step away. The air is cold and tight, and the smack of her boots against cobblestone travels through it quicker than a telegraph.

"Sister, please," entreats the man. "What sort of neighbor would I be if I did not at least hold open the door for you?" And with that, the man lifts his arm.

The arm elongates, emerging like a column of smoke. It stretches twice its length, then thrice, then four, five times too long. As it reaches, the man's coat sleeve lengthens, too. The arm stretches past Baba Yaga and across the square and up the granite steps, until at last it arrives at the synagogue door. Fingers close upon the brass knob with a *tap, tap, tap.*

By now, Baba Yaga knows she is not speaking to a man at all.

"On second thought," Baba Yaga says, "I think I'll visit the rabbi tomorrow." She shields a white bean in the small of her palm and watches it spin, pointing the way home to me.

But when Baba Yaga looks back up, she notices the man's other arm. It, too, has begun to stretch, skinny and birch-like as kindling. It has stretched so long and so far that Baba Yaga cannot see the end of it—vanishing in the very same direction that the white bean has pointed.

"What fine daughters you have." The Longshadow Man smiles. "Such soft hair."

Baba Yaga begins to run.

Denikin's men come at dawn.

The first Jew to die is a boy, seventeen, running home to warn his father. One of Denikin's soldiers shoots him in the head. They drop him in the town well to rot.

There is no such thing as a ghost of the dead.

Yet suffering has a way of begging to be remembered. Sometimes, as a story. Sometimes, as a wraith.

Today, they say the air in what used to be Gedenkrovka is heavier than it should be, so altered it presses damp on the skin. They say pain can be passed in the blood. A sorrow great enough can alter an ancestral line, can make itself visible in the body even generations later, even once the name of the sorrow is forgotten. How long does it take for the body to realize it is safe? Does it ever?

Can a restlessness be a ghost? Can a pair of hands?

There are no ghosts of the dead. Your grandfather does not sit at the foot of your bed and sing. Do not be stupid. You do not see a child in a Victorian gown by the window. These are mirages or devils. The dybbuk possessing your husband is simply his anger mixed with drink. There are no ghosts of the dead.

And yet, this *is* a ghost story.

There are no ghosts of the dead. But events? Events, if they carry enough wailing, can leave a mark. Can squeeze themselves into terrible shapes, grow arms, legs, a head on which to wear a hat, feet on which to follow you.

Events—they have a way of coming back.

CHAPTER THIRTY-EIGHT

GREEN FELT CURLED AT the pool table's edges as a striped thirteen rolled across like a palm-sized Saturn. It was nearly 7:00 a.m. The Chameleon King had been in the bar since four, dropped in Fayetteville, Arkansas, by a long-haul trucker named Joe Pill who'd played Vivaldi's "Four Seasons" on loop the journey through. Before that, it had taken two rides from the Crescent City to Baton Rouge. Another three into Mississippi. His charioteers had included a pair of aging sisters on a day trip to buy parakeets in the city (*Never get married,* they'd counseled, *get birds instead*), a stripper with a questionable pile of dead squirrels in her trunk, and a retired cop with a *Love It or Leave It* American flag bumper sticker. Every face, every name, every grip on the wheel and head tilted toward the radio, the Chameleon King had memorized. Stored away. Tanned and salted and saved for later like a scrap of meat.

"You thinking about someone special?" his opponent heckled.

Snapping to, he realized he'd been twisting chalk over the tip of his pool cue for a good two minutes. He was pretty damn sharp at pool, a sport of subtle, studied musculature—but Clarence Utah wasn't, and it was Clarence Utah's body he was living in tonight.

"Just hashing out that next chapter." He shot for a corner pocket and missed.

Clarence, he'd decided, was a struggling novelist from Tulsa, in town to research a book about a snake hunter in the Ozarks.

"Y'know, I was thinking I might write out my own life story one day. They say anyone can write a book." His pool rival, a barrel of a man with a brass tiger's head belt buckle, sank four shots in a row and went for the eight ball.

"Do they, now."

"Seems like nothing to it." He aimed, shot, and the black ball vanished into the table's belly.

That sounded like the sort of comment Clarence Utah wouldn't take kindly to. Maybe he wasn't in the mood to play pool anymore. Instead, he could be in the mood for a fight. Was Clarence a sore loser? Sure, why not. The Chameleon King scowled, grabbed the man's beer out of his hand, and downed it.

"What the hell, man!"

He smashed the Budweiser bottle on the barroom floor. The shattering felt like bells tolling inside him, as if a loud enough sound might wake him up. Might frighten off the ghosts, the dissonance too much for Benji to stomach. Might sever a line in the ground between who he had been and who he would be.

The bartender dragged him from the bar by the scruff of his coat, but not before he managed to nab another beer off a neighboring table and lift twenty-three dollars, unseen, from the tip jar. He was out of tobacco, so he dug a butt from the ashtray by the stoop and smoked that instead. A ring of pink lipstick haloed the filter from whoever had discarded it there. It was sweet, like a Jolly Rancher. Clarence Utah melted off him and dispersed with the smoke.

Isaac had been awake all night. That old rabid fox scrabbled hungry in his lungs, preventing him from sleep. *Keep moving,* it hissed. *Forget the house with the terrible yellow feet. Forget your ι name. Forget.* He held out a thumb.

"If you see God, you'll know it, you hear me?" the lady, who'd introduced herself as Jo, said. Her hands on the steering wheel were dirty, like she'd been digging carrots out of a garden. Fat raindrops fell on the windshield of her Toyota pickup, and she flipped on the wipers. "I saw Him when I was a real teensy thing, you know? Just a girl, back in Little Rock. But you're never too young to lay your eyes on the holy light of the Lord."

He'd quit riding trains after Benji died, replaced the rails with thumbing it and trust in his own two feet. At times, he missed the lonesome miles on a freight train's back. The screech of brakes too loud to talk over. But hitching had its own perks. The stories. The people. The strange one-act plays performed in the front seat of a rusted-out jalopy, as if a truck cab were a confessional booth. Anonymity had a soothsaying effect on folks. There are things you can tell a stranger you wouldn't tell your own mirror. Trust a secret to a friend, and you'll see that secret balanced on their lips for the rest of your days. But tell a secret to a hitchhiker, and they'll do you the service of taking it away with them when they leave. Carry that tender part of you off to another state, another highway. One small exorcism, performed with a foot on the gas pedal.

Isaac rolled up his window against the rain. "Don't know if I'd recognize Him if I saw Him." Hubcap, curled in his lap, gnawed at a piece of beef jerky the woman had dug out of the glove box.

"Oh, you would, you'd know, honey. When I saw Him, He was a frog. A lumpy little bullfrog with only one leg. I was seven, eight, somethin' like that. My dog had the thing in its mouth, then pop, bit the leg clean off. I picked up the critter and took it to a puddle. And when I put it in there, it looked

th those two bulgy eyes, and I knew it. I *knew* who
ng at. The heavenly Father Himself! You ever just
hat? You ever find the answer, I mean *the* answer,
out in front of you?" Jo squinted, then brushed a
flannel over the windshield to clear the condensation
gathering on the glass.

Answers . . . An answer is a flat tire on a back road. A dead-end
alley. As soon as you know anything for certain, the wandering and the wondering stop. No marvels anymore. No holiness.
Nowhere left to go. Where to find holiness, Isaac didn't rightly
know, but it sure as hell didn't come from answers.

But questions—those were another matter. Ask a question,
and an endless map of potential unfurls before you. North,
south, east, west, an interstate of unknowings, each with their
own exits and truck stops and bends in the road. You can wander along a question your whole life and never need to stop.
When he was on the bum, Isaac could wake up every morning
not knowing where he'd be that afternoon. Not knowing where
he'd sleep that night. And that kept him pressing on—the curiosity. A holy ignorance.

He'd thought he'd found an answer in the cursed old house.
An answer to his debt. An answer to his poverty. That maybe
if he could make a year's worth of dough, get a little ahead of
himself, he could crawl out of his hole far enough to do Benji
right. Give him a real funeral. Buy back his guitar. Even get
some of the kid's songs out there in the world. A small legacy.
He should have known that all an answer does is force you into
a cage. The little fox in his chest scratched, scratched, scratched.
Suddenly the walls of the car felt tight as a vise.

"Hey, baby, can you pull over? My knees are getting stiff, I
think I best walk for a while," he said.

"In this? You crazy?" The rain had turned silver with velocity,
making the car roof sing like a rattlesnake's tail.

"I don't mind a little weather," Isaac said. "Thanks kindly for
the lift."

He was glad he didn't have his pack with him. Nothing to get wet that mattered—though Hubcap disagreed, yowling as her fur matted with rainwater. He buttoned her into his tux jacket, and she curled up against him for warmth as he made his way down the black glint of the road, Jo's taillights shrinking into the distance. Though it was still only late morning, storm clouds padded the sky with false twilight. Beyond, fog like a lake of mercury. Whatever lay ahead was invisible—each step, a question. His hair stuck to his temples and his shoes sloshed with each footfall.

After a few miles, a chill began to take hold in earnest. It began at his toes and worked its way up, stiffening him inch by inch as if he were a candlewick being lowered into wax. The many sleepless hours had left him raw. Each shiver passed through him like a thunderclap, and he clutched Hubcap tighter, grinding his teeth to keep them from chattering. But this was *right*. He wasn't meant to be comfortable. To sleep in a bed, a roof overhead. How quickly a bed becomes a grave . . .

An hour passed. Then another. Surely, there must be a town or a truck stop soon. Early on, an eighteen-wheeler had passed him by, but that had been the last trace of humanity he'd seen. By now, the rain had given way to an icy sleet, encasing each grass blade in a silvery shell. It made the roadside glitter as if sculpted from glass. A wet, bone cold had crawled its way into Isaac like a weevil, but he shut the sensation out. Oil drills rose and fell. Vultures circled overhead, gouging dark gashes in the sky. Eventually his eyelids grew too heavy to keep them open, so he stumbled forward blind, blinking every so often to keep on track. His legs were numb. If only he could find an overpass or a thick stand of shrubs, he could tuck away from the storm and dry off, warm up, sleep for a spell—but the road threaded on and on, embanked by nothing but sky. *One more step*, he willed himself. *Another. That's it.* He would not be an Orpheus. He would not be Lot's wife, turned to a pillar of salt. He would not look back. Memory, it was nothing but a leash.

He was shaking so hard now that his steps were uneven. And this time, it wasn't from restlessness. His pale lips abandoned their blush, giving way to blue. Ringlets of his hair had frozen rigid enough to snap. Eventually, his limbs too stiff to keep moving, he collapsed under a billboard, leaning up against the chrome pillars. Whatever road he was on, he was on it alone. No cars passed. No lights in the distance invited him into a new city. If only he had a shot of whiskey and a hot cup of coffee—what luxury that would be . . . Isaac could almost feel the fantasy's warmth in his chest, spreading through him molecule by molecule.

Where are you going? Heaven or Hell? He could just barely make out the words on the billboard above, beaten by rain. Dial 1-800-kno-truth.

Heaven or hell . . . Isaac thought. What if there were other options? Liminal spaces, where the dead never died, but merely hovered in time. An ouroboros of a moment, forever swallowing its tail. Some memories, they must be so potent they never really end. They just keep looping back on themselves to be relived and relived. Was that where Benji had gone? A pocket universe where he was forced to plummet from that ladder again and again ad infinitum? Isaac closed his eyes. Cold draped over him like a mourning veil, but after a while, he could no longer feel it. The soft twang of guitar strings buzzed, somewhere just out of sight. He'd failed Benji. He'd let him die. Worse—he'd let him be forgotten. And now he'd left his sister to die, too. No wonder he felt like a ghost. They were more his people than the living were.

Where are you going? Heaven or hell?

Isaac sighed and his breath crystallized. He wouldn't need to call the number on the sign. He could find out himself. All he had to do was sit still and let the lacy frost settle. The only real way to pay his debt.

Isaac leaned back. He was tired. Tired of running. Tired of being haunted. Tired of stepping in and out of life after life after life. He could have been riding shotgun in Jo's truck right now, the radiator blasting heat. He could have been heading somewhere with a good meal, a warm bed. If given a do-over, maybe that's what he'd have chosen. But the choice had already been made—and a good showman plays to the audience he's got. A frigid wind rose, but Isaac had grown warm.

"Hey there, Fresh," echoed a familiar voice. "You ready to catch that Westbound train?"

He closed his eyes.

CHAPTER THIRTY-NINE

A TRAIN'S RATTLE FILLED Isaac's head. Or no, not a train . . . and not in his head, either. The sound yanked him back. He blinked. A farm wagon split through the fog as if parting the Red Sea. It was hitched to a sturdy black workhorse and stacked with hay bales, a man in a wool coat at the reins. Relief he didn't know he was holding washed through Isaac in a tidal wave. It wasn't his time yet. That coffee and whiskey, warm meal, warm bed . . . perhaps it was waiting for him after all.

"*Hey*," Isaac mouthed, his voice a wisp. "*Hey*," he tried again, this time sending a pinball of sound pinging through the cold. The driver turned a head and stopped. He raised an arm, and Isaac strained to lift his own in reply.

"Buddy, could I get a lift?" Isaac rasped. The driver grunted a nod, and Isaac flinched as he pulled himself off the ground. Pins and needles shot through his joints.

"You get tagalongs often?" Isaac asked.

The man shook his head.

"Where we headed, big guy?"

"Home." The driver pressed his lips into a line beneath a bushy mustache.

"Not a big talker," Isaac said through chattering teeth, "I respect that."

Wherever the cart was headed, it was *somewhere*. That was good enough for him.

They rode in silence, Isaac and Hubcap in back with the hay. He pressed up against the bales, which were miraculously dry in patches and released a sweet and heady perfume as they jostled along the highway. It was all he could do to stay awake.

After a while, a dense yellow light pierced through the sleet. It hovered bodiless ahead of them, a small sun. Growing closer, a dark rectangle emerged around it, as if the light were a painting held within an ornate frame. A gas lamp, Isaac realized, hooked onto the door of a looming wooden gate.

Isaac had thought they'd been driving along a state through highway, but as he drew nearer, he saw that the road led directly to the gate, ending abruptly at the latched door. Did this gate enclose a ranch? It would be a strange place for one. Isaac had made it as far as oil country, where the land had been pilfered so deeply not even a toothy radish would grow. Perhaps it was some sort of religious sect, a doomsday cult awaiting a messiah on a comet's back. Or could be a gated community of oil barons, hiding out in the desert with the wealth they'd bleached out of stolen Native land. Whatever the place might be, insular communities rarely took well to damp strangers without luggage. No matter. He'd make sure he wasn't a stranger at all.

The air must have grown warmer, because the frost on his clothes and hair had melted, and his limbs felt surprisingly limber. He threw back his shoulders and whisked his sodden curls from his forehead. The gates opened, letting the wagon and its passengers through. His identity dispersed like a gas, ready to rearrange and fill whatever container it needed to.

As soon as they crossed the threshold, sound splashed through the rain like a loose bull. Children squawked, their boots squelching in mud. Women's voices darted like shuttles on a loom, while men quarreled in that sacred cadence reserved for political squabbles. Hooves thudded low drumbeats into the ground as laboring beasts shuffled impatiently in place, punctuated by the clatter and jingle of commerce.

As the wagon carried him deeper, images emerged from the fog in pieces. A thatched roof. Then, a slab of brick peeking through chipping stucco. Sellers' signs swinging on squealing hinges: a giant pair of spectacles; a wood-burned sketch of a sewing machine; a basket of painted apples inked radium green. Beside the stores, lamps on tall iron posts. Other carts like this one, filled with tin jugs and wooden pallets, oxen at the helm. The fog pulled back from shape after shape, giving the illusion that the town was not being revealed, but *created*, manifested piece by piece for his benefit alone.

The cart stopped, and Isaac hopped off the back, dipping around front to toss the driver a flattened nickel. "A good luck charm," he said. "You hang on to that." He patted the horse on the nose and bid them both adieu. A few paces off, he spotted a man of his own rough size and scanned him quickly for posture and habits, adjusting himself to match. He wouldn't be able to convince anyone up close, but a casual glance would register Isaac as someone familiar, one of their own. He was glad for his timeless, albeit baggy, dress jacket, sopping though it was; everyone in the town sported antiquated attire, so his rags fit in. Their garb was too colorful to be Amish, but otherwise not dissimilar. Men wore long gray beards and heavy wool coats with collars turned up against the wind. The women were wrapped in a panoply of striped and plaid and dotted shawls. Baskets dangled from their elbows, abundant with fruits and cheese. *Benji would have eaten this place up*, Isaac thought. He could almost see his friend's shamrock eyes flash with eagerness, ready to jaunt straight into the center and start shaking down strangers for all the ballads and poems and stories they knew. *Just think, a joint like this*, he would have said, *it's like the Golden Record on the* Voyager—*sung and sealed and shot into space*, *a culture caught in a bell jar. And we get to be the lucky aliens to listen to it.* Benji had always been a sucker for the odd and obsolete. Must have been the time traveler in him.

The wet ground grabbed at Isaac's shoes as he made his way into the town square. Hubcap scratched at him from beneath his coat.

"Hey now," he whispered, "if you'd rather walk through the muck, I'll drop you right now."

She rearranged herself, glowering.

The town was shaped in a great circle, with all the shop fronts turned inward toward a central clearing, now ankle-deep with mud and growing wetter by the minute. A watering well punctuated the interior, surrounded by a jumble of farm stands and pop-up booths selling milk, glossy plucked chickens, stoneware vases, potatoes the size of a fist. Hunger tightened a knot in his belly. As he passed a stall stacked high with golden bread, Isaac palmed a honey-glazed pastry speckled with walnuts. He'd left his last pressed nickel with the cart driver, so he dropped a pebble in the sweet's place instead. He took a bite—and spat coughing onto the ground. The center was rotten through with maggots.

Something smacked Isaac hard in the back of the head. He spun, just in time to see a red ball splat in the mud. Three young boys chased it down, skidding to a halt about fifteen feet from where the ball had landed. The fastest two seemed around eight years old, with a smaller child of four or five stumbling to keep up. All three wore peaked hats and rough woolen trousers. One of the older boys had a cigarette drooping from the corner of his mouth.

"Sorry," one boy mumbled, grimacing at the mud they'd splashed on Isaac's pants leg.

"Sure you are." Isaac raised an eyebrow.

The little one caught up, panting. He sneezed and wiped the snot with the back of his hand. "Elye, Papa told you to let me play! You promised."

"I *am*, it's not *my* fault you're too clumsy to catch it."

"I am not clumsy!"

"Go get it then."

The young boy shook his head.

"You *scared*?"

"No!"

"Then go get it."

"*You* go get it."

Isaac spared a glance at the ball, which had landed at the foot of the brick well. He jolted at the sight of the raised image on the well's front: a two-headed eagle, wings outstretched. It was a common symbol in many a coat of arms and national flags—he knew this—but the coincidence still tinged Isaac with unease. He didn't want to think about the matching blue bottle, nor the man who carried it. He pried his eyes away.

"Hey, squirt," Isaac said, nodding at the boy with the cigarette. "You're too young for that shit, why don't you put that out?"

The boy snorted. "I'm older than you, Yaga."

Isaac's stomach dropped. "What did you call me?"

A sharp voice hollered from the market's edge and the boys scattered. He must have misheard the kid. He was tired, his senses warped. Still, there was something uncanny in the way the children frolicked in the open square, unhindered by the storm. In fact, not one of the townspeople held umbrellas nor shivered against the rain. It was as if they couldn't feel it at all.

Isaac could handle hunger. He had before. He could endure aching cold and exhaustion. But while he would happily abandon his comforts, his vices were another matter. Crossing the swamped square, he eased up the stairs to the general store, praying to find a tobacco counter within, and hopefully that cup of hot coffee.

"... thirty rubles? Thirty! Why don't you take my horse, too? Take my house. Here, I'll give you my trousers, take it all."

Two men blocked the counter, one spindly as a piece of straw, the other short with shoulders too wide for his seam-split vest.

The narrow man had a needle of a finger extended toward the cashier, a white-haired gentleman in round spectacles.

"Feh, it's a fair price, Zurach," the cashier bickered, swiping away the accusatory finger.

"Fair price! Do you hear this, Reb Mendl? Thirty rubles for a coil of rope? A fair price if it were spun from pure gold, maybe."

"With a golden lasso, perhaps you could finally catch yourself a wife!"

The tension popped like a balloon as the men collapsed into laughter, and Isaac nudged his way past. He scanned behind the counter for a turquoise pack of American Spirits, or even Pall Malls, but they didn't seem to sell either.

"Say," Isaac interjected, "none of you gentlemen have a smoke I could skin off you for a dollar, do you?"

Their laughter snuffed out like a wet match.

"You," the spindly man, Zurach, said, redirecting his pet finger to aim straight at Isaac's nose. "Why are you here?"

So maybe he'd overestimated his chances of blending in. The three men assessed him with suspicion.

"He's come for the Happening," the man called Reb Mendl whispered. "Hashem has sent a witness." His eyes were wide below caterpillar eyebrows.

"That's enough," Zurach barked—but not at Isaac. He was staring down at his companion, trembling with fury. "There is no Happening. Not today. Not yesterday. Not tomorrow. You should cut out your own tongue for such blasphemy." He turned to Isaac. "You, leave."

The shop owner slid out from behind his counter and brushed the two men off with an easy flick of his wrists. "Is this how you treat a visitor? Would you greet the prophet Elijah with such hospitality?" He looked Isaac up and down, frowning. "Look at his shoes, worn through like a child of Israel in the desert! Come, let's get you dried off and into a warm pair of socks."

The proprietor led Isaac to a small table in the back of the shop. With silent glances over their shoulders, the two customers left. They forgot the disputed rope on the countertop.

"You must be frozen through," the man tutted. "Don't mind those two asses, they don't remember what being cold and wet feels like. Many people have forgotten around here."

Outside the store windows, rain fell undeterred.

Isaac readied himself for what was sure to follow—questions about where he'd come from, who he was, his occupation and reason for visiting. He spun a game show wheel in his head, each sliver bearing a different name, a different life. They ticked by, choice after choice. A cousin come calling. A traveling doctor. A building inspector. A lost Mormon missionary. Tick, tick, tick, the identities churned past, but when the wild wheel finally stopped, it landed on Isaac Yaga himself. *No.* Isaac shuddered. He spun again.

"Here," the man said, handing Isaac a thick wool blanket. "Now give me your shoes and coat, I'll dry them on the stove out back." He obliged, and the man shuffled into the next room. As soon as the shopkeeper was out of sight, Isaac pocketed a handful of roast nuts and two tins of pickled sardines—one for him and one for Hub—before settling at the small table.

As soon as Isaac wrapped the wool around his shoulders, all the exhaustion he'd been staving off poured over him like melted butter. An oily animal musk clung to the shawl's fabric, enrobing him in an invisible pasture full of grazing sheep. Warmth crept through him. His bones could have been made of lead, they were so heavy. He let his arms fall at his sides. He barely registered Hubcap wiggling free from his shirt, nor the return of the shopkeeper, who lay a dish of cream at the cat's feet without question.

"It's good you've come," Isaac thought he heard the man say to him. "It's good to bear witness." The red stage curtains of his eyelids fell.

He startled awake to the clang of bells.

The crates and shelves throughout the store cast long forests of shadow along the floor. The room was empty, and his coat lay folded on the tabletop beside his dried, freshly oiled shoes and a clean pair of socks. How long had he slept? Even Hubcap was gone, probably feasting on plump sparrows under a porch somewhere in the town. Outside, a slip of purple evening had dusted in among the clouds.

The bells rang again.

Isaac dipped behind the store counter and popped open the cash register, which had been left unlocked. Inside were rows of red and yellow and green bank notes. The customers, they'd been bickering about *rubles* . . . In his fatigue, he'd glazed right over it. Where *was* he?

He left the useless foreign tender where it lay, gathered up his belongings, and stepped back into the square.

The bell tolled once more, and Isaac found the villagers scurrying toward a tall, grand building at the town's head. Sellers abandoned their wares, and the shops in the outer ring emptied as everyone made their way in the same direction. Isaac followed. Though it, too, was constructed of whitewashed brick, the tall building was festooned with ornate pillars and high, arching windows, sprawling with the majesty of Grand Central Station. A clock was inlaid like a diamond beneath the highest central arch, the diameter as wide as Isaac's arm span. It tolled two o'clock beneath green glass. Far below, a set of ivory-and-mahogany checkerboard doors opened to admit the crowd.

A conflicting motion caught the corner of Isaac's eye, back toward the commons from where he'd come. He turned to see a woman scurrying in the opposite direction—not to the ornate building, but away, toward the market's edge. She clutched a bundled infant to her chest and dragged a delicate girl with long raven hair along by the hand. There was something unbearably *familiar* about the family. It was as if they were old characters Isaac had once played, figures whose eyes he'd wept with, whose voices he'd sung through, whose feet he'd leaned on in wandering. The woman caught Isaac's eye. A chill passed through him at the glance. *Desperation.* A need so wide, no fury nor deception in the world could mask it. It wrapped around her like a noose, like she was an animal in a trap. This woman, she was prepared to gnaw off her own leg to be free.

The little girl with the black hair clutched a doll, dangling from her free hand. Though it wore a different set of cotton clothes and lacked the ruffled collar and black tears that Isaac's mother had painted on, its scarlet shoes and whittled hands bore an unmistakable resemblance to the Drowning Fool. Isaac took a step closer.

Then someone in the crowd jostled against him, pressing him through the doors and into the building. When he tried to look back, the woman and her children were gone. The great doors closed.

He found himself in a cavernous room. Benches squatted in stripes across a stone floor. In every corner, silk curtains with burgundy tassels dripped thick as amber. But the room's true pride was a golden tower, javelining skyward nearly two stories tall. It was wrapped in gleaming filigree, scrollwork and vines and winged beasts of paradise entwined in an intricate tangle, fit for a tsar's palace. The tower's crown was inscribed with Hebrew lettering, topped with a two-headed firebird, rubies in her beak.

It's a synagogue, Isaac realized. Though his mother had been raised Jewish, he'd never set foot in a shul before. A memory returned to him from childhood—passing by a temple while their family toured in Montreal. He'd tugged on his mom's hand, drawn toward the grandeur and cantillation billowing from the open door, but she'd yanked him away as if she couldn't bear to hear the music.

Women and small children were funneled up a flight of stairs into a separate section, while Isaac remained below with the men and older boys. He spotted the bespectacled shopkeeper a few seats away, his head bowed. Rows ahead of him, the boy who'd had the cigarette turned around and stuck out his tongue.

All throughout the synagogue, people were praying. The prayers—no two sounded the same. It was difficult to parse in the jumble of voices, yet whatever was being spoken, it wasn't Hebrew. Isaac leaned nearer to a looming bear of a man beside him to listen.

"Mosheh Leiser, Mosheh Leiser, Mosheh Leiser," the man muttered, one incantation among hundreds in the hollow, holy room. He spoke the words with a practiced ownership, patting his own chest. Slowly, other voices teased themselves loose. *Shmuel Genzl. Sarah Rovner. Chaya Rabinowitz.* Each person, holding a name to their chest like a shield.

The big man beside Isaac faltered. "Mosheh . . . L . . . Mosh—"

A snow-bearded man in a black hat approached, whom Isaac took to be the rabbi. He laid a hand on the large man's shoulder. "Yes. You are Reb Mosheh Leiser," he nodded, smiling.

"Mosheh Leiser," the man repeated.

Five minutes passed. Ten. The chanting, steady as the rain.

Just as a headache began to tell Isaac he'd sat still too long, a *pressure* urged toward them from outside the synagogue. It felt as if some invisible battering ram were pushing against the walls. The weight deep-sea divers endure beneath the blackened depths. Isaac's ears popped. As if in opposition to the force, the chanting rose. *Asher Tisman. Leib Cohen. Zidel Koenig.* The names snarled into one another, mingled and knotted and twisted. The pressure increased. *Shimon Ackerman. David Feldsher. Esther Frum.* Louder and louder. Their hands pounded upon their chests. *Yosef Geffen. Motie Adler.* Isaac's own name knocked against his teeth, thirsty to join the others, but he wouldn't speak it. There were too many names. Too many stories. Too many lives flooding into his body at once. He was oversaturated. They dragged at him like endless small, reaching hands begging to be clasped. All the while, the outside force pushed and pushed and pushed. There was a danger in it, an energy built of distilled dread. He had to get out.

Isaac crept from the bench and slinked toward the entryway. He yanked loose the double doors just enough to slip his skinny ribs through, diving past whatever force had been urging against the temple.

Outside, he sighed in relief. The rain had let up, and the air was brittle and dry. The doors pounded shut behind him.

"You shouldn't worry so much, you'll give yourself an ulcer. That's what my zayde says."

The boy from the ballgame had followed him out. He perched on the temple's stoop, knee cocked, assessing Isaac with a curious squint. Hubcap reappeared like a promise and the boy tugged her tail. She hissed.

"You got a smoke I could bum?" Isaac asked.

The kid passed him a cigarette and lit it with a match.

"So," Isaac asked, taking a grateful drag. "What's with the names?"

"The prayers you mean."

"Sure, the prayers."

"If we remember our names, we win."

"Okay. Tally. Whatever the fuck that means." Isaac shrugged. "So what's yours?"

The boy scrunched up his forehead. "My name . . ." He stared off into the middle distance, as if trying to recall, then shook his head. "It's good that you're here. It is good to bear witness."

Bear witness. There it was again.

"What do you mean, 'witness'? Witness what? The service in there?"

The boy knocked his heels against the stoop and shook his head. "It's coming."

"What's coming?"

"The Happening."

"And that's what I'm supposed to watch?"

The boy huffed, exasperated. "Not watch. I told you. *Witness.*"

Isaac tightened his coat around himself. A clawing wind had filled the gap the rain had left, and in the distance, new storm clouds were gathering. "What's the difference?"

"Well," the boy pondered, chewing on a fingernail. "Watching is just seeing. You can watch something and walk away after like you were never there. *Witness* is a testimony." He looked up. "With a witness, it could be like we never died."

The pit returned to Isaac's stomach.

"You're a weird kid, you know that?" he said, far more flippantly than he felt. On the horizon, the storm clouds had darkened. The edges were crisp and uncanny.

"Watch this!" the boy said, jumping up to traverse a stone step like a tightrope. He held his arms out to either side for balance, a lip bit in concentration.

But Isaac wasn't looking. He was staring at the storm.

Dense clouds tumbled over themselves as they gathered and swelled. They rolled closer. The color was off—not gray and cottony like a cumulus, nor a wall cloud's bruised blue black. These were sooty and thick, the color of charcoal. They weren't clouds. They were smoke.

"Something's on fire," Isaac said, starting down the steps.

The boy continued his high-wire act. "That's silly. Nothing burns here."

Light flickered through the smoke pall. As Isaac watched, the mass clarified and split into dozens of small, clean shapes. It became a row of men on horseback. The silhouettes torqued into focus until Isaac could make out the edges of their military sashes, blackened torches in their fists. Stallions' hooves lifted and fell.

Isaac startled as the boy wrapped his arms around his neck, hugging him from behind like a cape. "Don't worry, Yaga. I was scared the first time, too."

Isaac's mind reeled, desperate to reconcile with what his eyes were telling him. Had hours of cold and fatigue driven him to hallucination? He tried to blink the mirage away, even as the ground on which he stood trembled with the horses' footfalls.

From within the temple, the chanting continued. Names blended into one another, a single amorphous song.

"We have to go," Isaac said, fear setting in. Whatever was coming this way, he didn't want to be here when it arrived. He stood up, grabbing the boy by the arm.

"You're being dramatic," the boy said as Isaac started down the steps. He wriggled, trying to pull free.

"Are you nuts? Stop it." Isaac pulled again.

The boy shook him off, standing back with his arms crossed. "No."

The hazy soldiers continued their approach. Definitely men now, not smoke. One carried a flag trisected by a white, blue, and red stripe. Many held rifles. They'd grown near enough for Isaac to make out their features. Some were obscured by long yellow whiskers or thick black beards. Some, shadowed under fur hats. And amid the soldiers, ordinary men, too, ragged with poverty, their fists labor-calloused, dirt caked into their collars.

In the center stood a familiar man in a crisp peaked cap, a wool coat. Unlike the rest, this man stood still. The others flowed past him like water. Flowed *through* him. The man nodded, lifting his arms to gesture at the scene around him like a magician easing in an audience. *Welcome,* the gesture seemed to say. *We have a marvelous show for you tonight.*

"*Cu-caw! Cock-a-doodle-doo!*" The kid beside Isaac jumped up and wagged his elbows at his sides, taunting with a rooster's crow.

"What are you doing?" Isaac hissed. "We need to go. *Now.*"

The boy looked Isaac in the eye, his stare defiant. "The Happening will always come. There is no running. But you still have to yell. You have to mock and laugh and scream. Even though it always ends the same."

White wisps rose around the soldiers' feet, slithering up in singed tendrils. As they passed through the village, house after house burst to ash. The baker's cart. The grocery where Isaac had rested. Loose tumbleweeds erupted into burning balls of flame. Had Isaac been looking to the east, he might have seen a familiar sod rooftop bob by the tree line before scurrying out of sight on two straw-colored legs. The soldiers were near enough now that Isaac could feel the heat of their torches. See the men's faces, which flickered with firelight. Their uniforms, flaked with an ash as blanched as snow. Beside Isaac, the boy reached up and took Isaac's hand.

"Are you ready to bear witness?"

The phantom smoke descended until it was all Isaac could see.

Two states and one hundred years away, Thistlefoot halted. As if following an unseen call, the house turned to the east. The floorboards shuddered.

"*Gey vayter,*" Bellatine directed, oblivious to a faraway, slowing heartbeat. A heart that pumped the same blood hers did, coded with the same history. She pointed to the road, but Thistlefoot paid no heed. A snowflake landed on Isaac's cheek and did not melt. The house began to run.

CHAPTER FORTY

THERE'S A SCENE IN *The Drowning Fool* where our hero dies.

One night, he comes upon the Green Woman of the Wood, who lurks in every moss pillow and atop every sycamore and beneath every oak leaf, and he asks if she would like to hear a joke.

But, little clown, she says, *I have heard all your jokes.*

Well, that won't do! says the Fool. The odd thing about jokes is you can only hear them once. A joke has to be new and fresh and surprising to make you laugh, and in that way, it is the most alive story there is.

Aha! But surely you have yet to see me juggle, the Fool says. *I will toss in the air these three golden fruits, and gravity will seem like nothing!* And from his sack he pulls a golden pear and a golden peach and a golden nectarine, which levitate over the puppet's wooden hands with invisible wires.

I do not wish to see you juggle today, says the Green Woman, *because I have already watched you juggle fruit and bottles and telephones and step stools. There is not an object in the world I haven't* seen you throw and catch in the many times you have visited my forests.

The Fool is not deterred. *Why, then,* exclaims the Fool with a grin, *I will dance my silliest dance for you. Happy silly or sad silly, it can be your choosing.*

But again, the Green Woman shakes her head. *Dear Fool,* she says, *I have seen you dance all your dances before.*

The Fool is dismayed, for if the Green Woman has heard all his jokes and watched all his feats of gravity and seen all his dances, then every forest on Earth must have tired of him, too.

You should be proud! says the Green Woman. *You have traveled every woodland on this earth and beyond. You have laughed and juggled and danced to every tree and water tower, every songbird and airplane. Why, I can't think of anyone else alive who can boast such a feat!*

Can it be true? Is there nothing new to discover? Is there no punch line left to reveal?

The Fool walks out of the forest and across a cornfield and through a murky paper-mill town where the sky is black with smog, and he realizes that the Green Woman is right. He's been to all these places before. He's told his jokes. He's tossed his golden fruits and danced. Eventually, he reaches a riverbank and falls, weeping, to his knees.

Why are you crying, Fool? asks the river.

Don't taunt me, the Fool says. *You know full well why I'm crying, just as you know all my jokes and tricks and dances.*

I'm sorry, says the river, *but I'm afraid I don't. You see, with the Moon gone away, my current has become awfully unruly. I'm very cold and very deep, and I rarely see visitors. Everyone is afraid of me.*

At this, the Fool perks up. *So . . . we haven't met before?*

The river confirms that no, they have not.

Oh! says the Fool, leaping up. His red shoes shine bright as October apples. The black tears on his cheeks are dark diamonds, glistening. *Dear river, would you like to hear a joke?*

I would like that very much. Please, come tell it to me.

And so, the Fool wades into the icy river. To his ankles. To his hips. To his throat. The water covers his head. It floods into his lungs, drags him down to the rocky riverbed. And the Fool is laughing, laughing all the while, because he knows that there is one last place he has not voyaged. One last joke left to tell. One final punch line.

His red shoes slip off, one by one.

CHAPTER FORTY-ONE

BELLATINE'S HANDS REGISTERED THE black speck before her brain did. It began as a fire-ant itch pricking her palms. The itch gave way to heat.

Thistlefoot had been sprinting for hours, but now it slowed, coming to a stop beneath a peeling billboard bearing omens from the afterlife—*Where are you going? Heaven or hell?* On the ground, a dark heap. An interruption in the miles and miles of flatlands bleached colorless by frost.

By the time her brain caught up enough to realize what she was looking at, she was already clambering down the ladder toward the fallen shape.

"What is it? What did you find?" Winnie called from above— but Bellatine didn't hear her. Instead, she was running toward her brother, who lay stiff and pale as blight.

Thistlefoot knew. It brought me here.

Thin snow had settled on Isaac, making him shimmer in the dawn light. He looked just the way he had nearly three months ago, when she'd first found him asleep at the shipping terminal in New York. Back then, his rakish, muddied suit and sharp angles had conveyed a happy-go-luckiness like a good-time gambler, a trickster god, a traveler with a story. Now, he only looked small.

Her hands were blazing, an ebony heat as if they had been dipped in molten iron. The pain was so bold she almost doubled over, but she forced herself on. As she drew near, Hubcap sprang hissing from behind the billboard. She paced before her companion, the fur on her back raised to needles. There were paw prints looping the ground around Isaac, hundreds layered one atop the next. She must have been circling all night. Guarding him.

Yearning sprang up in Bellatine, a rope tied to each wrist pulling, pulling. She had felt this kind of singe before, but it didn't make sense here. Embering like this only seized her when there was something large to animate, like a kill strung up in a hunter's truck or a taxidermied black bear in some dusty museum. A deer by the roadside, split open with decay.

An Embering like this could only come for the dead.

Isaac was so skinny she could see his ribs through his T-shirt. His eyes were open. A web of ice spidered his lips.

No. No, no, no.

Bellatine broke forward through the circle of paw prints wreathing her brother like witching salt. Her footsteps burst the frost into steam. She fell to her knees, her hands ringing like bells in a burning temple. No breath fogged from Isaac's parted lips, nor bid his chest to rise. Hovering her right palm over her brother's heart, she could almost touch the silence, a siren song beckoning. The grass where she knelt had begun to smoke.

Just as she was about to thrust her hand to Isaac's chest, a memory of the deer on the roadside intruded. Entrails glistening as it moved toward her. Its terrible wail like a wheel breaking free of the axle. *I can't,* she thought, even as her hands drew nearer, *I can't.* But then her finger grazed the sharp rut of Isaac's collarbone. It was stinging cold. Waxy. Nausea rioted through her. Nothing could be more wrong than this. Nothing. This was her brother. Alone. Broken. In need of care. In defiance, she pushed the mewling deer from her mind. *She* was the one in control. *She* made the rules—not her hands. Not the dead. Not whatever cruel higher power had cursed her with the Embering. Little did that demon or deity know, when a tool found its way into Bellatine Yaga's hands, it was hers. And it would bend to her will.

The youngest living Yaga thrust her hands down upon Isaac's chest and her body became an inferno. Embering flared up from her blood, through her shoulders, down her arms, past her hands. It pushed into Isaac, who shuddered with the force. Ice crystals dissolved on his cheek. His coat dampened with melt. She splayed her fingers, pressing down, listening.

"Come on, you asshole," she hissed through gritted teeth. "Don't do this. Don't leave. Not again." Tears formed but lifted into steam before they could leave her eyes. She let the Embering spike hotter and half feared his body would catch fire beneath her hands, but she didn't let up. Closer, closer . . .

She felt a low twang like a cello string being plucked. Someone else was there with her. *I see you, malyshka,* a voice in her murmured. *I see you. He belongs to me.*

She pushed the Longshadow Man away. Focusing only on her hands, she searched deeper, heat scurrying through each atom of Isaac's body, careening down corridors of veins and capillaries, screeching against his bones. Closer . . . The Embering vibrated.

I see you, the terrible voice moaned again.

Do you? she snarled back. *Then watch this.*

And there, at last, she found it.

A drumbeat.

A pulse.

Tha-thump. Tha-thump. Tha-thump.

A worm of dread writhed in Bellatine's throat. What if she

brought forth some alien Isaac? A *not-Isaac*. Something from that Other Place, all dressed up in an Isaac suit, prim and buttoned as a young groom. She imagined spindled, yellow-tongued demons curled up inside her brother's chest. Creatures who yowled like sick goats. Zoos of the dead, flooding into Isaac's abandoned body as if it were a carnival ride. Would she even be able to tell the true Isaac from an impostor, after all the faces she'd watched him don and shed, his awful human carousel . . . ?

And even if he returned right, did she really want Isaac back? Her brother, the liar. The huckster. Her brother, the idiot who'd run off and gotten himself killed. The brother who could never bear to stay. His pulse quickened.

Yes. She surrendered. *Yes.* She wanted Isaac back just the way he was.

His heartbeat was bolder now. It thudded against her hands, hollow like a stone thrown down a mining shaft. Like a car backfiring on a dirt road. A firecracker gone off too soon in the hand that held it. There was a sorrow in the sound, as if something missing and dearly searched for had finally been declared lost for good. The ghostly voice in her head snuffed out, and so too did her hands' desperate burn. Isaac stirred beneath her touch. He blinked.

"Christ," he rasped, pulling himself up on his elbows. "I need a cup of coffee."

And it was then that she knew she had her brother back. Whole.

A cackle erupted from Bellatine's throat. Isaac had walked through death in the same way he must have walked through train yards and ghost towns. He had hitched his way out of the afterlife—and all he wanted was a cup of coffee.

Clasping a hand over her mouth to catch the madcap mirth, she realized: *He doesn't know he was dead. And he isn't going to know. Not today. Not tomorrow. Not ever.* Because she would never tell him.

Isaac looked around with a flick of confusion. He took in the ashen circle, the sooty scrub grass, the singed tatters of his clothes. "What hap—"

"You shouldn't smoke before bed," Bellatine interrupted, snatching a cigarette butt from the ground next to him. "It's dangerous. If you'd been indoors, you could have burned the house down."

He squinted, as if trying to sweep dust off a half-forgotten memory.

"You're lucky I got here when I did," Bellatine insisted. "Your coat was smoking like a chimney. Must have fallen asleep with it lit."

"Fell asleep . . ." he echoed, his voice still hazy with that Other Place. The sound made Bellatine shiver. He looked up at her, as if noticing her for the first time. "What are you doing here?"

"Saving you," she said.

"Saving me?"

"Yes," she said. Her voice cracked. "We're family, right?"

Isaac's brows furrowed with such perfect, jagged surprise that she nearly started crying all over again. He hadn't expected anyone to come for him. That lonesome hollow of his heartbeat, the butter-thick melancholia she'd felt as she'd laid her hands on him . . . He never thought he'd be saved, because he didn't think there was anyone to care.

"Come on," she said, reaching out to him. "Let's get you that cup of coffee."

He took her hand and she helped him to his feet. Hubcap yowled. From behind them, she could hear Winifred calling her name. The world was still there.

"The town," Isaac asked, casting a glance over his shoulder. "Did you see it?"

"What town?" There had been nothing but oil fields for miles.

He rubbed his temples. "Nothing. Never mind."

What do the dead dream? Bellatine wondered. She supposed she would find out eventually.

⁂

"Here," Bellatine said, handing Isaac a steaming mug. "Sorry it's not coffee. Seems we're out."

He sipped the green tea absentmindedly. Hubcap was curled in his lap, nuzzling against him. She purred, but Isaac's attention was on the window, where a flap of plastic had blown back, revealing the world outside. His eyes, fixed to the horizon. Searching.

"Is he all right?" Winifred whispered, appearing beside Bellatine.

"He'll be fine," she said. She hoped it was true.

Wind knifed through the gap in the plastic, passing through Thistlefoot like breath over a flute. It whistled through the eaves, almost as if the house itself were trying to speak.

As Bellatine walked back toward the kitchen, she caught a glimpse of herself in the hall mirror. Her cheeks were bright. Her hair, lustrous and thick. Even the bones of her face seemed softer, younger, and the worry lines that had begun to creep along her brow and eyes had vanished. She traced her lips, her throat. Every inch of her skin was rosy and smooth. Only her hands themselves remained unchanged—still as rough and worn with callouses as they'd ever been. Hands with memory. Hands with knowledge. Hands that could be of use. A smile teased at her mouth. She didn't stop it.

CHAPTER FORTY-TWO

IT WAS NEARLY SUNDOWN by the time they reached the Walmart lot where Bellatine had told the Duskbreaker Band to wait. When Thistlefoot had first broken into a sprint, the bus had tried to keep up—but the wheezing engine was no match. Now, Shona sat on the bus' hood, her legs splayed on either side of the horse-skull fender as she chewed on a corn dog. Sparrow was leaning against the bumper, dragging a bow across their fiddle to pass the time. Thistlefoot shimmied, lowering to roost.

"The prodigal son returns." Shona glowered at Isaac.

He shrugged, lighting a cigarette. He hadn't spoken much, but minute by minute the old hawk-gleam in his eye had grown stronger.

Rummy emerged from the bus, a toothbrush dangling from his mouth. As soon as he got near Isaac, he halted as if he'd hit an invisible wall. Bellatine could only imagine the energy he must be picking up from her brother right now. A radio broadcast from the beyond.

"So," Sparrow said, trilling on the E string of their fiddle, "now that the circus is back together, what's next?"

Shona finished her corn dog and reapplied her cherry lipstick, blotting it with a paper napkin. "I hope you enjoyed your little constitutional, Pinocchio. Where'd you dash off to, anyway?"

"It doesn't matter," Bellatine said, too quickly. "What matters is we're all here now. And we need a plan."

"The plan," Shona said, "is to kill him."

"By 'him' I'll assume you mean the other guy and not me," Isaac said on an exhale of lavender smoke. Good. He was talking.

"Hard to kill Longshadow before we know what he and his creeps even are," Rummy interjected.

". . . A *when*," Bellatine muttered. Memories of the previous night's visitation careened back.

"How's that?" Shona said.

"'I am not a what, I am a *when*,'" Bellatine recited. "That's what he said."

All day, the encounter had hovered just out of reach, a dream she'd forgotten upon waking. She'd risen with a hazy sense of dread she couldn't place, her jaw sore as if she'd been clenching it—but no memory of why. Rather than dwell, she'd thrown herself straight into more post-battle repairs, resetting segments of joinery loosened in the jump. Then Thistlefoot had started bolting toward Isaac. The midnight apparition sank even further from her thoughts while she gripped the railing, panicked, not knowing where the house was dragging her—or what it might be fleeing. The visitation felt like years ago, as if an entire life span had taken place in the time between. She glanced at Isaac; in a way, it had. But she could see it all now: The doorbell's chime. The samovar billowing fragrant steam. The butler of living smoke. The man who'd sat across from her, as sterile and precise as a scalpel. She recounted it all aloud as the others listened on.

"And out the window," she added, "there were flaming buildings. I'd forgotten, but I saw the same thing in the cemetery, after I was poisoned. The buildings weren't *there*, really. They were like a mirage."

"Somewhere you've been before?" asked Sparrow.

She shook her head. "They were old, foreign. The architecture looked a little like Thistlefoot, but different. And there was a town square, with a clearing in the center. A marketplace."

Isaac wrinkled his forehead, as if trying to reclaim something lost.

"What I don't understand is why, if the Longshadow Man's spent all this time tracking us down, did he breeze right in and out of the house without leaving a mark?" Shona asked. "Why not destroy the place outright?"

"I don't think he was fully there," Bellatine said. "Nothing seemed quite solid, and—"

"It wasn't time," Isaac spoke up. "The Happening isn't here yet."

"The what?"

"Tiny," he continued, "you said there was a pogrom in Gedenkrovka. When?" He was growing agitated.

"1919, but I don't see how—"

"What was the date?"

"I don't know. Hold on." She clicked on her phone, returning to the website where she'd found the shtetl record. "December first."

"That's in three days," Rummy said.

I am a when . . .

Bellatine read on. "*The start of the pogrom occurred at sundown on Monday evening. After weeks of loose threats, along with the execution of a local stone carver accused of colluding with the Bolsheviks, the December massacre began with the murder of a seventeen-year-old boy, shot dead in the street. This was followed by the burning of a nearby mill and the murder of four other Jews. By morning, the majority of the town had been burned. Forty-two Jews were dead, twelve injured. The rest were driven from the town, fleeing to Cherkasy and Smela.*

Among the refugees, eighty percent died of famine or disease within the following year."

"And you think the Longshadow Man is connected to this pogrom?" Shona asked.

"Yes," Isaac said. His voice rang with a certainty that sent a needling chill up Bellatine's spine. Some knowledge came from study, Bellatine knew. Some from trial and error. From hours spent tinkering in the workshop, collecting splinters. Some knowledge was taught, handed down by mentors or friends. Some came from mistakes. But where had Isaac's knowledge come from? Not, she feared, from the living.

Thistlefoot wriggled in the parking lot. Setting sunlight dappled its whitewashed walls, and the chimney stood with stark clarity against the sky. A relic. A living memory of a bygone place. A slaughtered people. A town singed from the map. The house was a walking memorial. The lone survivor. *One last stain . . .*

Truth traveled through her like a bullet. What kind of beast cultivates mobs out of common citizens, using fear as bait? In the real world, these weren't the traits of monsters. They were the traits of men seeking power. Traits of war. The Longshadow Man had shown her the burning shtetl with pride. He'd spoken to Isaac of eugenics, to her of cleansing a nation, the anathema of genocide. His weapon wasn't a gun, wasn't a knife; it was a charming invitation, a toast to a better tomorrow. It was fear at your back. Illa had written of seeing flickering soldiers, of feeling a flame-bearing dybbuk crouching on her chest. Bellatine had mistaken these visions for the girl's own mental baggage— but what if they were more than that? What if those traumas had grown bodied? All this time, Bellatine had thought the real world had abandoned her. That she'd been dragged into a fantasy realm, ruled by magic. But she was wrong. The world and its cruelties had been there all along. The Longshadow Man, this dybbuk and his wraiths, he wasn't a *who*, or an *it*—he'd told her this outright. He was a *when*. An event made manifest.

"He isn't connected to the pogrom," Bellatine realized aloud. "He *is* the pogrom."

"Excuse me?" Shona said. "What exactly are you saying here?"

"I'm saying," Bellatine said, buzzing, "why does a ghost have to be a single person? What if there could be a ghost of an experience? A point in time so broken that it becomes something else? Something solid?"

Rummy nodded. "If all it takes is a single disaster to create a living house, then what would an entire massacre unleash?"

"One last stain," Bellatine continued. "That's what he kept calling Thistlefoot. What if Thistle is the only survivor? Even those who made it through the pogrom would have died off by now. And the town itself was burned."

"He's completing his massacre," Sparrow filled in. "Completing himself."

"We need to know more," Bellatine said. "More about what happened."

"We could find someone else to translate the rest of the papers," Rummy said, "and hope there's something useful in them. But that's a gamble."

"It's not enough time," Isaac said. "He's going to try for us sooner."

Us. Something in the word landed on Bellatine like a dragonfly, glossy and strange. For once, her brother wasn't planning for an *I*. He was planning for *we*.

"How do you know?" Shona asked.

"Come on," Isaac said, "where's your poeticism? What do memories *want*?"

Sparrow flopped down on the concrete. "Hell if I know. A ham sandwich?"

"They want to be remembered," Winifred murmured. "Commemorated."

Isaac tilted his head. "This kid has literal rocks for brains, and she gets it."

Bellatine was relieved to see the reference pass over the

Duskbreakers unquestioned. And twice as relieved to see Isaac's acerbic bite returning.

"And re-creating itself on the anniversary is the ultimate remembrance," Rummy followed.

Shona cast a look at Thistlefoot. "By finishing the job."

Isaac snapped his fingers in affirmation. "Tally. He won't be able to resist."

Bellatine imagined Thistlefoot engulfed in blue flame. Imagined its walls crumbling to ash. The house was more than her salvation from herself. It was her ancestor. Her family.

"We won't let it happen," she said. "We'll fix this."

"Not everything can be fixed," Rummy said gently.

"Then we'll run," Bellatine insisted. "We'll do things Isaac's way this time. We'll run and keep running and not look back until he's given up."

"And let him keep hurting people?" Shona said, anger rising. "Every mile he's tracked you, he's left casualties in his wake. The longer you stall, the more civilians die."

"But if he finds us, *Thistlefoot* will die! *We* could die!"

"I'll burn that house to the ground a thousand times myself if it means saving one innocent life," Shona spat.

"Cool down, everyone." Rummy held up his hands, his shoulders soft. "We're all on the same side, remember?"

"What I don't understand," Winifred said, "is if he's a manifestation of a specific memory, a specific event, why does he target random people?"

"They aren't all random," Bellatine muttered. He'd confirmed it. She remembered now . . . "Li Fen."

"And Nina," Isaac said.

"He's covering *our* tracks. Going after people we've been in contact with."

Sparrow tapped at their jaw. Internal gears spun. "If Isaac is right about the anniversary, Longshadow's mirroring the way trauma behaves in the brain, neurologically speaking. Traumatic memories *do* grow stronger on the date of the event; it's called the Anniversary Effect. But of course, you don't think of your worst moments just once a year. They're there all the time. Those kinds of memories replicate. Bloat and warp. Take over."

Isaac wrung his shaking hands. "They want to be told and retold—like all stories do."

"It's about the memory, for him," Sparrow said. "The repetition. Maybe in some cases, it doesn't matter who the people are, they're just a means of acting out a scene."

"And with those you knew," Rummy added, "he's doing damage control. So his version of the story can be the only version."

"He's duplicating himself," Shona picked up. "Forcing the smokefed to perform new versions of the pogrom."

Sparrow nodded. "Reenactments."

"If that's true, how do we even know he'd stop repeating history if he caught Thistlefoot?" Bellatine asked, desperate.

"We don't," Rummy said.

"Yes we do." Shona said. She threw up her chin. "Because we're going to face him—and kill him."

Rummy exhaled. "No more running."

Sparrow's eyes flashed. "No more running."

Behind them, Thistlefoot bobbed on its haunches. A great feather shed from its belly and floated to the earth. It turned in the breeze, rolling off like a strange, downy tumbleweed. Bellatine trembled.

No more running.

"Back in Green Mount Cemetery, there was a funeral for a woman named Anne Bratcher," Winifred interjected. "Well, if you could call it a funeral. Only her husband attended, and the priest. During the service, they said she'd perished of demonic possession. That they'd attempted an exorcism but failed."

Shona squinted at Winifred. "You're a little *rosy* for a job in a cemetery, aren't you?"

"Oh, I didn't work there, I used t—"

"Used to live nearby," Bellatine interrupted. "What's your point, Win?"

Winifred crinkled her nose in thought, and Bellatine pushed away the startling urge to lick it. "What if an exorcism could work for this?"

"Come on," Sparrow urged. "Exorcisms are nothing but an excuse to beat on mentally ill folk and keep little girls in line. Trust me, I've seen it."

"Maybe so. But in this case," Isaac said, "the demon's real."

An exorcism. Even if the Longshadow Man was an event incarnate, he was still a ghost, wasn't he? And couldn't a ghost be banished?

"You mean exorcise the smokefed?" Bellatine asked. "Attack the passengers?"

Winnie shook her head. "Even if they could be harmed, I doubt that would affect the Longshadow Man. It would be like stepping on a worker bee to kill the queen."

"But exorcisms cleanse a *body*—and the Longshadow Man himself isn't *in* anyone."

"Your house," Shona said. "It's alive, right? Freakish, but alive. If the Longshadow Man steps inside, isn't that like a possession?"

"No," Bellatine blurted. "We aren't letting him in."

Sparrow patted her shoulder. "Honey, sooner or later he's barging in, even without an invitation to dinner."

Bellatine's heart sank. She dug the black-and-white photo out of her overalls pocket—Illa, Malka, their mother, and the legless Thistlefoot behind. Her thumb brushed over the speckled image, as if the subjects might return from the dead to speak the answers aloud.

Isaac snatched the photo out of her hand. He squinted. He kept staring, silent, for a long while, as if his mind had stepped off into another room.

Shona snapped her fingers next to his ear. "Hey, *zonzo*, we're in a conversation here."

Rummy shushed her, which she protested with a toss of her ponytail.

Bellatine's throat constricted like a fist. Was her brother slip-

ping back into that Other Place? What if, like all her Emberings before Winifred, the awakening was only temporary, and
he was about to vanish back into that unbearable mannequin-
stillness?

"The Drowning Fool," Isaac muttered. He tapped a spot near
the center of the picture. Then, thrusting the photograph back
at Bellatine, turned on his heel and strode purposefully toward
Thistlefoot.

The Drowning Fool? If he hadn't just had one toe in the River
Styx, Bellatine would have slapped him. Even now, he still only
cared about the tour. About making his money.

"The show is *over*, Isaac," she grumbled.

"Not the show," he said, pointing back at her. "The puppet."

Isaac flung a leg over the lowered stage and hoisted himself
up. He vanished into the parlor. Dragging sounds followed.
Vinyl against wood. The click of the road case opening.

She looked down at the photo, studying the spot Isaac had
tapped. Young Illa peered back up at her, her crow-black hair
rivering down her shoulders, a doll dangling from one arm.
The doll . . . that's where Isaac had been pointing. She looked
closer. It was a large doll, a good eighteen inches tall, wearing a tattered cloak and trousers. A male doll. Had that been
common? His face and hands were carved of wood, and as she
looked closer, a nauseating familiarity overtook her. He was so
small in the photograph, she hadn't noticed. And the black-
and-white, it had camouflaged what would have made the figure recognizable in an instant—his bright red shoes.

Isaac reemerged with the Fool in hand.

"Mira told us she'd had him since she was a girl . . . That he
was older than the other puppets," Isaac said. "But we never
asked *how* old."

It was true. They'd never known where Mira had gotten
him from as a child. How long he had been in the family. *The
Fool* . . . Bellatine realized. He had *been* there. He would have
seen everything.

"Wake him up," Isaac growled.

Then, he tossed the Fool into the air. The puppet spun, his rag-wrapped arms and legs splaying out like his body was a star taking its place in the firmament. As if pulled toward a magnet, Bellatine raised her hands. The Fool made his descent—landing firmly in her strong, present grip.

Heat. It surged through her, thick as burnt sugar and fizzing. The puppet convulsed, but she couldn't drop him. The Embering had her now, had both of them, and it would complete its work. She felt herself tumbling through the fibers of the Fool's ruffles and coat, into his wooden cheeks, down through the whittled angles of his joints. *Thump thump. Thump thump. Thump thump.*

She gasped. The Fool dropped to the floor. Then he stood and dusted off his shoulders.

"Jesus," Sparrow whispered. Shona took a step back.

The Fool straightened his hat, though it was sewn onto his head. He bowed to the east, then the west. *"Hello, fine travelers! Would you like to hear a joke?"*

Isaac hopped down from the stage. "No jokes today, friend," he said, kneeling in front of the living doll. "But we would like to hear a story."

"Oh, have I the story for you!" the Fool exclaimed. *"How about a story of a whale that lives in the belly of a man? Now, that's a story!"*

Bellatine took a breath. Her lungs, miraculously, were working. Her vision clear. "We're looking for a particular story, actually," she said—though her voice felt as if it were coming from someone else. "Do you know the story of the house on chicken legs? Of Gedenkrovka, and what happened there?"

"Oh, my good people," the Fool cried, *"I can juggle! I can sing songs from any nation! I can make you laugh so hard you will forget to breathe and go into the next life, still laughing! Why ask for a story so sad when you can hear a marvelous one instead?"*

"Please," Bellatine said. "This is the story we need."

The Fool sighed. *"Very well. Sometimes the story you need is not the story you might want. I respect this. But I warn you, there are no jokes in this story. Yes?"*

"Yes," Isaac said.

The Fool took a deep breath, puffing up his miniature chest. *"There is a shtetl called Gedenkrovka, in the Smiliansky district of the Cherkasy region of the Russian Empire,"* he said. His voice was smooth and dangerous as a river. *"In this village lives a woman,"* he continued. He closed his painted eyes, as if in remembrance. *"Her name is Baba Yaga."*

CHAPTER FORTY-THREE

THE FOOL WILL TELL it well, I have no doubt. All the right flourishes to make you lean in closer. All the right riddles and all the right rhymes. But come now, you've been with me all this way. What sort of storyteller would I be if I abandoned you to another soothsayer in the final hour? No. Stay with me. After all, I was built to be hospitable.

Here it is: my final origin. This version, it is not like the rest. It is not dressed up in finery. No ornate bows tied around its throat. No vanilla dabbed on its wrists to perfume it sweeter. No eggs hatched or crows felled. No monsters but the monsters of our own making. No beautiful lies. No folktale. Only what happened, plainly told.

And as for you—you have only one task. Come. Sit at my hearth, which burns and burns and does not stop burning. Hear the wind move through me as a family once did. Bear witness.

There is a shtetl called Gedenkrovka, in the Smiliansky district of the Cherkasy region of Imperial Russia. There is nothing exceptional about this place. It is a shtetl like all other shtetls—a market town, abundant with merchants and tailors and cobblers alike. It sits on the road from Shpola to Cherkasy, only seven versts from the railroad station of Vladimirovka, allowing commerce to flow freely as cow's milk. The Jewish families here, of which there are three hundred fifty, give or take, live comfortably. No disturbances have ever sullied Gedenkrovka. During the Great War, it was untouched. While the October Revolution saw peasants plundering other villages, the people of Gedenkrovka remained unbothered to fast for Yom Kippur and sound the shofar. Along the town border, the Christian peasantry is passive, friendly even. There has always been peace between the Jews and the peasants. There has always been peace between Gedenkrovka and God. Nothing ever happens in Gedenkrovka. Nothing ever will. There will be no pogrom here. This belief, unshakable.

A girl child is born. She is given a name, but the name does not stick. From the beginning, the girl behaves like an old babushka, curmudgeonly in her ways and insistent on solitude. She prefers to sit alone with the chickens while the other children play. When Reb Asher Tisman comes by with the weekly dairy, she haggles him down to nothing like a grown man would, though she is small and feral as a barn cat. *Little Babushka Yaga,* the women tut, *she has no patience for the other children. Perhaps she will grow backward, sweetening with time.* But Babushka Yaga does not. As she ages, the bitterness and the nickname follow her, until the name has worn itself down and smoothed like a worry stone, small enough to fit on a tongue: and so, Baba Yaga came to be.

Baba Yaga marries late. The matchmaker joins her to a man who talks little and thinks little and has little hands and feet like a rat, and who is rarely home, which suits Baba Yaga just as well. He moves his new wife into a small cottage near the edge of town, and leaves straight after for a monthlong journey, selling tin roofing to the wealthier families in other cities (a luxury I, myself, am not afforded). A few days home, a month away, and so it goes. This becomes the way of things. There is no great love between wife and husband. So, when word comes that he has been taken by influenza on a trip to Odesa, Baba Yaga weeps for one day and one day only, and that is that.

By now, the year is 1919. It is not so very long ago, though my tellings make it seem so. Funny, how becoming a story strips away the realness of a thing. The hereness of it. But this is the year of the pop-up toaster and the shortwave radio. Buster Keaton makes his silver screen debut. The Great War is finally ended with the Treaty of Versailles. Behold, the industry and progress. Behold, the trenches deep with dead. A modern age arrives with flashing lights and gunpowder, rumrunners and ticker tape. In America, the land of Baba Yaga's descendants, jazz swoops through Chicago. Ford Motor Company changes hands, from father to son, a new generation of invention. Engines and trumpets blare.

For Jews in Russia, time moves more slowly. They study the Talmud. They work until Sabbath and then they rest. In larger cities, gentile cities, people cluster into cinemas, but here, it is the synagogue that is full.

The widow is left alone with two daughters. Illa, the eldest, is sharp like her mother and taken to cruelty. She is an angry child, and though she does not know why, she often feels as though there is a starving crow living inside her, trying to peck its way out. Illa keeps a tobacco tin near her bed full of dead wasps. Sometimes she catches one still living and plucks off its wings. Baba Yaga would do anything for Illa and her happiness.

The younger daughter, Malka, is only an infant. She is rosy and fat and grows fatter each day. Baba Yaga gives her gifts of honey and rosewater and a small, soft scrap of silk. Illa gives her a wasp's glossy wing. To feed her daughters, Baba Yaga keeps a brood of chickens, whose eggs she takes to market to sell or trade. As she sits in the market, she listens, and as she listens, she steals stories to take home to her daughters. Together, they are content.

Today, it is nearly winter. Twigs snap brittle from the trees and fall to the frosted earth. Illa is weaving a new scarf for her little clown doll and Malka is learning to scream until her mother gives her a finger dipped in wine. Beyond my eaves, wolves sleep without stirring beneath a quartered moon in Pisces, invisible in winter daylight.

"Mama," Illa demands, "you need to sing. I hate your singing but my doll likes it."

And so Baba Yaga sings. Malka stops crying to listen. Illa closes her eyes, letting the rasping notes of her mother's voice fill her up, though she turns her face away so she won't be caught enjoying it. Baba Yaga does not have a beautiful singing voice, nor do her notes hold the key, but she sings without apology. It is an old Yiddish song about a ghost trapped within a lantern and the lamplighter who loves her. The song is good and honest, and most of all, the song is theirs.

I give you this image as an offering. A moment of stillness. See how Illa grows frustrated with the weaving and snaps the yarn in her teeth? See how Malka wiggles her toes and gurgles? She is not speaking yet, but she may soon. See how Baba Yaga keeps singing, as she tosses purple carrots into a soup pot crowded with chicken bones? These are the moments we must dwell on, when we can. They are not stories. Bless them, for how un-storied they are. A holy unhappening.

The following day, Baba Yaga sends Illa to the neighbors to fetch a bag of feed for the chickens. She is late returning. No doubt dawdling with Miriam the neighbor girl, muddying her new skirt. When Illa finally comes home, she is empty handed.

"Where is the feed I sent you for?" Baba Yaga asks.

Illa struggles to catch her breath. "Mama, Miriam's father

says there are men coming. Men with guns. He says they are here to teach us a lesson."

"Feh," Baba Yaga says, "he is telling you scary stories. You've seen the soldiers, *shefele*. They are mean and drunk, but have they ever done us harm?"

"What about Reb Haim?" Illa glares, hands on her hips. "The soldiers killed him."

"Reb Haim told everyone with ears that he was a communist," Baba Yaga huffs. "If you poke a finger into a dog's cage, don't be surprised when you get bitten."

But still, unease weighs on Baba Yaga's shoulders like a yoke.

Denikin's men swarm the morning market. This is not unusual in itself, but there is a strange tightness in the air. Usually, the soldiers would be perusing the goods, taking what they wanted, intimidating the merchants with bawdy jokes and idle threats. Today they touch nothing. They do not walk nor move, but hover by the market's edge. A sea of held breath.

There is one soldier Baba Yaga recognizes. Andrei, a broad-nosed man with low eyebrows and large floppy limbs like a dog's ears.

"Andrei, what is happening here?" Baba Yaga asks him.

He does not answer.

"Andrei," she demands. "Speak to me."

But he only looks ahead and blinks, as if Baba Yaga were a buzzing fly.

"We have orders to follow, Jew," he says to the air. "You understand." His voice is hollow. Many of the soldiers have battle rifles stiff against their shoulders. Others have hands in their pockets, pistols' outlines swollen against their thighs.

The silence is gamey and thick like spoiling meat. Baba Yaga can feel her heart beating in her mouth. One soldier barks an order. Then, a flash of gray. A table overturning. Another. A shot rings loose in the icy air. Reb Elazer's son, only seventeen, has tried to run—an attempt to warn his father, no doubt. The fishmonger is home ill with a head cold. Josef is a good boy. Now, Josef is lying facedown in the snow. The back of his head is gone.

It is here that the story truly begins.

Baba Yaga's basket of eggs slips from her hands and the eggs break. Yolks run out into the earth.

What follows: flame and blood. A brick is thrown through a window. A leg is removed from the body. A child's brains are dashed with a stone. A house burns to ash with a family barricaded inside. All I can do is tell you this story in vignettes. In flashes of light. Pain, it is not the sort of story with a beginning, a middle, an end. It is only bursts, one after another after another. A mill's wheel turning flame instead of water. A wailing man, his pregnant wife's open belly in his arms. A dead cow, entrails hot and dark. A teenage girl begging on her knees.

Young Josef's body is dumped in the town well. The water goes poison with rot. On the brickwork, the two-headed eagle chokes, thirsty.

And somehow, still, there is a refrain within the heart of Gedenkrovka. *There will be no pogrom here. There will be no pogrom here. There will be no pogrom . . .* As if chanting it might rewrite a history already in motion.

Those who escape the initial attack run to the synagogue for sanctuary. They lock themselves within the great doors. For a moment, they believe they are safe, here in God's house. But not even a house can be a savior. I should know. There is a subtle difference between locking an enemy out, and an enemy locking you in. When the local peasants arrive to join the soldiers, they surround the synagogue for three days and nights. Those within do not sleep, nor have water to drink, nor food. They are tortured until they are not, at which point they are killed. God, not wanting to watch, closes his eyes.

Baba Yaga is not there. When the others run to the synagogue, she slips away. Runs back toward the forest—where Illa and Malka and I, still unhatched, wait for our part of the story to begin.

"Get in the loft. Hurry and be quiet. Illa, get under this blanket and don't talk." Baba Yaga tucks her family into the crawl space of my rafters. Together, we wait. Malka coos, sucking on the corner of the blanket. Illa's eyes are wide with fear. She clutches her doll to her heart.

"Mama, will you sing to us?" Illa asks.

"Tomorrow," Baba Yaga whispers. "I'll sing to you tomorrow, *ziskayt*. But now, we must be quiet."

In the distance, we hear celebration. Glass shatters and a whooping follows, as if a firework has erupted, rather than a life. The shouting grows nearer. Against my floorboards, I can feel Illa trembling. Malka, little miracle, has fallen asleep.

Another shattering of glass. A crackle of flames. Judging by the voices' nearness, they must be at the Nodelman house two doors down, where young Miriam lives. "Come outside, filthy *zhyd*," a man shouts in Russian, the slur putrid in his mouth. By the sound of his accent, he is a peasant, not a soldier. Baba Yaga recognizes his voice—Stanislav Egorov, a farmer who often bought eggs at her booth. He is a new husband, with a wife taken a mere two weeks prior. Baba Yaga had congratulated him only days ago, and he had beamed with pride.

There are new sounds now. A woman's voice begging. A child's choked sobs. And then, two gunshots. After that, only the clink of bottles meeting in cheers.

Illa presses her hands over her ears. "Mama," she whispers. "Mama. What's happening?"

Baba Yaga pulls the blanket tighter around her small family.

The *pogromtshiki* arrive at the second house, that of Reb Berish and his wife. Someone kicks the door in with a military boot.

"*Dobriy den*, good afternoon," one of the men shouts. "Is anyone at home? Come out, we will not hurt you."

There is another crash—someone has thrust the butt of his rifle through a window. At the shatter, baby Malka's eyes fly open.

"A good *zhyd* cooperates with the tsar. Why hide if you trust in Russia?"

Crack—a chair snapped over a knee. Malka's eyes grow wide.

"Things will be worse for you if you hide."

We listen as Reb Berish's home is ransacked, but *baruch Hashem*, there is no one home. Only the silver Sabbath candles, passed down for five generations. Only the precious kopecks tucked beneath a mattress, which were to pay for a journey to America. Only a photo album. Only the makings of a life. They must have lit the house aflame, for the air grows so thick with smoke, Baba Yaga must hold her breath to keep from coughing. Illa uncovers her ears to cover her mouth. Malka's face contorts, her little forehead creasing, her tiny nose flaring. Then—she begins to cry.

"Hush now, darling, hush, please," Baba Yaga hisses. She bounces Malka against her. "Be quiet. You must be quiet." But Malka's wailing only grows.

The soldiers' shouts grow nearer. They are coming here. I will be the third house. I know this. So does Baba Yaga. And still, Malka cries. They do not hear her yet, as the wool blanket muffles her. But soon, they will.

"Please, please," Baba Yaga begs. She rips a breast from her shirt, pressing it to her baby's mouth, but Malka turns her head. She cries louder.

The soldiers are nearly here now. Baba Yaga can hear their laughter scurrying like weasels over the snow. "Shhh," she pleads, shoving a hand over Malka's mouth. "Shhh, it's all right." Baba Yaga's heartbeat thuds in her ears. Her vision has gone stark white with terror. Illa, sweet little snakebite, dear Illa, she has buried her face in her mother's lap. Do not look, Illa. Do not listen. Malka continues to cry. It is muted, but not silent. Not nearly silent. The soldiers have arrived at the door. Malka's face is smothered beneath her mother's hand. A hand as gentle as lace when it needs to be, or strong as iron. The knuckles, slightly over-plumped from cracking. Fingertips calloused from labor. A hand that might carry an entire story in its cupped palm. The hand presses down. Malka squirms beneath it. It presses harder.

Three men enter me. Two, soldiers, their postures as rigid as bayonets, trained into formality. The third, Egorov, tagging along for the fun, no doubt. A story to tell his new wife, how he defended Russia. A few shiny gifts in tow.

Malka's ribs expand and contract. Expand and contract again. She whimpers and her mother's hand shakes. Grinds down over the infant's nose. Her mouth. The pressure so firm, Malka's milk teeth break through the gum.

One of the men is holding a lit torch, and I flicker red and black. The firelight makes the men's shadows stretch across the walls, their arms impossibly long, as if they could reach all the way up to Baba Yaga and her daughters, crouched in the loft, without their legs leaving the floor.

The men destroy the furniture and loot the cabinets, though there is not much to take. They search in the pantry and inside the fold-top benches, and they overturn the beds and the tables.

"*Slushai!*" someone barks from outside with a general's confidence. The looters stop, snapping to attention. More commands follow. After a small eternity, stretched out like their shadows, the soldiers turn and leave, Egorov with them. As they do, they hurl a torch through my kitchen window. Their footsteps crunch in the snow, growing quieter and quieter. Baba Yaga counts their distance in breaths. One. Two. Three. When she reaches a hundred, she lets a single moan ooze free.

"Oh, my little *mameles*," she gasps, "you were so good, so very good." She runs a hand down Illa's hair. She lifts her other hand from Malka's face, which is wet with spittle. She brushes her cheek. The child does not stir.

"Little hare," Baba Yaga whispers, pinching her cheek. But Malka does not flinch, nor smile, nor breathe. "*Little hare,*" Baba Yaga says again. She is shaking the girl now. She is slapping her face. Illa watches, no longer trembling, her eyes open and fixed. "*Little hare, little hare, the men have gone, do you hear me? Wake up!*" But a hare does not wake, and neither does a child.

"Mama," Illa whispers, "the fire."

Below, the torch's flame has spread. It crawls up my walls, an unbearable itch.

Baba Yaga does not hear her. She stares at Malka. Her feet and hands are so very small! Her eyelids, nearly translucent. Each eyelash, delicate as an ice crystal. Malka is to be one year old, next month. Baba Yaga imagines the celebration. What a wonderful day it will be! She will sew a new pair of mittens for Malka and let her eat all the honey she wants. Why, there they all are now, gathered in the parlor. Illa is dancing. Buttery rugelach bake in the oven—are they burning? No, no, they are perfect and golden and sweet. Malka is making a strange sound—a first word! Yes, she's sounding it out, she is saying . . .

"*Mama!*" Illa has begun to cough. Smoke blackens the room. "Mama, help!"

Help? Why would Illa need help when she is dancing so beautifully?

"*Mama!*" Illa sobs. "I can't breathe."

Baba Yaga's head snaps up. She sees Illa, trembling in the loft. She sees Malka. And at once, she sees her story as it is.

There are moments for sorrow and there are moments for

rage. Both, born from grief. Sorrow is long-lasting. It can become a companion if you let it. A stray cat who refuses to leave your side. There will be time for sorrow, as sorrow, like a cat, has many lives. Rage is brief. It ravages the body like a house fire, consuming and powerful. This—*this*—is the time for rage.

Baba Yaga howls. Her voice is half her own, half Lilith's voice, night-monster, keeper of children. She clutches her baby, limp, to her chest.

"Mama," Illa coughs.

Baba Yaga descends from the loft and crosses through me. Smoke becomes ephemeral shackles, encircling her ankles, twisting and re-forming into new chains. She passes through the bedroom, where the mattress gapes open with a bayonet's gash. She trails into the kitchen. Fire licks up the lace draperies and gouges black streaks in the wooden planks. It catches her skirt, but she walks through it as if she cannot feel the burn.

Baba Yaga falls to her knees. She lays Malka on the floor beside her, as if asleep. Illa watches from the ladder, the blanket still tight around her. When her mother closes her fingers around the flaming head of the torch, all Illa can see is light. Baba Yaga's hands blister and steam. A black spark. It travels up her arms and through her body. A punishment: let these hands never be of use again. A prayer: let these hands bear us through one thousand burnings.

The mother turns back to her elder daughter. "You will *live*."

A great whoosh of air passes through my body, sucking all the fire from the walls. First, the pale rims of each flame, then the golden middles, and finally, the blue core, one after another pouring into Baba Yaga's hands.

When she slams her hands down onto my floor, heat floods out from her and into me. It rushes along the floorboards and into the walls, bursts up into the rafters and screams through the foundation. *"Shem HaMephorash,"* she moans, that same name tucked beneath the Golem of Prague's tongue, God's ineffable name that moves lifeless clay into waking. How does one describe this feeling? The sensation of being born?

I stand. Behold, my blasphemy. A grieving so furious it has pushed God aside and become its own god. My legs are strong and new, already hungry to run. And so I do. I run from the row of houses, past bodies bleeding in the snow. I run past the synagogue, soon to be rubble. I run past a row of trees, dangling with terrible fruit. I run past the cemetery, where stones are already being wrenched from the earth, and past the watering well, deep and fragrant with corpses. I run past Gedenkrovka, past the great forest and the Vilshanka River, toward something new.

Meanwhile, back in the village, something else is born. A larger memory. A *suffering*, coalescing into a bodied form. The dybbuk turns his many heads to the west, watching me go. Then, he devours everything that remains.

The fire in my body has been snuffed out—all save for the lonely torch itself, glowing in Baba Yaga's grip. Ahead, the clay cookstove sits cold and empty. She unlatches the door and tosses the torch inside. She stokes it with wood and scraps of yarn. She kisses Malka on one eye. Then the other. She kisses her mouth, and each small fingertip. She kisses Malka's feet, still unwalked upon. She kisses her ears and her belly. She sings to her, an old Yiddish song about a lantern and a ghost, and as she sings, she places Malka within the hearth. The fire cradles her like a mother. Then, the child disappears.

"Mama, are we safe?" Illa whispers.

Baba Yaga pauses. "Yes. We are safe."

She shuts the hearth door. Malka's flame burns for one hour. Then one day. One year. It has not stopped burning since. And I have not stopped running.

You were warned. The story as it is—it's not the story as we wish it were. But then again, it is not a story at all. It is our world. A dead child is a dead child. A massacre is a massacre. Memories must be told. Hands beget hands. Mothers beget children, who beget daughters of their own. Generations pass, and suddenly, we forget. Our descendants are born yearning and they do not know why, for they have forgotten. Their hands are full of fire. Their legs are trembling to flee. The body remembers. The soured air remembers. We cannot forget. I cannot forget. And if I am to remember, so too, I vow, will you.

CHAPTER FORTY-FOUR

THEY WERE BLESSED WITH a windless night. Isaac felt the stillness settle on his shoulders. The eye of a storm.

"Hey, Pinocchio."

Shona swung a leg over the windowsill, joining Isaac on his perch. Her thigh bounced down on the spot where, mere days before, he'd left the pressed nickel. Handprints still disturbed the dust where he'd launched himself loose.

"You aren't trying to slip out on us again, are you?"

"Nah." He took a long drag. Exhaled. A magenta sky stretched over the flatlands wide and taut as a motel bed. Gravity had always struck Isaac as a tenuous force. Elastic like a rubber band. One day, if he pulled hard enough, it might snap and let him fall into the sky.

"Then you won't mind if I join you."

Out here in the flatlands, they could have been anywhere. He didn't even know what state they'd landed in. Somewhere in Oklahoma or Missouri. The American Expanse. They'd marched Thistlefoot forward until they found a place with no other houses, no factories, no highway or truck stops. No civilians to trade their names for numbers on a list of casualties. Maybe they weren't in real America at all anymore, but myth America, the America those lifer hobos he used to know would sing about. An America of tumbleweeds and graves built from rust. Of land that stretched on and on and never reached a border checkpoint. Of old rails where no trains ran anymore and ghost towns with cattle bones draped on the fences. Was this, Isaac wondered, the America his ancestors had imagined when they'd sailed to Ellis Island? Was this the America where they'd envisioned the Yaga bloodline would end, after all it had survived? He thought not.

Out on the ledge, Shona helped him uncoil some of the barbed wire they'd dug out of storage, leftover from Bellatine's remodeling. They nailed it below the window in strips—a deterrent against anyone climbing in. Isaac was careful to avoid the barbs as he worked. He didn't intend to see any of his blood spilled here. Not yet.

"That's right. Make sure the tin's secure. No, not on the knee; how's Thistle supposed to bend? We're making armor, not a splint." Bellatine tossed orders at Winnie and Rummy on the ground below. A few yards out, Sparrow tinkered behind the bus, arranging an alchemical octopus of propane tanks and rubber hoses.

"You knew she could do that, huh?" Shona asked, passing the wire to Isaac. "Make things come alive?"

Isaac didn't answer.

"It's okay, I get it. Family business."

He took a nail from between his teeth where it dangled next to his cigarette and drove it into the siding. The preparations helped quiet some of the restless fox-scratch in his ribs, but he couldn't help but feel it was nothing but busywork. If the dybbuk wanted to send his shadows in, no amount of thorn and armor would keep them out.

"You think it's true?" Shona continued. "What the clown told us?" In the house behind them, the Fool lay lifeless in his case, a mere object once again.

Isaac nodded. "I know it's true."

"How?"

"Gut feeling."

It was the only answer he had, and the amorphousness of it felt sticky and thick in the back of his throat. Isaac never took any word at face value. A full tank of discernment and skepticism had kept him alive all his years on the road. But the Fool's story felt different. He had the distinct sensation that he'd heard parts of it before. No, not heard . . . *lived*. Glancing back through the window at the cookstove, Malka's fire reached long, red fingers over the clay, light slipping through the bricks. Isaac blinked away. He'd spent all day trying to keep his eye off the flames, but his attention kept wandering back like a moth. A death call.

"This place is fucking cursed," Shona muttered.

"So leave," Isaac said.

She chewed on a hangnail and spat it overboard, wiping her lipstick-smeared thumb on her jeans. "Always the charmer, Yaga."

He did want her gone. More than anything, he wanted her to leave—and to take him along with her. They could vanish together into some strip-mall flyover state and spend the next week fucking in a cheap hotel room and drinking Jack Daniels from the bottle until the money ran out. Then they'd go on the bum, sleep under the stars, ramble the same lines as T-Bone Slim and Leon Ray Livingston until they'd two-stepped out of enough cops' clutches to wear their boots straight through. Freedom, that's what it would be. No quick-footed ghosts but the ones he was already chums with. No past. Yet even as the fantasy billowed brighter, some anchoring whisper held him in place. *Bear witness.* He drove in another nail.

"This doesn't belong to you," he grunted. "You're uninvolved."

She stared at Isaac, and he felt like she was looking right past his skin and into his bones. It was a look *he* was usually the one imparting. "Maybe if more *uninvolved* people had stood up back then, the ending might have been different." She unwound another coil of wire and bent it around a nail.

"It's just a house," he said. He almost felt guilty, as if Thistlefoot could hear the slight. It's bad luck to insult the doomed. But saying so made it all feel simpler. *Just a house*, slated for demolition.

"Not to the Longshadow Man, it isn't," Shona countered. "And if that evil leech wants something, it's my job to get in his way."

"You're an idealist," Isaac said, scornfully.

"No." Shona said. "An idealist thinks they're going to win."

A coyote barked in the distance. Then another, and another, until the pack broke into a chorus, reverberating through the quiet dusk.

Sometimes, when he closed his eyes, he saw flashes—a boy chasing a ball. A looming brick building, crowded with benches. A storm cloud of tangled limbs. But whenever he tried to recollect more clearly, the thoughts wriggled away like tadpoles into the red recesses of his memory.

Shona twisted to crack her spine, then leaned her back against the window frame. The hem of Isaac's poached jacket flapped beneath her own.

"I'm never getting that coat back, am I?" he asked.

She reached out and brushed a lock of hair from his eyes. "If we both survive, ask me again."

Just before daybreak, the Duskbreakers left to take their posts around the perimeter, a quarter mile out. Shona in the eastern third. Rummy in the west. Sparrow between the two. They would scout for a smokefed mob and, if anyone drew near, reconvene in the bus to take down whoever tried to approach the house. Isaac and Bellatine would stay with Thistlefoot. They were done fleeing. They were lying in wait.

"Longshadow doesn't like to get his hands dirty," Shona had

counseled as they'd planned for the day ahead. "He has others do the heavy lifting for him. If he doesn't have people to influence, he loses his main weapons."

"So the deeper we can boogie into no-man's-land, the better," Sparrow said.

"I'll be able to sense the smokefed coming," Rummy assured them. "I missed their attack before. Being near Bellatine . . ." He rubbed his neck, rueful. "It threw too much static in the mix. But with some distance, I'll be clear."

"Our little radio tower." Sparrow pinched Rummy's cheek.

At Bellatine's insistence, the Duskbreakers had taken Winnie along, with orders to get her somewhere safe and out of the fray. She'd argued, but Bellatine wouldn't hear it.

"You want to live," she'd said, holding the girl's silvery face in her hands. "So live. I'll find you when it's over." They kissed, and Isaac saw his sister press a small wooden spoon into Winifred's hand as they parted. Winifred tied her hair ribbon around Bellatine's wrist.

This was the language of goodbyes. Parting gifts to be returned upon reunion. Unkeepable promises. Isaac recognized the motions. He'd exchanged endless trinkets while on the road. Hundreds of empty vows. Some with girls who thought he'd only be gone a little while, or at least were polite enough to pretend. Others with old friends he'd met by chance in a train yard or busking spot. Some with strangers he'd shared a beer or a con with. *I'll see you down the line*, they'd say. And if Benji was there, his friend would grin, shake the chump's hand, say, *Don't worry, baby, you always meet twice.* But what happens after that second meeting? What happens when history has already looped back on itself? After that, there's no guarantee.

In the dim light of the attic loft, Bellatine readied for the Longshadow Man's arrival. She moved quickly and methodically, as if she were not a woman, but a machine. *It's only a room,* she told herself of the loft, suppressing the icy trickle of unease that threatened the nape of her neck. *You've been in here a hundred times. Nothing's changed.* Yet even so, she couldn't help but hurry as she worked, desperate to leave the crawl space and its memories as fast as she could.

How do you kill a memory? The question thrummed alongside her pulse as Thistlefoot bobbed restlessly in the cold. She leaned into the heave and drop of each sway and matched her breath to the rhythm. The measured oxygen helped her head clear, her panic calm. *This is your house,* she insisted to herself, *not his.* Hadn't Thistlefoot been awakened for this very task? To protect her family from this same threat?

"Teach me how to help you," she whispered, descending the ladder. The wood was warm from Malka's fire, and heat prickled all too familiar on her fingertips. Shame washed through Bellatine then and she scurried down faster. The Fool's story flashed and replayed like a dark filmstrip. Maybe she'd been right all along. The Embering *was* a curse. An inheritance bred from violence and ghastly sorrows. That's why the house had always felt familiar. Why the Longshadow Man could drill into her head when her power flared. They were all flames born from the same spark. Relics of the same horror. Was that why Mira had always treated her like a monster? Had she known where the Embering had come from? Or, like the smokefed turning on the innocent, like the peasants around Gedenkrovka who stood at the soldiers' sides, was it simply easiest for Mira to revile that which she didn't understand?

She'd taken out her phone and pressed CALL before she could convince herself otherwise.

It picked up after the second ring.

"Yes, Bellatine? Do you need something?"

Bellatine let out a breath she hadn't noticed she was holding. "Hi, Mom."

"I'll be honest, this isn't the best time to chat, call me tomorrow, or Wednesday if you—"

"I love you."

Silence ballooned on the line.

"Bellatine, what's going on?"

"Nothing. I—"

"Is it your brother?"

"Isaac's fine, I told you. It's nothing. I just . . . wanted you to know."

She could hear Mira's measured breathing, aloft on satellite waves.

"Well. All right then. I appreciate that."

"I hope you have a good day. Go back to what you were doing."

"Bellatine, I don't under—"

She hung up before the lump in her throat had a chance to rise to the surface.

"Voilà." Isaac dumped a clatter of junk onto the floor, a mix of items from the pantry and garbage. He crossed his arms.

Bellatine picked up a clay jug, blowing dust off the rim. The air made a hollow trill as it passed over the opening. "What is this?"

Isaac sighed. "Let's call it *improvisation*. Here." He tossed her performance clothes at her. Had the past two months of tour gone as planned, they should have remained stiff and blanched, save for a gentle thinning at the knees, yellowing at the armpits. Instead, brown specks dotted her collar where she'd scrubbed blood away with bleach. The knee, threaded shut from tearing open on the Estey factory steps. *The best-laid plans . . .* She'd always hated that idiom. It implied that people had no control, no ultimate power over what plays out. Bellatine didn't agree. It took organizational skills and elbow grease, but you could take the reins in any situation. Or at least, that's what she used to believe.

"Put them on," Isaac urged.

"Why?"

"*White shroud*," he insisted.

They'd dug for exorcism rites online, landing (to Bellatine's deep skepticism) on KaballaKween.com, which paired mystic advice with coupon codes for rosé wines, all splashed across a glittery lilac background. But what the website lacked in gravitas, it made up for in high-quality scans of what looked to be ancient rabbinic texts. In one such document, white shrouds were listed as the exorcist's traditional garb, symbolizing their purity of spirit. Bellatine's fingertips prickled. *I'm not pure,* she thought. Her pulse quickened once more.

Isaac rooted through the pile, emerging with Bellatine's hammer. He snatched up the clay jug, and with a reckless swoop, knocked the bottom out. Isaac pressed his lips to the mouthpiece and trumpeted into the bottomless vessel, which amplified the sound like a bullhorn. In the corner where she slept, Hubcap's ears pricked up. Isaac nodded, satisfied. "Shofar."

"Isaac . . ." With each moment, Bellatine's heart sank deeper. Now it was so low in her ribs that the weight of it threatened to drop clean from her body and vanish through the floor. "I don't think . . ." She faded into silence. What were they doing? This felt like playing make-believe. They weren't holy. They weren't pure. Nothing in this house was. Maybe the Longshadow Man was right to want to erase it all.

Isaac interrupted her thoughts. "Did you put armor on Thistle's claws, or just feet and legs?"

"Not the claws, but why—"

"Good. It says a possession has to leave the body from under the big toenail. Now hurry and put those on." He slinked out of his own trousers, then climbed into a spare pair of white linen pants. "We'll start rehearsal as soon as you're dressed."

"Rehearsal?" Her pulse was raging now. It batted against her jugular like a June bug rattling against a window screen. *Tap. Tap, tap, tap.* "Not everything is a play, Isaac. You can't charm this monster away with makeshift props and luck like you would with an audience." Isaac's junk pile rattled as Thistlefoot continued its nervous wriggling.

"Listen," Isaac said. "You ever hear of a *tulpa*?"

The word didn't sound familiar. And she didn't have time for one of Isaac's riddles.

"The name comes from Buddhist mysticism," he continued, not waiting for an answer. "The idea is, if enough mystics focus on manifesting an imaginary creature, their belief in it will make it real. They'll sit in a big group and meditate on this one idea, this one character, until it shows up. Thought affecting reality."

"So you're a Buddhist now?" she said, lifting an eyebrow.

"The way I figure, this is true of anything," he pressed on, smoothing his white T-shirt. "Is God real? Fuck if I know, but Joan of Arc had enough faith to let herself burn at the stake. When people believe in something, believe in it so much that it informs their life and death, it may as well exist because it's changing the physical world. At that point, it doesn't matter whether God is real or not. The belief, and the action that follows belief, makes the story true and alters the world to match. Acting's the same. If you can get the audience to believe that you're the character, if you can suspend that disbelief, it rips a hole right through space. Because in that moment, in that room, if the work is done right, it isn't a shared delusion. It isn't a story. It's real."

Bellatine plucked what looked like a jar of dried parsley from the pile, dislodging a pair of pruning shears. "Thrilled to be spending my final night on Earth listening to a theatrical lecture over a pile of trash."

"You *aren't* listening," he barked. Bellatine flinched. "What happens when you fear something? When you believe it can hurt you?" Again, he pushed ahead without waiting for a response. "You give it power. Didn't you hear what the Fool said? When Thistlefoot stood up, so did the Longshadow Man. When Thistlefoot started running, who started running after?"

He did.

"By running from him," Isaac said, "by putting all our fear and attention and belief into running—"

Bellatine flicked a glance up toward the loft, where the other preparations lay. "We make him more real."

Isaac nodded. "And guess what." He held up the broken jug. "I *believe* this is a goddamn shofar that is going to banish a demon. So unless you have a better idea, let's do a fucking exorcism."

"But all *you* do is run," she countered. "It's all you've ever done."

Isaac's eyes fell to the floor. "Maybe there are certain things I *want* to make more real. More . . . alive." He looked brittle again then, as he had when she'd found him. For a moment, the blue-lipped memory shadowed his face.

"So," she said, thumbing her overall straps. "You're not a Buddhist."

A smile played at his lips, and the death-shadow vanished. "No. My buddy Benji taught me about that. He was a wiz with this stuff—myths, monsters, legends. If he were here, he'd probably flip open that big songbook in his head right to some ballad that had all the instructions we'd need."

"You've mentioned him before," Bellatine said, carefully.

"Yeah." Isaac paused. "He died."

There was so much about Isaac she still didn't know. There was so much of her he'd never been around to learn. And now, they may never have the chance.

"Listen, kid—" he started.

"Yeah?"

"It's been . . . These past three months . . ." He cleared his throat. "This tour, you think it was worth it?"

Bellatine stared at him in disbelief. Then, she burst into laughter. It winged through Thistlefoot like a flock of jays and the house jerked in surprise at the sound. "No way, man!" She laughed past her breath and when her breath was gone, she kept laughing. Isaac broke into a grin, and soon, he was laughing, too.

Her phone buzzed. Bellatine answered.

"They're coming," Rummy's voice echoed on the line. "Definitely feels like a mob. We'll keep them occupied, but he won't be far behind."

"Okay. Thanks. And hey"—she lowered her voice—"how's Winnie?"

"She's safe. And she'll be waiting for you when you're done. Give 'em hell."

"You too." She hung up. *She'll be waiting for you . . .* She remembered Winifred's face, haloed in pale light as they wove through the Lantern Parade. Remembered her mouth, cool and sweet, as she'd kissed her after the rock fight, their bodies tangling against the wall. Perhaps this could all be worth it after all.

Bellatine sucked in a long breath. "Gimme that, will you?" She took the jug in hand and blew. A low moan sounded. "Raise the lantern?"

Isaac nodded. "*Kill* the ghost."

The chime above the door began to ring.

CHAPTER FORTY-FIVE

OVER THE YEARS, THE people came. Some arrived with sickness, disguised as a gift. Some came starving from lands blackened with blight. Others, choking beneath a dictator's bootheel. Some arrived shackled in the bowels of terrible ships (one such ship sprouted wings, and tried to fly). Potatoes went to rot, and so they came. Houses of prayer were burned, and so they came. Children and sisters and brothers were thrown into gas chambers, and so they came. Villages were plundered, so they came. The people dreamt, and as they dreamt, they believed, and their belief grew into oceans, into sails, into a good, strong wind to carry them toward that land called America. When they arrived, they found more of the same. New hungers. New tyrants. New suffering. Old brutalities. The soil, already dark with blood. But for one brief, suspended moment, there in the liminal breaths between *here* and *there*, there was hope.

And what did the people bring with them? Trinkets. Candlesticks. Babies birthed on rancid decks. Coins sewn into coat linings and photographs of beloveds they would never see again.

Languages, folded into the suitcases of their tongues. Gods and demons and superstitions. And other keepsakes—those they didn't even know they carried. Stowaways, with claws buried in their backs. Memories. Stories. Ghosts.

Children were born and raised among the stories, and their children, and theirs, until the stories were forgotten. The ghosts, forgotten, too. Now, a boy whose great-grandfather ate fistfuls of grass to survive drives his rusted-out Chevy in circles between the high school parking lot and the rotary, just to hear the engine purr. A girl whose grandmother was forced into soldiers' beds—a *comfort*, they called her—stays out at a party until three a.m., plays spin the bottle for hours. These, small celebrations. The joys of forgetting. Of running the gas tank to empty just because you can. Of wearing red lipstick and curling your hair, kissing someone, and then walking away whenever you choose. Generation by generation, we forget. Only the body remembers. The body, and the ghosts. Flickers of flame.

At the first ring of the owl-talon bell, Thistlefoot's cabinets flung open in unison, flapping like clipped wings.

At the second ring, Bellatine realized she had stopped breathing. She could feel the presence on the other side of that door, the weight of one hundred years pressing in. She tried to dispel the notion of being buried alive.

Isaac caught her eye and nodded, his cat wisping around his ankles.

Ready? he mouthed.

No, her heart thundered. *No, no, never.* "Yes," she whispered.

The third bell chimed. Thistlefoot was vibrating, as if standing still took all the house's power. An arrow drawn back in a bow and held. Held. Held. Bellatine brushed a palm against the wall and let a small trickle of heat pour into the house. The trembling lessened.

When the fourth bell chimed, it came as no surprise. The Yaga siblings didn't answer. There was no need. For as soon as the ringing dissipated, the Longshadow Man sifted through the door like smoke.

Bellatine released her breath.

"Children," the Longshadow Man called. "Where I come from, it is customary to greet a guest. American hospitality certainly *lacks*."

Isaac stepped forward. "Pardon, but I heard it was ill luck to shake a guest's hand over the threshold. Brings in bad spirits."

"We wouldn't want that," the Longshadow Man said with a smile, smoothing his lapel. He inhaled deeply, his nostrils flaring. "Ah yes. Lovely to be back. So many precious moments here . . ." He ran a finger along the windowsill, flicking away a speck of dust. "I can still smell them."

The room shuddered and rearranged. Bellatine's eyes took a moment to adjust; superimposed over the living room, a second living room lay. Furniture that hadn't been there a moment ago blinked, translucent. Dim shapes moved over the space—a woman's outline. An infant on her hip. An older child. The mirages went through the motions of sweeping, eating, sewing, as if an elaborate shadow play were being performed along the walls. A broom handle swelled and shrank in silhouette. Thread stretched in a flat black line, lifting and falling as a shadow hand moved a shadow needle through penumbral fabric.

Focus on what's real, she told herself. Without her wooden spoon to reach for, Bellatine ground her feet into the floor. Felt the solidity there. She slipped her hand into her pocket and drew it out, full, hiding it behind her back.

"Such an honor to see you again," the Longshadow Man purred, turning to her. "And you listened to my humble request— no more evasion. I am pleased."

Bellatine said nothing. Ancestral shadows continued to roam over the walls, somewhere outside time.

He opened his arms. "You understand, I take no pleasure in this day. I am simply completing a task. It is ugly work, making our world brighter. Stronger. More *pure*. But we do it because we love our people, and we fear God. We blot out the stains."

"Listen to yourself," Isaac chided. "Your dialogue sounds like it was written for a Nazi in an Indiana Jones movie. You might consider rebranding."

The Longshadow Man snapped his fingers, and tiny flames sparked along his trimmed nails.

"Ah yes. Isaac Yaga. The resurrected."

Confusion flicked across Isaac's face. And then, worse. Recognition.

"And Bellatine Yaga." The Longshadow Man turned. "The cursed one." His smile didn't reach his eyes. "I have tasted your shame. It is bitter as wormwood. Sticks to the teeth." He moved one step closer, and it took all of Bellatine's willpower not to recoil. "I can take it from you, you know. Your burden."

She hesitated.

"What do you mean?"

"What is this curse if not another soiled relic? An antiquity?" He lifted his fingertips to his mouth, still burning, and flicked a tongue through the flame. It sizzled for a moment before he pulled back. "Let me relieve you of it. Of the curse, and its wretched child." Thistlefoot creaked.

"We didn't know . . ." Bellatine's voice softened. "I didn't know what had happened here. I thought this house was . . . good."

"There is no shame in being led astray," the Longshadow Man cooed. "We are all taken in by devilishness. By those who wish to sully us."

She cast her eyes up at him. "It was a mistake."

"Tiny," Isaac cautioned.

She drew closer to the Russian. He did have a certain *allure* to him. He was sleek and strong. He was in control. Imagine, to master that kind of discipline. To be both the bridle and the hand that tugs the reins. Imagine, the Embering nothing but a memory. Or no, not even that. Forgotten.

"You can make me normal?" she asked. Cautiously, she circled the ghost. He was so tailored. So crisp. Like a man who could deliver on his word.

"Yes, child," he hissed. "Yes."

"Don't listen," Isaac said. "*Tiny.* Stop."

"Please," Bellatine said, arriving in front of the Longshadow Man again. She held out her empty hands. They were trembling. "Show me what to do."

The dybbuk strode forward—and collided with the air.

The wreath of salt she'd let silently spill from her fist caged him where he stood. It encircled him, unbroken. Bellatine raised her eyebrows at her brother. "Well? How was I?"

Isaac winked. "Stanislavsky would be proud."

The Longshadow Man showed his teeth. "*Insolence.*" On the walls, the shadows writhed.

Isaac revealed the clay jug he'd hidden behind a stack of books, lifted it to his mouth, and blew. The tekiah blasted through the little house, and Thistlefoot bucked. Bellatine snatched a crumpled sheet of paper from her pocket and began to read the hand-scrawled psalms. "*They kneel and fall, but we rise and gain strength—*" She stuttered through, regretting the rush with which she'd noted it down, letters bunched and scrambling together. "*His—his mouth . . .*" She was faltering. Her tongue felt like rubber, clumsy and fat. "*His mouth is—is . . .*" The Longshadow Man tried again to step forward, but stopped at the rim of salt.

Isaac broke off the shofar's call and snatched the paper away. "*His mouth is full of oaths and deceits and guile,*" he announced. The Longshadow Man grimaced, and his limbs began to flicker, like the shadows on the walls. An arm gone, then reappearing. A leg. It was working. "*Under his tongue is mischief and iniquity,*" Isaac yelled, his voice low and unyielding as the shofar call itself. "*He sits in the lurking-places of the villages, he slays the innocent,*" *his eyes spy on Your army."* Isaac's voice rose louder and louder. A hole began to ripple out from the demon's chest. *"He crouches, he bows down, and—"*

Suddenly, the Longshadow Man lifted his head and spoke with Isaac in unison. *"An army of broken people shall fall by his signals."* From his breast pocket he drew a blue bottle full of liquid. Bellatine reached out, but it was too late. The Longshadow Man hurled the bottle toward the ground, the two-headed eagle gleaming. It burst on the hardwood floor. Vapor filled the air.

CHAPTER FORTY-SIX

ATOP HER LOOKOUT ON the scaffolding of an abandoned oil drill, Shona snapped open a hunting knife and touched up her lipstick in the metal's reflection. If their scheme worked, she shouldn't need a blade. But if something went wrong . . . well, she'd rather exit this life looking sharp—and gripping something sharper. Her silhouette cut into the sky like a dark flag.

"Time to bloom, mornin' glory," Sparrow said, their voice crackling over speakerphone. "We're almost under you."

Shona tilted her freshly painted lips toward the mouthpiece. "Not yet. Not till I see where the bastards are coming from."

Listening from within the bus, Winifred cast an inquiring glance at Rummy.

"I can't tell," he said through gritted teeth. "It feels like they're everywhere. In my whole body, like bees."

Winnie laid a gentle hand on Rummy's shoulder. "Thank you, by the way. For lying for me. It's better Bell thinks I'm safe."

"No prob—" Rummy buckled and vomited into an empty water jug.

"Lovely," Sparrow groaned.

He wiped his mouth with the back of a hand. "There's got to be a whole parade of them." Sweat beaded on his brow.

"All the more reason for me to stay and help," Winnie nodded.

"More the merrier," Sparrow agreed.

The smokefed would come. They would come fuming, come clawing at their own backs, come like a carnival choked with bells and streamers of soot, eager to draw Thistlefoot into the open. But they mustn't reach the house on legs—not until the Yaga siblings had dealt with the Longshadow Man. Not until they'd had a chance to turn the tides.

From her makeshift crow's nest above, Shona caught a smudge moving in her knife's lethal point. Not the mirror image of the approaching bus. Nor Thistlefoot, a mere fleck in the distance. This motion came in from beyond that, farther east. She pivoted to look.

"Let's go," Sparrow hollered up, leaning their head out the driver's-side window as they pulled up beneath.

"Hold on. There's something . . ." She trailed off, squinting. "I can't quite tell. It seems like—" And then she was scrambling down the scaffolding.

The smokefed crested the horizon.

They undulated, a swarm of fire ants. Hive-specks, converging into a single joined mind: fear. It was this fear that choked them as they scuttled through the dead grasses. Fear that hitched onto their backs, spidery and gaunt, the weight of which bent some onto all fours while others trampled the weaker of the mass. Fear wisped up from their skins in tendrils of smoke. Made them throw their names away like rotten fruit, to be devoured by the faceless hunger of their passengers.

Shona pounded on the bus door, and Sparrow pulled the lever, swinging it wide. "Found 'em." She shoved Sparrow aside to take the wheel.

"How long do we got? Where are they?"

"A couple minutes at most. They're coming from the east, two dozen of them or so."

"Two dozen?" Rummy whispered. "That can't be right. There's got to be more." Whatever nausea had gripped him when the mob overtook them in New Orleans was nothing compared to what swam through him now—waves of static, jagged as glass. Winnie helped him to his feet, blotting his face with a rag. In the distance, early-morning fog rolled over the plains like a low sea.

"Ready for your big showstopper, sunshine?" Shona said to Sparrow.

Sparrow rubbed their hands together. "Operation Milkman, here we go."

Rummy collapsed with his forehead against Winnie's shoulder and whimpered.

Shona frowned. "Sorry for this, buddy." She revved the engine—and they spun with a dizzying screech, bulleting in the direction of the smokefed.

In the back of the bus, Sparrow threaded a series of rubber tubes out the windows, which waggled like yellow tongues as the bus bounced over rough terrain. The hoses all led back into the same source: a metal tank, nearly as wide as a human torso.

"If Doctor Longshadow can play pharmacist, so can we. Sedative gas," they explained to Winnie, twisting a nozzle on the tank's crown. "Should put the crowd to sleep faster than a Brahms symphony."

"I like Brahms," Rummy moaned.

"You want a little puff of it for the road?" Shona called over her shoulder.

"Kinda . . ." Rummy said, miserable.

"What can I do?" Winnie asked. She was fidgeting, working the hem of her sleeve into tatters. She had no interest in being decoration. In standing still. She'd stood still long enough.

"Put this on." Sparrow tossed her a black handkerchief, embroidered with butter-colored flowers. They tied a matching one around their own face, covering the nose and mouth. Winifred followed as the others donned bandannas of their own.

The smokefed were fifty yards off now. At the front of the pack, a bearded man howled—more animal than human. A woman in pressed blue jeans and a ruffled church-worthy blouse tore her hair loose as she ran. It came out in bloody clumps in her fists. Two lanky teenage boys followed behind, their skins smoldering pearl white. Clinging to all of them: passengers, long and bright as needles.

"Here goes," Sparrow said. "Hold your breath." They turned the tank nozzle one more rotation, and the hoses swelled with gas. Wind shrieked through the equine skull's teeth as the bus barreled along the crowd's periphery, leaving a purple cloud in its wake like a venomous centipede. The speed—it still felt unnatural to Winifred. Moving *against* the Earth, not with it as she'd always done. She could sense the planet slowly rotating in the opposite direction, as if the wheels were carrying them backward in time, fleeing the rising sun.

"*Milkman, milkman, take my cup,*" Sparrow sang. "*When my man is away—*"

"*Come fill it on up!*" Shona hooted from the driver's seat.

Rummy let out a weak laugh.

Across the plain, Thistlefoot bowed. The sound of a bell echoed from far off like distant birdsong, four long chimes. A shadow rippled.

"It's starting," Winnie called. "Is this working?"

As the gas dispersed, the question answered itself. Row by row, the smokefed staggered. The family at the front had already collapsed, twitching on the sod. Behind them, a cluster of young oil workers swayed and sank to their knees. Five. Then ten. Then twenty smoke-sick bodies blinked and fell, their bleached panic emptying into unconsciousness. Silence spread across the flatlands, save for the Duskbreaker engine's steady purr.

Sparrow whistled. "Lord Almighty. They're cute when they sleep."

"How long should this stuff last?" Shona asked, circling back to make sure they were all down. The smokefed's chests rose and fell, their mouths twitching as if calling out in dreams. Their harmless passengers oozed against the ground in hazy pools.

"Fifteen minutes with the one dose," Sparrow calculated. "But I'll spritz 'em with a little bonus every so often to re-up."

"Good." Shona looked out across the field. Only the tip of Thistlefoot's roof was now visible in the distance, a shivering patch of weeds. "We have to give them all the time we can."

Through the cracked bus windows, Winifred watched the skyline. Vultures circled the house, waiting—though if the ghost indeed fell, the scavengers would be disappointed. Memories, as Winnie had come to learn, didn't make for much of a meal.

Out in the endless stretch of Middle America with no mountains to interfere, only frost-blanched scrub root and red dirt, one could gaze out as far as the horizon's ripened curve. The morning fog had spread, coating the earth like the skin of an unpolished plum. It tumbled toward them. A low unease threaded through Winifred's belly.

"Something isn't right," she whispered.

"Not right like 'a boogeyman sent a possessed army our way,' or some other kind of *not right*?" Sparrow asked, sealing off the tank.

"The fog . . ." Winifred knew weather patterns. She'd spent eons witnessing the roil and convulsions of the skies. She'd been worn down by thousands of water droplets, falling, evaporating, re-forming, falling again to gather as dew. But that fog, it was too dense. Too swift.

Rummy screamed on his cot, hands flying to his face. "Make them stop," he cried, tears streaming down his face. "Too many, too many, *too many*."

Shona called over her shoulder, still behind the wheel. "Shhh, shh, it's okay. We got 'em, see?"

The mist seemed to swell, swallowing the land as it neared. Though the sun was leaking higher in the sky, the fog only swirled faster. Thicker. It blotted out the light.

Almost like smoke.

The miasma unzipped, splitting into fragments.

"Go, go, go!" Winifred yelled. Shona slammed into reverse as Sparrow dove for the metal tank, turning it to full blast.

The mist billowed toward the bus—and from within, the passengers appeared. They clung to a sea of human bodies, wrapped in smoke. Pale white tendrils licked out from lips, ears, wafted in thin curls from the corners of hazed eyes. The passengers smudged at the edges, converged to envelop the mass as if it were a single vaporous organism crawling over the earth.

And the closer it drew, the louder the buzzing. Voices snarled, one matted oration: *"We—hands torches—we—belly growls, the hunger—what if the food spoils—jobs gone—they take everything—how our veins are bright white wheat swaying—remember—there were so many—candles—swaying—bodies—swaying—"*

Gas wheezed out of Sparrow's yellow hoses, crumpling the first wave of attackers—but there were more behind them. The violet-colored sedative and the unholy smoke collided like two great phantoms.

"I can't see," Shona said, squinting through the windshield.

"We have to make a barricade!" Winifred shouted. "Keep driving! Anything to block them off."

Shona grimaced, veering into reverse, cutting off the smoke-fed. The mob reared back. A few more seconds earned, Thistlefoot that much closer to escape. Would those moments be the division between triumph and failure? They could only hope.

There was a thump against the bus' nose. Shona slammed on the breaks.

"I'm cranking the gas," Sparrow yelled. With the vehicle now stationary, the mingling fumes had begun inking through the windows. "Cover your mouths! Don't breathe it in!"

Sedative spewed from the hoses, dousing the smokefed. Those in front dropped cold, the rows behind, wavering. *Run,* Winifred prayed silently to Thistlefoot at the horizon's crest. *Run. Loyf.* She could almost taste Bellatine's voice, that guttural demand on her lips. Her voice itself, another kind of prayer.

Thistlefoot ran. It blinked out of sight.

More fumes slithered through the bus' cracked windows. The air tinged with the scent of singe and rot. Hay, moldered in rain. Beasts of burden split at the belly. A familiar perfume. It poured off the new throng of smokefed, reinforcing them, reinfecting, overpowering the sedative until only the cruel smoke remained. Shona ran to Rummy and helped him hold his bandanna over his face. Sparrow leapt from window to window, wrenching them shut. The bus began to rock, back and forth, back and forth, as the crowd struggled to push past.

Winifred looked frantically to her comrades. Their chests had begun to heave, their faces reddening. One by one, they dropped their hands from their mouths and took involuntary gasps. The bandannas were no use. First Rummy—white etching through his closed eyelids, creamy swirls appearing beneath his skin. Then Sparrow, who coughed into their velvet sleeve before snapping their head back, growling with blighted lungs. Shona held off longest, her muscles straining as she worked to hold her breath—but even she eventually folded. She slumped, and Winnie saw the imprint of what could only be a passenger squeezing around her middle.

Whatever distance they'd wedged between the Yagas and the ashen mob, it would have to be enough.

Winifred shuddered. She waited for the poison to take her. It would be all too fitting—an end like this, like her namesake's. Typhoid-ridden, from ill water. Smokefed, from toxic air. Winifred Hadley was destined to repeat her death again and again, just as the Longshadow Man was cursed to bring about the same massacre in perpetuity. Time, looping back again and again, unchanging. She shut her eyes. She waited.

She kept waiting.

A jarring crash sounded as Sparrow's large body cracked against Rummy's cot. Shona hissed, her lipstick stark as fire against a smoke-sick face. A blade glinted in her hand. She lunged forward.

When you look like someone else, Isaac's advice echoed, *it's easy to think you're them. But you're not. That other girl . . . she's in a box. Dust. You're not dust.*

I'm not Winifred Hadley. I'm not Winifred Hadley. A fevered mantra.

Winnie's eyes flew open. Isaac had been wrong about one thing. She may be alive—but she was *also* dust. Earth. Stone. And the thing about stone?

It doesn't need to breathe.

Winifred acted fast. Her eyes, clear blue. Her cheeks, silvery as granite. She leapt between Shona and Sparrow, and as she did, the blade slid between Winifred's ribs.

Granite, typical, unmoving granite, feels nothing. No joys. No sorrows. An eternity of nonbeing. There is no difference between pain and pleasure to one who is accustomed to nothingness. Any sensation becomes a celebration, for sensations are proof that you are here. Alive. No longer a blankness. So when the metal seared red-hot into Winifred's chest, she felt it as she felt all things: as a conversation. The wound was only a feeling, just as the smoke was a feeling. Not good, not bad, simply a message from the world to her flesh. The danger, only a feeling. Nothing. She relaxed, pulled the knife from her body, and cast it aside. What harm could a pinprick do to the Earth itself?

Startled by the interference, Shona snarled and backed away. Rummy had risen behind her and stumbled toward the bus windows. "Get out. We have to get out," he was muttering. Sparrow bashed open the emergency exit, and within moments, all three had torn their way out and vanished into the mob.

"Wait!" Winifred cried. Her voice was swallowed by the horde. Grabbing Shona's banjo like a mace, she followed after, a blond ringlet sticking to her dampened cheek. Below, the sea of smokefed flowed on. She stepped into the fray and swung the banjo wide. It wouldn't stop the crowd. She was small, and it was vast. But they wouldn't stop *her* either.

You cannot kill a stone.

All the while, the trio once known as the Duskbreaker Band vanished into the milky haze. They lurched forward, limbs of a monstrous body. Beyond the horizon: an old house, drawing them like a magnet. They moved as one.

CHAPTER FORTY-SEVEN

ISAAC'S PULSE QUICKENED AT the blue bottle's shattering. His muscles coiled tighter beneath his skin. His shoulders hunched on instinct. *Symptoms of fear,* he thought—and then he thought nothing. He only felt. The room vanished, and all he knew was a weight bearing down on him. All he saw was white.

Vaguely, he sensed someone at his side. His sister. She had fallen to her knees, an apparition squatting on her back. Its vaporous body was nearly human, with arms so long they knotted twice around Bellatine's neck. She didn't notice the creature—enraptured only by her hands, which she dragged across the floor as if trying to smear off something filthy. As she did, the rough wood caught on her skin and tore, leaving trails of blood behind. *"I don't want them. I don't want them,"* she moaned.

"Hey there, Fresh."

Isaac stumbled back. He spun, looking for the voice's origin, but saw no one. Only a wisp of pale fog trailing over his shoulder.

"I knew you'd let me down again."

This time, Isaac found the speaker. Hubcap grinned. She licked her teeth.

"First, you killed me," the cat said in Benji's voice. Isaac covered his ears, but the hissing accusation only grew.

"I'm sorry," he muttered. "I tried—"

"And now you leave your debt unpaid. Do you know what becomes of an unpaid debt, Fresh?"

A gap. It leaves a gap.

"That's right, baby boy. A gap. And a gap must be filled, ain't that right? You take a life from the bright ol' cosmos, the cosmos gonna snatch one right back."

He felt his head turn involuntarily to the side. Bellatine was scratching at her hands, weeping, flesh clumping under her blunt fingernails. *"I don't want them, I don't want them."* The figure on her back purred.

"It would be a shame if someone else had to pay for your mistake."

Terror thundered through Isaac in white bolts. Tiny. It was going to be Tiny. He'd let Benji die. He'd created a gap. Now the scales were going to balance themselves. Panic stung in his nostrils and throat. It stank of burning hay.

"Hardly fair," the Longshadow Man tutted from within the salt circle. "If only there were a way to keep her safe . . . Another trade, perhaps."

Hubcap had crouched next to his sister, though he hadn't seen the cat move. The feline opened her razored mouth and vomited dust. She croaked. "I have come to bury you."

Thistlefoot's walls tightened. An ache rippled up Isaac's spine. Somewhere, he could hear the soft sound of an infant crying. Too small. Too trapped. He had to run. He had to run and never, never stop running. He had to pay his debt.

"There is another option," the Longshadow Man whispered. "Another life you could offer." The house creaked as if protesting. "All you need to do is set a match."

"*I don't want them. I don't want them.*"

Her hands, killers. Her hands, the product of death. Death begets death begets death. Bellatine moaned into the floor. With each drag of her hands, they seemed to grow larger, more unmanageable. "*I don't want them.*" She'd touched Winifred with these hands—what terrible stains had she left behind? She'd touched Isaac, an unholy necromancy. There would be a price. There was always a price. And soon, Thistlefoot would be gone too and there would be no more haven for her. *Haven.* There never was a haven. This house was just as cursed as she. Both abominations.

Kerosene. A lighter. That's all it would take to erase them both. There would be no peace. Not as long as her hands remained. Not as long as Thistlefoot walked. No peace. Only her and her hands, which now multiplied upon themselves, filled the room, smothered her. She was drowning beneath a river of hands, searing hot as coals.

Not safe. Debts must be paid. The gap. The gap. The gap.

Isaac lurched toward the pantry, digging in a storage trunk for something, anything, to make the terror stop.

"That's right," Hubcap seethed, "a simple transaction. The house for your sister's life. What has this hovel brought you but danger? What has it brought you but suffering upon suffering?"

Creamy fog distorted every shape into a twisted plague. On one wall, Benji's silhouette plummeted from a train car, then returned, then dropped, then returned, on endless loop. On another wall, a village flickered and crumbled under mounting shadow flames. His own shadow joined, buckled with burden. Torment after torment. Nothing to trust. Nothing but the bottle of whiskey he'd dug from the trunk. Yes, this would do. It would burn fast.

"It is time to collect." The Longshadow Man's voice slithered in unison with the talking cat. The sound hooked into Isaac's bones, hollow as the grave.

He'd pay his debt. Then it could be over. Over, at last.

⁂

Through an ivory fog, Bellatine saw Isaac rise and stumble away. A passenger drooped from his back. Thistlefoot reared, and she dug into the floorboards to hold on. Her fingernails splintered. *Monsters.* She and the house alike. It bucked again, and Bellatine slid sideways. She thudded into the wall, her elbow cracking against plaster. Thistlefoot was moving her, tilting her across the floor.

"Stop!" she growled. "I don't belong to you!"

Another twist, and the house flung her to the left. She reached out to catch herself, gripping the doorframe. Heat leaked from her fingers into the wood, and for a moment, the weight on her own back lightened. Wasn't there something she was supposed to do? *Logic. Return to logic.* She strained for the part of herself that could notch a perfect dovetail joint. Could tell the angle of a pine board even without a laser level. Could solve any problem with a tool in hand. A tool . . . She'd prepared supplies, but for what? She couldn't remember now. The only memories that mattered were the screaming deer, rotting by the roadside. The death chill on her brother's skin. Her twice-great-grandmother's crime, her doomed hands pressing down, down, down in the dim attic crawl space. *The crawl space. That's where I hid the* . . . The miasma closed in once more. Thistlefoot tossed, hurtling Bellatine toward the bedroom. She groaned as her shoulder struck the wall with a sharp pop. She pushed it back. There was only one tool that could clear her head. One action.

Wrenching herself up, Bellatine dove through the doorway. The ladder hovered ahead of her, enrobed in blurred mist. She scrambled up, hand over hand, leaving crimson prints in her wake.

Monster, the voice in her head croaked, unyielding. *Monster.* With each rung, weight pressed heavier on her shoulders. Arms, not her own, were pulling—but she pulled back.

Reaching the entrance to the loft, Bellatine dragged herself inside, falling at the vinyl crate's feet. *No,* hissed the shadows in the walls. *Evil, it's evil, evil, you are evil, hands evil, evil touch, evil girl.* She pushed through the dissonance and unlatched the case, throwing open the lid. She reached in. Her hands, as she knew they would, met softness. A spark awaited her. Coal-black heat. She drew the Fool to her, even as every shadow beneath her eyelids screeched with accusation.

The Embering arrived like a venom. It burned up her wrists and into her mouth. It wasn't as strong as she was used to, still muffled within Thistlefoot's four walls, but the smoke-fear spiked her strength enough for the Embering to take hold. As it moved, she could feel it burn her fear away, drop by drop. Her legs grew solid beneath her. Her heartbeat slowed, pumping blood that fizzed with fever. Each screaming shadow ebbed until nothing more than scattered light. The choking arms let go. Her head was clear and angry and *hers.* When she looked to her hands, her wounds were gone.

On the ground below, her brother and his passenger had stumbled into the bedroom. Isaac held a lit match between his long, pale fingers. In his other, a bottle of whiskey. He splashed the liquor onto the bedsheets, then dropped the flame. Bellatine didn't bother with the ladder. She dropped from the loft and flung herself toward him. The Embering still pounded in her palms. Isaac watched the fire rise, mesmerized. Flames danced in reflection within his empty eyes, smoke swirling beneath his skin. She reached him. Grabbed his wrist. And then breathlessly, she slid her hand into his and held on tight.

Dark warmth flowed into Isaac's hand and shot through his arm. He flinched, yet whatever had newly grabbed him wouldn't let go. *A debt is a debt,* Hubcap hissed, but she had begun to blink in and out like a bad TV signal. Heat rippled past Isaac's arm and into his throat until he could taste it. The talking cat contorted into static. A few yards away, something meowed, and Isaac squinted. Was he seeing double? Hubcap, another Hubcap, crouched wide-eyed behind a pile of clothes. The hair on her back stood on end. Isaac's fear recoiled. It shrank and shriveled within his veins. The ache in his back abated, weight evaporating in waves. As the hand in his squeezed tighter, the taunting, phantasmal feline before him faded into nothing and was gone. Only the real Hubcap remained, cowering among the laundry.

Isaac smelled smoke. Saw a burning bed, flames rising higher.

"Shit!" he yelped. He grabbed the bedding and balled it up, smothering the fire. "I liked that pillow!"

At his side, Bellatine groaned with relief.

The Longshadow Man remained in the parlor, trapped within the salt circle. His polite veneer had shed, and he looked broader. Clearer. The lines and angles of his body had grown more solid. He was becoming more real.

Isaac grabbed Bellatine's face. "Are you okay?"

She nodded.

Outside, coyotes yipped in the distance, drawing nearer. No . . . not coyotes. The voices were feral but human. The smokefed. They must have made it past the Duskbreakers. They were coming.

"*Chiiiildren,*" the Longshadow Man called through the open door. He spoke like he had all the time in the world. "Such a mess." He clucked, looking around the ruined room. "I like a job complete and clean. We will try again."

Isaac glanced around for the makeshift shofar until he

spotted the jug a few yards from the salt circle, shattered into pieces. He slumped against the singed bed. He was tired. So tired he felt as if he could burst into powder and float away. They couldn't destroy the Longshadow Man. You can't destroy an act of destruction.

Something stirred. It was low to the ground and bright, and at first, Isaac mistook it for a child.

"Good day, friends, would you care for another story?" The Fool flipped over and stood on his head. *"Once, Baba Yaga went to the bookbinders, in search of a recipe."* With a wobble, the little doll walked forward on his hands. The Longshadow Man looked down at him, snarling. *"When Baba Yaga arrived, she asked for the oldest recipe book in all of Gedenkrovka, and the bookseller, he said— whoops!"* The Fool flopped over, landing on his belly. His red shoe skidded through the circle of salt.

The binding broke.

The Longshadow Man straightened his hat. Then, he stepped over the salt line and brought his shoe down hard on the Fool's head. There was a crack. Bellatine took a sharp breath.

"The bookseller said," the Fool squeaked through a shattered cheek, *"'But, Baba Yaga, everyone knows that the oldest recipes in Gedenkrovka are—'"* Once more, the Longshadow Man lowered his foot, this time with more force.

"'—the . . . the oldest recipes in Gedenkrovka . . .'"

"Silence," the Longshadow Man snarled. He ground the puppet's head into the floor. "Take that name from your mouth and burn it."

Why was he wasting time on the toy? It was frivolous—but he seemed determined to mute the little doll.

It's the story, Isaac realized. *He's trying to stop the story.*

How do you ruin a people? Is it with fire? Is it with bullets? You can drag a man through the street tied to the back of a horse. You can incinerate a village. Can line families up in rows against a brick wall and fell them, one by one, like a forest. But all it takes is one survivor, and the story lives on. One survivor to carry the poems and the songs, the prayers, the sorrows. It isn't just taking a life that destroys a people. It's taking their history.

That was why the Longshadow Man needed to burn Thistle-foot. Because the house remembered. Kill the story, and you kill the culture.

You can't destroy an act of destruction.

But if the story lives on? The whole story—not only the death of a place, but the *life*? Then the slaughterer has lost.

Bear witness, a voice inside Isaac hummed. Suddenly, forgotten images slammed back into him. The shimmering village with its thatched roofs. The grocer who had warmed his coat and boots by the fire. The boys and their ballgame. The synagogue . . . its chorus of names. *Shmuel Genzl. Sarah Rovner. Chaya Rabinowitz . . .* The Longshadow Man thought these names were dead, erased by time and by cruelty. Merely sounds, with no *body* to inhabit. And he was right. But not for long.

"Isaac," Bellatine said through gritted teeth. Her gaze shot between the shattered Fool and the Longshadow Man, who took another step, leaving the broken circle of salt behind. "Isaac, we need to go." The Longshadow Man came toward them.

But Isaac wasn't there anymore. Only the Chameleon King— and he had begun to change his colors.

CHAPTER FORTY-EIGHT

BEFORE HER EYES, BELLATINE'S brother transformed. He fanned out his shoulders, broadening himself to twice his normal width. His arms lifted into foreign angles. The lines in his face rearranged as he twisted the corner of his mouth, the lift of his eyebrows, the apples of his cheeks. Within a moment, a stranger stood before her.

"Dybbuk," the man who had been Isaac growled. "Have you forgotten me?" He stepped back into the parlor, toward the Longshadow Man, into the light.

"My name is Mosheh Leiser. And I am not gone."

The Longshadow Man shuddered. For a fleeting moment, he wasn't a man but a mass of shadows, passengers, writhing in their shell of a coat.

That's when the room tilted. Shouts broke through the walls and through a gap in the boarded window. Bellatine looked out—and saw an army. Hundreds of people thundered over the plain, twinned by lanky, smokefed creatures that rode the men and women like stallions. Shona was among them, a passenger's gaseous fists tangled in her hair. Rummy, too, who frothed at the mouth, holding his head in his hands as he ran. Sparrow, white smoke leaking over their obsidian skin, leapt onto Thistlefoot's leg and began to climb. A laugh of despair boiled up in Bellatine's lungs.

Isaac transformed again. Narrow, this time, but shorter than his normal height. His stooped posture resembled that of a man who'd spent hours laboring over a table, as some of Bellatine's own colleagues had developed after lifetimes in their workshops.

"I am Reb Yoneih," Isaac said, "and you will not forget me."

The Longshadow Man tried to move forward, but his legs had slipped into translucence. They flickered. His feet dissipated and blurred, losing their shape. Whatever trick Isaac was playing, it was working.

Someone pounded against the wall. Sparrow had scaled the leg all the way up to the porch, with others close behind. It would only be moments before they broke through. She and Isaac would be more than outnumbered. They would be dead in minutes. Bellatine's mind raced. Making things, that was her language. Spoons and nightstands. The slender neck of a cedar lamp, a room's rough timber frame. Creation. She needed to keep the smokefed out—but what good were her skills now, empty handed?

Your hands are not empty, an inner voice urged. A lingering Ember fizzed in her knuckles. Her eyes fell again on the Fool, split and silent on the parlor floor. Before she could talk herself out of it, Bellatine darted back into the bedroom and up the ladder, where the vinyl road case full of puppets waited. She leaned over the cast of *The Drowning Fool* and, sucking in a last shuddering breath, thrust her hands inside.

The Fox with the little green vest and the garnet eyes.

The Mayor with the purple sash.

The Tailor at his sewing machine.

The Moon.

The Green Woman with willow arms and legs.

The Girl with No Face.

With each new awakening, Bellatine's power surged brighter. Light poured through the youngest Yaga. Not a burn, but a brightness, peeling back layer after layer of doubt. One by one, the puppets careened into life. They rose. But she didn't stop there. The Embering rioted from her with such untamed joy, she couldn't stop it. She didn't *want* to stop it. Her hands fell on the vinyl case, and it grew long, wet fangs. She touched the wall and it rippled with scales. Then the loft's ladder as she made her descent, each rung undulating like a tadpole. Outside, the pounding grew louder, but Bellatine didn't listen. Sunlight poured from beneath her nails and from the ends of her hair. She trailed through the house. A vase of flowers spat belladonna poison from its blue lips. The pantry door broke from its hinges and inchwormed behind her. She touched everything, and everything she touched awoke. Stretched. Looked up to their maker.

"I need you," she begged, breathless. "Help me."

The Chameleon King shapeshifted again, letting Reb Yoneih melt away. Sarah Rovner took his body now. He remembered her huddled in the women's section of the synagogue. Her eyes too close together, her nose tilted left, her hands worrying at a rash on the side of her cheek. She'd been delicate and prone to illness, he knew, from the rough red patches around her mouth. But she'd had a life. When Sarah landed in Isaac's body, she filled every inch of him. Her cheek itched. Her heart yearned for the sweetheart she had lost to the Eastern Front. She smacked Isaac's lips together, remembering the taste of sweet apple kugel.

"I am Sarah Rovner," she and the Chameleon King said as one. "You *will* remember me."

The demon roared. His right arm fissured into a dozen fuming tendrils. They reached, smoking, and then snuffed out.

Sarah Rovner vanished, and Bull the blacksmith appeared. Isaac's muscles ached at the notion of a hammer descending hundreds of times upon an anvil. Next, Zurach, the spindly man from the grocer. Isaac flexed his hands, recalling the man's sharp, accusatory finger. He spun between faces and bodies, name after name after name. Ten. Twenty. Thirty lives slipping in and out of his own. In the gaps between changes, the Longshadow Man regained his solidity and tried to step forward, but then Isaac changed shape again, and the dybbuk would wail, another part of him multiplying before threading out of sight. The carousel of faces turned and shimmered. Had he been on the streets, a hat for tips at his feet, the crowds would have fallen to their knees in madness and wonderment. Isaac ignored the protestations his bones had begun to make. He'd never been so many people before. He'd never let himself float so far away.

Vaguely, he was aware of motion around him. Wood cracking. Outside forces pushing in, while strange, impossible protectors kept the dangers at bay.

There had been a boy with a cigarette. His face came back in pieces, first the nose, the eyes, the round ears pinked with cold. What had the boy's name been? Perhaps he'd never said. No matter. Isaac's knees stung from scrapes, collected in endless ballgames and chases of tag. Scrapes that, for the boy with the cigarette, never had a chance to heal.

"You will not forget me."

The Longshadow Man's torso divided, his creatures scrabbling through his chest as they stretched like dough—thinning, coiling, tangling. He, they, screeched like steam escaping a kettle.

Another transformation, and Isaac felt himself returning nearly to his own body. His face was his own. His gestures, familiar and practiced, yet with a youthful, feminine precision. *Illa.* This was Illa, yes, he remembered now. The little dark-haired girl by the edge of the wood, there with her mother. He shimmied into her, marveling at the similarities between his motions and hers. She had never been forgotten. She had been with him, in each small mannerism and each cruel, broken promise. An echo.

"What has come to pass cannot be changed," the Long-shadow Man rasped.

"Yes," Isaac agreed in Illa's voice. "It cannot be changed. But it can be told."

He shook Illa loose from him and focused. It was time for one final performance. A grand finale. The Chameleon King grinned. He winked at the dybbuk, who flickered into terrible illusions before him—a pile of bodies, their arms and legs severed; a burning farm; a dead dog swollen with rot; a looted cemetery. Memories, yes. But not the *only* ones. Isaac focused on his feet first, making them buckle under years of labor. Then the knees, one tilted in, both creaking in winter rains. The pelvis, the hips, cocked to balance a heavy basket, or a soft, fat child. Isaac twisted his hands into working hands, which could knead dough without tiring or gently comb a knot from a little girl's hair. Capable hands, like his sister's. When he reached the face, he tried to remember every final detail. Not as he'd last seen the woman, famished with desperation, but as she'd appeared in the photograph. Steady. Unyielding. Standing on the threshold of her life, yet unknown, which rippled out like a river before her.

Isaac's voice was loud and unbreakable. "My name is Baba Yaga. You will *not* forget me."

All around Bellatine, a battle raged. She had wrestled her way out of the house and onto the porch, where *The Drowning Fool*'s menagerie kept the smokefed at bay. Everything around her shimmered with life. She gripped the banister for steadiness and it writhed into a garter snake, encircling her wrist like a gauntlet. Cresting the lip of the stage, Shona dove at her, and Bellatine pressed her hand to her chest, heat surging. Shona's eyes went wide, then blinked as the creature clinging to her disappeared, bursting into soot.

"You with me?" Bellatine asked, surprised at the lightness in her throat.

"I'm with you," Shona gasped. "We tried to hold them off to buy you time. I'm sorry."

Bellatine cast a glance over her shoulder. Through the window, she saw her brother, his eyes closed, body precise as a clock—the Longshadow Man thrashing in agony before him.

She gripped Shona's arm. "You gave us exactly the time we needed."

Sparrow barreled toward them, and she thrust a palm to their shoulder. Sparrow gasped, then slowed, their passenger gone. Their rattlesnake earring wriggled like a caterpillar.

All those years, Bellatine had thought she was alone.

(She brushed a fingertip over the owl ringer, and it opened its talons, slashing at a man who rammed at the door.)

She thought she'd been abandoned.

(The Girl with No Face kneeled and handed her rose to a frothing woman. The thorns stabbed through the woman's hand.)

She wasn't alone.

(The Green Woman clicked her tongue, and a murmuration of starlings dove at the horde.)

She had never been alone.

"My name is Baba Yaga. My name is Baba Yaga. Baba Yaga. You will not. Will not forget."

The Longshadow Man's solidity wavered. His body clambered over itself, grasping. He was nearly all smoke now. A white pall undulating in place.

Something called to Isaac then, and he turned away, leaving the dybbuk to gnash against his scattering outline. The crying had returned. It was soft, smothered, but it pulled on Isaac with the might of a fishing hook in a flounder's mouth. It was a *baby*. How had a baby come here? Who had left a baby to cry alone in this house? Desire dragged him through the bedroom, past the low ladder leading up to the loft, past the pantries, into the kitchen. The crying, it came from the stove. Flames batted against the clay and strained toward him. *My child*, he thought, *my little hare, come to me.* He reached out. He turned the iron latch. The door flung open—and with that, a flame soared loose.

"What's that noise?" Sparrow called over the clamor. Bellatine's ears rang from the Embering, which poured from her like a hot spring, but another sound cut through. An infant's cry. She listened closer. Her brother's chanting had stopped. *Isaac.* Had he succeeded? Or had he been silenced?

"Stay here," she called to the Embered and the two Dusk-breakers among them. Then, she sprinted into the house.

Whatever form the Longshadow Man had once taken had eroded. Shadows twisted against the walls. Some with too many tongues. Some with maggots plopping fat onto the hardwood floor. Some made from knife blades pressed to a belly. He seemed to be merging with the house itself, and Thistlefoot shuddered with each incarnation.

"Shhh," Bellatine soothed, dragging a sparking finger along the walls. *It's okay, dear one. You are my home and I am yours. I am here.* Isaac wasn't in the parlor, so she pushed ahead. The bedroom, too, was empty, but through the final doorway she saw him. He walked strangely, with a gait that was not his own. The crying was louder now. *Malka's stove.* Sobs rose from the fireplace. And there, ahead, Isaac reached for the latch.

"Wait!" she started to call, but before the word left her throat, he had flung the door open. Fire shot free. It whooshed past Isaac, knocking him back, and careened over Bellatine's shoulder. The sobbing had risen. It was nearly deafening, endless. All the wailing that had been stifled, free now and riotous. The fire bounded through the bedroom and into the parlor, where it shattered into a firework of light. Flames stabbed through what remained of the dybbuk, swallowing him into ash. He fizzed and crackled. One last hand snatched at the empty air before vanishing.

Outside, the howls of the smokefed quieted and went still.

Fire clung to the walls and draperies. It lapped along the floor.

"Isaac," Bellatine coughed. Smoke blackened the air. "Isaac!" She ran to him, pulling him up from the ground—and when he looked up at her, it was Isaac himself looking back.

"Hey, kid," he sighed. "How you doin'?"

"Tally," she choked, relief washing through her.

Isaac grinned, but hacked as the smoke thickened. "We gotta get out of here," he said, pulling himself to his feet. The ladder cracked and fell in the bedroom, chewed through with heat.

"But Thistle . . ." The great house creaked, shaking, and the rush of air as it moved only stoked the flames.

"We have to *go*," Isaac urged, grabbing her arm.

"No!" she shouted. "There has to be a way to—"

"Kill the lantern," he interrupted over the rising smoke.

Bellatine froze.

"Kill the lantern!" Isaac persisted. He tightened his grip.

Bellatine took one final look around the room. She memorized every inch she could. The old, leaning beams. The warm oak. The scuffs in the floor, worn down from a century of footsteps. *You are mine, and I am yours,* she thought.

Ah yes, little human, and so it shall be! a creaking voice in her head replied.

She turned back to Isaac. "Raise the ghost."

They wended past tall columns of flame. As they ran, the fire seemed almost to part to let them through.

"Wait!" Isaac blurted, pulling loose. He trilled a birdcall through his teeth, and a moment later a yowling Hubcap tore toward them, scrambling up Isaac's pants leg to nestle under his arm. Only then did they continue, bursting through the front door.

Bellatine sucked in a lungful of oxygen, sweet as ice. Behind them, a crash sounded as a ceiling beam collapsed. She fumbled at the crank to drop the ladder. With the heat surging above them, they lowered themselves down rung after rung. Cinders drifted past like fireflies. Below, Shona and Sparrow shouted their names, reaching up with bloodied hands to help as the Yaga siblings descended into the meadow.

The smokefed were scattered in the grass. They blinked at one another, dazed. Shook themselves out, fear no longer squatting on their shoulders, then trailed back to their own homes, to their own memories. Rummy rested unconscious, yet steadily breathing, on Winifred's lap. The stone girl wiped dried blood from his forehead, watching with bright eyes as the Yagas and the rest of the Duskbreakers staggered toward them.

Once they'd reached a safe distance, Bellatine fell to her knees. Tears tumbled to the ground—but she would not look away from the burning house. Isaac knelt beside her, an arm around her shoulder. No matter how she shook, he refused to let go. Across the clearing, Thistlefoot scraped and moaned, bucking like a rabid animal as the fire spread. It had chewed through the roof, devouring the garden, and slicked the feathers from its haunches. Sparks flew from the stage, catching stray tumbleweeds alight. They rolled across the flatlands, churning wheels of fire. Red welts charred Thistlefoot's long, golden legs. Yet the house did not flee. It suffered, and it mourned, but it did not run. Neither did Bellatine, nor Isaac. They stayed. They bore witness. The time for running, ended.

All the while, Malka's crying remained. It filled the sky and the earth. It galloped unencumbered, an immutable wailing. All the tears of which she'd been robbed. All the fury a century could hold. She cried, and she cried, and she did not stop crying, and even after the legged house had fallen to dust, still she cried, and no one silenced her.

CHAPTER FORTY-NINE

I HAVE ONE THOUSAND origin stories, but only one ending.

My ending is ash.

Do I wish it were different? Of course! I am no martyr and have little interest in noble pursuits. I would rather be living, as would we all. But oy, the story is the story, and not even I, master of changes, who from wood became a house, became a beast, became a flame, can change that.

What, you are surprised to hear me still speaking? If so, you have not been paying attention. A house can be burned. A story cannot. What is a house but a container for a life? What is a life but a container for a story? When a container is broken, it does not destroy the contents. It sets them free.

There is a version of your world, almost exactly the same as your own, in fact, where houses come alive. Where memory leaves a mark. And here, like in your world, every house that has ever been lived in is haunted. Haunted with births and with feasts, with piano notes, with arguments, with promises kept and unkept. Haunted with footsteps pattering along the kitchen tile. Haunted with insomnias and telephone calls and spilled glasses of wine. All the makings of a life.

Here, there live a brother and sister. This detail is important. The *living* of it. Before they were born, long before but not as long as one might wish, there was all too much dying. When the brother and sister tumbled into their bodies, they did not know it, but this past death was already there, tucked into their blood. A memory. A birthright. As they grew, the memory grew with them. It took its own shape within each child. The boy child ran and ran and could not stop running. He slipped out of himself and into others, disguise after disguise. He did not know why he was running—only that to stop would be fatal. Every cell evolved to flee an army that had long since stopped following.

In the girl child, the memory pooled in her hands. Her hands remembered griefs that the girl herself did not. They boiled with remembering and with the remembering came refusal. *We will not touch death again,* cried the hands. And so, the hands became an anti-death. A life-maker. They longed furiously to untouch the sorrows of the past, but the girl child did not know of those particular sorrows—so all she could feel was the longing.

I will ask you these: What happens when the walls we raise outlive the dangers they were built to keep out? At what point does a fort become a cage?

I'll tell you what came after. I'll recite it as a folktale, for you have earned this much. It's a tongue that makes sufferings taste sweeter, more possible to bear. And it makes the joys more bearable, too. Thus it begins:

A man stands over a pine casket. The casket is empty. Were one to come upon the funeral, which no one will, they might mistake it for a dream or a mirage—this lone, narrow man in a black suit, a matching cat at his feet, mourning over a coffin by a railroad in the desert. While the casket is empty now, it will not be empty for long. The man places a silver coin upon the railroad track, and he waits, and the cat waits, until at last a train passes by and spits the nickel out, flat and gleaming. The man kisses the coin. He sings a song into the grave, though he is no singer, not like the emptiness in the coffin had been. He drops in the coin. Somewhere along the phantom Westbound line, a gap closes.

A month passes. The young man is weary. He has visited every pawnshop from Arkansas to Arizona. His boots have worn down. His black hair is matted and his pockets nearly empty—but at last, his search is ended. In the back of a junk store somewhere near Stillwater, he finds an old familiar guitar. The strings are rusted and the fret board dimpled from playing, but when he strums it, the sound is warm and clear. He hasn't much money. He haggles until the clerk gives in, and at last, leaves with the guitar in tow.

The following morning, he drops it on the stoop of a shelter in Oklahoma City, a note tied to the neck:

For a kid who needs a time machine. x B. S.

The man turns. He walks away and the black cat follows. In the distance, a bus idles, waiting. On the back of the man's coat, an old coat he once had and now has again, is stitched a curious shape. A horse skull, wreathed in vines.

Meanwhile, another story: There is a theater in the northern forests of Vermont. It ripples with velveteen curtains and paper lanterns strung from the roof. The theater was built by two strong hands, the same hands that had built the pine casket. Each night, the seats are full, and a menagerie of strange, whittled puppets take the stage. People make pilgrimages to this place. They travel over rivers and oceans, down the spines of mountains, over sacred stretches of highway. *This puppeteer, she is unlike any other,* they whisper. *A master. Why, it is almost as if the puppets move all on their own.*

A show is about to begin. The lights fade. In their seats, the audience holds one collective breath. Behind the velvet curtain, there is shuffling. Final props to straighten, cues to set. A woman hovers a silvery finger over the lighting board, slides a toggle. Headphones tamp down her yellow curls. "Rigs on deck," she whispers to the puppeteer, leaning in so her lips graze the sharp of the puppeteer's chin. The puppeteer smiles. She flexes her hands, already growing warm. "Strings ready." And then, a violet spotlight pierces the proscenium.

The puppeteer appears on the stage, four puppets in her arms. One, a lion with a goat-hair mane. One, a glossy black crow. One, a little blue hare. The last, a miniature house, lofted on two golden chicken legs.

"Once, not so very long ago," the puppeteer says, "there was a fierce lion and her two daughters, who lived in the most marvelous house." She sets them down, presses a hand to each of their hearts. "The lion's name was Baba Yaga. And this is her story."

The puppets stir.

My ending is ash. This is true. But it is not *their* ending. Nor is it the story's end. For as long as it is remembered and told, the story remains. The silencers have lost. And as long as those who suffered, whose mothers suffered, whose mothers' mothers suffered in the icy throes of winter's blood can now find joy, small as it may at times be—there is victory.

If a story does its job, it doesn't ever end. Not really. But it *can* change. This is the nature of folktales. They shift to fit each teller. Take whatever form suits the bearer best. What begins as a story of sorrow can be acknowledged, held like a sweetheart to the chest, rocked and sung to. And then, it can be set down to sleep. It can become an offering. A lantern. An ember to lead you through the dark.

ACKNOWLEDGMENTS

A WHOLE LOT OF people went into making this book (and, well, making me)—without whom *Thistlefoot* would never have grown legs. I give endless thanks to:

My parents, Michael and Helen, and my brother, Rustin, for a lifetime of love.

Cassandra de Alba, Meagan Masterman, and Colin Hinckley, aka The Autumn People, for being the spookiest, sweetest writing group and enduring my whining without ever once sacrificing me in a blood ritual; blessed be the bones. Double thanks to Cassandra for being *Thistlefoot*'s first civilian reader, live-texting me things like "no more doorbells!" in acute distress. Kirk Murphy, all rooftop doughnuts and curling prowess. Rose Alexandre-Leach, who accidentally waterboarded me with champagne when the book deal came through. Monika Grist-Weiner with cemetery spells and quilt scraps. Evan Johnson with letters tied in twine. Riley Goodemote with a bottle of wine on the doorstep and all that came after. Extra gratitude to Matt Rivers, train hopper extraordinaire, for teaching Isaac and Benji how to ride—and for supporting me through the drafting process with absolute belief and encouragement while I freaked out. Thanks to poets Heather Madden, Julia Story, and Simeon Berry for being such encouraging mentors and powerful friends. Otis Gray for the writing sessions in his tricked-out van parked in the alligator swamp. Brooke Bullock, who welcomed me into her beautiful, quiet home, where I wrote so much of this book. Katherine Arden for generously lifting me up by helping me find an agent. Sarah Jane Young for carpentry know-how and research. Jeremy Radin for the melancholic, very Jewish Zoom conversations. Shoshana Bass (heiress to a puppet empire!) for puppetry direction, knowledge, creation, and general brilliance, and Sandglass Theater, whose work inspired the rod-puppet designs of *The Drowning Fool*. Brilliant creatrix Maria Pugnetti for skillfully crafting the *Thistlefoot* touring shadow scrolls, and Gilbert Ruff for the enchanted box that holds them. Louise Glück, who gave my first book a chance, thus making the life I now lead possible. Captain Vivian Cutpurse, the fiercest pirate on the seven seas (yes, she's a cat). And to the billion others who let me spin plot ideas by them, listened to me gripe, shared their (very niche) knowledge, and celebrated with me.

I am also indebted to the following stories and authors, from which I drew inspiration, education, and magic: Isaac Bashevis Singer and Sholem Aleichem, whose vibrant shtetl stories helped bring Gedenkrovka to life. *A Treasury of Jewish Folklore*, edited by Nathan Ausubel, from which the Longshadow Man's eternally reaching arm was adapted. *Photographing the Jewish Nation: Pictures from S. An-sky's Ethnographic Expeditions*— an incredible collection of images that helped me travel back in time—and Chaim Buryak's extensive shtetl research on jewua.org. Endless forgotten folktale tellers who, over centuries, whispered Baba Yaga stories in kitchens and around fires so that she might travel through time and space to reach me. Libba Bray's Diviners series and Leigh Bardugo's Six of Crows duology for teaching this sorry poet how the heck to pace a fiction plot—while providing an escape from the drudgery of pandemic life (I think Bellatine would fit right in with Evie and the gang, and Isaac would make a dastardly member of the Dregs . . .). Ray Bradbury and Angela Carter: the devils on my shoulders pushing my prose to be as candy-coated and purple as I damn well please. To *Buffy the Vampire Slayer*, the greatest story ever told. And forever and ever to Kelly Link—whose stories have always felt like permission. Like a homecoming. Like getting onto a carnival ride where the theme is, somehow, the inside of my own brain.

A parade of thanks to all the amazing dedicated people at Anchor Books for laying their hands on *Thistlefoot* and Embering it to life: production editor Kayla Overbey, proofreaders Lyn Rosen and Rima Weinberg, text designer Christopher Zucker, publicist Julie Ertl, marketers Annie Locke and Sophie Normil, editorial assistant Zuleima Ugalde, Altie Karper (who helped Gedenkrovka find its true name), Yuliana Konovalova, Daryna Yakusha, Sonia Bloom from the Yiddish Book Center, cover designer Mark Abrams, cover artist Andrea Dezsö, and copy editor Shasta Clinch (who surely possesses some laser-minded superpower). And my deep thanks to the Mass Cultural Council for providing genuine, tangible support to artists like me.

Extra hollering gratitude to my agent, Paul Lucas—thank you for believing in me from the get-go, for guiding my words into the world, and for encouraging me to write this book; and to my editor, Anna Kaufman—it truly feels like fate brought us together, and boy howdy am I glad that it did. How lucky, to have a brilliant editor, an ideal reader, and a sweet pal all in one.

And lastly, humbly—to the people of Rotmistrivka, the real Gedenkrovka. May your memory be a blessing.

ABOUT THE AUTHOR

GennaRose Nethercott is a writer and folklorist. Her first book, *The Lumberjack's Dove*, was selected by Louise Glück as a winner of the National Poetry Series, and whether authoring novels, poems, ballads, or even fold-up paper cootie catchers, her projects are all rooted in myth—and what our stories reveal about who we are. She tours nationally and internationally performing strange tales (sometimes with puppets in tow) and composing poems-to-order for strangers on an antique typewriter with her team, the Traveling Poetry Emporium. She lives in the woodlands of Vermont, beside an old cemetery. *Thistlefoot* is her debut novel.